A VISIBLE DARKNESS

Michael Gregorio are Michael G. Jacob and Daniela De Gregorio. She teaches philosophy. He is interested in the history of photography in the nineteenth century. They have been married for over twenty-five years and live in Spoleto, a small town in central Italy. *Days of Atonement*, their second novel, followed *Critique of Criminal Reason*. *A Visible Darkness* is the third novel in the Hanno Stiffeniis series.

MICHAEL GREGORIO

A Visible Darkness

faber and faber

First published in 2009
by Faber and Faber Ltd
Bloomsbury House 74–77 Great Russell Street London WC1B 3DA

Typeset by RefineCatch Limited, Bungay, Suffolk
Printed and bound in the UK by CPI Mackays, Chatham ME5 8TD

A CIP record for this book
is available from the British Library

ISBN 978-0-571-23787-6

2 4 6 8 10 9 7 5 3 1

This is the way the Germans are made. There's no man so mad, but he'll find someone who is ready to follow him.
Heinrich Heine

'Three of them can consume a dead horse in three days.'

Linnaeus might have been describing famished wolves or bears emerging from the forest in desperate search of winter nourishment, but savage Nature was not the subject of his dissertation.

Flies . . .

That's what Linnaeus was talking of.

And as I left the house that morning, I spotted another corpse in the garden.

The lawn and flower-beds had become a cemetery in recent weeks. I had buried a rat, three field-mice and a squirrel, intending to hide them from the eyes of Helena and the children. I knelt down to examine the creature more closely. Half hidden beneath one of the rose-bushes, a fair-sized stoat in what remained of its red-brown summer coat.

It had not been there the previous evening when I returned from my office in town. Yet overnight, it had been reduced to a skeleton, more or less. Four or five bluebottles were fighting over the last shreds of flesh, darting in, teasing at the fat where the ears had been, pulling at the gristle as they flew away, but never going very far. The bared, pointed teeth made no impression on those ravenous creatures. They seemed to have no notion of fear. Armageddon had arrived for the stoat in some form or other; the flies had done the rest in no time.

It seemed to verify Linnaeus's claim.

In the past few days I had been reading everything that I could lay my hands on regarding flies and filth. Count

Dittersdorf's library had yielded up Linnaeus, and other useful things as well. But this particular essay was a revelation. Where they came from, what they ate, the cycle of their existence, how fast they could reproduce. They came in all shapes and sizes, and he divided them into a regular army of species and sub-species. The familiar *musca domestica*, the yellow-striped *scathophaga stercoraria,* the larger *calliphora vomitoria,* and a hundred others. The Latin names spoke volumes about their filth, their habits, and the danger that they posed.

Lotingen was infested with them.

My home was besieged by them.

They filled the air, settled on every surface, seemed to multiply like the locusts in the plague that was visited on the ancient Egyptians according to the Bible. They crawled around the eyes and the mouths of my children, and there was nothing I could do about it. I had taken refuge in books, hoping to find some news which would tranquillise my own misgivings, and end my wife's fears. So far, I had found nothing. On the contrary, what I read called forth questions that I had never previously considered. How many days would it take, for example, for the same three flies to consume the corpse of a man, a woman, or a child?

Each day was hotter than the day before.

Walking along the dusty road to town each morning, I had begun to notice a host of creatures that I had never seen before. Strange winged ants with metallic shells the colour of brass, which attacked and ate the smaller flies and midges. Larger beetles with hard green carapaces lurked in holes that they had dug in the rock-hard banks of the lane, darting out to catch the ants which ate the flies. It was as if Nature had declared a universal war between its constituent parts.

And here was the evidence in my own garden.

It was hard to imagine such destructive ferocity in any creature, let alone one that was so small, but those blue-bottles showed no intention of leaving the corpse alone while anything edible was left on the bones.

Had the flies consumed the fur, as well?

Linnaeus had said nothing regarding the horse's hair.

I made a show of examining the roses, in case Helena was looking out of the window. The blooms were dry, opaque, brittle. At the merest touch, the petals would fall to the ground like autumn leaves. Strands of a cobweb glinted like harp-strings in the sunlight, and, as I looked more closely, something else that Linnaeus had written returned to my thoughts.

He spoke of Nature's *'inevitable revenge'*.

Trapped in the fine silken threads, twisting this way and that, a fly was trying desperately to free itself from the mesh. Rainbow-colours flashed off its shining black armour. One wing was beating in a blur, its tiny legs pushed frantically against the silk restraints.

Like a tightrope walker, a spider ran out to watch.

With a sudden dart, the spider leapt forward. Part of the thorax disappeared inside the spider's maw, and the victim bounced more furiously on the imprisoning thread. In trying to break loose, it seemed to tie itself up even more securely.

A rose-petal fell to the ground, and the spider pulled back, watching.

The captive fly made one last effort to escape.

With a sudden jerk, it appeared to take flight.

Just as suddenly, it twirled and twisted, spinning round and round the vibrating silk, and all the fire went out of it. I saw the devastating effect that the spider's attack had had. The part of the body that had been caught for an instant in the spider's mouth was flaccid and flat, all the colour gone, as if it had been sucked dry.

One rapid final dart, and the fly was gone.

I was tempted to call Helena, and show her what I had just seen.

Would she believe me if I told her that it was the self-same fly that had caused her to scream the night before? Would she be pleased that it had fallen prey to a more terrible spider?

I dismissed the idea.

3

The sight of that voracious spider would distress her all the more.

The baby was due in a month, or so.

Since the invasion of the flies three weeks before, Helena had roamed the house with a leather fly-swatter in her hand, her mouth set hard, determined to eliminate every buzzing thing that came within striking distance. The windows were now kept constantly shut, and Helena would reprimand Lotte if a door or window were left ajar. The air inside the house was stale and putrid, as if something organic had been pushed beneath the sofa and left to rot. The children stayed indoors; they were not allowed to play outside. Helena was afraid for them, she admitted.

I was afraid for her, instead, though I could not bring myself to tell her.

One day, while reading an article in a French publication – the writer claimed that one fly alone could hatch a million eggs – I suddenly realised that Helena was standing close behind my chair, and that she was reading silently over my shoulder.

'Does it mention that they are the eyes and the ears of the Devil?' she asked, her eyes never shifting from the page.

I threw the article aside, and jumped up. I meant to comfort her, but she shrugged me off, half stumbling away, her left hand on her greatly swollen belly, her right hand holding out the fly-swatter which had become a fixed extension of herself.

'They *are*, you know,' she murmured.

Her hand smashed down to take another insect life.

Last night, she had wakened the house with a cry that set my heart racing.

Lotte came running into the bedroom from the nursery, and I jumped down from the bed. Helena was bending over the cot of baby Anders. The night was hot, but Helena was as cold as ice. Her hair was a wild burning bush of chestnut curls. Her expression was that of a Medusa who had seen her own face in a mirror.

4

'What is it, ma'am?' Lotte implored.

I took my wife by the arm, trying to lead her back to bed.

She pushed my hands away. Her eyes were wide and fixed on the baby. She had seen a huge black fly crawl into his mouth, she said at last. And it had not come out again.

Lotte glanced at me, and shook her head.

A *nightmare*, she mouthed without speaking.

There was no fly inside the child's mouth. Nothing had happened, if not for the terrible vision which had wakened my wife. Lotte nodded towards the cot where Anders continued sleeping. He was the only one in the house who did not wake up. His face was serene, his breathing regular. Having finally got Helena into bed again, I searched high and low for the monstrous black fly which had cast its dark shadow on her imagination. I told her that I had killed it, too, but I do not think that I managed to convince her.

As I gazed on that spider in my garden – the leg of the dead fly jutting from its jaws like a bent piece of wire – I had to wonder whether Helena's dream had been not simply a distempered nightmare, but the vision of a real and terrible danger.

I went to take a spade and quickly buried the stoat, waving off the flies that circled around it in an angry swarm, nipping at my hands and face and neck, as if to take from my flesh the nourishment that I had just deprived them of. Then, wrapping a damp handkerchief around my face, breathing in the essence of lavender in which Lotte had soaked it, I went out quickly through the gate, turning right along the lane in the direction of Lotingen and the procurator's office.

The closer I got to the town, the worse the stench became, despite the lavender, despite the pressure with which I held the cotton to my nose.

By the time I reached the East Gate, I could hardly breathe.

The hot sun had only partly dried the river of yesterday's filth which covered the cobbles leading in the direction of Gaffenburger's abattoir. Beneath the solid crust, there was a semi-liquid mulch. And fresh beasts had been driven into

Lotingen that morning, adding their own deposits to those of yesterday, and all the days before. The street was a dark brown carpet, and all above was a dense dark cloud of flies and other insects. If one attempted to pass that way, they would rise up, buzzing angrily at the intrusion, then fall back where they had come from.

The insects frightened us, but Spain terrorised the French even more.

They were facing a new kind of war down there; the Emperor's answer was to send more men. Prussia had been subdued, while Spain had not. The campaign was a bottomless pit into which they were pouring money, men and arms. For over a month, the number of soldiers passing through our streets had been growing day after day. The Emperor's finest were going to Spain; the worst would remain in Prussia.

French horses fouled our streets, as did the cows and the sheep that fed the troops. If an animal dropped dead, they left it there to rot. Bones and carcasses littered every yard of the way to Gaffenburger's stockyard. Wagons crowded with French soldiers rolled in swift succession down to the port, and every imaginable thing was left behind them: the remains of food and drink in every form. Solid, liquid, fully or partly digested. It was a common sight to see defecating French buttocks hanging out over the end of a cart. The flies swarmed in their wake, fell hungrily upon the sewage. Lotingen was sinking beneath a tide of filth. Myriads of insects floated on it, and flew above it. The French would not clean up after themselves. No Prussian would clean up after the French. And to make things worse, the gentle breeze from the sea which generally tempered the summer heat was nowhere to be found.

How long had it been since our lungs had breathed fresh air?

Linnaeus had been quite clear on this point: foul air and filth make flies!

I strode across the bridge.

As a rule, I go straight on, passing along Königstrasse, following the southern wall of the cathedral, then crossing over the market square to my office, which is on the far side, opposite the French General Quarters.

Instead, I turned sharp right.

Fifty yards down the lane stands the yard of Daniel Winterhalter. If one has to travel anywhere that the public coach does not go, and if one does not happen to own a horse or a trap, then a call at Winterhalter's is inevitable. He always has a fine selection of horses and a range of phaetons, flies and berlins for hire.

I went in through the arch, feeling better now that I had made my decision.

In the corner of the empty yard – most of the coaches had already gone – stood a most unseasonable carriage for the north coast of East Prussia. Winterhalter must have regretted buying it a thousand times: an ancient landau painted the same colour as the filthy sludge which fouled the streets outside.

'Has anyone beaten me to it?' I asked him, pointing.

Winterhalter was rubbing down a fine bay with a wire brush, chasing away the flies as he finished his stroke, in a sort of intricate ballet in time with the horse's swishing tail.

'It's the last one left, Herr Stiffeniis. And not the best, as you can see. *They* requisitioned all the rest first thing this morning.' He pulled a glum face. 'I just hope they decide to pay, that's all! If you aren't going far, it'll get you there and back.'

'Not far,' I said, giving thanks to God for the unserviceable state of the landau. 'How long will it take to get her ready?'

I knew how long it would take. The minute we had finished haggling over a price, he would put one of his older hacks – certainly not the fine bay stallion – between the shafts, adjust the halter, invite me to climb up, hand me the reins, and remind me to use the whip with urgency and frequency.

Five minutes later, I was rolling back the way I had come. I had made a decision, and would leave the procurator's office in the hands of my clerk for the morning.

2

Manni spoke out boldly.

'As cold as Mamma's hands!' he cried.

We had been on Mildehaven beach a couple of hours.

In their first excitement the children had dug a hole in the sand. Then, I took them down to paddle in the sea. Manni splashed and shouted, while Anders cried whenever a drop of water touched his face or hands. They soon forgot the flies and the smells that we had left behind in Lotingen.

Exhausted after their hard labour, they lay down on the sand and ate the picnic lunch that Lotte had prepared for us. Then, I organised a game of Similes to keep the children busy. Süzi won the first point, though there was a heated dispute about it.

'As round . . .' I proposed.

'. . . as a thaler,' she answered immediately.

I was forced to produce a coin from my pocket to settle the argument in my daughter's favour. The apple that Manni held up in defence of his own simile was a less than perfect circle. When silence fell again, I posed the next question, and Manni came up with that disconcerting answer.

'As cold as Mamma's hands!'

My wife sat staring silently out to sea.

The sun was hot, the gentle breeze coming off the sea was refreshing. The water inside the sand bar was flat, blue, warm. The waves broke on the *haf*, but they were nothing more than a gentle ripple with a harmless white crest on the smooth surface of the Baltic Sea. The idea of taking them for an excursion to the beach had been an excellent one. There could have been no better view. No better sky. No cleaner air.

Despite all this, Helena's hands were cold. It happened when she was afraid of something.

But what was she afraid of?

I looked all around the vast expanse of empty sand.

There were three or four other coaches on the sands that day, but they were tiny black dots in the far distance. Sea-gulls were poking along the waterline in search of rag-worm, wrangling noisily over knots of tangled sea-wrack and the encrusted mussels that had been washed in on the morning tide.

Helena had heard what Manni said, though she did not say a word about it. She sat in rigid profile. Beads of perspiration sparkled on her brow and along her upper lip. Her hair was swept upwards, trussed down with a blue velvet ribbon. Her gaze never shifted from the sea. She had worn the same smile all the morning.

'You must pick an object which is cold by nature, Manni,' I explained. 'Or one which is cold by circumstance . . .'

'But they *are* cold,' he shouted defiantly.

'Come along,' I said, jumping up, bustling more than was necessary. 'That hole must be filled in before we can go home. Help your sister, Manni.'

Süzi obeyed at once.

Manni watched for a moment, then fell to work at her side, using his hands like outstretched pincers. The word-game was forgotten in an instant.

I brushed the sand from my hands and clothes, then took a few steps towards Helena. She was sitting up straight – gown stretched out before her, her back resting against a little scarp of eroded sand where the dunes gave way to the beach. I sat myself down on the top of the mound and swung one leg over her head, as if I might have been playfully sitting on her shoulders.

'Almost time to be getting back,' I whispered in her ear.

As I spoke, I pressed my knees gently against her arms. Then, I laid my hands on either side of her head and rested it back against the pillow of my stomach. Her up-tilted eyes looked into mine. It was the first time she had shifted her gaze from the thin line of the horizon where the dark blue sea and the pale blue sky collided. She closed her eyes and smiled more softly for a moment.

I rested the point of my chin against her forehead, and began to massage the muscles in her neck. Then, I slid my hands down the length of her arms. Her hands were poised upon her swollen belly, as if to protect the creature growing there from whatever the world might throw at it.

Before I could place my hands on hers, they slid away beneath her armpits like frightened deer retreating to the safety of the forest.

'Manni's right,' she murmured. 'My hands *are* cold.'

'What is wrong?' I asked her, resting the palms of my hands on the bulge of her womb. A month or so, and it would all be over. Maybe everything would be gone by then. Filth, flies, the French, as well.

Helena's hands shot out, and caught hold of mine.

In that moment, I felt the chill of cold sweat on her damp palms.

Her head pulled away. She stiffened, gazing out to sea again. It was as if a dark cloud had suddenly appeared in the summer sky, threatening to pitch a thunderstorm upon our heads.

Farther along the beach, three French soldiers came tramping noisily out from the dunes. Laughing and cat-calling to one another, they made their shambling way down to the water's edge.

Manni and Süzi froze like frightened squirrels.

The soldiers had not seen us. They were gesticulating, shouting, pointing towards the waves which gently lapped upon the shore, as if they had never seen the open sea before.

I did not move.

I did nothing that might attract their attention.

I took Helena's cold hands in mine, and I pressed them hard.

Then, I turned to the children.

'As soon as you have finished, we'll be going home,' I encouraged them.

Their eyes flitted from the far-off soldiers to me, then back again.

The sound of my voice must have reached the Frenchmen. Two of the soldiers turned and looked in our direction, while the third man never took his eyes off the sea. One of the two took a step our way, raising his hands to cover his eyes from the direct rays of the sun. He stared at us for some moments, then he turned back to his companions.

'They had the same idea,' I whispered to Helena. 'A peaceful day at the seaside, that's all.'

'I heard their wagons passing by all night,' she said, as if I had not spoken.

Was that the source of her uneasiness? The fact that the French army was on the move?

'What's happening in Spain should make our own lives easier,' I said, intending to reassure her. 'They like us well enough at the moment.'

Helena's fingers tightened into fists.

'Do you really believe that?' she hissed.

'They mean us no harm,' I said.

The soldiers were making more noise than my children had done. They laughed and shouted, passing a bottle of wine between them.

'I am not speaking of the French,' she said. She turned her head, her eyes looked up into mine. 'Not those three. Nor the rest of them. You understand the real danger, don't you?'

A vein was pulsing rapidly in her temple. She was like a lamb who has caught a glimpse of the butcher's knife. It pained me to see her distress, yet I did not understand the cause of it.

'What is it, Helena? The insects, the foul air, the filth . . .'

'It is not that,' she said quickly, looking down the beach again.

Two of the men were naked now, their bodies gleaming white in the sun. They were dancing by the water's edge, touching the sea with their toes, as if they meant to enter it and swim, while the third man seemed to be trying to dissuade his companions from such a bold enterprise.

'What worries me', she said more slowly, 'is what may happen *here*. Spain will put ideas into Prussian heads. And now, the French are weaker. That's what frightens me. You know what they are like, our countrymen. If one of them comes up with a wild scheme, he'll find a thousand who are ready to follow him.'

At her side, the baby was sleeping beneath an umbrella. Anders turned on his blanket and let out a tiny whimper.

'It's time to go,' I said, standing up, helping Helena to her feet, lifting up the baby, making haste to gather our things together and put them in the carriage, encouraging the children to do the same.

The soldiers had come out of the water. They were jumping up and down to warm themselves. Soon, they would start looking for a new amusement.

Within two minutes, Helena and the children were sitting quietly in the landau. Having removed the horse's nose-bag and hung it on the nail at the cart's end, I climbed up into the driver's seat, cracked the whip, jerked on the reins, and we turned our backs on Mildehaven beach.

Forty minutes later, I pulled hard and the carriage stopped before my door.

There was a miasma hanging over Lotingen. The sun had brought the untreated sewage to a fiery ferment. The children jumped down and ran quickly into the house, as I told them to do. In Helena's case, such speed was out of the question. I helped her to the ground, while Lotte came out and took the baby from her arms. When, at last, my wife's heavy, fragile figure reached the door and entered the house, the children waving from behind the windows that Lotte did not dare to open, I felt as though I had sealed them all inside a tomb.

As the carriage gathered speed again, I felt the spattering blows of insects on my brow. I had arranged to meet Gudjøn

Knutzen at four o'clock that afternoon, but I did not relish the appointment. Nor the thought of what we would be doing. We had been collecting 'evidence' – so-called – for the past two weeks. Fortunately, this would be the last occasion.

Tomorrow the trial would begin.

As I walked away from Daniel Winterhalter's yard, stepping carefully through the filthy streets, I felt my angry stomach surging up into my throat.

3

Gudjøn Knutzen was waiting by the steps outside my office.

My clerk was in his usual state: grey hair standing up on his head as if the comb were still waiting to be invented, his clothes as spruce as a strolling tinker's. His wheelbarrow contained a well-worn shovel and a set of scales that had once belonged to his grandfather.

'Which way today, Herr Stiffeniis?'

'The Berlin road,' I announced.

He did not ask me why I had not come to work that morning. He did not care. He let out a loud sigh of resignation, and began to trundle through the streets behind me with his wheelbarrow.

I had adopted a scientific method of working, a proven French method, in the belief that the French themselves would not be able to ignore such carefully documented facts. Each day, Knutzen and I would take ourselves to one of the main roads leading into town, looking out for what I called 'fair samples', that is, deposits of varying sizes – large, medium and small – which I could add to my statistical record.

As we made our way through the town – I with my ledger under my arm, Knutzen pushing his wheelbarrow, both dressed up like bandits with handkerchiefs tied over our noses – I consoled myself with the thought that this would be the last time that I would be obliged to make a public spectacle of myself in the interests of the tiny commonwealth of Lotingen. The following day, those shocking statistics would be made public. The French would *have* to act upon them.

'That's a good one,' I said, as we turned the corner into Berlinstrasse, though we had ignored a thousand similar hazards as we passed through the besmirched and stinking streets on our way there. Lotingen seemed to be sinking under a rising tide of horrid filth. Fresh cow-pats steamed like erupting volcanoes everywhere you looked. It was impossible to pass along the road without soiling your boots, impossible not to carry the mulch inside wherever you went.

Knutzen grunted, and took out his scales.

He dropped them with a clang, then reached for his long-handled shovel.

'Smells like rotten tripe,' he growled, as he shovelled it up.

He held up the scales and moved the balance-weight across the iron bar.

'It weighs precisely two pounds, nine ounces,' I read from the gauge. In my notebook, along with the weight, I added a brief description of the nuisance: *dark brown, fresh, extremely runny*.

While Knutzen dropped the contents into his barrow, I stepped back, waved the flies away, then moved ahead, looking for another decent specimen. I did not need to go two yards. I had decided from the start that six examples weighed and recorded each day would provide sufficient data for a statistical report that might end the squabbling which had divided the town for the past month.

'Over here, Knutzen.'

Again, he loaded the object onto his scales.

Again, I recorded every detail: *nauseous, fly-plagued, 3 lb 2 oz*.

'Stinks worse than the last one,' Knutzen muttered as he turned the plate of the scales and let the contents slide with a lurch into the wheelbarrow. 'Bloody flies!'

He stood back from the cart with this exclamation, waving his shovel at the cloud of insects circling there, scattering droplets of liquid excrement in a scything arc from which I quickly distanced myself.

'My wife was complaining again this morning,' I confided, instantly regretting it.

'Who isn't,' he muttered grimly.

This glum taciturnity is one of Knutzen's traits. I had acquired him with the office, there was nothing to be done about it. How many times had I thought to send him packing? I would have preferred a more sociable underling, but who in Prussia had the courage to turf a widowed father out of a job? He was in his fifties, a slovenly man of low birth and no manners, with only three things on his mind: his children; the animals that kept them alive; and the promise of a state pension when he reached his seventieth birthday. If I remained in Lotingen so long – and I had no wish to leave it – Knutzen and I were destined to pass many more years in each other's company.

'I hope that you'll remember, sir?'

I knew what he meant. His salary was nearly due.

'I will, of course.'

He nodded once. It was the only thing that concerned him. Where the money came from was a matter for my conscience. My meagre expenses had been strictly limited by cuts in the State economy after the Compromise of Tilsit; I would have to pay him his half-salary out of *my* half-salary. Did he thank me? He did not. The sixth cow-pat went slopping into his wheelbarrow.

Knutzen turned to me. 'That's your lot done, sir.'

As I closed my ledger, he shovelled three or four more shovelfuls into his barrow.

'Back to the office,' I announced.

The relative enthusiasm that Knutzen had shown while we were choosing and weighing the cow-droppings went out like a light. An expression of sullen resignation took its place. I knew what he would be doing for the next hour. That manure would be spread on his vegetable-patch. Then, having milked his cow and made the round of his duck-run, collecting eggs, he would feed the piglet that he was fattening up to sell to the

French. At five o'clock, he would return in a huff to the Court House and seat himself in the small closet at the end of the hall, ready (but not particularly willing) to usher in any visitor who had business with the law until closing-time.

Together we returned towards the market square.

What would Lavedrine have said if he could have seen me?

The French criminologist and I had been thrown into fierce competition the year before as we struggled to solve a crime that was one of the most perplexing in the annals of recent Prussian history. Was he back in Paris, I wondered. What smiling sarcasms would flow from the Frenchman's lips if he could see me now, collecting cow-dung in the streets with the same concentration that we had employed to analyse the scene of the Gottewald massacre?

The town was busy. I met numerous acquaintances, and was obliged to nod and wish them all a bright good afternoon. They looked at me, glanced at Knutzen and his wheelbarrow, then quickly moved away. And the more I tried to hurry him forward, the heavier his barrow seemed to become. The stink of the stuff in his cart hung upon us like a poisonous fog. Flies flew all around in a dense, black cloud. I stopped at the water-pump in the market square, and washed my hands, but I could not rid myself of the clinging stench of faeces.

'The smell is corrupting the weave of my clothes,' I muttered.

My only hope was that Lotte would have some marvellous country remedy for unpleasant odours that modern science had not, as yet, dreamt up.

'Hang them out to air,' Knutzen advised me gruffly.

While he pushed his cart away in the direction of his home, I went up the stairs to my chambers to pass the remainder of the day in the company of the file relating to the case which had obliged me to compile those revolting statistics: Keillerhaus *versus* Gaffenburger. First, I would make my final computation. Then, I intended to write my opening address to the court.

Apart from the loud ticking of the Dutch clock, the only sound in the room was made by the agitated rustling of tiny wings. How many flies had managed to find their way into my office, I could not begin to estimate, but I blamed Knutzen. The window looking out on the market square was open. It had been left that way all through the long, hot day.

I sat down at my desk, and cursed him again.

While we were walking out, I had asked him the usual questions.

Had any mail arrived? Had anybody called at the office?

'Nobody, sir,' Knutzen said.

Yet, clearly someone had been there. On the desk lay a book. It was a slim volume in a pale, expensive pig-skin binding. I picked it up and read the title.

A Most Remarkable Phenomenon of Spontaneous Creation.

4

'The court of Lotingen is *finally* in session.'

That accentuated adverb was not a part of the ritual announcement. And perhaps Knutzen's short temper was justified that day. As a rule, there are no more than five or six casual onlookers when the district assizes are called on the last Friday of every month in the Pietist meeting-house on Fromborkstrasse. The cases to be tried are generally matters of the dullest sort, petty theft, domestic wrangling, drunkenness, disturbing the peace.

'Procurator Stiffeniis presiding!' Knutzen added.

The eyes of at least a hundred people turned in my direction as I made my way out from the minister's vestibule, crossed the hall, and took my seat behind the raised altar-table, which had been cleared for the occasion and covered with a crimson damask drape. The eager excitement of the throng crushed together in the narrow pews – many of them seeing me in my judge's toga and black cap for the very first time – and the grumbling of those less fortunate who had come too late to claim a seat and found themselves obliged to stand at the back of the hall, was the true measure of the civic importance of the case.

'Silence in court!'

Knutzen had to shout, calling for order several times again before the proceedings could commence with any sort of reasonable dignity.

On the right-hand side of the bench stood the plaintiff. Wearing a three-quarter-length coat of dark blue wool with a double row of brass buttons despite the persistent summer heat, studded leather sea-boots, his three-cornered nautical hat tucked beneath his arm, his face as dark, brown and wrinkled as a fried walnut, Fritz Keillerhaus looked every inch what he proudly claimed to be: a ship's captain, who was used to ruling a crew of ruffians, alone and unaided in the pursuit of behemoths. On the other side, Augustus Gaffenburger, the owner of the Lotingen slaughterhouse, and the defendant in the case. They wore matching theatrical expressions of anger and impatience on their faces.

I cleared my throat, then read out the deposition which had given rise to the dispute.

'On the 20th of July, in this, the year 1808, after making repeated complaints – in the first instance, directly to the accused; in the second place, to the civic authorities of the town – I, Fritz Keillerhaus, captain (retired), do hereby solemnly swear and affirm that no action was ever taken by either party to correct the wrong that I have suffered. Indeed, the nuisance has grown steadily worse. Therefore, and most reluctantly, I feel obliged by honour to sue for the payment of substantial damages incurred as a result of the continuing assault upon my property . . .'

'By his cows!' Captain Keillerhaus burst out impulsively.

'We know the nature of your grievance, sir,' I answered briefly. 'We are here to settle the matter. The essence of a fair trial is that after your complaints have been fully stated, the accused should be given the opportunity to refute them if he can. Allow me to finish, and we will get on with business!'

Captain Keillerhaus looked down. For one instant, I thought he might be going to spit. He did not. Which was fortunate. It is an offence to expectorate in the presence of His Majesty's magistrate in the performance of his duties, and even more so when the court makes shift in a consecrated chapel for want of any better assembly-room. I would have been obliged to fine him for it.

'. . . *continuing assault upon my property,*' I resumed, '*damages which have been estimated in the region of five hundred thalers.*'

I turned to Captain Keillerhaus again. 'Do you stand by your statement, sir?'

'Of course I do!' he snapped. 'I'd not have made it otherwise.'

'Very well,' I said, deciding to ignore the rudeness of his reply, which had caused titters from some of the women and knowing smiles and laughter from many of the men who were present in the room. I turned to Gaffenburger. 'What have you to say, sir? How do you respond to the charge brought by Captain Keillerhaus?'

'Captain Keillerhaus is looking for trouble,' he said, 'and hopes to make a profit by causing it. He seems to be convinced that I am rich.'

Loud laughter came from the public gallery.

Gaffenburger's slaughterhouse was one of the largest business enterprises in Lotingen. The defendant's grandfather had set up in a small way sixty years before. At that time, most people would have considered it a public utility of the first importance. The present owner's father had enlarged the main building and constructed a network of holding-pens where the restless animals could be calmed down and watered before the fatal moment arrived when they would go to meet the executioner's knife. Augustus Gaffenburger had inherited the business from his father a decade before, and nothing much had changed for a while.

Then the French had arrived.

After the pacification of Prussia, the French garrison in Lotingen numbered anywhere between one and three thousand men – our port and estuary were the gateway to the northern plain and the Berlin road to the south – so there was now an unending flow of foreign soldiers passing through. There was a constant demand for fresh meat as a consequence, and the French were paying for it. Gaffenburger's business had

tripled in the course of the occupation, and if, as many people suspected, Napoleon was intent on invading Russia when the next campaign season came around, the necessity to slaughter even more cows and sheep, and feed up the French for the fight, was likely to make him a very rich man indeed.

Knutzen was obliged to insist on silence again before I could speak.

'Captain Keillerhaus,' I continued, 'tell us, if you would, what the substance of this complaint is.'

The Captain opened his mouth and a sound came out. 'Shhh . . .' He stopped, looked at the wooden altar-table behind which I was sitting, thought for an instant, then changed his mind. 'Droppings, sir.'

'What manner of droppings?'

'You know as well as I do!' he protested. 'How many men and women have fouled their precious boots in recent weeks? Shoes do not come cheap. Every time you walk out on the street it's an obstacle course to avoid stepping into the shhh . . . animal droppings. Of every shape and size, and all of them smelling like the Devil's own. I have counted them, sir . . .'

General laughter greeted this announcement.

'Silence in court!' Knutzen thundered.

The trial proceeded in this manner for an hour or so.

Having heard all the evidence, I donned my cap and began to read out the sentence which I had decided on the evening before. I was well aware of what I was doing, and I knew the risk that I was taking. The French authorities would be offended, but something had to be done, and I had determined to do it. A copy of my report would be submitted to them. For this reason, I made a particular point of citing a renowned French scientist to illustrate and justify my arguments. Could they ignore French logic?

'As reported by J. N. Hallé in his *Procès-verbal de la visite faite le long des deux rives de la rivière Seine, le 14 février, 1790*,' I began, 'and employing Monsieur Hallé's specific method of statistical analysis, we can say that the town of Lotingen, like Paris itself, is subject to the accumulation of rubbish and organic refuse to an alarming degree.'

I looked around.

There was a widespread nodding of heads.

No one could deny the truth of what I said, not even the French.

'It may be assumed', I went on, 'that this is the norm in any town in Prussia at the present time.

'In addition, Lotingen is subject to the daily transportation "on the hoof" of beasts from the countryside on their way to the slaughterhouse. According to the Gaffenburger abattoir records, upwards of fifteen hundred sheep and cattle are butchered there in the course of a normal working week. No precise information is available regarding the disposal of the usual remains, though butchers, tanners, soap-manufacturers, perfume-mixers, horn-carvers, button-makers, and the like, account for the general bulk of the comestible and marketable commodities which result from the killing of animals. Much else, in the way of blood, brain, intestines, inedible membranes, et cetera, finds its way, by one means or another, into the River Nogat and then, with the help of the estuary flow, into the open sea. Nature deals, we may say, with the matter that Man rejects . . .'

I paused, and looked around. All eyes were turned in my direction. I was hoping that the inhabitants of the town would be shocked by my findings, and from the looks on their faces I was not disappointed.

'But there is an *additional* nuisance,' I went on with particular emphasis, 'which Nature does not carry off by its own processes. I am speaking of the faecal matter which the sheep and the cattle deposit on our streets as they make their way to the Gaffenburger slaughterhouse pens. By means of statistical calculation, I have established that in excess of fourteen pounds' weight of untreated dung are deposited on each ten-yard stretch of every road leading into town every morning, where it lies in a deplorable state of nauseous decomposition for the next twenty-four hours, when the process is repeated. The pestering flies and noxious worms which are spontaneously born of this accumulating effluvia are a general nuisance, but, more importantly, are a serious threat to the health of every man, woman and child.

'No person in the town would deny the myriads of flies this summer.'

Again, these remarks were intended for the French.

'If we consider the distances from the four main city gates to the slaughterhouse, which have been accurately measured by myself – they extend for a total of 2,100 yards – then we are able to calculate that about 2,900 pounds' weight of animal *excreta* lies untreated on our city streets every single day of the working week. This is a vast, a staggering, amount of fresh, stinking . . .'

Before I could complete the phrase, the door of the meeting-hall burst open.

There was a beadle outside with instructions to let no one enter once the assizes began. Nevertheless, a French soldier in the green colours of a despatch-rider came striding down the aisles between the pews, his boots thumping hard on the wooden boards, his spurs jingling in the shocked silence. He was tall, bright-eyed, moustaches greased, his hair wound up in a pig's tail, three white stripes on his sleeve.

He drew up before the bench, saluted, and held out an envelope to me.

'Procurator Hanno Stiffeniis?'

I took the packet, examined my name in a curlicue hand, then turned it over and glanced at the seal. Unbroken, as it should be, but smudged, as if the wax had been pressed down rather too heavily, and with great haste.

'Who is this letter from?' I asked him in French.

Even in a public courtroom, limited privacy is possible if two men converse in one tongue while all those about them speak another.

'It is from the office of Lieutenant-Colonel Claudet, mon-sieur.'

I tore the seal and opened the paper.

Herr Procurator, please follow this messenger without delay.

'Has something happened?'

The messenger's mouth pursed in that peculiar down-turned expression by which the French signal their ignorance of cause or consequence. 'I cannot say, sir.'

'And where are you to take me?'

'*Les Quartiers Générals, monsieur.*'

Every Prussian knew what the French General Quarters was. Every man in Lotingen was in awe at the thought of being taken there against his will. The cellars, according to local legend, were the daily scene of tortures and beatings that the Holy Roman Inquisition would have blenched at.

I stood up, then sat down again.

My thoughts flew this way and that, like crows in a cornfield when a musket explodes in their direction. The French must have realised that they would be prominently mentioned at the trial. They knew well enough what the local population thought about them, their horses, their cattle and their dung. Was that why I had been so urgently summoned? To prevent me from speaking out in public?

I looked at Knutzen.

'The court is adjourned until nine o'clock tomorrow morn-ing,' I said. Though every person in the meeting-hall heard this announcement from my lips, Knutzen insisted on repeating it.

As I laid my judge's cap on the table, shook off my cloak of office and stepped down from the altar to join the French messenger, a stunned silence reigned in the courtroom.

All eyes were on me as I left the chapel in his company.

5

The door was ajar.

I could hear the rumble of voices on the other far side of the door, though I could make out nothing of what they were saying. I knocked and waited, but no one called for me to enter. And yet, this was the room, according to the French soldier who had led me there.

I knocked again, pushed open the door, and stepped inside.

An officer in a long-tailed jacket and brown riding-boots was standing before a desk, his shoulders turned towards me. He was tall, and very thin, a greasy yellow twist of a pig-tail drooping over his upturned collar below a bald flare of red scalp. He did not turn to face me, but continued speaking earnestly to someone on the far side of the desk that I could not see, his voice a rough, low growl.

'. . . a great deal of time and effort to hack it off. A piece of bone . . . Pure evil! Why would anyone . . . ?'

The officer turned his head, revealing the profile of a low forehead and a broken, beaky nose, and spun round on his heel to face me. I recognised him. That is, I had seen him as he mounted a horse or climbed into a coach outside the General Quarters, though I had never actually met him, or been formally introduced.

'Procurator Stiffeniis?' he enquired, staring.

His hand hovered in the air, a gesture that might as easily have been a rebuff as a welcome. He did not offer his hand for me to shake. Nor did he make any step towards me.

I dipped my head in a necessary semblance of respect.

'Hanno Stiffeniis,' I answered, letting my outstretched hand drop, slapping it against my thigh. 'I was administering an important trial. Was such an interruption necessary, sir?'

I took a deep breath.

'I am Colonel Antoine Claudet, newly appointed commander of this garrison,' the officer announced, blatantly ignoring my question.

His hair fell over his forehead in crisp, white curls, like a sheep in need of shearing. His left eye was closed and shrunken, which added a grotesque air to his long, plain face. Despite his height and his bright silver epaulettes, he did not make a good impression on me. His nose was large and red, as were his hands. His sharp cheekbones were streaked with purple veins. And then there was his unsightly eye. He had started out as an infantryman of the lowest class, I was convinced of it, and had spent so many years sighting down the length of a musket that he was unable to open it again. Seniority, persistence, and heaven knows what other dubious 'qualities' had moved him up through the ranks. But slowly, very slowly. He was one of those lowly individuals that the emperor Napoleon purposely chose to elevate above the legitimate rulers of the proud nations that he had crushed, a constant reminder of their humiliation.

How had we let ourselves be so easily conquered by such grubbing lice?

'May I ask what you want from me, sir?' I enquired.

Colonel Claudet gritted his teeth in a vain attempt at a smile. There was nothing cordial about it. Indeed, I thought, if I had judged him correctly, he was one of those men who exercised his arrogance on those below him, just as he suffered the arrogance of his direct superiors. And while I was a magistrate, I was also Prussian, a citizen of a country that he and his fellows had occupied and crushed.

'*I* did not ask for you at all,' he replied curtly.

He stretched his left foot out to the side, shifted his body after it in a sideways movement, and came stiffly to attention, allowing me to see the person sitting on the far side of the desk for the first time. 'I suppose you have heard of General . . .'

'Malaport. Louis-Georges Malaport.'

The voice from the far side of the desk sounded like the bubbling of a pot of porridge on a low fire. I knew the name, of course. Who did not? Malaport was in charge of the French troops all along the Baltic coast from Danzig to Königsberg. As a soldier, he had distinguished himself at Auerstadt, leading the final charge on the exposed left flank, which had sent our army running from the field. He appeared to be exhausted, worn out, aged. His shoulders were rounded and narrow; his head seemed over-large; his stomach was enormous. He sat very quietly, looking down at his hands, which might have belonged to an ageing aristocratic lady. They were small, pink, creased and wrinkled like paper made from crêpe, joined tightly together, as if to hold him anchored in that position.

Immediately, I was on my guard.

'General Malaport,' I echoed.

He looked up at the sound of my voice. His eyes were piercing, naked – small, bloodshot, translucent, grey.

'I have travelled a long way to speak with you today,' he said. He pointed abruptly to the chair which stood in front of the massive desk. 'Sit down,' he said, and gestured impatiently at me. 'You worked with an officer named Serge Lavedrine, we hear?'

General Malaport leant forward, rested his chin on his tiny joined hands, and closed his eyes as if to concentrate on my reply.

'Is Lavedrine in Lotingen?' I asked, surprised to hear the name of the French criminologist.

Claudet's mouth fell open, but the words that I heard did not come from his lips.

'He spoke very well of you, monsieur,' General Malaport replied, though he hardly moved, and did not open his eyes. 'I have read his report of your joint investigation. He praised your honesty and investigative abilities. We will need those qualities.' He flicked his forefinger in the direction of Claudet. 'Go on,' he said.

'The emperor has drawn up plans for Prussia,' Claudet continued quickly. 'He considers the Baltic coast to be of vital importance for France.' He hesitated, then added: 'And for Prussia, naturally.'

I might have asked him why, but he did not give me the chance.

'A deplorable state of inefficiency reigns out there. Thieving is the order of the day along the Baltic coast. It's been going on for centuries, of course, but now it is necessary, essential, I would say . . .'

'Get on with it!' Malaport grumbled, raising his head for an instant, as if his repose had been troubled by an impertinent fly.

'Certainly, sir,' the lieutenant-colonel agreed. 'The emperor's aim is to increase production. Those resources must be exploited to the full, but they will not be properly . . . that is, not fully exploited while . . . well, while what is happening out there continues to happen.'

The pig-like eyes of General Malaport opened wide. They stared malevolently at Colonel Claudet.

'Come to the point!' he snapped.

'Sabotage, Herr Stiffeniis. That is the point.' Claudet drawled on. 'Someone on the coast is intent on making trouble. He, or they, will baulk at nothing . . .'

Malaport's fist crashed down on the table.

'Murder,' the general said quietly. 'That is what we're talking about. It is compromising important French interests, and must be stopped. You will stop it, Herr Procurator Stiffeniis.'

I had read nothing of the sort in the newspapers, nor in the Court Despatches which had recently arrived from Berlin. Nor had news of a murder on the coast been announced in the *Bulletin militaire* which reports every week on the state of affairs in East Prussia.

'Have French soldiers been killed?' I asked.

General Malaport smiled wryly. 'It might be better,' he said. 'At least, the motive would be clear. We have no one with experience in these matters to whom we may turn. Unfortunately, Lavedrine is not available.'

He glanced at Claudet, then turned to me again.

'I've been looking through your file. Even before Lavedrine came to Lotingen, you were chosen for your investigative skills by the late Professor Kant himself. Königsberg, 1804, I think it was?'

I nodded, accepting the remark as the compliment he intended it to be, wondering whether he would be equally impressed by the case I had been working on more recently. One thing was clear: a murder hunt was on the cards. I felt a flutter of excitement. But an instant later, remembering the horror of the case which I had had to face the year before with Serge Lavedrine – the massacre of the Gottewald family – I felt less sure of myself. I would be obliged to co-operate with the French, but this time I would be working on my own.

'I am grateful for the faith that you express in my regard, sir,' I replied, 'but I cannot help you unless I know a little more. Who has been murdered? How was the crime committed? And why will French interests be threatened if the killer continues to go unpunished?'

Malaport slumped back against the chair, as if each question was a punch.

'You are correct, Herr Stiffeniis,' he said. He sat in moody silence, considering I knew not what, then he turned to his fellow-countryman. 'Leave us alone, Claudet. You have other things to do, no doubt.'

The most powerful man in Lotingen garrison glared at the most powerful man in northern Prussia. Then, the lieutenant-colonel saluted and strode stiffly out of the room, casting a black look at me. As the door closed more loudly than was necessary, General Malaport cast his tired eyes on mine.

'You know the Baltic coast, I think? You know what goes on up there.'

I sat up straighter. 'Many things, sir. Fishing, smuggling . . .'

'Important French interests, remember.'

'The docks and harbours, then. Trade and the English blockade . . .'

'Amber,' he interrupted me in a hoarse whisper. 'Amber is what interests the emperor.'

Amber had been on everyone's lips for a year. One night, a month or two before, a paper had been pinned to the door of Lotingen Cathedral, and to the doors of many other churches in the canton. A melodramatic gesture, but an effective one. Luther's ghost was walking the streets at night, the people said. He was pinning up his lamentations, trying to incite good Prussians to revolt against the foreign thieves. 'THEY ARE RIP-PING IT OUT', the title screeched. A rough drawing illustrated the theme: a large chunk of Baltic amber cut in the shape of a human heart. The Prussian eagle was imprisoned inside the resin, like a dead fly. And a threat. 'FRANCE MUST PAY!'

I had been surprised by the motive for such anger. There were a thousand more important things that the French had ripped from Prussian hands. Our pride. Our liberty. Our independence. But then I thought of the ancient amber necklace that my mother had worn on every important occasion in Ruisling. The handles of our best knives and forks were amber inlaid with silver. So was the candlestick on my bedside table. The mouthpiece of my father's pipe, the handle of my pocket-knife. If one had made an inventory of the Stiffeniis estate, there would have been a thousand items, large and small, which were decorated with amber from our Baltic shores. The portraits of my ancestors hanging up in the library were framed in sculpted amber. The paintings had faded, but the amber was as bright and fresh as the day it had been polished and set. Its very permanence seemed to highlight the weakness of the flesh that those ostentatious frames contained.

'France has plans for the amber industry,' he said.

He did not say what those plans might be, though I could guess. Was there one crucial event in the history of my country – the financing of a war, the purchase of new cannons, new ships, new horses, swords and pikes – which had *not* been paid for with amber from the Baltic Sea? Was there a single item representing the wealth, the history and the culture of Prussia in the collections of other nations that did not contain a piece of amber? Was it any surprise that the French were interested?

'A corpse was found in Nordcopp yesterday morning,' General Malaport went on. 'A young woman. One of the amber-workers. She may not have been the first to die. Nor will she be the last, I fear.'

'What makes you think that she was murdered, sir?' I asked. 'Gathering amber on the shore is not the safest way to live. The waves of the Baltic Sea . . .'

Malaport's hand came down flat on the desk, but there was no anger in the gesture.

'Waves do not butcher bodies,' he said. 'You'll be in a better position to judge when you have examined the corpse for yourself. What is happening in Spain has not gone unnoticed here in Prussia. I want to know whether Prussian rebels are involved.'

Helena's frightened voice echoed in my mind. The words that she had pronounced on the beach. Despite censorship of the papers, news from the Spanish peninsula was on everyone's lips. The fact that it was supposed to be kept a secret made it all the more disturbing. The Spanish *guerrilla* were getting the best of the emperor's finest. And though we might admire their courage, we quaked at their methods. Was it possible that men who wore the Cross of Christ around their necks could strike in such a manner? They went from bad to worse – hamstringing horses first, then the men who rode them. And the revenge that the French extracted was even more horrendous. There had been a massacre in Santa Maria del Cruz. One hundred Spanish women and children had been hanged. The peasant *guerrilla* might go home victorious one day, but they would find no one to welcome them. Their cooking-fires had been extinguished for ever.

'Nothing of the sort will happen here,' I had promised Helena.

She had been silent, never once taking her eyes off mine.

'Can you be certain, Hanno?' she had said at last. 'You think you know the French. But do you know your countrymen? I am more afraid of what our rebels may do. There will be no end to it. That's all I know.'

Had Helena been right?

'You are a magistrate, sir,' General Malaport emphasised. 'By helping us, you may protect the less hot-headed of your countrymen. Innocent people are bound to suffer if violent repression of a rebellion is necessary.'

Did he understand the risks of the situation in which he was placing me? Did he know how many Prussians had been murdered by their neighbours as they walked home after speaking to a Frenchman?

General Malaport smiled thinly. 'I know what you are thinking, Stiffeniis,' he said. 'I'll order Claudet to set a close watch upon your family here in Lotingen while you are away.'

He rose without a word, walked to the window, and gazed out over the market square. He was even shorter than I had estimated. Round and bloated above the waist, his legs were thin and curved like carriage-struts. There was nothing palpable which denoted authority in his physique, yet something had induced Napoleon to hand the man a general's baton. I could only pray that it was his intelligence.

He turned abruptly and stared at me.

'If you have no objection, sir, you will leave immediately.'

My thoughts flew instantly to Helena.

'My wife is ill,' I said. 'I am reluctant to leave her in a state which . . .'

The fat on Malaport's forehead corrugated into a frown. 'Is the lady dying?' he asked. He was not being sarcastic. Rather, he was informing himself of the situation, and I was forced to smile. He seemed to be a man of extreme judgements.

'My wife is pregnant.'

'Pregnant?' he said with a dismissive wave of his hand. 'I thought you were talking of something serious. Your wife has a doctor, surely? He'll play her fool while you are away. When is the child expected?'

'In a month,' I murmured.

'If all goes as I expect,' he charged on, 'you'll be home in a couple of weeks. I do not see that as a reasonable objection. You will be serving France, but Prussia will thank you for it. I have already spoken to the district governor. Herr Count Dittersdorf agrees with me. You will report to Colonel Richard les Halles who is in command of the area, though you should consider your authority to stem directly from me. I will be keeping a close watch on the situation. In the final analysis, I'll hold you responsible for the investigation. Do you understand what I am saying, Stiffeniis? Do as you wish, but try not to step on too many toes. A coach will be leaving for the coast at five o'clock. Make sure that you are on it. *Bon voyage.*'

I had been dismissed.

Yet one thing prickled me as I walked to the door.

'Herr General,' I said, turning back to face him, 'we have a serious problem in Lotingen. The French army is at the root of it.' I told him of the situation in the town, the filth on our streets, the danger of an epidemic which was on everyone's lips. 'If I help you, sir, will you help the town in return? Not all French soldiers are en route to Spain, after all. Couldn't the ones who remain be set to work to clean the streets after those who are departing?'

General Malaport pursed his lips, then nodded twice.

'First, I want results on the coast, Herr Stiffeniis. Good day, monsieur.'

I closed the door, and walked out into the hall.

'Stiffeniis.'

I met the eyes of Colonel Claudet as he stepped out of the shadows. He had been sent out, but he had not gone away. He had something more to say to me.

'Remember, monsieur,' he warned me, 'you can weigh *la merde*, you can discuss it in a Prussian court of law if you like, but the streets of Lotingen will not be clean until it suits *me*.'

'Herr General said . . .'

'Herr General watches his own back. I watch mine. I advise you, sir, to watch out very carefully for yours. *Bon voyage, monsieur.*'

With an ironic salute, he turned and walked away.

The French needed me, but that did not change the facts. I would not be working *with* them, I would be working *for* them.

I walked home in a daze through the narrow streets.

What if the child were born before I could resolve the case?

6

The Baltic Sea was breathing in our faces.

I felt its salty presence tickling at my nose and coursing down my gullet.

I had spent the last three hours in a corner of the coach with my head propped on my hand, eyes closed against the dust kicked up by the horses on the bone-hard highway, sometimes sleeping, otherwise pretending to sleep.

We were going to a place called Nordcopp, I and my travelling companions.

The appointment had been set for five o'clock at Lotingen town cross.

Having kissed Helena goodbye with less passion than I truly felt – Lotte and the children were looking on – I had walked back to town, my leather travelling-bag hanging from my shoulder. The road was empty, except for swarms of flies, which nipped at my face, neck and hands.

The carriage was waiting.

Pulled by four stout horses, it was grey with dust, though painted black, and it appeared to have travelled many miles that day. I quickened my pace, taking stock of the vehicle as I approached. It was not the sort of carriage that generally ferried passengers along the coast road. A large square box with stout wheels and great leather suspenders, it was a transport wagon of some sort. On the roof, as well as a mound of valises, bags and sacks, there were a number of metal tubes, some wooden crates, and a set of oversized drilling bits. The French had deemed that I should be conveyed *not* as a passenger worthy of care and consideration, but as just another piece of heavy equipment that needed to be moved up to the Baltic coast.

There were three other passengers, and all of them were French.

I announced my own name; they fired back with a rapid cannonade of French double names and surnames which went straight over my head. No doubt my name had been equally quickly forgotten. As the coach pulled away, the luggage on the roof began rattling, shaking and clanking, as if a dozen blacksmiths had been hard at work up there. My companions shouted angrily at the driver, but there was nothing to be done, the man shouted back. The road was full of holes and ruts after the long, hot summer.

The other passengers were soon engaged in heated discussions. They were talking of their experiences in Spain. Their tales of the campaign froze the blood in my veins. In one instance, thirty French troopers had been caught in ambush and cut to bits with scythes and pitchforks. In another case, the throats of five French officers had been slit by *guerrilla* warriors posing as peasants in a country *taberna*. Their still-beating hearts had been ripped from their breasts, and French blood had been quaffed as if it were the finest Madeira wine.

I closed my eyes, thinking of Helena, and the tribulations she must suffer in my absence. The children, the unborn child, the flies and insects, the foreign occupants, the stench which hung over Lotingen. I recalled the details of our parting. Of necessity, I had told her of my meeting with General Malaport.

'I must go to the coast,' I announced. 'A woman has been murdered there.'

'Do you know who she was?' she asked. 'Was she married? Did she have children?'

'I only know that she was employed collecting amber,' I said.

'She was Prussian, then.' She placed two fresh shirts in my bag, and closed the strap. 'There, that's everything. Except for the promise you must make me.'

37

'To be back soon . . .'

'No, no,' she protested. 'I want something else from you.'

She had made me promise that I would find the killer before the baby was born.

When not pretending to sleep, I sat in silent isolation looking out of the carriage window. The road was unusually busy, the travellers almost exclusively French. While we drove north and east, French troops, cavalry and baggage-trains flowed by in the opposite direction. There was nothing surprising in that river of marching Frenchmen – though it did make the direction being taken by my travelling companions all the more mysterious. After serving two years in East Prussia, where they had besieged the city of Königsberg, then mercilessly crushed a more recent rebellion in Kamenetz, the marching troops were going down to Spain. I had seen the same battle-worn faces every day for the last month as they marched or rode through Lotingen, turning left towards the interior on the long road that would lead them eventually to Paris and beyond, or wheeling right towards our port and the galleys which would race them to Spain.

As dusk came on, a heavy sea-fog rolled in off the sea, and the coach slowed down to walking-pace. Not long afterwards, we turned off the main highway, heading out towards the shore along a sandy lane. The Frenchmen grew ever more anxious, shouting up to the driver, warning him to take care of the 'beak', and go more slowly. I did not ask what they were referring to. As I was climbing up into the coach in Lotingen, handing my bag to the coachman on the box, I had caught a glimpse of a long, slender object made of metal. Rolled up in heavy canvas, it had been tied to the vehicle with a great many ropes. The further down that lane we went, the more loudly this metal tube began to clank and judder as it pulled against its moorings.

On every occasion, French conversation died in an instant.

Their eyes rolled up to the ceiling, they spoke in worried whispers, and the man sitting next to the window dropped the sash, leaning out to see that nothing had come adrift above us, reaching up to check that the ropes were holding, calling to the driver, ducking back inside to announce that all was secure, and that, despite their worst fears, nothing had happened to upset their plans.

Plans?

One thing was clear to me: their military careers would be at stake if any damage were done to the 'beak'. At the same time, I began to feel that they feared for more than just their careers alone. They spoke of the officer that they were delivering it to as some sort of ogre, who might eat them all if any harm came to his metallic plaything. It gave me unexpected pleasure to hear the thrill of fear in their harsh voices.

Suddenly, a loud shriek split the night.

Leather brakes bit harshly on the steel rims of the wheels. The carriage creaked, rocked, skidding from side to side on the sandy surface of the road. The smell of burning took the place of salt and sea air. Above our heads, instruments, tools and boxes began to clash like warring bands of medieval knights locked in a battle to the death, coming to a crashing, rowdy climax as the vehicle lurched to a sudden halt.

My travelling companions flew into a fit.

They leapt down onto the sands before the coach had fully stopped.

I did not follow, but remained where I was. I was going on to Nordcopp after all, and I dared to hope that the rest of the journey would be more peaceful without them.

'*Les forets!*' one man shouted. '*Avez soin des forets!*'

'*Descendez mes instruments très vite!*' another voice demanded.

I heard the studded boots of someone up on the roof, the repeated calls for their valuable cargo to be unloaded, and carefully, too. I stared out through the open window, wondering whether I ought to get down and offer them a hand, but then dark shadows ran into the circle of light that was cast by the coach-lamp. They would have no need of me. Indeed, the local helpers seemed to be more efficient and orderly. A voice stood out above the others, issuing orders in a sharp, commanding tone, while a succession of boxes, packages, bags and more unwieldy objects were handed down from the roof to the hands now reaching up to receive them.

I took complete possession of the empty vehicle, and closed my eyes.

'Paralysed with fright, are you?'

The accent was French, though the language was German.

I opened the eyes. A head was poking in through the door, a dark silhouette against the sulphurous light of a lantern.

'Or are you deaf?'

Wisps of sea-fog hung about his face and hair like drifting pipe-smoke.

I sat up quickly. 'Colonel les Halles is expecting me in Nordcopp,' I began. 'The sooner I get there . . .'

'You are there,' he snapped in bulldog fashion. 'And I am he. Now, get out quick, monsieur, or that carriage will take you straight to Königsberg.'

I made haste to jump down from the coach, embarrassed to be told by a Frenchman what a native Prussian might be expected to know. So, this was the ogre that my fellow-passengers had been speaking of, the one with whom General Malaport had told me that I would be required to work.

He was shorter than myself, more square, robust, rugged. His head was a cube, his close-cropped hair as white as salt. And yet, he was not old. Certainly, he had not passed forty. There was a piercing, challenging, brutal quality to his rude stare, as if he were summing me up for future use.

'Procurator Hanno Stiffeniis,' I announced. That 'get out quick' still stung, and I thought it best to meet his rampant arrogance with disdain.

'I know who you are, monsieur,' he replied brusquely. 'I do not know what you may yet be. But we have work to do. The stink of the Baltic Sea will not cover the stench of the *fräulein* for very much longer.'

He turned away, shouting to the man on the roof of the coach. 'That drive shaft! Break it, and I'll break your neck!'

As I retrieved my leather satchel from the ground, he turned to meet the other new arrivals, informing them that their instruments would be stored in a hut close by, warning them that nothing should be touched without his say-so.

He exercised authority like a bludgeon.

'Coach clear, Monsieur le Colonel!' A soldier saluted.

Les Halles grunted, and waved the man away.

'It's too late to do anything tonight,' he said, his voice gruff and low, as if he were accusing us of coming late on purpose, just to frustrate his plans. 'You'll start first thing in the morning. We rise at five.'

He raised his lantern to my face, let out another dismissive grunt, then turned away, stumping off into the fog. 'Follow me,' he shouted.

We trudged after him in silence, each man carrying his bag or valise. It was heavy going; the sand was very fine, damp with fog, and it clung to our boots like lead. A dark structure loomed up suddenly. A wooden hut. There appeared to be others dimly glimpsed in the shifting half-light.

Colonel les Halles kicked his boot against the frail door.

'*Entrez, messieurs!*'

He might have been urging assault troops forward on a suicidal mission.

Was he capable of conversational speech? Every word was an order. Every order was to be obeyed. Was I alone in hearing the sarcasm in his voice? Or was it a question of Prussian sensibility, and nothing more?

One of the newcomers pushed past me, hurrying forward into the light and the shelter. 'This is *true* French hospitality!' he exclaimed.

I followed him up the wooden steps and took a few wary paces into the room.

We might have been aboard a whaling-ship. The edifice was ribbed and panelled like an upturned boat, the wood as shiny as metal, green-tinged where damp had made its home in the grain. The wooden roof was low, the room was small, and it seemed even smaller, crammed with sets of drawers fixed along three of the walls. Heaps of tools and instruments were stored above the drawers. Those drawers were narrow, as if they were used to hold maps and drawings, each marked with an iron letter from the alphabet. There were picks and hammers hanging from hooks. Large boxes containing screws and nails, all the paraphernalia of carpenters and woodworkers, were ranged on top of the drawers. In the centre of the room, a large table was illuminated by a hanging oil-lamp. Bread, cheese and wine had been set out on trays.

There were four soldiers standing around it. Their eyes slid over me and settled on the newly arrived Frenchmen. Greetings and names were quickly exchanged, together with more particular enquiries, regarding their journey and the state of the empire. The words *Spain* and *guerrilla* were like magnets to men who were isolated on the extreme northern coast of the continent.

I stood apart, holding tight to my travelling-bag, like a lost pilgrim, uncertain to whom I might address myself. But Colonel les Halles had other plans for me. He had taken up a position at the far end of the room, well away from the feast.

'Stiffeniis,' he called. 'Come over here.'

I went to stand beside him.

We were like a small private island; the other officers composed a larger, more convivial land mass some way off across the wide sea.

'I received a note regarding you from General Malaport,' he began, then stopped abruptly. 'First, let me see your orders.'

As he spoke, he slipped the cape from his shoulders. His uniform was stained and spotted. Mud had dried in places, as if he had just recently stopped working, and then in such a hurry that he had had no time to restore his finery. Only the stripes on his sleeves and the silver epaulettes on his shoulders proclaimed what he was. In the days to come, I would understand that this was what he wanted his underlings to think of him: he was a commander, he was ready to soil his hands, having no time for social nicety. He put first things first, and all the rest flew out of the window.

'You have left a wife and three young children in Lotingen,' he said, taking the letter that I held out to him, folding his arms, settling his bulk on the edge of the table, staring at me out of dark, hooded eyes. 'Your wife is expecting a fourth child, I've been informed. It cannot have been easy for you to leave them there, not knowing how long it will take to . . . to resolve the situation here.'

It was the first word of ordinary humanity that I had heard from his lips. Was there a Madame les Halles waiting for him in France? Was there a child who could squeeze a drop of tenderness from the heart of Colonel les Halles?

At my back, I heard the start of a small welcoming party for the new officers. Bottles were broached and exclamations of appreciation were made, concerning the unexpected quality of the German wine, the excellence of the dried sausages and the pickled herring.

He was keeping me well apart, I realised, singling me out, marking me off from the others. I was his Prussian guest, though that did not mean that I was to be generally made welcome. I waited in silence while he cast his eyes over my letter of commission. When he had finished, he handed it back to me. 'Carry this letter with you always,' he warned. 'It will be your passport here. You won't go far without it.'

'Without your assistance, I will not go far, in any case,' I said.

He did not reply immediately.

'Do you know what is happening here on the coast?' he asked, his voice low and guarded. His eyes flashed into mine.

'General Malaport told me. That is, he spoke of a woman,' I replied obliquely, taking my lead from my interlocutor.

His thin lips creased into a bitter smile.

'I like your answer,' he said. 'I can only hope to God that Malaport has chosen wisely. I will not hide it from you, I would have preferred a . . .'

'French magistrate?' I interrupted him.

'What else?' he answered quickly. 'But that is hardly the point. Get this fixed firmly in your mind, monsieur. My only concern is for results. I asked the general for a man who knows Prussia and understands the Prussians. Malaport has sent you to me. I had no voice in the matter. My work is being hampered, I want the obstacle removed. I will not permit interference with my plans. If you are not successful, you'll be sent packing. They can send me someone else, or I'll do the job myself.'

I felt the urge to smile, though I was careful to conceal it. How would such a man manage to ingratiate himself with a nation of Prussians who hated the occupying forces on sight?

'You, sir?'

'Me, sir. Or someone *like* me. A man whose only aim is the good of France. A man who will stop at nothing to achieve success.' He made no effort to hide his pride, or his single-minded drive. 'Do you understand what I want from you?'

He looked up suddenly, glanced over to the table where wine was being consumed in quantity, then back at me.

'Did you tell *them* why you were coming here?' he asked.

I shook my head.

'I do not discuss the emperor's business with the first man that I meet,' I replied.

'Keep it that way,' he said, as if the declaration had won me some sort of grudging consent. 'You will reveal your findings to me alone. They will discover the motive for your presence here soon enough. They are mechanics. They have more important tasks to occupy their thoughts. I will keep them busy. They must only know what is necessary.'

'Different tasks, nothing in common,' I summed up.

'On the contrary, monsieur,' he snapped. 'All of you have one aim in common. Your roles may differ, Herr Magistrate,

44

but all of you must strive to make Nordcopp a place which is safe and efficient.' He lowered his voice a key. 'Murder and commerce do not make good bedfellows.'

He stared at me in silence for some time.

'I want to show you something,' he said, turning to the desk behind him.

Something that might have been a child's game had been roughly tipped from a box. The pieces were distributed higgledy-piggledy over a board painted yellow and blue, as if a careless boy had knocked the models over, then gone to bed without bothering to set them in place again.

'These are my dreams,' he announced quietly.

At my back, the welcome party grew louder. Glass clinked on glass, more drinks were poured, conversations were eagerly pursued with mouths full of bread and cheese.

'What do the pieces represent?' I asked.

His eyes darted in my direction, dancing in the lamplight, apparently amused by the naivety of the question. They spoke of a sharp intelligence, but little kindness. He looked down, moving the pieces carefully, placing some on the broad blue field, shifting others onto the narrow yellow one. There was a fixity in his concentration, a gentle care in his handling of those frail objects which surprised me. His large head inclined over the table, carefully surveying the positions that he had chosen. The silvery hair on his head had been cut back almost to the bone. The dark stubble on his jaw was longer, as if he had forgotten to shave that day.

'Those toys would delight my son,' I said.

He picked up one of the pieces as if it were a precious jewel.

'The real pleasure is to see them grow,' he said. 'Soon the game will begin. For the moment, we are content to plan. But the work goes ahead and nothing must delay it. No one. This coast will never be the same again.'

He set the model down, and gazed at me.

'Herr Magistrate, I want you to do something for me.'

I nodded, expecting to receive some further peremptory order.

He paused for a moment. 'Go over to that table. Help your-self to a glass of red wine. A very large glass. Drink it off in a single draught. Then drink another. As soon as you've done that, monsieur, you must follow me.'

I looked at him in disbelief. Was this some sort of bizarre joke?

'I am not a great drinker of wine,' I began to say.

His forefinger appeared in a flash in front of my eyes. It was stubby, strong, the fingernail black and broken.

'Drink it!' he hissed. 'You'll be needing it. They will start their work tomorrow, but you will start tonight.'

7

I obeyed without a word of protest.

Something in his manner warned me that it would be futile to resist.

I walked across to the table where the French officers were eating and drinking, took a firm grip on a warm bottle of red wine, filled an empty glass to the brim, then poured the contents straight down my throat. I took a deep breath, poured out another draught, then drained it off in the same fashion. On the far side of the room, les Halles nodded slowly, as if some ritual of initiation had been carried out to his liking.

I studied his face for a moment, defiantly poured myself a third glass of wine, and emptied it off just as quickly.

The French officers watched with indifference. I might have been a condemned man, availing himself of a final request before the sharp axe fell. The colonel's staff must have known what was in store for me, yet no one uttered a word to warn me what it was. One of the officers who had travelled up from Lotingen took a pace towards me, his mouth full of bread, his eyes round with surprise.

A voice spoke out, and stopped him in his tracks.

'This way, Herr Stiffeniis,' the colonel called.

He swept a lantern from its hook on the wall, and threw open the door.

As I walked towards him, he addressed the men in the room.

'By the time I return, you will be in your bunks, messieurs,' he said. 'My adjutant will show the new men where to sleep.'

No one said a word. They were going to bed, whether they liked the idea, or not. Colonel les Halles had decided.

'If you are tired today,' he added, 'you'll be exhausted tomorrow. I intend to work you to the bone.'

He stepped back, and ushered me out of the door.

The fog was as thick as a fire burning damp peat.

Dimly, I heard the murmur of conversation picking up inside the hut, the clink of glasses, a toast of some sort. For one moment, envy possessed me. I had eaten nothing since leaving Lotingen, and the wine was burning a hole in my stomach. The hot fumes rushed to my head.

'Are we going far, Colonel les Halles?'

'Not far,' he growled, holding up his lantern.

The light glowed like sulphur. It hurt my eyes as I trailed behind him.

The night was warm, the damp air seemed to cling to my skin. A light breeze ruffled the hair on my neck, and I shivered. I was, I realised, a trifle inebriated. And yet, I thought (one of those blatant idiocies for which drunkards are renowned), a spinning head and a sheen of sweat on my brow were better than the gut-wrenching stink of excrement on the streets of Lotingen.

My thoughts flew home to Helena.

Her battle with the flies, her efforts to keep them away from the children and out of their food. If I could just conclude this case, I thought, I might be able to make capital of my success, and force General Malaport to take steps to resolve the situation.

I felt a sardonic smile form on my lips.

Was this what it meant to be a Prussian magistrate? If I were able to solve the problems of the French, would it result in a thinner layer of *merde* on the streets of my home town, and fractionally less fetid air for my children to breathe?

The colonel stopped in front of the last hut, and held the lamp up.

'Tell no one of what you are about to see.' He stared at me for longer than was necessary. 'Is that quite clear, monsieur?

The details, I mean. You must act with circumspection.' Still, he held my gaze. 'Are you ready?' he asked, as if he were inviting me to leap into deep water from a great height.

'I am here for no other reason,' I said.

As he unlocked the door and ushered me into the room, my nerves were taut.

I was not prepared for the fetid smell, and had to swallow hard. A tangy stench of organic decomposition seemed to have worked its way into the wood from which the hut was built. You might consume it with fire, but you would never wash it away. An animal might have been rotting under the floorboards.

And what was that object laid out on the table?

In the gloom, it looked nothing like the body of the woman that I was expecting to find. Indeed, it looked more like a very large badger.

Les Halles held up his light.

'Blast their eyes!' he cursed. 'Somebody has been here.'

I did not hear the rest. My eyes were drawn to the object on the table in the centre of the room. It was draped with a cloak of animal pelts. Some were brown, others black and every shade of grey. Was this furry winding-sheet made of rat-skins? Only the head and the face remained exposed.

I corrected myself.

What remained of a face . . .

The conversation I had interrupted in Lotingen that morning came to my mind.

'. . . Pure evil! Why would anyone . . . ?'

Les Halles set his lantern down on the edge of the table.

The light revealed a forehead that was blue, the skin pulped and split. A thick crust of blood had congealed in a black sheet across the woman's left temple. Her left ear was a solid lump of blood, which had dripped down onto her slender neck. The nose was turned up at an angle that was obviously unnatural. But below the nose, all was a mystery. There was a gaping hole where the lower half of the face ought to have been.

49

'You won't see much if you stand dithering there,' les Halles called sharply. 'Come closer, man. You'll need more light. There ought to be some candles.'

While he rummaged on the shelves which ran the length of the far wall, I stood beside the table, alone with the body. He wished to illuminate it, render it more terrible, more indelible in my mind. He fumbled in the gloom, while I prayed that he would not find what he was looking for. There was too much light for me as it was. I cringed at the task which lay before me. No sight is worse than a lifeless corpse, except the spectacle of a woman who has been hideously mutilated.

'What do you make of it?' he called over, roughly opening drawers, slamming them closed again.

'That wound is terrible,' I managed to say.

He returned with a fistful of candles, muttering beneath his breath, lighting them from the lantern-flame, setting each candle firmly upright in a pool of its own wax along the table edge. Like the high altar in a church. The orange light swelled, casting dancing shadows on the brutalised face. The sunken cheeks seemed to quiver with animated life.

'What's this?' les Halles exploded, as he set a candle down beside her head.

I looked where he was pointing.

A trail of stones had been laid out on the table like a halo.

He snatched one up, held it to his eye, then threw it to the farthest corner of the room. 'I gave strict orders that no one be allowed in here,' he hissed. 'They are devils. They come and go as they please. God knows how, but they do it. There's no stopping them . . .'

'Of whom do you speak?' I asked.

I was unable to look away from that devastated face.

'The Prussian girls. They must have wormed their way in here, covered the body with that vile thing, then laid these baubles out on the table. Thieves, the whole blasted pack of them!'

'I'm sorry?' I said.

50

Faced with a corpse, he seemed more interested in bits of stone.

'This is amber,' he replied, as if he were spitting out nails. 'Unpolished amber! These women are barbarians, monsieur. They'll steal it and sell it, yet they believe in every legend that is spoken about it. This, I suppose, is some sort of pagan funeral rite. Somebody's going to pay for this . . .'

I raised my eyes and stared at him.

'Would you punish this woman's friends because they care?' I asked.

'I don't give a damn about her friends!' he exclaimed. 'There are more important issues. One of my men has been seduced. How could they get in here without help? That soldier has disobeyed *me*. Do you see now, Herr Magistrate? Do you understand the gravity of it? They wrap my men around their little fingers. If those girls know what happened to her, everyone in Nordcopp will know.'

I looked down at the damaged face.

Which religion prescribed the strange manner in which that corpse had been laid out?

'A ritual, you say? What kind of ritual?'

Colonel les Halles shook his head. 'This cloak is supposed to save her from the Baltic cold when she's laid in the ground. The amber will buy a seat near the fire in their Valhalla.' He blew his lips together noisily. 'You Prussians are master storytellers. This coast has more tall tales to its name than a children's nursery.'

He spoke of barbarity as if he were an apostle of civilisation. Why would he not allow the women to mourn for their comrade who was dead?

'What was her name?' I asked, unable to tear my eyes away.

I heard him rustling in his pocket, the sound of a paper being unfolded.

He had written out her name. He had no idea who she was.

'Kati . . . uscka . . . Rod . . . end . . . ahl,' he grunted, struggling with the syllables, as if the foreign name were hateful to him.

I leant over the body, looking closely at the bruised and battered forehead. The head had been struck twice, I judged. The greatest damage was concentrated in the area above her left eye. The eye was closed, the skin bulging, purple, the eyelid grossly swollen up, black with blood. A further blow had dug deep into the bridge of her nose. Had the blows been delivered by a hammer? The blunt edge of an axe? The weapon had been heavy enough to stun her, though the initial attack had not killed her. She was still alive when the butcher began to carry out the mutilations on her unresisting body. Blood had flowed freely down her face and neck, and curdled in her hair. Her heart had gone on beating for quite some time. The battered brow and broken nose told their story of violence, but what was I to make of the yawning emptiness below?

It was as if her face had collapsed in upon itself. She might have swallowed the pieces. Her upper lip drooped down into the formless space where her mouth ought to have been. A wild beast might have torn the lower part of her face away with a single, ripping bite. The red-raw pit stretched from earlobe to earlobe, encompassing what had been her mouth, her chin and her throat. Scraps of flesh, tangles of nerves, fragments of bone, torn gristle, muscle and shredded cartilage had been roughly hacked away, as if by a demon surgeon.

Why attack the face alone?

There was nothing instinctive about it. I had no doubt in my mind. The attack had been carefully planned, premeditated, then put into effect. Those flaps of skin hung loose inside the cavity of the face because the central prop had been torn away, taken out as a single piece. That human face had been – the word took on a strange, perplexing significance – *mined*. It appeared as if some insane anatomical engineer had drilled and emptied the lower half of her skull, hollowing it out, removing only the deposits that interested him, leaving the rest alone.

Holding my breath I edged closer to the chasm.

'The jawbone has been cut out,' I murmured, angling my head, taking advantage of the flickering candlelight to verify the point. 'I am not an anatomist, but . . . well, you can see the damage clearly enough. These tissues here . . . They would have held the jawbone fixed in place. They are dangling in shreds, like strips of torn paper against the inner walls of the larynx. The teeth are missing, too.'

The teeth . . .

Not one remained in the upper jaw.

'Where was she found?' I asked.

Katiuscka Rodendahl had been found on the beach beyond the military boundary. She had not presented herself for roll-call at the start of the working day, but no one had attached much importance to that fact.

'They pass through our pickets like shadows,' he added. 'She probably left the compound during the night, as many of them do. We search the ones who leave by the gate, of course, but it's the Devil's own job. I can hardly trust my men. These girls have a way with lonely Frenchmen far from home.' He laughed sardonically. 'They make for Nordcopp village. No one there would chase them away. These girls have money . . .'

'Is that why she was murdered, do you think? For money?'

A grumbling laugh rumbled out from his throat.

'Amber is more valuable than money, Herr Procurator. Gold comes cheaper. We carry out random body-searches and they yield significant results. But for every piece that we find on them, another bit goes out unnoticed. The traders in Nordcopp are waiting to buy it from them. Amber-trading is against the law, but when did the law stop people trying? Thieving is an art on the Baltic coast. If you hope to stop the theft, you must change the method of collection. And that's what I intend to do. There'll be machines all along the coast.' He made an extravagant gesture with his outstretched hand towards infinity. 'Machines don't steal.'

I had nothing to say on that count.

'Well?' he growled again. 'Don't you want to see the rest of the body?'

I wanted nothing less in the world.

My hand was shaking as I threw back the fur coverlet.

The corpse was naked. And cold, though I barely touched it. The orange glow of a million candles would never warm her up. The body might have been sculpted in grey marble that was veined and mottled with impurities. Light bounced off the taut surface of her skin, leaving shadows in the rolling contours of her well-formed muscles, firm breasts, strong arms, powerful legs. No outward damage was apparent. None at all, indeed. It was as if the torso and the limbs were of no concern to the person who had killed her.

'She was handsome,' the colonel murmured quietly. 'Most of them are.'

His eyes were fixed on the triangle formed by her stomach and thighs. A thicket of curly dark hair cloaked her sex. I had heard men gossip over pipes and ale, naming the peasant girls, pronouncing judgement on the qualities which proclaimed that this or that maid would make the perfect wife and bear a dozen children.

I thought of Helena's slender arms, tiny wrists, long neck. Her bulging belly made her seem more fragile still. This woman and my wife did not belong to the same species. They might have come from different worlds. This girl was a big, strong physical presence, even in death. I put all thoughts of Helena aside, and tried to think of nothing but the woman stretched out on the table.

There were no open wounds on the body with the exception of some half-healed nicks on her hands and arms. She had cut herself while working, probably. Like a priest preparing for the Holy Communion, I put on a pair of thin kid gloves which I took from my pocket. Beginning with the arms, moving over the hips, I continued down along the legs, applying pressure with my fingers as I went, searching for broken bones, producing a volley of light cracks as I tested the joints.

'*Rigor* makes the joints stiff,' I murmured. 'So far, she appears to be uninjured.'

Placing one hand over the other, I pressed down hard at various points along both sides of her ribcage, then over the sternum and the breastbone.

No sounds came at all.

'Nothing,' I said. 'Apart from the visible damage to her face.'

The colonel watched suspiciously as I removed my gloves and reached for my shoulder-bag. I took out my drawing-album, and released a piece of graphite from the narrow silver tube that Helena had given me several years before for my birthday.

'What now?' he asked.

'I want to sketch her,' I said. 'The corpse will rot. She must be buried soon.'

'What's the point? Will anyone want a picture to recall her by? In this state . . .'

'The sketch is for my own use,' I explained. 'I will need to remember her as she is. Professor Kant . . . my *maestro* maintained that the exact physical details of every crime are revealing, especially if comparisons are called for. There may be others . . .'

'I hope there won't be!' he exclaimed sarcastically. 'You are here to prevent it from happening again.'

I did not speak, I was busy moving the graphite point over the paper.

'The killer went to work on the face,' he said, pointing to her forehead. 'When I first saw her, I thought that she had fallen from a great height. A heap of bones was found farther down the coast shortly before I arrived. Another amber collector, they say, who fell off a cliff. But there was no cliff near the spot where this one was discovered.'

'This one?' I repeated coldly. 'Do you mean Katiuscka Rodendahl?'

Were all Prussian women nameless in his eyes?

'This one here,' he confirmed. 'No rock did that.'

I nodded, continuing with my work, finishing my sketch of the profile of her brow, her fractured nose, and the jagged contour of the unnatural cavity below. As I worked, I wondered about the shape of the part that was missing.

'Was she married?' I asked.

'None of the girls . . .' les Halles began to say, but then he stopped. 'There are no Prussian men inside the camp. Not one, except for yourself.'

'Was she naked when found?' I asked him next.

'Not a stitch of clothing on her.'

'Did you examine her back and shoulders?'

'Not a mark. No wound. Nothing, except for the damage to her face.'

'Did you find her yourself?'

That question provoked a laugh. 'Do you see me as a man with time to stroll along the seashore, Herr Stiffeniis? I've been here four months, and I have hardly had the time to take a piss! She was found by one of my men.'

'What is the name of the soldier?'

'Pierre Grillet,' he hissed, as if reluctant to reveal so little.

'What sort of a man is he?'

'First-rate.'

His answers were becoming shorter, as if he resented being questioned. The fact that I was a Prussian, a civilian, and a magistrate who threatened to block his schemes, went ill with him, I suppose.

'May I speak with him?' I asked carefully.

The colonel was silent for a moment.

'My men work very hard. Most of them will be sleeping. You can have a word tomorrow morning,' he conceded finally. 'I'll send him to you.'

I thanked him, wondering at the same time whether concern for his men and their sleep, or a reluctance to allow what I asked, had inspired his answer.

I put my album away, picked up the hanging shroud, and was about to cover the body again, but the left hand of les Halles shot out and seized my wrist.

'What do you think you are doing?' he said, separating

56

his words like a teacher telling off a boy who has been too bold.

'This body has been deprived of every dignity,' I said. 'I see no reason for her to go naked into the ground.'

'You have not done yet, monsieur,' he said roughly, pushing my hand away.

'What do you mean?' Did I need to explain to him what must be obvious to any man with eyes? 'This woman was killed by blows to the head. The lower half of her face has been ransacked by a maniac. This corpse can tell us nothing more.'

'I know why she was killed,' he snapped back. 'I know who did it. I cannot put my finger on the man, but I can point you in the right direction. This body will confirm what I am about to say.'

He raised his hand to hush me.

'She was trafficking in stolen amber,' he pressed on. 'She was murdered for it. Instead of paying what she asked, the smuggler struck her down and took it for free. She spoke out of turn, perhaps. She may have threatened to give his name to me. He made an example of her. A warning to all the other amber-girls. Keep your mouths shut. That was the message. That is the path you must follow. The illegal trade in stolen amber. Prussian thieves and smugglers . . .'

'General Malaport did not tell me you had solved the case,' I interrupted. 'Why did he bother to send for me?'

Irony was alien to les Halles, it seemed.

'I can tell you that, monsieur,' he replied assuredly. 'The coffers of the army are low. Now, Spain is stretching our resources. A drawn-out war in a poor country costs vast amounts of money. That's where Prussian amber comes into the equation. Nordcopp will yield ten times as much to us as it ever did to you.'

'I do not see your point,' I objected.

'There's one small problem,' he nodded at the corpse on the table. 'A Prussian slut has been murdered, and diplomacy

57

dictates that a Prussian magistrate should examine the case. We want nothing to do with the business.'

'A Prussian slut?' I repeated his phrase slowly, as if savouring the words. 'So much for French diplomacy.'

'Don't bandy morals with me,' he snarled. 'I was not born a colonel in the emperor's engineers. My words are rough, my thinking rougher. I know the tricks of the poor. They steal a silver thimble and swallow it, knowing that they'll shit it out in a day or two. Amber is a jewel, and a stomach is a bank-vault. Open her up, Herr Procurator Stiffeniis, and see what's in her entrails. And while you're about it, stick your finger into every hole that you can think of. If I were you, I'd put my gloves back on.'

That night, I perpetrated the final indignity on the corpse of Kati Rodendahl.

The search did not prove fruitless.

8

A noise disturbed my sleep.

A dull blow repeated at regular intervals.

A bludgeon beating me slowly into consciousness.

I listened in the darkness of the empty hut.

An echoing *thump*, the drawn-out rattle of chains, a brief pregnant pause, a teeth-clenching rasp of metal sliding on metal, then another resounding *thump*. I might have been in Paris once again, watching public executions from the foot of the guillotine in the Place de la Révolution, but no coarse cheers went up as another once-noble head fell into the waiting wicker basket. Instead, the chains began to jingle and clank, metal sheared once more, and that *thump* pounded out again.

I sat up, felt around for my boots in the darkness. The leather was cold to my touch, slick with damp. A jolt of pain racked my shoulder as I stood up stiffly. I had not undressed the night before, but slept in the clothes I had worn all day. I did not need to drag myself from any warm cocoon; I was already wearing it.

I unlatched the door and stepped outside.

The sharp chill of the early morning was unexpected.

A dense white fog rolled in off the sea.

Instinctively, I slipped my hands into my pockets.

My fingers closed around the piece of amber that I had removed from the mutilated corpse the night before. I held the nugget up, recalling last night's labour in all its horror. Though diabolical, the colonel's intuition had been correct. The dead girl *had* hidden a stolen piece of amber about her body. She had tucked it deep inside her sex. Larger than a plum, even I could see that the stone was valuable. It was a ravishing gold colour, as if it had been cleaned and polished, with darker veins of red threading through it.

More surprising still was what that piece contained.

A female wasp in the act of laying her eggs. A stream of tiny bubbles squirted from its tail like the trail of a shooting star. The insect was large, its thorax swollen. Each detail of its body and wings was as perfect as the day that it had died. Its front legs pushed forward, as if it had been seeking desperately to break free from the dripping resin that had fixed and drowned it.

Had a thousand years gone by?

More, perhaps?

Scientists in Prussia and abroad had recently begun to study amber, claiming that God's Creation might be better understood by examining the plants and creatures which it contained, claiming, indeed, that the Garden of Eden itself had once existed somewhere on our Prussian shores.

The memory of the insects in my garden returned to mind.

Flies, ants, beetles, attacking and devouring anything that could be eaten. I did not pretend to be a man of science, yet there seemed to me to be nothing which distinguished those living insects from the creature trapped inside that piece of amber. That wasp could be dated to the birth of the world, they said. Insects had survived for aeons. Like us, they had persevered. And yet, I thought, insects had no visible conscience, showed no mercy. Eat, or be eaten, that was the law of Nature. They had consumed the corpse of every creature born since Adam and Eve.

A cold shiver ran across my shoulders.

Would they persist when I – when *we* – had turned to long-forgotten dust?

I shook these strange ideas from my head. I had a case to solve. I must begin by establishing the facts. Had the girl been murdered as she tried to smuggle her treasure away from the coast, as Colonel les Halles believed?

He had shown me the death certificate the night before.

Naked body of a woman found on Nordcopp shore. Aged thirty, give or take a year or two. Deceased as a result of blows to the head. Whether accidental or intentional remains unclear. Grave damage to the face inhibits easy identification. Savaged by animals after death?

Signed & sworn, this day, 11th August 1808.

The report was written in French. It had been signed with an illegible scrawl by the company doctor.

Here was another source of information.

A brief note had been added in the same hand, identifying Kati Rodendahl as one of the amber-workers from the camp.

I let the piece of amber slide back into the safety of my pocket.

'It is evidence,' I had insisted. 'It may prove useful.'

'Keep it safe,' les Halles had warned me, giving in at last, reluctantly allowing me to carry it away with me. 'That piece of amber was stolen from us. It belongs to France.'

A narrow plank walkway linked the seven huts which stood on the crest of the dunes. Somewhere below was the beach. I could hear the sound of waves. I was fifty yards away from the waterline, though I did not know it. The dense white fog shrouded the scene that would, otherwise, have presented itself to my sight. All was still and silent, except for that endless sequence of repeated sounds: the rattling of chains, the shriek of metal, the concluding *thump*.

Far out to sea, the fog merged with the grey waters of the Baltic Sea. It was impossible to say where one began and the other ended. Further out, however, I could see a silhouetted gold-edged horizon, and I caught a glimpse of a sail – a fishing-boat? – a mere flash of white in the far distance. Suddenly, a bar of pink shot into the sky. Other bars shot off at different angles as the sun floated gently upwards like a wedge of honey-coloured amber. It had no more power to heat the world than the glimmering stub of a distant candle. And where the weak light could not penetrate, the sky above the fog was dark blue, shimmering into coal-black.

The noise did not cease.

Somebody was already hard at work.

It might have been a procession of ghostly Teutonic knights in rusty, clanking armour, going home to rest in some funeral crypt after a midnight roust. The Order had ruled the Baltic coast with an iron fist for centuries. They had been the first to organise the gathering of amber, the first to regulate the trade. Control had passed to local lords, then, finally, to the Hohenzollerns. Now, the French had laid their hands upon our riches.

With a start, I realised that someone was lurking at my shoulder.

I am tall, but the man was taller. And he was thinner, too. His blue woollen jacket rucked up in folds where his belt pulled too tightly at his waist. His face was the ashen colour of lye soap, his features utterly undistinguished, except for two thick-lidded eyes which peered back at me without blinking. They reminded me of the unseeing black buttons sewn onto the pale cotton face of my daughter's rag doll.

'I am Pierre Grillet,' he announced. 'I was told that you wanted to speak with me.'

'The soldier who found the body on the beach?'

'The colonel said to take you in to breakfast,' he said, though he did not confirm or deny what I had said. He simply turned and walked away, taking great long strides along the narrow walkway of rotting planks.

I had eaten nothing since leaving Lotingen, and I was famished. I followed him willingly to the hut at the far end of the row.

He threw open the door, then stepped aside to let me enter first.

The aroma of toasted corn hung in the air in wisps of blue smoke. Coffee had become a rare commodity since the English set up their blockade of the Channel, but toasted corn will do for men who have forgotten the taste of anything better. I looked with yearning at the breakfast table, the plates piled high with fresh bread. French officers were making short work of the feast. Every man in the room stopped eating. All of them stared at me, and not one word was said. It would have been impossible to hold a private conversation.

Reluctantly, I turned to Grillet.

'It might be better if we speak out here,' I said.

'As you prefer, monsieur.'

There was something sly and insinuating in his reedy voice.

'You speak good French,' he added, as he closed the door on the tempting smell of food, and we turned our faces to the fog once more.

The compliment spurred me to be brusque. 'Just tell me how you found the body. Make it short, and keep it simple. For the sake of a foreigner, do you understand me?'

He nodded, sniffed, began to speak.

'Three days ago, I was scouting up along the coast. It was shortly after breakfast. This time of day, more or less. I'd been on duty all that night, so I had the morning off. I'd gone about a mile in that direction,' he pointed away to the east, 'when I came upon her. She was lying face down on the beach. As naked as Eve before the Fall. I wondered what was going on, of course. It isn't every day that you find a . . .'

'You have told me what you saw,' I said. 'Now, tell me what you did.'

He cleared his throat. 'I called out to her, that's what I did. But she did not reply. I guessed what was up, of course. Like I said, a naked woman lying on the shore. And way above the waterline. She hadn't been swept ashore. I went up close, and prodded her leg with the toe of my boot. When she didn't move, or cry out, I ran back here and reported what I'd found. I didn't even turn her over. No idea what she looked like. I didn't see her face until the sergeant came and rolled her over . . .'

'And you were alone when you found her?'

'Just me, monsieur.'

He had no one to corroborate his story. What he told me was what he wished to tell me. It might be more or less than the truth.

'What were you doing on that stretch of coast?'

'I went to bathe,' he replied.

Soldiers are not the cleanest men in the world.

'Do you often wash?' I asked him.

'Tuesday, or Wednesday, as a rule,' he said. 'I'll not wash this week, though. Not after what happened.'

'Do you always go to the same spot?'

'No, sir. I'd never been so far along the shore.'

'Why did you go so far off this time, then?'

He pointed down to the beach. Beneath the blanket of fog, the noise of the work went on unbroken. 'The sea is dirty here since they started digging. You go in white, but you come out blue.'

'Blue?' I quizzed him.

'There's something hidden under the sand and pebbles. It's a blue clay, one of the girls was telling me. It breaks up into powder when they pierce it, and turns the water into a sort of blue dye. There's a phrase for it in German . . . *blaue Erde*, I think they call it. That's where the amber is found.'

'Did you kill her?' I asked him bluntly.

He was the first to admit that he had seen the body. He had been alone, and was in an area beyond regular French military control. He could have murdered her without being seen, then fabricated the story of happening by chance upon her body. It was a perfect cover. In his apparent openness, he appeared to be above suspicion.

His small eyes opened wide with shock.

'Why would I do that?' he protested, his voice rising sharply.

Clearly, he did not like being questioned by a Prussian. And by a Prussian magistrate even less.

'I can think of a few good reasons,' I replied flatly. 'She was young and fit. She may have been a beauty before someone went to work on her face. Did she refuse to let you have your way with her?'

He pulled himself stiffly to attention, but he did not answer.

'Why was she naked, Grillet? Did you tear her clothes off before you raped her?'

His cheeks were two inflamed red spots.

'I'll speak to the colonel about this,' he muttered.

'The colonel ordered you to speak to *me*,' I snapped. 'When I have finished, you may tell him what you wish. Why was the woman . . .' I stopped, corrected myself. 'Why do you think that she was naked, then? What logical explanation would you give for that fact?'

'That's obvious, sir,' he spat back.

'Not to me, it isn't.'

He sighted down his long nose at me before he spoke.

'They're whores, sir. Every last one of them! They won't consort with us, not openly, but they won't stay put at night. I'd been on duty, as I told you. We guard the compound where those women sleep, or they'd all be off to the village, and half of them would never come back. We've lost many in the last few months . . .'

'Lost, or gone?'

The idea that there might be other bodies struck me forcefully. The fact that les Halles had not informed me of the situation seemed like a grave omission. Did he suspect what I suspected? Was he covering up for his men? Did he believe that one of them was guilty of this murder? And of other murders, too?

Grillet shrugged. His bony shoulders grazed his ears. 'They could be anywhere, sir. They are here one minute, gone the next. Smugglers head for the Russian border, I have heard. That's where the women may have gone.' He grunted mirthlessly, and

I realised that he was laughing. 'If that's the case, we may catch up with them. Moscow. That's where we'll be heading next.'

Unless they send you off to Spain, I thought.

'You have not answered my question,' I said. 'What do you believe may have happened to the dead girl's clothes?'

He seemed to relax a fraction. 'I've got two ideas on that front, sir,' he said, then he made a loud clicking sound inside his mouth. 'Either she was trying to swim out, or . . .'

'Swim?'

'That's right, sir. They do it all the time.' He pointed to the east. The fog had almost disappeared at the far end of the beach. A group of huts raised on stilts seemed to float above the waters of the lagoon half a mile away. 'The women live down there,' he pointed. 'They swim to the shore at night. I reckon she met with something in the water. Some sea-monster probably dug that hole in her face.'

'Oh, yes?' I encouraged him.

'A basking whale, or something similar. Catch that fish, I bet you'd find a bundle of rags in its guts. Like Jonah in the Bible.'

Against my will, I let out a chuckle. 'That is an ingenious explanation,' I complimented him. 'But you mentioned two possibilities. Let's see if your second is as clever as the first, Grillet.'

'Thieves,' he said, and added quickly, 'Prussian thieves.'

What else? I should have expected it. If I asked a Frenchman for an opinion, he would tell me that the guilty party was certainly a Prussian.

'Prussian thieves, indeed!' I challenged. 'Excluding myself, I have not seen a single Prussian man in this encampment. Or are you talking about the Prussian women? Do you suspect the girls of murdering their workmate to rob her clothes?'

'Not just her clothes, sir.'

He looked at me attentively, as if considering how much to tell me. Wondering, perhaps, if he had been too quick to tell a Prussian magistrate where he laid the blame for the murder of a Prussian girl.

'Monsieur Magistrate, the situation here is complicated. We are French soldiers. We have no wives, no women of our own. And there are no whore-houses nearby, like you'd find in a decent town. Some of these girls are up for it, though. Why would *we* kill them? You could buy all the girls on Nordcopp shore for a *napoléon d'or*! Dead girls are no use to any man. No use to us, nor to the colonel.' He jerked his thumb decisively back over his shoulder. 'But for *them* it's different!'

'Who do you mean?' I asked.

His eyes fixed mine again, and held them. 'The local men, monsieur. There are Prussians living near to the shore. They have a different trade with the women. Stolen amber, monsieur. There's a motive for you! The girls must put some by. They're always trying to smuggle it out under our noses. They'd have to try and sell it to someone, don't you think? Those men have wives and women of their own, they are not like us. What's a dead Prussian wench to them?'

'Are you suggesting that the girl was murdered by a smuggler?'

'I am, monsieur.'

I nodded, thinking of the amber in my pocket.

'Let's say, Grillet, for just one moment, that this idea of yours is correct. The girl broke out of the compound and swam to the shore, intending to sell her amber to a local man, and, for some reason, he murdered her.'

That piece of amber was worth a lot of money. But Grillet's reasoning was faulty. Kati Rodendahl had never been given the opportunity to sell it. She'd been murdered before she got the chance to make a trade. Whatever it was, the motive was not theft.

'Why would the killer strip the body naked?' I challenged him.

Grillet looked at me for a moment, then he smirked. 'Why not, monsieur? If you have stolen a life, you might as well steal her clothes. And every other thing that she had hidden about her person.'

Did Grillet know Kati's secret?

Did all the French soldiers on the shore know where the girls hid their amber?

'What *things* are you speaking of?' I asked him.

He was still smiling. The roots of his teeth were black with the stains of tobacco wads. 'I'm guessing,' Grillet went on. 'She might have had a ring, earrings, a sacred medallion. Depends on whether she was planning to leave, or not.'

'It is certainly possible,' I conceded.

'Then again,' he pressed on, 'if a deal had been already struck, he might have cheated her. If she threatened to report him to the colonel, he might have killed her to protect his identity. For me, it's Prussian business,' he concluded emphatically, and he appeared to believe what he said.

I did not react.

Grillet proposed that Prussians were killing the girls for profit, or to maintain the secrets of their illegal trade in amber. But what if the nationalities were changed about? Might the French be staging murders for political reasons known to themselves alone? Might the French officers – and les Halles himself – be involved in the conspiracy? The idea that girls had run away to Russia was plausible, but was it true? What if they had died like Kati Rodendahl? What if the bodies had never been found? If the French could frighten the women into avoiding any contact with the smugglers, wouldn't it be to their own advantage?

Was that why they had sent for a Prussian magistrate? In the hope that he would find a Prussian scapegoat? Was that why Malaport had called for a man whose wife was in the final stages of a difficult pregnancy? Knowing that I would agree to anything for the sake of a quick and easy passage home?

The sun was burning off the fog like a bright phosphorescent flame.

'Very good, Grillet,' I said, shading my eyes. 'Colonel les Halles will be told that you have answered all my questions.

Now, where can I find the women who work the amber? Her friends, for instance. I'll need to speak with them . . .'

'You cannot,' Grillet interrupted brusquely.

'Cannot?' I frowned.

'Colonel les Halles is on the beach with the engineers who arrived last evening,' he said. 'The new machines are being set up. His specific orders. No one can go down there today. Excepting the builders and the colonel himself, that is.'

'What about the women?'

'Confined to their cabins. There is no way to reach them.'

Was he about to inform me that I would be confined to my hut, as well?

I skipped to the next point on the agenda that I had set myself for the day.

'I mean to speak to the company doctor. Where can I find him?'

Grillet's French was rural, his pronunciation more heavily accented than the norm, brutal in its directness. '*Le médecin n'est pas ici,*' he said.

'Not in the camp?' I repeated.

'He lives in Nordcopp. Three miles inland.'

I was surprised. Did Colonel les Halles allow his officers to live in the town?

'That's half an hour by horse,' I insisted stubbornly. 'However slow the nag may be.'

'The horses are on the shore, as well, monsieur. There's heavy stuff to be moved about down there.' He paused, like a wrestler looking for a better hold. Then, he leapt to the attack again. 'If you want to go, you'll have to walk.'

The trace of a sardonic smile graced his thin lips. I had met this sort of insolence before when working with the French. They might need me, but they were not prepared to help me overmuch.

'Just point me in the right direction,' I said, ignoring the provocation.

He looked inland. 'Follow the track leading out of the main gate. It will take you straight to Nordcopp by way of Nordbarn.'

'Nordbarn?'

Grillet settled the strap of his cap more comfortably beneath his chin.

'You asked about her friends, monsieur,' he volunteered. 'Those women up in Nordbarn used to work down here on the shore themselves. They may have known the woman that you are interested in. And now, monsieur, if you've done with me, I'll have my breakfast.'

He placed his hand upon the door and pushed.

The smell of French bread and toasted corn wafted over me again.

'Will you come, too, sir?'

I peered inside and met the suspicious glances of the French soldiers. They all knew who I was. They also knew that I had just interrogated one of their number. My stomach ached with hunger, but I did not go in.

'Thank you, no,' I said.

I would eat Prussian food.

Nordcopp was not so very far away.

9

The sun beat mercilessly down upon my head.

It was three miles to Nordcopp, even less to Nordbarn, according to Grillet, but it seemed like thirty as I tramped along the narrow rutted carriage-track which had brought me to the Baltic shore the night before. Fishermen and the people who worked the local amber were reputed to dwell there, but I saw no man. Grillet had also warned me that the area was rigorously patrolled by French troops, but I did not meet a single soldier.

I seemed to be going nowhere, beating time in the middle of a desolate wilderness, a vast expanse of rolling sand-dunes crowned with withered clumps of stunted grass. The only sounds that shattered the persistent shrilling of the wind were the sharp shriek of an occasional solitary gull high above my head or the softer piping of an unseen curlew. As time dragged on and nothing changed, I began to wonder whether Moses himself could have led me safely out of that desert.

Then, a stunted laurel bush appeared like a mirage on the horizon.

I reached it, and I saw a stand of slanting ash trees further off. Sheltering in their lee was a cluster of low broken-backed roofs. I counted five huts as I approached, five long buildings covered with salt-blackened thatch that was hanging almost to the ground. They were set in a horse-shoe which enclosed a small bare space, and leant so close together that the villagers must have heard their neighbours rutting.

Nordbarn.

The settlement was like a primitive fortress. There was one way in and out, a narrow passage that pointed towards the coast. That was where the amber came from. That was where the French soldiers came from. In ages past, the Baltic Sea had been the local people's only source of livelihood, the source of all the dangers that they faced. I could only hope that they would not see me in the same menacing light.

My ears were throbbing. The sensation had been annoying me for quite a while, long before I actually saw the place. The noise increased in intensity, the nearer that I came to the village. It might have been the droning of a hive of bumble-bees. Or the streets of Lotingen at midday, I recalled ruefully, when the clouds of flies and midges were most bothersome.

Yet, no fly troubled me.

No droning bee was anywhere to be seen.

And suddenly the throbbing ceased.

A wooden shutter was thrown back, a face looked out.

I froze on the spot.

Let them see you plainly, I thought.

They would see a man who had not shaved since the previous morning. A man whose hair was tussled by the wind, and stiff with sand. A man who had slept all night in the rumpled, sweaty clothes that he was wearing. I began to regret my slovenliness. Would I look to them like a magistrate who had the power to conduct an important criminal investigation?

The shutter closed with a bang.

Diffidence was probably normal in that place. Especially knowing that one of their number had been murdered. Then again, there was the fear of strangers which such news might be expected to arouse.

I began to stride more purposefully towards the village.

My German tongue would convince them that I meant no harm.

I passed through the gap between the huts and emerged in the heart of the hamlet.

I could feel eyes upon me, though I could not see them. There were movements behind the narrow window-slats as I planted my feet in the centre of the open space. Then, like an actor in a tragedy, I cleared my throat, and began to introduce myself to my invisible audience.

'My name is Hanno Stiffeniis, Procurator to His Majesty the King . . .'

A gaggle of geese came waddling around a corner. Wings held wide, beaks up and gaping, they screeched, slithered and slid to a halt in front of me, like troops running out from a besieged fort to repel an attack. A large pig came snorting after them, with two less corpulent swine hard on its heels. The door of the middle house opened slowly, and a man appeared in the doorway.

He stepped out into the sun. He was squat and built like an ox, though aged.

'I must speak with the women of the village,' I announced.

'What do you want with them?' he barked, his voice coming in great choking gasps. He raised his head at an angle, as if to see me better. His left eye was milky white with cataracts. His skin was scarlet, his face round. Bald on top, he had sparse white whiskers sprouting from his chin like onion roots. There was something of the terrier-before-the-baiting-starts about him.

'I wish to ask them some questions,' I said.

The man twirled his forefinger in the air. 'There's lots of women working here,' he sighed. 'You'll need to be more exact, Herr Magistrate. What exactly is your business with them?'

He dropped his aitches, rounded his consonants. He was intelligible, but only just. And I felt that he was toying with me. He knew why I had come. For all I could tell, he knew everything that there was to know about what happened on the coast.

'A woman was found the other day down on the beach. She had been murdered. I'm trying to trace anyone who may have known her . . .'

'Best place to start,' he wheezed loudly. 'The beach, I mean. Bet them French soldiers could tell you what you want to know.'

I was surprised by this bluff reply. Anger was a better word for my reaction, though I struggled not to show it. I did not intend to start my enquiries by telling this upstart why I had not begun my investigation down on Nordcopp shore.

'Her friends work here, I have been told. I want to talk with them.'

I employed the peremptory tone that any magistrate might use, though I lacked the power to command that I had once possessed. I knew it, and so did he. Since the coming of the French, the authority of every magistrate in Prussia had been diminished. Even a humble village elder might decide to question it.

But he did not. He smiled as if something privately amused him, turning away with a nod of his head and a theatrical gesture of open-handed welcome, inviting me to follow him into the building.

I might have stepped through a magic mirror. It was day outside, but everything inside was darkest night. A fire burned at one end of the room – weak flames, a great deal of malodorous smoke coiling up from damp wood. The temperature was intolerably hot. Lanterns hung from low beams above the heads of a score of people working there. All of them were women, and they were bent over strange machines, like winkles attached to a rock in the sea.

I looked in horrid fascination at the faces staring into mine.

Wherever I glanced, I saw raw stubs where fingers, hands and arms should have been. There was a distinct disproportion between the number of limbs in that place and the number of faces. Many of the women lacked an arm, or part of it. A very young maid sitting close to the door had one leg only. Two whole hands attached to the same body were in very short supply.

One woman in particular caught my attention.

I might have been staring at the body I had examined the night before.

Stained teeth and jagged grey bone poked out of the left side of her face where her cheek ought to have hidden them. Her purple tongue lolled out, before she sucked it in again. The entire left side of her face had been roughly tacked together, the skin stretched tight, but never tight enough. I would not have employed the surgeon who had treated her to make a sack of jute for me. Her eyes were fixed on the old man, like a dog that was waiting for a bone. She raised a mangled hand – the thumb and a finger remained – slicking away the saliva that dribbled from her sagging mouth and ran along her jaw and chin.

Could that creature speak? And how did she manage to eat?

'Get to it!' the old man wheezed.

The woman pressed hard on a treadle, a grinding-wheel began to twirl, and she bent forward, huddling over her work. All the other women did the same. The hive of bees began to drone again.

Could the wealth of Prussia come from such a dark, dank hole?

Those people looked as though they had lost a battle, and been badly mauled in the fighting. Was this how amber was processed before it went to market? By women with ravaged limbs and half-formed faces?

In the centre of this den stood a wooden table. A basket of apples, two loaves of bread and a stone flagon of small ale had been laid out there. Would their wheels stop whirring for half an hour to permit them to eat and talk together? Or would they take it in turns, first-come-best-served, in some hierarchy of merit or terrible disability that I could not divine?

'Over here, sir,' the master gasped, making his way to a larger machine which stood close to the fire. It looked more complicated than the others. He placed his hand on one of the wheels with a show of proud tenderness.

'I'd invite you to sit down,' he whispered hoarsely, glancing around the room, 'but then you'd have to earn your living.'

I had never seen the inside of an amber workshop. Like any other manual trade, I imagined that it would require a steady hand, and a sharp eye. But this man's hands were twisted with arthritis, and one of his eyes was as white as chalk. He peered at me, but I did not think he could see me very well.

'I can speak well enough on my feet,' I replied. 'Where are these women?'

With surprising agility, the man seated himself astride the machine as if he were riding a horse. Resting his hand on a sort of pommel, he turned to look at me, a parody of a general posing for an equestrian portrait.

'Why would the French send a Prussian magistrate here?'

He unlatched the button of his collar as he spoke, and a bluish-grey goitre spilled onto his chest. It was like a second head that swelled and bobbed as he wheezed, 'What's up, sir? Ain't you never seen the scrofula before?'

He seemed amused by my discomfort. I had observed the same sort of defiance in my father's serfs. The master might own their bodies, but their souls and maladies were their own private business.

'Never let them think that they know better,' my father said to me one day.

He had a score of tied serfs on his estate, and one of them had just claimed that there was one thing the master could *never* do. My father grabbed the knife from that man's hand, gripped the large striped sow between his knees, and drove the blade deep into its windpipe. Red blood gushed over his shoes and his new silk stockings, spurting across his yellow waistcoat and into his face, but my father did not flinch.

I took my lead from this example.

'I've seen worse things than your swollen crop,' I said.

Kati Rodendahl's face flashed before my eyes.

Then, I could not help myself, I glanced in the direction of the horribly disfigured woman that I had noticed immediately I entered the house.

76

She stared back at me with sullen fixity, and I quickly looked away.

'Would you rather speak to the French?' I challenged him. 'It's all one to me.'

It was not the same, of course, and he knew it. He pulled a wry face.

'Let's waste no time,' I snapped. 'Which women here knew Kati Rodendahl?'

He pointed to the woman whose ravaged face had unsettled me twice.

'Hilde knew her, sir. But she can't tell you nothing. She's lost her tongue, so to speak,' he sneered. 'You'll have to speak with me . . .'

I stepped forward, pushed him hard in the chest, and knocked him from the saddle. The women stopped working, their treadles ground to a halt.

'If you hope to continue in this trade,' I warned him, 'you will co-operate with me.'

All eyes in the room were riveted on me, as if they thought that I intended to harm him. I towered above their master physically, but my dominance was of a different sort. The weight of centuries pressed down heavily on that man's round shoulders. The French had freed their serfs, they had forced us to do the same, but he would always be an underling. I had it in my power to take away all that he had slaved to obtain, and he knew it.

I motioned to him to get up.

'Name, age, place of birth,' I snapped.

His head bent dutifully like the man who had dared to challenge my father.

Hans Pastoris was fifty, so he said, though he looked like one of the wrinkled ancients who had spied on Susanna as she emerged from her hot tub. Born in Silesia, he had started life as a farm-boy. After the widespread destruction there in '78, he had fled to the Baltic coast to seek his fortune, working as an eel-fisherman near the village of Palmnicken until the local amber trade had sucked him in.

'I became an expert grinder in time,' he concluded.

'High living got you that goitre, I suppose?'

'It will choke me sooner or later,' he wheezed. 'If no one kills me first.'

'Every person here is crippled,' I replied bluntly, looking around the room.

The fire had not gone out of him.

'The Baltic Sea's a sharper, Herr Procurator,' he said. 'Calm and flat, then along comes a wave and it's swept you off your feet. First instinct is to save the amber. While doing that, you finish up on a rock, or your leathers fill with water. You cut yourself to ribbons, or you drown, an' that's a fact. Drowning's bad, but cuts are worse. You keep on working, see, then your hand or leg turns black. Mephitics, necrotics, them surgeons have a name for everything. Have to cut it off before it kills you. It's wet leather that does it. Stinking cow gets in your blood. Down on the beach they need women that are strong and whole. There's a dozen accidents a month . . .'

'And the injured come here to work?'

'If it wasn't for me,' he added piously, 'they'd perish.'

I did not swallow this saintliness. He offered the women the chance of survival, but they must slave hard for it. I was under no illusion that he shared his profits equally with his workers.

'What happened to her?' I asked, nodding to the woman he had called Hilde.

Pastoris regarded me for a moment. 'That face is nought to do with the Baltic,' he said, shaking his head. 'These girls know there's amber beneath the pebbles on the shore. Some of them dig where no one's ever dug before. Some of them use explosives to get to it. But gunpowder don't play games, sir. Blew up in her face, it did.'

Could something similar have happened to Kati Rodendahl?

I immediately dismissed the notion. The face I had examined the night before had been sectioned with a precision that explosives did not possess. A surgical knife had been used with great skill. And there was no sign of burnt flesh.

'Can I speak to her?'

'I wasn't lying, sir.' He leant close, his goitre swaying like a turkey's. 'There's not much left inside that mouth of hers. Hard enough for me to understand her. She could only have got the powder off a Frenchman, and he got clean away. Amber's a capricious old divinity. Makes you rich, or strikes you dead for trying.'

'Does she know that her friend is dead?' I asked.

Pastoris nodded. 'News of that sort travels.'

'Who brings it?'

A sack was hanging from the beam above his head. He set it swinging wildly with a backhand swipe. 'French soldiers come here every morning, bringing amber to be buffed. Weighed when they bring it in; weighed before they carry it off again. And while they're waiting, they amuse themselves by frightening the girls. Had a real lark, they did. A body lying on the beach. Naked, dead. An amber-girl. Raped, robbed, and cut to bits, according to them. They had my girls in tears. Half of them are talking of leaving here. I sometimes wonder if the French are doing it themselves – killing off the girls, I mean – to drive the others away. What with these machines and all.'

What Pastoris was saying clearly contradicted what les Halles had told me.

Did les Halles know what his men were up to?

Then another thought occurred to me.

Would the soldiers dare do anything unless les Halles gave the order? Might the death of Kati Rodendahl serve his purpose? Could he be trying to frighten the girls into running off, exploiting the murder to his own ends? He had told me himself that he would have no further use for the female amber-workers as soon as his engines were up and running.

'Tell me what the soldiers said exactly.'

'Said?' Hans Pastoris grinned. 'A figure of speech, sir, if you'll pardon me. They don't speak much German, we don't speak much French, but we can mime all right. Then again, ounces are ounces, pounds are pounds. We may count in different languages, but the figures look the same on paper. Any fool can mime a female dead and naked.'

As he spoke, his stubby right forefinger slashed across his throat, his eyes rolled up in their sockets, then his hands formed two imaginary ample breasts. Then, he glanced at Hilde again.

'She knew what they were on about. She got ears, she heard Kati's name. The others would have told her if she hadn't. I saw the fear in her eyes. In all their eyes! Who can blame them after what happened last time?'

'Last time?' I repeated.

He nodded. 'Kati ain't the first. She won't be the last.'

'Kati Rodendahl was murdered,' I said.

'So were the others.'

Grillet had spoken of amber disappearing, girls running off in the night. 'Are you inventing tales, like the French, Herr Pastoris?' I asked.

He shook his head.

'Girls go missing all the time,' he said. 'It's been that way down here for a good while, sir.'

'The French know where those girls have gone,' I said. 'One of the soldiers told me that they may have run away with bands of smugglers. He said that most of them are bound for Russia.'

Pastoris smiled grimly. 'I am mighty glad for them, then. But what about the bones, sir? What do the French have to say on that score? Skulls and bones found down along the shore, Herr Procurator. No one cares a fig about them. The French may say they've stolen amber, but that is what they always say! Call them thieves, and that's the end of it. Since that new colonel arrived, they don't fuss themselves no more about Prussian girls. He's got orders. Machines, they say. He plans to do away with us all.' Pastoris shrugged his shoulders. 'They want our amber, but they don't want *us*. And the cheaper it comes, the better. They'd kill off all girls to save a schilling. Would? Have done, if you ask me! Them two ruffians that came the other day, for instance.'

He stopped abruptly, aimed a sharp-eyed glance at me.

'Do you know their names?' I asked him.

Pastoris dug into his pocket, pulled out a notebook, waved it in the air. It was a vile-looking thing with a worm-eaten cover. He licked his thumb, began to leaf through the grimy pages. 'They make me register every single thing,' he complained. 'Who brings the amber, who takes it away. That day they were Jacques Pillard and Robert Margiot.'

He turned the page to me. The names were written in a small neat hand, together with the amount of rough amber that they had brought: eight pounds net. The note was dated 13 August 1808. Three days previously. The same evening they had taken five pounds and seven ounces of polished amber away with them.

'They thought it funny, sir, the way that Hilde was weeping and slobbering.'

I thought, instead, that it would make a good argument to present to les Halles when I saw him next.

'Let me ask you something,' I said, putting my hand into my pocket. 'What do you make of this?'

I opened my palm and showed him the amber that I had extracted from the corpse.

Pastoris plucked at it greedily, held it close to his whitish eyes. Then, he weighed it in his hand, and felt the surface with his fingers like a blind man.

'Nicely buffed,' he murmured. 'This is amateur work, of course. The girls on the shore rub it down with pumice to take off the marine deposits. To give a buyer a rough idea of its potential. In the hands of an expert polisher, it would make a beautiful brooch, for instance. Then again, there's something makes it far more valuable.'

'What's that?' I asked, though I knew, as every Prussian must.

He held it up to the lamp. 'Can you see that insect trapped inside? It's big. A serious collector, someone interested in curiosities, would give his right arm for it, sir.'

'Where would one find such a man?'

He raised his shoulders and his goitre bulged beneath his chin. 'Nordcopp's the place.'

'Do the women go there?'

'There and back in a spit and a cough,' he replied. 'One of the soldiers would let her in and out in exchange for a quick . . . I'm sure you can guess,' he added with a smile that showed the gaps in his teeth, jabbing his right forefinger rapidly in and out of a hole that he formed with the thumb and forefinger of his left hand.

'Who would she seek in Nordcopp?' I pressed him.

He handed back the amber with a shrug of his shoulders.

'She'd know exactly who to give it to.'

'Who?' I insisted again.

'I cannot tell you who,' he said. 'Only where.'

Nordcopp was a forty-minute walk away, he said, along the same rutted carriage-track.

'And while you're there,' he called after me, 'be sure to try the fish soup. It's as good as the amber, but a sight less dangerous.'

I thanked him for his help, and continued tramping on through the sand.

10

Long before I saw the place, my lungs got wind of it.

Fried fish, salt fish, fish boiled and baked. And everything in between, from fresh to foul. The air was more malodorous than the cattle-besmirched streets of Lotingen. There were flies as well, though not so many, nor so big as the ones that I had left behind me. But hunger rebels against such niceties, and I lengthened my stride towards Nordcopp.

This trading-post was known to the Ancients. I have since read up on the place. They considered it to be a sort of Mecca, where all the greatest craftsmen in the world came in search of amber for their workshops. A highway made of tree-trunks, the Amber Road, once stretched to the Mediterranean Sea in the south, and it was regularly tramped by Roman, Greek and Arab traders. Amber was a rich spring from which a mighty river flowed. A thousand streams branched off to every city in the known world. The Romans carved the amber into religious idols; the Greeks chose to fashion fertility *phalli*. In Italy the heirs of the Renaissance jewellers have long been famed for their tabernacles encrusted with amber and precious stones. In Catholic Danzig they still make rosary-beads to count off *Pater Nosters*, though amber Bible-covers are the pride of Protestant Königsberg, where the Pietists hold sway. In Russia, Orthodox churches are panelled with it. And even in the Temple of Atheism, Paris, the sacred stuff is moulded into buckles and gaudy hairpins for harlots and ladies *à la mode*.

Everyone has always wanted amber, but nowadays the French want it most of all.

Napoleon subdued the rest of the continent, while we pleaded neutrality. But we had amber, so he invaded us. For a year or more, the supply of amber has flowed in one direction only. As I stood before the gates of Nordcopp, I knew that carts and ships packed with *succini prussici,* as amber was called in the Latin tongue, were travelling towards Paris at that very moment.

It might be the colour of honey. It might be red, like a blazing sunset. Straw-yellow, like wine. Or the deep, dark brown of mahogany. Whatever the hue, it was worth a small fortune. The stolen riches of Prussia would pay French soldiers' wages while they fought in Spain, and provide them with firearms. Spain would soon be crushed by the power of amber. Then, when Napoleon was ready, he would turn his sights on his only ally, and our Prussian amber would conquer Tsar Alexander as well.

Nordcopp was far smaller than I had expected, but more full of people than I could have guessed. A crowd of men were pushing their way towards a wooden watch-tower. It was so ancient, it seemed about to topple and crush them all. I joined the throng, and began to thrust with equal determination. On either side, tables of baked fish, stuffed eels, trays of bread and cakes, jugs of ale, legs and wings of roasted chicken were being offered for sale, their virtues loudly proclaimed, as I shuffled towards the guardians of the citadel.

A group of French gendarmes were blocking the entrance, armed with muskets. One of them – a large, fat man with an oriental moustache – was staring hard at me. 'Oi, you!' he called, his bayonet flashing close to my nose. 'Your face is new. What are you doing here?'

Before I could answer, the man began to provide answers for himself.

'Amber, is it? Come from far off, too, I suppose.'

He hardly seemed interested as his face heaved close to mine. His uniform was smart enough, but his breath stank of half-digested fish, and my empty stomach rolled.

'Where are you from, then?'

'Königsberg,' I said on impulse.

He nodded back. He did not ask my name, or demand to see my papers. New arrivals were pushing up against my back and they all seemed bent on entering the place as quickly as possible. All around me, I heard muttered complaints in German. No one moaned too loud, however. They did not intend to be held up by me, or by the guards.

'A bit of business, a plate of fish soup, and I'll be on my way,' I said in French.

His heavy hand fell on my shoulder. 'Don't rush, monsieur. Enjoy yourself. Every coin you spend in a Prussian shop will help to pay French taxes. You'll be body-searched on the way out, so make sure you get a receipt. And if you haven't got a bill of sale, have some loose change handy in your pocket,' he added with a wink.

I was tempted to pull the written order of General Malaport from my pocket, and wipe that smile off his face. Instead, I pushed on silently through the narrow entrance-gate as he lifted his bayonet and waved me on.

Was Pastoris correct? Were the French in Nordcopp a party to the illegal trade in amber? How would les Halles react if I returned that night and gave him a name with an acute accent on the final syllable, instead of the Prussian name that he seemed to expect?

Nordcopp had once been a fortified village. The wooden watch-tower above the entrance looked down on a maze of narrow by-ways, and I was quickly carried into the heart of this labyrinth. The wattle walls were ragged, worn with age, the grey timber frames of the houses rotten and pockmarked with shell-holes. Evidently, the French had bombarded the stronghold before they sent marauders in to secure it. It was the sort of rank-smelling medieval warren that had all but disappeared in Prussia. As the pride of the nation grew in the wake of reforms of the great King Frederick, hovels like these had been flattened. I might have stepped back into a former time in history. The buildings were dark and low, the straw roofs barely higher than my shoulder, packed so close together that the traders and the open drains all ran stinking downhill in the same direction. On either side of this fetid alley, waist-high counters were loaded with jars and strung with beads, which gleamed and glistened in the half-light, like candles in a church.

We might have been pilgrims jostling our way from one chapel to the next in search of sacred relics or papal indulgences. Each man in that thrusting company had one thing only on his mind: amber. In the first alley, I counted seven tiny shops, like troglodytic holes in the wall. Each cave was crowded with men, heads bent low as they examined the merchandise on offer. Their muted voices were a constant buzz, broken suddenly by a loud exclamation, or a vile expletive, as a deal was made or rejected.

Two or three times I tried to enter a shop, hoping to see what was going on in there, but the backs seemed to stiffen, and elbows suddenly became dangerous weapons. I was forced to pull back on each occasion into the lane and swim with the tide, hoping to find a shop that was less furiously busy.

How should I go about asking questions without provoking suspicion?

It was dark and cramped inside those caverns, and I was ill-equipped for the part that I had chosen to play. Many of the men crushing up against the sellers' tables held a tiny lamp in their hands to make the task of choosing easier. Thin beams of light flashed this way and that as each man cast around, frantically seeking what he was after. Many a customer had a magnifying-glass that he clamped to his eye by exerting the muscles in his cheek and brow.

They looked the part of professional amber-traders, whilst I did not.

I felt as out of place as any novice must.

It might be wise, I thought, to find some place where I could eat, and take more careful stock of my position. The smell of grilling fish was overwhelming. Blue smoke swirled and drifted above the heads of the milling crowd. Was there a tavern or a chop-house nearby? Was that where they were all going? I followed the throng down another narrow alley without finding the place. Tavern? I had the impression that these people ate with their eyes, and that the object of their hunger was one thing, and one alone.

Like vultures, they seemed to feast and gorge on the sight of amber.

More than once I was obliged to stop while the man in front of me concluded his business with a dealer on the threshold of a shop, and money changed hands. On another occasion, I was brought to a sudden halt behind a man who began to piss against the wall. An obstinate seller continued to dangle a string of amber beads in front of his face, while he emptied his bladder. 'By the Lord, Herr Franz!' the merchant insisted. 'Are they not the finest matching set of natural rarities you have ever seen?'

Franz thrust his member back in his pants, and grunted dismissively about them being rather too 'natural' for his taste. As he moved away, the salesman began to look around more keenly. He did not try his arts on me, but settled instead on the man behind me. 'Just the job for you, Ludwig. Aren't they perfection? Step inside, do, sir!'

Was I marked out in some way? Everyone appeared to know everyone else, but I knew nobody. 'Anything for me?' was the phrase that I heard most frequently on the lips of the customers. They would stop for a moment by a doorway, look in over the heads of the men who had got there before them, then call out loudly to the shopkeeper: 'Anything special, Harald? Anything lemon-coloured?'

I was quick to learn, or so I thought.

I stopped before a shop that seemed less crowded than the others. There were only three men inside. 'Anything for me?' I called out.

The seller raised his head. The purchasers turned around. They stared at me in a manner that, I am sure, was intended to be hostile. They did not say a word. The looks that they exchanged were eloquent enough. *Who is this intruder?* I held their gaze for a moment, then quickly moved away, carrying my embarrassment off with me.

Halfway down the next alley, I stepped out of the surging flow to take a closer look at the sparkling array of goods on open display. Various lumps of amber and a jar full of beads like large beans were laid out on a plank of wood blocking the entrance to a tiny den. I leaned close, and I was greeted by a jab in the ribs from a man already positioned there. Voices from behind began to shout more loudly, 'Get a move on!'

The owner looked up and flashed a winning smile at the man beside me.

'Herr Gusmar! Welcome back, sir! Do come in.'

Was that the secret? Would traders only speak to men they knew, customers they had dealt with before? If that was the case, the best thing for me to do was search out the gendarmes, make my identity known to them, then question these people while slapping Malaport's order in their faces. But what if the soldiers were in cahoots with the amber-dealers?

'Come with me, sir. The real thing. Prize goods only.'

The voice seemed to rise up from the earth, like shifting gravel. I looked down. She was not much taller than my daughter, Süzi. That is, she barely reached my waist. But this child's hair was an artificial flaxen colour streaked with grey, as if she had dyed it badly. It was tied up in a thin tail at the nape of her neck, like a newborn kitten's. Her voice was shrill and seemed to rattle in her throat. Her hand was small, but it clutched at my hand like a blacksmith's vice, and refused to be shaken off. In the lobe of each ear, a bit of rough-cut amber shone.

The strangest little girl that I had ever seen.

The only female I had noticed in Nordcopp that morning.

Wearing a white gown with many strings attached, she might have been wrapped in swaddling clothes. Yet everything about her contradicted everything else. Do little girls have grey wrinkles? The lines ridged at the corners of her mouth, and hung in heavy folds beneath her eyes, which were over-large, red-veined, rheumy like a grandmother's.

'They won't sell *you* anything,' she declared. 'They can't.'

There were people buying and selling amber everywhere in Nordcopp.

What did she mean?

I looked around for assistance, and was roughly pushed aside. I was creating a bottleneck. The cork threatened to explode as the pressure built up in the alleyway behind me.

'Get a move on there!' someone shouted violently.

'Follow me,' the child hissed. 'Before you get yourself arrested.'

There was urgency in the voice, crushing strength in the fingers.

'Call the French,' another voice insisted. 'They'll move him on quick enough.'

'Gendarmes! Gendarmes!' the cry went up.

A French soldier appeared at the end of the alley, waving his bayonet in the air.

'There's amber here for everyone,' he shouted. 'Calm yourselves down!'

His execrable German caused a general laugh to go up.

'We have to get off the street,' the child insisted, tugging at my sleeve, charging forward towards the gendarme, brushing hard against the wall, barging people out of the way.

'Well done, Erika!' the gendarme called. 'Caught another, have you?'

She skipped to the left without warning, pulling me after her, cutting through a narrow breach in a wall. Though limping heavily, she was extremely agile. Three pigs squealed in fright and skittered away to the corner. Underfoot the earth was mushy, the smell of filth unbearable. We were in the wreck of what had once been a house. Though the walls still stood, the roof had collapsed and left the building open to the sky.

I tried to free myself.

'Let go of me!' I shouted, but the demon child would not release my hand.

Grim tales of the countryside rang in my head, tales of wanderers waylaid by beautiful maids, toothless crones, or smiling children, lured to their deaths in the name of Prussian hospitality.

'Will you not leave go?' I grabbed at her wrist, struggling to throw her off, as if she were the Devil himself. As I swung her around, she crashed against the wall, and I heard the rattle of her bones.

The pigs squealed, and ran away to the other corner.

The child breathed heavily, leaning back against the wall, looking up at me.

'Near tore my arm off, you did,' she complained. And yet, there was a hint of a smile on her lips. 'My hands are as strong as an eagle's claws. Did you feel the force, sir?'

'What do you want from me?' I looked at her intently, struggling to suppress a wave of revulsion. I was eager to get out of that foul pigpen.

'You're after amber,' she said, panting after the tussle. 'I heard you say so to the soldier on the gate.'

Had she spotted me so soon? Had she been following me?

'This town is full of people selling amber,' I replied.

'They'll never sell it to you,' she answered quickly.

'My money is as good as any man's.'

'I told you, sir,' she said sternly, staring into my eyes. 'The Nordcopp guild don't ever deal with strangers. I can help you, though.'

Nothing in her manner was childish. Indeed, she spoke to me as if I were a child that had to be protected.

'How can you help me?'

She kicked out at a pig that came too close. 'I know where amber's freely sold, sir.' She looked at me coyly. 'Is that all you're looking for?'

Incredulity robbed me of speech. I had just been propositioned.

'Amber is my only interest,' I murmured in reply.

'Ours is the very best,' she said. 'Our prices are the lowest. And if you're hungry, why, we'll sell you a bowl of fish soup, too.' She jammed her hand up to her mouth and suppressed a girlish giggle. 'I heard you tell that story to the guard.'

'Amber that is not controlled by the French, or the guild?' I asked. 'You know the punishment for stealing amber . . .'

'There's profit here for everyone,' she replied with a shrug. 'The guild don't care. Their own business is flourishing. And the French take a cut from everyone, legal or not. That gendarme knew where I was leading you. I'll have to grease his palm before the day is out.' She laughed shrilly. A harsh metallic sound. 'He don't care if you buy amber, or the little jewel between my legs.'

I had always thought of amber as something sacred, ancient, mysterious. A gift of God, a blessing on mankind. Instead, it seemed to affect the people on the coast in a way that was unwholesome. In Nordcopp every soul was blighted with evil intentions, or marked by their consequences. The corpse of Kati Rodendahl flashed before my eyes again. The face of Hilde, the woman who worked for Pastoris. The speech and manners of this child blotted out any presumption of innocence. Had all the females on the coast been seduced and ruined by amber?

'Amber, sir?' Her head tilted to one side, smiling, taunting. 'The finest in Prussia! And the best fish, too. Don't let the opportunity get away.'

'Very well,' I nodded, pulling my hand away as one of the pigs in the ruined building attempted to lick it.

I would never have found the entrance without her help. One wall of the pigsty appeared to have been struck by a shell. A narrow, jagged fissure, just wide enough to admit a man, had cracked the wall diagonally from top to bottom. We passed through, and into the yard of yet another house that had also lost its roof. Now it was home to hens and ducks and geese. Erika pushed a tattered canvas aside to reveal a gaping hole.

'This way, sir,' she said, and her hand reached out.

I hesitated for an instant, then took her hand in mine.

The bones were small, the skin hard, very dry, and crinkled like the bark of a tree. As I stepped into the dark cavity, that hand was all I had to guide me. It might have belonged to a woman who was a hundred years of age. Indeed, I shuddered, wondering whether she had been transformed by the darkness.

But her voice rang out and broke the spell: 'Million of years ago,' she said, 'the Teutons dug this hole. If they were under siege in Nordcopp, they'd sneak out this way, then attack their enemies from behind. The exit's closed off now, of course, but we still use the storeroom underground.'

I did not care to guess what use they made of it.

It stank like a cess-pit, a reservoir where all the filth and carrion of Nordcopp had been collected and left to rot for centuries. It was blackest night down there, and I held on to her hand more tightly. Three or four times we altered course, veering left, then turning right. At every twist and change, my faith in Erika was severely tested. Was I out of my wits? No one knew where I was. Hans Pastoris might have guessed. But who would ask him? No one knew what I was doing there, not even the creature in whose hands I had placed my life. I was beneath the ground already. It was damp, cold, the musty air clogged my breathing. If I never surfaced again, who would know of it? Was I going stupidly to my tomb?

But then I sniffed a reassuring smell. Beyond the mouldy fetor of decay and physical corruption, something appetising flavoured the air.

'Fish,' I murmered. And as I spoke, my eyes began to make out a glow in the distance, a shimmer of light, which gave solidity and substance to the slick, damp walls of the tunnel. My ears strained too, catching the echoing rumble of far-off voices.

A shriek from Erika froze the blood in my veins.

Her high-pitched cry rose and fell like the wailing of a wolf. Was it a signal?

If so, I was dead meat for any man who was armed and waiting to rob me.

She pushed on faster, pulling harder at my hand. I could follow, it seemed, or she would leave me behind. I tried to resist, digging in my heels, sliding on the slippery floor, but I could not stop myself. We were running headlong down a slope, I realised, for we burst into a dimly lit chamber, and the floor reared up in front of my face like a wall.

She turned to me, but did not say a word.

My breath came back in gasps.

We were in a stone vault, that had once been plastered. Now, it was stained dark green and ugly brown with mould and damp. Lanterns hung at intervals around the walls, reflecting light on the faces of the people who turned to stare suspiciously at me. They sat at tables piled with lumps of what looked like glistening honey.

Or globules of blood which took in light, and gave off even more in a flashing, sparkling array.

The aroma of boiled fish was inviting.

A large copper cooking-pot dangled from a hook above a blazing fire. Another large pot stood by the side of the hearth. It was covered with a lid, as if it had just been removed from the flames.

I congratulated myself on my good fortune.

But what would a real amber merchant do to establish his credentials? Would I be able to persuade the people in that cellar to accept me as one of them, having failed to do so in the shops and streets of Nordcopp? And how might I steer the conversation towards the piece of amber that I had recovered from the corpse of Kati Rodendahl? How did a piece of amber find its way from the seashore to an underground cellar in Nordcopp where they also sold fish soup? That was what I wanted to know.

Seven or eight men were seated at rough trestle tables. Each one had a plate of soup, a lighted candle, and a small pile of amber on the table-top. They might have been playing some mysterious glass-bead game together while they ate, but it didn't take much to see that each man was locked in his own private world, scrutinising the pieces laid out before him in mystical concentration. No one said a word. The trick seemed to be to take a nugget, hold it up to the candle, peer at it intensely for a while, then set it down, and repeat the operation with the next piece. No man raised his spoon to his lips. Indeed, they did not seem to care if the fish went cold, or rotted on their plates. They were famished for amber and nothing else.

'Have a seat, sir. I'll only be a moment.'

Despite her hampering leg, Erika skipped quickly across the room towards a tall woman dressed in a soiled white apron. She was wearing a large red turban on her head. Waving a large cooking-ladle in the air, this woman was clearly the high priestess of the place. With one hand firmly planted on her hip, she watched the vestal approach with a welcoming smile, and they began to whisper together, the child stretching up on her tiptoes, the older women bending low to meet her.

I sat down at an empty table, and looked around me.

The fellow at the next table called out: 'Can I have some more?'

Had I been mistaken? Were they there to eat, after all?

'With you in a moment!' the tall woman called back, turning to the fire.

She lifted the lid of the pot that was cooling on the hearth, dipped her ladle inside, and began to stir it around. The sound that this action produced said nothing good about the contents. She might have been stirring a saucepan full of pebbles as she made another large sweep with her ladle.

The customers looked up at the rattling sound.

'I'll have some, too,' another man said.

Were they crabs, cockles, oysters, clams? My stomach felt like an empty cavern, and the air was rich with the smell of fish. 'Can I have some, as well?' I called, and my voice was louder and more urgent than I had intended.

Erika darted back with the easy grace of a maimed cat on the prowl, making a wide, lolloping sweep around the other tables before she reached mine, looking to see how each man was getting along.

'I'll take your order now,' she said. 'Then, Marta will dish up what you are hungering for.'

There was a look of unconcealed excitement in her eyes. They were dark green with sparkling points of light. She was playing the part of a coquetting waitress, but that image of a hunting cat refused to go away. The feline was closing in for the kill, and I could not shake off the feeling that I was the mouse. 'I told my mother what a fine gentleman you are,' she added. 'I said she'd better treat you well. So, you just tell me what you'd like to have, sir.'

'Isn't there a list?' I asked.

Erika smiled uncertainly. 'Just tell me which colour you'd prefer.'

I was silent for a moment.

'I have . . . no particular preference,' I said.

This vague order sent the wrinkled child spinning away. She crossed the room and spoke again in whispers to the cook. A minute later, the woman in the bright red turban came over to my table carrying a bowl of fish soup. She set it down with a smile, then she sat herself down on the bench opposite me.

'Welcome to Nordcopp, sir. I am Marta Linder. We've not seen you before. What are you looking for exactly? Erika couldn't say for certain.'

I spooned the broth into my mouth, and chewed on a piece of fish.

She watched me attentively. 'About the amber,' she specified. 'Is it the shape, the weight, or the colour that interests you the most? Just name it, and I'll have the girl bring it over.'

They were selling amber under the cover of serving fish.

What had Pastoris said? The French were most particular about the weight. They weighed the amber when they brought it to his workshop, and weighed it again when they came to carry it off. So, weight was important. But was it the most important factor? The French took it to Pastoris to be cleaned and polished. Were shape and appearance more important, then? And how would one choose between two pieces of amber which were exactly the same weight and shape?

'Colour,' I decided, removing a fishbone from the tip of my tongue.

The woman was past her prime, but she was still handsome. A row of black kiss-curls was stamped flat across her forehead

96

by the weight of her red turban. She pursed her lips, her eye-brows arched as she studied my face.

'Oh I see,' she said. 'You are a jeweller. I should have guessed. And from Königsberg, Erika tells me. So not a whole-sale trader. Quality is what you're after. Is that right?'

I returned her smile, as if to confirm her deductions. At the same time, I had to say something. 'The fish is very good,' I commented, raising the spoon to my mouth again to put an end to the conversation, swallowing bits of haddock and eel, and the thin broth in which they were swimming.

'I'll show you something really tasty,' the woman declared. 'Ten pieces. All the same size. As smooth as pebbles from a fast-flowing stream. Oval in form and slightly smoky. A deep, dark red. That colour never is truly transparent, sir.' She leaned closer, and peered into my eyes. 'A great lady will want to wear them day and night. Can you imagine the beauty of a necklace made from those fine baubles?' She kissed the tips of her fingers. 'Dragon's blood. The name they give to the finest rubies. But you know that, of course. These are a thousand times prettier than the purest Indian rubies. You'll make some-thing fit for a queen, I'm sure of it.'

'There aren't so many left,' I joked, thinking of Marie Antoinette, and the horde of noblewomen who had lost their heads in France. 'Great ladies,' I explained.

She did not smile. Perhaps she hadn't heard me. Someone in the room called for more, but she didn't shift.

'Erika!' she shouted over her shoulder. Then, she turned to me again. 'She'll be very pleased with you, sir. She knows she'll get her share. She did bring you down here, after all. And as it is your first time here, you can have her when you have done your trading. It won't cost nothing extra.'

Her words affected me like the shearing of a metal blade against a whetstone.

'Is that the way to speak of your daughter?' I managed to say.

Marta Linder stared at me as if I were a branded fool.

'Do you want to see my amber, or not?' she asked me coldly.

'It won't change colour while we're speaking, surely?' I challenged her. 'Tell me, Marta. What is wrong with the child?'

'The *child*?' she mimicked.

I lost my patience. 'Erika. Your little girl,' I said.

'Erika ceased to be a little girl a while back,' she replied, and laughed. But then her expression softened, as if the artist who had drawn her face had rubbed it with a cloth, and instantly sketched in a more accommodating look. She lowered her head, and whispered across the table. 'She's mighty popular with the gents. You'd be surprised, sir. There's many a man who'll go with her.'

I recalled the French soldier in the street above, and his allusive words to Erika.

'Sex, is that what you are speaking of?'

She stared at me for some moments, her black eyes twinkling. 'What else, sir?'

'Is that why the French soldiers don't bother her? They think she's bringing men down here for . . . for . . .' I could not find a suitable word. 'To cover up the fact that you are selling amber? They think instead in terms of fish. And flesh . . .'

She seemed amused by what I had said.

'Nothing in Nordcopp is what it seems, sir. Amber, fish, flesh; each man has his preferences. Especially regarding amber, sir. It must be big, or bright. It must be round, or flat. *De gustibus*,' she said, surprising me with a Latin idiom she must have picked up from one of her clients.

She laid her hands flat on the table, and leaned forward.

'Do you want to see them, then? The red ones, I mean. Colour of blood . . .'

I nodded. 'Let's start with the blood.'

As she rose and turned away, I thought I heard her muttering, 'Thank the Lord!' under her breath. She went across the room, murmuring to Erika as she passed. The girl was stirring the pot of boiling fish, but she stepped aside quickly. Marta Linder glanced cautiously around the cellar, then stretched her hand behind a cupboard and retrieved a little packet from

98

some secret hiding-place. As she came back to my table, she untied the strings that held this bundle closed. Sitting down again, she shook the contents out on the wooden surface.

My appetite for fish dissolved as I stared at those stones.

The colour was truly spectacular, as she had promised. She lifted the candle, shifting it across the table. The variegated colours – light and dark – seemed to ripple and flow like fresh blood spurting from a vein.

'They are very beautiful,' I said, whispering despite myself.

'Just feel them, sir!'

My hand stretched out mechanically. I took the nearest piece between my thumb and forefinger and held it up to the light. Like every man in that room, I had succumbed to the passion for amber in an instant. I must have looked as dazed, seduced and ravished as they did.

'Smooth,' I murmured. 'And warm to the touch.'

'A lover's kiss on a slender neck.'

'Have you been long in the trade, ma'am?'

I held the piece of amber close to my eye, as I had seen the other customers do.

'In this trade . . . no, sir,' she murmured softly with a wilful smile.

I did not need to ask what trade she had been in before.

I picked up another piece of amber. A stream of golden bubbles deep inside the oval nugget caught the light. Each bead was somehow like, but quite unlike, the other pieces in the set. 'This one would make a wonderful ring,' I said for want of saying something.

'Oh, I wouldn't split 'em up,' she said quickly.

I set the bead down on the table, and sat back, tapping my fingernail against my teeth, wondering how to bring the conversation to a head. Should I ask her directly if she had ever had any dealings with Kati Rodendahl?

'Don't you like the colour?' she asked.

'The colour is pleasing enough,' I said, thinking of the startling colour of the piece of amber in my pocket, 'but . . .'

'But what, sir?'

'I was looking for something brighter. Yellow, perhaps . . .'

'The colour of piss? Or more like what a dying old lady coughs up?'

She smiled no longer. She had seen through my pretence, and shrugged off ingratiation like an uncomfortable cloak. Her face seemed angular, her eyes sharper and more inquisitive. I thought I could see a marked resemblance to the daughter. Her hand reached out and slid the candle to one side. Then she sat forward, filling the space, her breath hot in my face.

'One word from me,' she said, 'and these gentlemen here will rip you to bits. They don't take risks. Your corpse will rot with the rats in that tunnel over there. Out with it! Who are you?'

'I am a magistrate,' I admitted, my voice barely audible. 'And I'm investigating a murder. One of the girls who gather amber on the coast was . . .'

'What are you doing *here*?' she hissed. 'Shouldn't you be out *there* looking for answers? What do you want from us?'

'I need to know . . .'

'Ask the French squaddies how she died,' she seethed before I could finish.

'You know something that the French do not,' I pressed on quickly. 'That is why I am here.'

Her eyes glistened. 'What do you want to know?'

I picked up one of the fine amber beads that lay glistening and forgotten on the table, and held it in front of her nose. 'Somebody sells you amber like this. Who brings it to you?'

She pursed her lips, but she did not reply.

'Does it come from the girls on Nordcopp shore?' I asked.

Her eyes flashed angrily. 'Why don't you ask them who they take it to?'

Had she done business with those girls in the past? Was there some lingering insult, some outstanding debt that still rankled? She seemed to have neither time nor pity regarding them.

'You have not answered my question,' I said. 'Who brings it here?'

'I have my suppliers,' she snapped, 'and that's the end of it!'

Our huddled conversation made no impression on the other people in the room. Doubtless, when a deal was being struck, they all held huddled conversations of their own.

'Someone in Nordcopp takes pleasure in chopping women into pieces,' I said. 'I want to stop him. The French do, too. Unless I catch him soon, they'll come through here like a howling gale. Wouldn't it be wiser if you talked to me?'

She stared sullenly at me, but still she would not speak.

I swept my hand slowly around the room.

My eyes went with it, looking at the tables, the entrance to the tunnel, the seated men, the fireplace where her daughter tended the pots. 'I could have brought the French here with me,' I said as my eyes locked into hers. 'I could have brought ten gendarmes. But that was not my plan. I don't want them involved in this affair.'

'A Prussian working for the French?'

She pronounced each word as if it fouled her tongue.

'A Prussian trying to save the lives of Prussian women,' I corrected her.

As I spoke, I reached into my pocket and closed my fist around Kati Rodendahl's piece of amber. 'Who would be interested in a piece like this one?' I asked, unclenching my fingers slowly to reveal what was hidden in my palm.

She stared for a moment, as if she could not quite believe what she was seeing.

'Where did you get it?' she whispered, stretching forward.

I grabbed her hand, twisted hard at the wrist and pressed her skin into the flame of the candle. 'It came from the body of a murdered girl. Now, tell me, ma'am. Who would she have tried to sell it to in Nordcopp? Would she have come to you?'

I felt hot breath on the nape of my neck.

'Let me see it.'

The strange voice of Erika sounded in my ear. She darted forward and plucked the amber from my hand. She lifted it to her nose, sniffed it like a squirrel that has found a nut, then began to turn the piece in her fingers and examine it from different angles by the light of the flame.

'This is not our usual trade,' she said, cocking her head to one side, stepping back from the table. 'But I know who handles stuff like this.'

'Who?'

'Follow me,' she said, clasping the amber tightly in her fist.

I stood up quickly, while Marta Linder caressed her burnt flesh and cursed me under her breath.

'I'll handle him,' Erika whispered to her mother. She led me towards the tunnel entrance without a backward glance, still clasping Kati Rodendahl's amber treasure as she darted forward into the pitch darkness.

I reached out, caught hold of her slender arm, but the girl kicked out, and tried to shake herself free of me. 'Why are you pulling at me?' she screeched.

'Give it back,' I warned her, catching hold of her hand.

'Just let me hold it for a bit,' she whined, like a child who has taken possession of another's doll, and doesn't want to give it up.

I could hear her breathing, but I could not see her in the dark. I did not like the situation. That creature knew her way around those tunnels. I did not. If she could shake me off, I'd have trouble finding my way out. If that bit of amber was so valuable, I might have trouble finding her again. She struggled, but I felt her warm musty breath on my face. The air was tainted by the salty smell of her sweat.

'The dead girl owned it, didn't she?'

Her voice sounded heavy and sad in the gloom.

'Was she bringing it to you?' I asked her, easing my grip on her arm.

She let out a loud sigh. 'No one in their right mind would come down here with a piece like this, sir. But I know . . . There are people in Nordcopp who'd do anything to get their hands on it.'

'Who?'

No answer came from the dark.

Suddenly, she breathed in sharply. 'You think that she was killed because of this jewel, don't you, sir?' she said.

'It is very likely.'

'You are wrong.'

'What do you . . .'

She did not let me finish. 'He'd have known where to find it,' she said. 'He wasn't interested in amber. He'd have turned her inside out for a gem like this one.'

Her argument struck home. The killer had had the opportunity to rip the corpse apart in search of what he was looking for. *But then again*, I thought, *if he did not want the amber, what* did *he want from Kati Rodendahl?*

'How much might this be worth?' I asked her. 'And who would buy it?'

I saw a gleam in the dark, stretched out my hand, and plucked the amber nugget away from her.

I might as well have uncaged a bear.

Erika let out a howl and leapt on me like a fury. Her hands were everywhere. On my shirt, clinging to my jacket. Her boots dug into my knees, and scraped my bones. She scrambled after that piece of amber, climbing all over me like a beggar's monkey, though I held it out beyond her reach, trying to fend her off with the other arm. Her nails clawed at my eyes, raked my cheek, ripped at my mouth.

'Give it here!' she screeched.

I twisted and turned, throwing her off, kicking out as she tried to attack me again, holding her at bay as I edged back, following the tunnel upwards, never stopping until I reached the derelict house, the pigs, the hole in the wall, the street, and safety.

As I rejoined the throng, her screams and swearing followed me. There were scratches on the back of my hands, and I felt the dribble of blood on my neck and throat. On the corner at the end of the street, there was a public water-pump. While washing my wounds and cleaning my face, drying myself off again with my pocket handkerchief, I cursed that little demon. The moment I did so, I realised the folly of it.

Could I invoke anything worse than the affliction God had given to Erika Linder in the instant that she came into the world?

12

I did not know the doctor's name or his address.

Grillet had told me that he could be found in Nordcopp.

'It shouldn't be hard to find him, sir,' he had said. 'The settlement is small. And there's no one else.'

The obvious place to start my search was in the French guard-post.

I made my way back to the main gate and the watch-tower.

There were three soldiers in the guard-room, which contained enough air to sustain one life alone. One of them was blowing clouds of blue smoke from a long clay pipe. Another man was gnawing on a black-pudding sausage, while the third, a sergeant, was fast asleep behind a desk, his large feet resting on the table-top.

The man with the pipe was the soldier who had spoken to me as I entered the town an hour before.

'Been robbed already?' he asked. 'Been fighting, have you?'

Erika's nails had evidently left their mark.

'Two of us were scrapping over the same bit of amber,' I nodded. 'They told me there's a doctor here in Nordcopp. Do you know where I can find him?'

He did not know. Nor did the man with the sausage. And neither of them seemed inclined to wake their sleeping sergeant.

'This doctor attends to the workers out on the coast,' I insisted.

The man who was eating tore off another piece of sausage. 'There's a doctor's sign down that way,' he growled, swallowing pork and words, pointing out of the door with what remained of the sausage.

On a map the town of Nordcopp looks no bigger than a spot of filth that a fly might leave behind. In reality, it is a swarming, seething labyrinth of narrow lanes that twist and turn like wriggling worms in a fisherman's bucket. It is like a living organism: small and compact on the outside, crammed to bursting with intestines, arteries and veins, each smaller and narrower than the one before.

Outside the door, I turned to the left, then followed a dark, winding, surprisingly empty alley to the very end, where it opened into a cramped and irregular little square.

This space was dominated by the crumbling façade of a very old church.

Had I been a Roman Catholic, I might have cried miracle. The name of the temple was cut into the lintel, CHRIST THE SAVIOUR. Next door, I saw the signboard hanging over a house that must once have belonged to the priest. Carved of wood, nailed together in the form of a star were two small arms and legs. When new, they might have been flesh-pink, but rain and damp had leached out all the colour. Those dangling limbs were pale ash-grey, except for more resistant spots of bright red paint which clearly signified blood.

I went across and pulled on a bell-rope.

What was a French doctor doing in Nordcopp, I asked myself. Did his presence there signify the dawn of a career which would eventually flourish on the streets of Paris, or was this the twilight of a military hack-bones who had been despatched to the farthest northern reach of the empire?

A vision in white opened the door. A stout old woman with long white hair and very large bosoms filled the doorway. Her face was extremely pale, her eyes bright blue. She was wearing a long white apron and matching linen bonnet.

'May I speak to the doctor?' I asked in exploratory German, wondering whether the French doctor had found himself a local housekeeper.

'Doctor's busy,' she replied in the uncouth dialect of the north coast.

'I'll wait for him, if I may,' I replied.

'Who shall I tell him's calling?'

'Procurator Stiffeniis of Lotingen,' I announced.

A resonating German voice called out: 'Herr Magistrate, come through.'

At the sound of the voice, the woman stepped aside like a stronghold door swinging partially open. I was obliged to squeeze through the narrow gap between the doorpost and her forbidding chest. The doctor was Prussian. I could not have been more relieved. And if I was eager to speak with him, it seemed that he was equally keen to talk with me. Had the wind changed in my favour?

It shifted again as I followed the matron into his room.

'Herr Procurator,' he greeted me, his hand closed tightly on the carved horn-handle of a surgical knife. 'What can I do for you, sir?'

I gaped in reply.

A young man was tied to the table-top by his hands and ankles. A farm labourer, I judged, from the filthy state of his shorn head and his collarless grey shirt. He looked to be no more than thirty years of age, and his trousers had been cut away. His lower left leg was the colour of the sugared swizzle-sticks that I sometimes buy for the children. The calf was fiery red, the foot bright purple, the toes a plump row of rotten black plums. Below the knee, the limb had swollen up to the size of a fisherman's over-boot.

'I . . . I had some trouble finding you,' I began to explain.

The doctor jabbed hard, and jerked downwards.

'I'll be with you in a moment,' he said.

A terrible stench engulfed the room, together with a scream that was barely human. Blood gushed, surprisingly rich and red in colour. Oily green pus came oozing out of the wound, thick and dripping, like warm lard.

The screaming died away in a dead faint.

Immediately, I felt the fish in my stomach begin to swim upwards.

But none of it made the least impression on the surgeon. To the sight, the smell and the sounds, he was apparently immune. He worked the knife in deeper, parallel with the shin-bone, filleting quickly, peeling away the dead skin and the rotten flesh, releasing the inner contents of a limb that looked for all the world like the leg of a statue that had been carved from yellow-veined basalt.

'Flat scraper number one, Frau Hummel,' he ordered briskly, without looking up.

The lady stepped over, picked an instrument up by the blade and laid the bone handle in his outstretched left palm with a mild slap. His thin white fingers closed around it, while his right hand held the other knife steady in the patient's leg. He slid the larger, wider blade inside the wound, then changed hands, extracting the smaller scalpel, which he gave over to the care of the lady. Then he went back the way he had come, working up from the ankle to the knee, opening and widening the incision.

'What were you saying, sir?' he muttered through his teeth, as more blood and pus came spurting out. The lady deftly dropped the used knife into a glass jar, then held up a large sponge of torn rags to absorb the noxious fluxes.

The stench was now intolerable.

With deft chopping strokes, he hacked away the muscle from the calf.

As this tissue slopped onto the table-top, the lady mopped and dropped the dead meat into a bucket, wiping her bloody hands on her apron, swatting at the flies, of which there were a number in the room. With a dull thud and the sound of something tearing, the blade struck bone. The doctor glanced at his assistant as he handed her the cutter, then he stared at me.

'Well, sir?'

'I came to ask for your help,' I managed to murmur.

'Hacksaw number two, Frau Hummel,' he snapped.

With another little slap, the saw was in his hand. An instant later, he began to hack and cut with a will. 'Help?' he grunted.

I swallowed hard and looked away.

With that infernal rasping in my ears, I concentrated my attention on the case of implements laid out on top of a chest of drawers, and read the label: *Surgical instruments of Herman Heinrich,* MD *Dresd.* The tools were arranged by shape and size: pliers and pincers for gripping flesh; sharp picks and pointed prodders of various dimensions, short to long; then, an armoury of surgical knives – some for paring, others for cleaving; and finally, a selection of saws, some small and fretted, larger ones for hacking. Above each item was a small label, neatly indicating the name of the maker, and date of manufacture. Had the man who was strapped to the mahogany table seen them before the operation began?

Instinctively, I looked across the room again.

Dr Heinrich stared back. In one hand he held up the saw. In the other, a severed calf and foot. He nodded sternly. 'There! Almost done. Just have to cauterise the wound and stop the bleeding . . .'

He must have spotted the expression on my face.

'Would you prefer to wait outside?'

It was very hot in the surgery. Despite the fine weather, the fire was lit, and I soon understood the purpose of it. The lady was coming towards the table, bearing a red-hot iron like a flat-ended poker which glowed menacingly in the thickening gloom.

'I think I better had,' I said.

No sooner had I closed the door than a raging scream announced that the patient had woken up. The sweet stench of burning flesh filled the house. Agonised shouting followed on, then great, gasping sobs. I had to cover my mouth with both hands to stop myself from retching, and would have welcomed another pair of hands to block my ears as well. Some minutes went by very slowly. The noise boomed suddenly louder as the doctor opened the door, then faded away as he closed it.

He had left the lady to cope with the patient's tears.

'A clod run over by his own milk-cart,' he sighed. He did not offer me his hand, but wiped away some unnameable remnant of gore on his apron. 'Best to have it off while the pain is fresh.'

'What a welcome surprise this is, sir!' I said with a genuine smile.

'Surprise?' he echoed, and his face seemed to darken.

'I had almost convinced myself that you were French. Your signature on the death certificate was . . . well-nigh illegible, to say the least.'

'I was in a hurry,' he replied brusquely, glancing pointedly at a ceramic clock that was hanging on the wall as if 'hurry' was his watchword.

His voice was strained and nervous, though he was young enough. His face was thin, his nose prominent, the skin of his cheeks taut and flat, his forehead broad. He wore his dark brown hair cut very short. His profession seemed to distance him, somehow, and yet, I thought, the doctor was hardly any older than I was. In his mid-thirties, I would have guessed. Only his eyes let him down. They were grey, dull, lacking in animation, as if he spent a great many hours alone in a room working closely on one thing only.

'You must be very busy,' I remarked.

'What can I do for you?' he said, ignoring any attempt at cordiality.

'The dead girl on the beach . . .'

'Another one?' he butted in again, as if such a discovery were not merely possible in Nordcopp, but highly probable.

'Oh no, sir,' I assured him. 'The same body, I believe. Three days ago . . .'

'I wrote it all in my report,' he interrupted me again. 'I had to certify that she was dead, nothing more. A cursory physical examination for form's sake. The colonel told me that a magistrate would be coming soon. A Prussian magistrate.'

He said no more, but his eyes were never still. If I had been measuring him, he was carefully measuring me.

'General Malaport insisted on it,' I began to say, then I baulked as I tried to find a convincing explanation for the general's decision. Could I tell him that the French high command believed that a public announcement of Prussian guilt would sound better if it came from a Prussian mouth, and in the German tongue?

'I had no choice in the matter,' I said.

'I understand your position,' he murmured dryly.

'I was the nearest Prussian magistrate to hand, I suppose.'

'I dare say,' he fired back, waving his hand dismissively, as if he did not care to know any more than I had already told him.

It made for a strange stop-and-start sort of conversation. We must have seemed like two poor musicians attempting to play a difficult duet together.

'May I ask how you became involved with them?' I enquired.

'If you'd care to step into my study,' he said, 'you will understand, perhaps.'

He crossed to the other side of the hall.

'We should feel flattered that they choose to favour us,' he added, drawing aside a red curtain, and pushing open a narrow door. 'Though I doubt that you *are*,' he muttered as he led me into the room.

The Prussian soul is a strange, volatile creature. One minute, we are hard and cold, impenetrable and distant. The next, an upsurge of national sympathy, and tender feelings for a fellow Prussian, break gently in upon our icy citadel.

'A drop of *aqua vitae* won't hurt,' he said, as I followed him inside.

I was no longer listening. I was staring at the walls. A collection of pale shapes hung from bright brass hooks. I realised at once what the future held for the man that I had seen tied down on the doctor's cutting-bench. Half of a left leg with an articulated foot was just one item in the vast display. We might have been inside a gallery of precious objects, but the forms on show were more macabre than they were artistic. There was a whole leg made of wood with metal pins in the knee and ankle joints. Segments of thighs made of plaster, I think. Calves and biceps beaten from metal, which served as moulds or models, perhaps. There were bunched fists, open hands, upper and lower arms, rough-shaped feet without toes. Splints made of wood and metal, braces, metal bands and other more mysterious props that made no sense to me. And all hanging up like pieces of armour in a baronial dining-hall.

'What are . . . they?' I could not find a suitable word.

There was a strong perfume of wax in the room, as if he spent long hours in there, reading or writing by candlelight, perhaps.

Dr Heinrich took two crystal thimbles and a matching decanter from a circular table. 'I have long been fascinated by human engineering,' he said, filling the glasses to the brim, pointing me to a horse-hair armchair. 'I fashion replacement limbs. There has always been a need for them here on the coast. That is what the French require of me. I am not merely a physician.'

He raised his glass in a toast, though he did not sit down.

'Have you been here long, sir?' I asked.

'I was born in this house,' he said. 'The practice was my father's. The Heinrich family of Nordcopp goes back a long way.'

'You must know the area well,' I said, intending to make the best advantage of his local knowledge.

'Better than most.'

He drained the contents of his glass in a single draught.

'It is fortunate for me,' I assured him. 'Local assistance is what I need. Your professional view of this case will be invaluable to me. I read your report, of course, but one thing puzzled me. You offered no opinion regarding the cause of death.'

Dr Heinrich raised his shoulders and blew out air.

'It could have been . . . well, just about anything at all,' he said. 'She was struck on the temple with a heavy object. A cudgel, a stone. Who knows? The blow stunned her, but it certainly did not carry off her jaw. I only hope that she was dead when the cutting started.'

'Indeed, the missing jaw.'

I paused, waiting in vain for him to offer some hypothesis.

'Not just the lower jaw,' I went on, breaking the heavy silence, 'the upper teeth as well. Why would anyone want to steal a jaw and a set of teeth? What purpose could such things serve?'

I could hear the note of pleading in my own voice.

He looked up at me. 'Like you, I have seen that stark barbarity and I can find no explanation for it.' He hesitated a moment, as if debating with himself. 'There is only one thing that any man wants in Nordcopp,' he said in a calm penetrating voice. 'Amber.'

He sank once more into silence.

I did not help him. I sipped from my glass and waited.

'It may not help you much,' he added some moments later, 'but this I can say. Her death was not an accident. It was nothing like the dreadful mishaps that take me down to the beach more often than I like.'

I grasped at this conversational straw. 'This morning on my way to Nordcopp,' I said, 'I saw a girl with her face blown away . . .'

His eyebrows shifted. 'Works for Pastoris in Nordbarn?'

'That's her.'

'Hilde Bruckner,' he confirmed. 'Now, that *was* an accident. Brought it on herself, the foolish wench! I was stuck with the task of trying to patch her up. She'll die if she comes down with so much as a cold.'

He had made a start, but he stopped again abruptly.

'That mutilation was caused by gunpowder,' I persisted. 'The person who told me also mentioned that a French soldier probably supplied it.'

'Really?' he said, busying himself again with the decanter.

That was it. He had nothing more to say. I had learnt twice as much from Grillet. And yet, I could not believe that Dr Heinrich was so detached, so apparently unconcerned about what was happening in Nordcopp.

I tried a different route.

'I suppose you see a lot of accidents,' I said, nodding at the casts on the wall.

'Farm accidents, like that man in the other room,' he replied 'Industrial accidents since the French arrived. The girls in Nordbarn sometimes manage to slice off a finger on those grinding-machines, having already lost a foot or a leg in the sea. Aye, that's the major part: the girls on the shore. Gangrene is as common as an ingrown toenail. Occasional explosions, loss of a hand or an eye. I do what I can, but it amounts to little more than chopping.'

'I heard another rumour coming here,' I said.

'You did?' he asked, as my silence stretched out.

I looked hard into his eyes.

They did not flinch away, as I expected. And yet, there was something flinty and fixed about the way he returned my gaze, as if he resented the fact that I obliged him to be sociable. As if he had decided for reasons of his own to say as little to me as possible.

'I heard that other girls have disappeared. Girls who harvest the amber. It is thought that they may have run away . . .'

'Oh, it's quite likely,' he said. 'They run away all the time.'

I sat forward in my chair, edging closer to him.

'They also say', I lowered my voice, as if to confide in him, 'that human remains have been found along the seashore. And that bones have been found in the sand-dunes. Have you heard such rumours, doctor?'

To my surprise, he smiled. It was the first time he had done so since I entered the house. 'Human bones are often found in this area,' he answered promptly. 'I have a small collection of my own.'

My heart seemed to leap inside my ribcage.

'May I see them?' I asked.

He went across to a large black dresser with carved panels, curly spindles and a dozen shallow drawers. 'I keep them here in my Cabinet of Curiosities,' he said, sliding out one of the drawers. It was six or seven feet long, a yard deep. It had been divided up into twenty-odd smaller spaces, none of which was shaped quite like any other, by an ingenious system of inter-lacing struts. The exhibits were of differing sizes: some quite tiny, others relatively large. I recognised a tibia.

'Did you find them all yourself?' I asked.

'I have bought one or two of proven local origin, but the others were found in the area by my father, or myself. A natu-ral philosopher, he started off this collection more than fifty years ago. He discovered this skull in the dunes out beyond Nordbarn.' He ran his finger around the rim of a large hole in the brow. 'It was made by a stone axe, I'd say. I have a decent watercolour of such a weapon somewhere in my print collec-tion. Our ancestors lived by hunting and fishing. Sometimes, when food was short, I suspect that they may have eaten one another.'

'How old are these bones, then?'

Dr Heinrich smiled. 'There you have it, sir,' he said. '*Exactly*, I cannot say. Accurate dating is the great curse of modern antiquarianism. My father used to make an educated guess, but that is hardly scientific, as I'm certain you would agree. There is a lively academic debate going on at the moment. There is no known method for judging the age of ancient bones. Being so resistant to decay, they are usually dated by association. If we find, say, a small skeleton in a tomb along with a round Roman shield and a short sword, we may safely assume that the contents, including the bones, date from Roman times.'

'And in the absence of such evidence?'

'Your guess is as good as mine.'

I took a deep breath. 'How many of these exhibits can be reliably dated?'

Heinrich lifted up the tibia and held it in his hands. 'I know what you are thinking, sir. You are asking yourself whether this bone, and others like it, might belong to women who have died more recently on the coast.'

'You are correct,' I admitted.

'And you are *wrong*,' he said with the measured authority of a collector. 'The bones found by my father and me have all been carefully documented. Regarding exactly where and when they were found, that is. Each one bears a label, and is carefully entered in the Heinrich catalogue. There is little room for doubt.'

He picked up a small hollow bone, held it to his eye and stared at me through the hole. 'This one, for example. It is very well-documented, sir. A *vertebra* amulet. It came from the crypt of the local church three years ago. The coast of Prussia has always been a violent place. Pagan tribes, Vikings, brigands, the Teutonic Order, all of them seeking amber. Then, the Poles, the Lithuanians, the Russians. Now, the French . . .'

'You mention amber,' I said. 'As a collector . . .'

'Not of amber, sir, I assure you. It costs too much for my humble means.'

'Still, you must have an opinion,' I insisted. 'For instance, regarding the creatures, flies and so on, that are sometimes found in amber. Were there men on Earth when those insects ruled the air?'

Dr Heinrich fixed me with an inquisitive stare.

'The Bible says that it was so,' he replied at last.

Hand in jacket pocket, my fingers caressed the nugget that Kati Rodendahl had been carrying. I marvelled again at its airy lightness, the smooth surface of the stone, the warmth that it seemed to emanate as I closed it in my palm. As it must have done inside the girl when she was living. It would have cooled down after her death. It was as if the amber had lived and died with her.

I pulled it from my pocket and held it out to him. 'I removed this from the corpse,' I said. 'Is this what the killer was looking for, do you think?'

The way Dr Heinrich swept it from my palm reminded me of Erika's hawk-like swoop at the honey-coloured bauble. He turned it over in his fingers, held it to the light from the window, shifted it from hand to hand as if to gauge its weight.

'A marvellous piece,' he said at last. Having opened his mouth, he seemed unable to stop. 'The colour, the size, the form itself, a perfect lozenge. Yet that is not all,' he said, looking up quickly. I had not seen such undisguised animation on a human face in quite some time. 'The insertion is absolutely unique. You may find wasps today, sir, but you'll not find one like this in God's Creation. They were drowned in the Flood. I myself believe that these creatures are far, far older. Older than mankind, in fact, despite what the Bible, that is, what Biblical scholars, say . . .'

He did not finish. His brow creased, he raised one eyebrow, and peered at me intently. 'When found, the corpse was naked, according to Colonel les Halles,' he said, his eyes fixed on mine. 'Evidently you have found her clothes, Herr Procurator.'

Had he been more open with me from the start, I might have told him. We were both obliged to work for the French, but that fact had not made us allies. We seemed, instead, to be standing on opposite banks of a very wide river, calling to each other from afar.

'Let's say, I found the secret hiding-place,' I said laconically.

'And the killer did not,' he concluded. 'Might that be why he vented his anger on the victim's face?'

13

Helena dearest,

I arrived safely on the coast and have now started work. I seem already to be making progress with my investigation, and I dare to hope that I will not be delayed here long. The French colonel in charge of the camp is doing everything in his power to assist me. And the local inhabitants appear to be more at ease knowing that a Prussian magistrate is asking the questions, and that he has their concerns at heart.

How goes it all with you at home? Is Lotte helping you, as she ought? And what about the children? Are they behaving themselves? I only pray that they are not too troublesome. They were so excited at the thought of a new baby brother. It will be a great relief for all of us – and most of all, for you! – when the child is born.

I miss you all, and Lotingen, too.

Has the situation improved . . .

I had never been good at writing letters to Helena on those rare occasions when I was away from home. I asked her only what I did not need to know, or knew already, and I lacked the courage to ask her what I really should have asked.

I wanted to say so much, instead I said very little.

I added a few lines regarding the general aspect of the coast and the state of the French camp where I found myself, assuring Helena once again that I would not delay my homecoming by so much as one single minute.

What more was there to tell that would put her at ease?

The door flew back on its hinges, crashing loudly against the wall of the cabin.

I looked up with a start.

A stubby forefinger was poking aggressively at my face.

'Tonight we'll dine together, Stiffeniis,' said Colonel les Halles. 'You can tell me what you have been doing all day.'

I had not heard him knock. Which is not to say that he had bothered to announce his arrival. Before he came, the only sound had been the muffled rumble of the sea upon the shingle shore below, the lesser rustle of a million pebbles as the retreating water tried to suck some back. If any knuckles had beaten against the door, I could not have failed to hear them. He barged in with the air of a superior officer who is inclined to see what his inferiors are getting up to in the privacy of their quarters.

And yet, it was difficult to think of him as my superior in any respect. His dark blue jacket was creased and crumpled. A pale tuft of lining sprouted from a jagged rip at the shoulder seam. His once-white trousers were stained, scuffed and filthy. His boots appeared to be sopping wet; he left a trail of sandy clots behind him as he entered the room. His face was wet with sweat. It had trickled down his temples and neck, and left white dribbles on his dusty skin. He might have come from some inhuman struggle which had wrung every single drop of every possible fluid from his body. Traces of fatigue were layered over his person. Oil, sweat, dirt and sand spoke out loud in spots and patches which dotted his skin and marked his clothes.

But the smell of him was worse. The damp, salty sea air, which had filled the hut before he polluted it, seemed like all the balms of the East in comparison. If the breeze had fought to get in through the cracks, I could easily believe that it redoubled the fight to get out and escape from him. The odour of his unwashed body inundated the atmosphere. And yet, clearly, he was pleased with himself. The expression on his face declared that a day spent mounting a new engine was a day well spent.

On my own face, I knew, a less happy expression reigned.

'I must finish writing . . .' I began to say.

Les Halles waved his hand dismissively.

'Finish it later,' he snapped, then conceded with brusque magnanimity: 'If it's on my desk by tomorrow evening, that will satisfy me.'

Evidently, he believed that the paper in my hand was meant for his eyes.

The urge to tell him that his professional concerns came a poor second to my domestic worries welled up in me, but I crushed it swiftly. The opportunity to dine with him, and tell him between mouthfuls what was on my mind, was too good to miss.

My letter could wait.

'I accept your generous offer,' I said, as if I had been invited to a formal dinner at the General Quarters. 'If you'll grant me the time to clean myself up, I would be grateful.'

'To judge from the stink in here,' he grunted, 'you've been crawling through the drains of Nordcopp.' He held up his hooded lantern the better to see my face and clothes. 'But be quick about it. When hunger takes hold of me, it tends to swallow up my patience. In twenty minutes, hut three.'

An invitation? It was an order.

'Most kind,' I murmured, as he went out, leaving the door wide open.

Was *I* the one who stank? Was *I* the one who needed to spruce himself up?

As I put away my quill and closed the bottle of ink, stowing them carefully away in the travelling *nécessaire* that Helena had purchased for my thirtieth birthday, I felt the anger welling up in me.

Should I wash?

A bucket had been provided for my ablutions. It contained cold water from the sea. The bucket was not particularly clean. Nor was the water fresh. In something of a passion, I stripped off the shirt I had worn all that day and the day

before, dipped it into the water and sponged my face, arms and chest with it.

What about my hair?

I wear my hair long, and loosely tied. It was dry, clogged and clotted with the sand that was carried on the persistent breeze. With a curse against French colonels and their sudden invitations to dine, I dropped down on my knees, took a breath and dipped my head into the bucket. Helena had put a towel into my bag, but I had acted without thinking. It was too late to start rummaging inside for a towel. I used the soiled shirt to soak up some of the water, brushing my hair back with my hands, tying it up tightly with the same strip of black ribbon that I had worn all day.

My beard?

Each attempt at improvement urged me on rashly to the next. And all in the desire to outdo Colonel les Halles. No Frenchman would outshine me. I shave each morning at home, but I had not shaved once in Nordcopp. I took the cut-throat razor out from my shoulder-bag, dipped the blade into the water – it looked less inviting every time I was required to use it – and made some darting correction to the stubble on my face and cheeks.

Again, I used the dirty shirt to rub my cheeks and dry my hands.

Now, what was I to do with the shirt?

I rolled it into a bundle, and stuffed it into the bucket, leaving it there to soak, while I went to look for the spare linen shirt that was rolled up somewhere in my travelling-bag. I had been intending to wear it the following week if the investigation dragged on so very long, but I was left with no choice.

Time was drawing on, but as I shook out the fresh linen, time stood still.

I held the garment to my nose, and took a deep breath. I closed my eyes, and inhaled the heady perfume of lilac and rosemary from Helena's garden. For one moment I was back in Lotingen. Thank Heaven for the little cotton bags of crushed flowers which Lotte always put between the clean clothes in the drawers at home to take the edge off the smell of burnt ashes. When the maid washed on a Monday, the entire previous week's supply of ashes went into the tub with the dirty garments.

I opened my eyes.

I pulled on the fresh shirt, carefully folding down the collar, knotting the linen bands in a fluffy bow at my throat. I was ready to dine. Except for the final touch. I took out a small ceramic bottle from my bag and unscrewed the stopper. The scent of Farina's finest *Kölnwasser* filled my nostrils with lime and lemon, orange and bergamot. While visiting Paris in 1793, I had purchased a perfume enriched with a distillation of rose petals from the shop of Monsieur Roget & Cie in rue Lerebours, and I felt sure that les Halles would have something of the sort. As I slicked my hands over my hair, luxuriating in the perfume, I could not help but smile. Hut three would be a battlefield of contrasting, competing scents: essence of Prussia *versus* the Grande Armée of essences of France. I trusted in Helena's good taste to bring me safely through the conflict. By the time I knocked on the door, waiting for his gruff call to enter, I had convinced myself that the skirmish was already won.

A small, square table was laid with a plain white cloth embroidered with only a regimental emblem. The plates of fine bone china were also white, and adorned with the same red heraldic badge. The cutlery was heavy silver: worn, but very ornate. There were two seats, one on either side of the table, which was loaded down with a basket of bread, two bottles of red wine, cut-crystal goblets, a large salver on which a long boiled sausage lay, another dish containing meat chops in a red sauce, and dishes piled with potatoes and beet. The sight and aroma would have made a favourable impression in an eating-house.

Only one thing spoiled the scene.

Colonel les Halles was seated at the table, a napkin stuffed down the unbuttoned neck of his uniform. He held a large chop to his lips with both hands, and gnawed on it like a starving hound. He dropped the bone noisily onto his plate, rattling his knife and fork, splashing gravy over the tablecloth. With a loud sigh, he picked up his wine-glass and consumed half of the contents in a single draught. 'You have used the time to good effect, Herr Procurator. You look and smell like another man. And much more pretty than the old one,' he concluded with a raucous laugh, as if greatly satisfied with these ironic remarks.

I stood there like a jilted bridegroom.

He wore the same uniform. The same filthy trousers. The same sodden boots. His short hair stood on end, as if he had tried to scratch the sand from his hair, then given it over as a hopeless task. He did not sit at the table so much as slouch, his boots stretched out to one side, his head bending low to meet the food and drink before his hands could bring it up to his lips. The spotted mess on his napkin reminded me of a large map in my office in Lotingen which showed the shoals of the Nogat estuary in red ink, the shifting sandbanks in brown. He eased himself into a more comfortable position, sitting further back in his seat, and his boots left half-moon clumps of mud and sand behind them.

The smell of his sweat was more acrid and penetrating than before. Despite the aroma of warm food, I realised that I would be obliged to inhale it the instant I sat down opposite him at that small table. No Essence de Lavande Provençale would save me, and my mind flew back to lunches eaten in peasants' cottages when I went out hunting with my father and my brother, thirst and hunger sweeping away decorum as the unwashed serfs and their earthy wives rushed to lavish their best on their master and his pampered sons.

'Sit down,' les Halles commanded.

I did as I was told. Could I doubt where the power in Prussia lay? He had ordered me to clean myself up for dinner; I had run to obey. If he told me to sit, I sat. While he, in his unspruced filth, looked complacently at my clean shirt, washed face and combed hair, then added harsher salt to the insult of carelessness.

'I did not know that Prussians were such fops,' he said, grabbing up a bottle in his fist, slopping wine into the goblets. 'You see the menu before you, Stiffeniis. Pork chops braised in Pomeranian wine. A bit vinegary for my taste, but there you are. Meat sausage in a vegetable broth to follow. Potatoes baked in sea-salt. All washed down with Saxon wine. The best of France and Prussia.'

He raised his glass. 'Taste it.'

As I carried the glass to my lips, the heel of his boot kicked out at my shin.

'Not yet. I want to propose a toast. Here's to the success of Richard les Halles's . . . now, what *shall* I call her? "Shale-drill" sounds tame, don't you agree?' He clicked his tongue, smiled, emptied his glass. '*Coq du mer*? Hm, that's better. Les Halles's Sea-Cock. With its long scrawny neck pecking away at the sea-bed. Will you drink to that?'

I raised my glass in the air, then drank a sip.

He sat forward, elbows on either side of his plate, and a nauseous stinking wave drifted into my face. 'You should have seen the way it pecked this afternoon! The Baltic tried to resist like a proud old Prussian matron, but I had my way with her. A bit bumpy at first, but once we struck the – what do you Prussians call it, *die blaue Erde*? – there was no stopping her. As soon as my engineers get their pipes into the water, and the engines start pumping, we'll be sucking up amber like *limonade*. When the sorting-racks come into play, a new era will begin on the north coast. I expect to draft a report of my success to Paris within the week.'

He drained his glass and fixed me with a smile, waiting to hear what I would make of his industrial success.

I raised my goblet again. 'I wish that you could build a machine, monsieur, that would suck up all the *merde* and flies from the streets of Lotingen, my home town. All the citizens, my wife included, would thank you for it.'

The expression of triumph on his face gave way to dark brooding anger.

I had surprised even myself by this sarcasm, and I immediately regretted it.

He jabbed his fork into a chop that was swimming in red wine.

'Give me your plate,' he snapped, holding out his other hand, opening and closing his fingers impatiently until I obeyed. '*Bon appétit*, Herr Stiffeniis.'

Without waiting to see how I might react to the food, he hunched over his plate, head down, his knife and fork poking from his closed fists like daggers, and began to wolf his food.

'You come from a family of aristocrats, I have been told,' he spluttered, glancing up, an over-large piece of meat in his mouth. He chewed it greedily, his lips and his teeth engaged in a complex grinding operation that ought to have resulted in the swallowing of his tongue.

I had no intention of stepping onto the thin ice of my personal life. I did not wish that man's ghost to cross the threshold of my home. Not even during conversation at the dinner-table. 'That is not quite exact . . .'

Les Halles thrust his fork at my face, a potato impaled on the prongs.

'Don't lie to me! I've got a file. It's all written down. After the Gottewald massacre investigation, Colonel Lavedrine reported on your character. Reserved in manner, sometimes brusque, it says. A tongue that is sharp, eyes that never flinch. You do not give yourself away, though your heart may be flailing wildly inside your breast.' The potato disappeared into his mouth. He drew the contour of my face in the air with his empty fork. 'You eat like a duellist, I would add, elbows close to your sides as you handle your irons, all very trim, no matter how tough the meat may be.'

He turned to the side and spat out the lump of meat in his own mouth.

'Inedible,' he said, 'but you eat on.'

I continued to chew. 'Our teeth make swallowing easier,' I replied.

He managed a smile as he ate.

'We come from different worlds,' he said. 'Anyone can see it. I will always be the unrepentant son of a Montgalliard sheep-herder. But you, Stiffeniis, even when you're hot and dirty, your hands black, hair knotted with sweat, you could ask a lady to dance and she would say yes. Aristocratic, as I said . . .'

Was it a compliment? Or was it the opposite?

'I own no land, nor have I ever served my country. I detest arms and armies. My principles . . .' I swallowed hard, having said more than I intended. I certainly did not mean to tell him that I had been disinherited by my landowning father. 'I chose to study the law, instead.'

His face became an ugly sneer. 'Whatever you say, you'll never cease to be what you are. What's the local term for it?' His eyes narrowed, his brow furrowed, he chased the word he sought across the ceiling. And all the while, he made the most appalling row as he chomped at his meat. '*Junker!* That is, a proud and privileged troublemaker.' He might have been reading from a book that claimed to describe the people and the habits of East Prussia. 'People like you were driven out of France. The ones who dared to stay lost their heads in Paris.'

I bit my lip. I could have told him a lot about Paris. I had inhaled a new perfume there in 1793. I had seen the French mob murder their king. In the Place de la Révolution, my spirit had been overwhelmed by a bewitching essence: the smell of human blood. An unknown aspect of my character had risen to the surface. I had been fascinated by the simple mechanics of Death. A lever was pulled, the guillotine blade fell, a life was carried off for ever. Nothing was easier, nothing was headier.

'You refuse to believe that men like me will change the Prussia that you hold so dear,' he went on, as if my silence pricked him. 'The new breed of French egalitarians may be rough, but we are ready, monsieur. We know nothing of good manners, and care even less. Our generals are men of the people, yet they can whip the hide off a Prussian army led by men with surnames as long as the Rhine. How did it happen? You do not voice the question, but I can hear it all the same. French peasants with a little technical education will build machines and mould the armies that will sweep your world away. Baltic amber – Baltic "gold", as you so proudly call it – is just a small part of the process. The Teutonic Knights made Prussia great. Well, now it is ours!' He halted for a moment, then drank deeply. 'Its only purpose now is to serve our purpose.'

I cut a piece of meat with my knife, carried it to my mouth with my fork, and began to chew it slowly. I would not answer with my mouth full. I would not give him that small satisfaction. And yet, I privately conceded, he was right. We were different, and not on account of our table manners alone. He saw Kati Rodendahl as an impediment to his ambitious plans; he wanted to see the murderer caught for that reason alone. Killers and their victims must not hamper the harvesting of amber. French interests would not be sacrificed for anything so human, or so petty.

'My only purpose', I said, intentionally echoing his own words, 'is to end the killing of Prussian women.'

He clicked his tongue, and shook his head.

'You fail to understand the situation, magistrate. The killer must be found because we want him found. You will find him, because you have been ordered to do so.'

The words flew out of my mouth before I could stop them. I was thinking of Lotingen, the filthy streets, the buzzing swarms of flies, the discomfort, the illness that the French had brought upon us like a plague, the threat that they posed to my wife and my children.

'Such blind indifference may work against you in the end,' I said. 'As it has done in Spain, sir. If Prussia revolts, well, I hardly dare to think of what we Prussians would be prepared to do. You called us storytellers, and it is true. But you should remember, sir, we like our stories grim.'

We stared at each other across the table.

'We are always looking out for danger,' he replied sharply. 'We crush resistance without thought or pity. But this is petty politics, monsieur. I am interested in one thing only: the amber of Nordcopp.' He let out a long sigh. 'I hate the stuff. Indeed, I cannot see its graces. What is it, after all? It is resin, nothing more. Centuries ago, it dripped from trees, then it solidified. Occasionally, a creeping insect was trapped inside. Which makes it more revolting, I say. The death throes of an ant, the agony of a spider! Only a mind profoundly cruel can admire it. And as for women wearing it upon their bodies . . . Amber does not come from the sea, it comes from Hell. It is the colour of sulphur.'

Of blood, I thought.

The sights I had seen that day came flooding back. The amber beads that Marta Linder had laid before me on the table. Like large red drops of congealed blood. Men's eyes lit up greedily, as if inflamed to possess them. Erika had attacked me like a ravenous hawk to get her hands on the amber containing the wasp and its eggs. She would have murdered me to have it. Certainly, she would not have hesitated to offer me the dubious joys of her tiny, monstrous body.

Les Halles wiped his mouth, planted his elbows on the table, and stared at me again with hard, stubborn eyes. 'So, let us be practical, Herr Magistrate. What have you found out today? What am I to tell General Malaport of his protégé's doings?'

I bit my tongue, and sat back in my seat.

It was time for the *redde rationem* to begin.

I could not refuse to answer him. Nor would sarcasm protect me. I told him first of my meeting with Hans Pastoris, and then of the woman working there, Hilde Bruckner, the friend of the girl who had been murdered.

'Her face has been ripped to shreds,' I said at one point.

Les Halles looked over the rim of his glass. 'What are you suggesting?'

'Gunpowder destroyed that woman's face. She was using it to search for amber.'

I saw him stiffen. 'The woman is alive. Or am I mistaken?'

'You are not mistaken,' I nodded.

'So, what connection do you make between the cases?' he growled. Clearly, the mention of gunpowder was not to his liking.

'You mentioned it yourself a moment ago,' I said. 'Amber. The woman working for Hans Pastoris was looking for it; the woman who died had already found it. But I was wondering whether what had happened to them both is indicative of a general trend . . .'

'I see no link,' he smiled back.

'Kati Rodendahl was mutilated *after* she was dead,' I replied. 'She did not blow herself up. But that is not my point. The point is this. Amber means wealth. Every man and woman on the coast wants their share. No, I was thinking of the person who provided that woman with gunpowder. As I have been informed, a French soldier . . .'

A riotous laugh erupted from les Halles. He choked, coughed violently, and I was bombarded by a hail of half-chewed bits of bread. 'Good God, Stiffeniis!' He raised his wine-glass and took a mighty swig. 'You almost did for me there. Still, I expect no less from you, I admit it.'

'No less?' I echoed, puzzled.

'It was only a matter of time before you put the accusation into words. I warned General Malaport of the risk. He'll throw the blame on us, sir. That is what I said. What else would one expect of a Prussian magistrate?' He slammed his fist on the table, rattling the crockery. 'Your French is excellent, monsieur, but do you know the popular expression among Parisians about going to work on your own balls with a hammer?'

I did not, and I told him so.

'You are the hammer; the balls belong to us!' He shook his head, then drank more wine. 'Soldiers are the same the whole world over. It is more than possible that my men trade gunpowder for sexual favours, but that doesn't mean . . .' He did not finish what he meant to say. He leaned forward, his face inches from my own. 'What we saw laid out on that table last is altogether different. It goes beyond amber. The killer was interested in her body. He took what he wanted, and he left the rest. Including the amber. He left her corpse on public display. Now, that's what I call evil. He meant to put the fear of God in every woman working on this coast. He intended to unleash terror, and chaos. Now, why would *we* want to do that?'

I had a theory. I had heard it from the mouth of Hans Pastoris in Nordbarn. The French were trying to make the women flee, rather than be obliged to drive them off the coast.

'Two of your soldiers, Pillard and Margiot, did exactly that the other day in Nordbarn,' I replied. 'They terrified the women there, talking openly of the girl who had been murdered . . .'

'Do you really think, Herr Magistrate, that they would brag if they had something to do with it?' he asked sarcastically.

'You threw a Parisian saying at me,' I replied. 'Very well, sir. Let me throw a Prussian proverb at you. "Put a wolf in a hen-house, leave the door open, you know which way the hens will run." I do not point my finger against the French . . .'

I heard no noise, but les Halles jumped up, raising his finger to his lips.

'What is going on out there?' he murmured.

In that instant, a fist rapped sharply on the wooden door.

Les Halles strode over to the door, and threw it open on a sea of faces.

The men drew back, as if they were contrite for having disturbed him.

I caught my breath: a different message was written on their faces.

'What is this fracas?' he growled. 'A problem with the barge? God be damned, I don't intend to go back in the sea at this hour . . .'

'Not the drill, sir,' a voice cried out.

'What, then?'

'A man has come. From Nordbarn, sir.'

I knew what had happened before I heard it from the soldier's lips.

14

'I knew that there was something strange in there. The pigs would not come out. They had already feasted.'

The voice of Adam Ansbach was thick and heavy, a sort of rasping, country sing-song. The young man had discovered a body in the pigsty, and he would lead me back the way he had come. His mother's farm was half a mile from the hamlet of Nordbarn, he said.

Colonel les Halles would not be accompanying us.

' "To each man his own task," ' he said tritely. 'Another proverb, Stiffeniis. Latin in origin, I do believe, though mighty popular with engineers. It looks to me as though your hard day's work will continue on through the night. Report to me as soon as you return.'

The women had been summoned from their cabins down on the shore. While I was in my hut, gathering my bag, I heard the roll of names being called. Over a dozen had been read off the list when I heard the ominous silence.

'Ilse Bruen?'

No answering female voice cried out.

'Ilse Bruen?'

The name hung as heavy as the pillow of fog which had slunk in from the Baltic Sea to suffocate the land.

'Provide horses for the procurator and his guide,' the colonel ordered.

I was glad of the offer though my guide was not so pleased, as I was soon to realise. He had little experience of saddle-riding, he said, and all his attention was given over to that difficult task.

'Can we go no faster?' I asked impatiently.

'Need to be careful cutting through the dunes, sir,' he warned. 'If the animals put a foot wrong in the fog, we might not get there. Follow hard on the tail of my mount, if you will. Should you lose sight of me, stop at once and call for me to come back. There are shifting sands off the main track. The French colonel would not be happy if we lost his horses.'

I took him at his word and rode attentively in his wake.

The fog was like a wet cloth that wrapped itself around our faces. The air was perfectly still. The horses made next to no noise on the damp, shifting sand. It might have been quicker to walk, though we would have been exhausted by the time we got there. I found it hard to believe that the boy had run all the way from the farm to the coast without a light if the way was as dangerous as he claimed.

We had been riding ten minutes or so when he fell back to ride at my side.

'The going's safer here, sir,' he said.

We rejoined the rutted, sandy track that I had walked that day to Nordcopp and back. While taking the short-cut through the dunes, I had wondered whether he might be exaggerating the danger as a way of avoiding the questions that I wished to ask him.

'We are getting close to Nordbarn Sheds,' he announced, his voice uncertain, low, as if the silence of the night imposed it.

'The place where Pastoris works,' I added, meaning to show him that I knew the general direction we were taking.

'Pretty close, sir. Our farm is more to the east, a bit farther on . . .'

'Are you ready now to tell me what you saw this night?' I interrupted him.

As I spoke, I was seized with doubts.

Had anyone told him who I was? Had the French bothered to mention that I was an investigating magistrate, that I would have to ask him questions, and that he was obliged to answer me?

He did not answer me, in any case.

Instead, he raised his hands to his mouth and let out a long, loud whoop.

Gleaming lights appeared like pinpoints in the swirling white opaqueness, waving gently as the lanterns signalled the direction for us to take. Voices sounded faintly in the distance, whooping back like a pack of ululating wolves

Some minutes later, we pulled up before a tumbledown house. Ignoring the large woman who wrested the reins from my hands, I stepped directly over to Adam Ansbach.

'Where is she?' I asked.

While riding there, I had examined the matter from a hundred different angles, and met with a thousand doubts. If the French had reinforced their guard after the murder three days before, how had this woman managed to leave the compound and reach that place in the fog at night? She must have known that Kati Rodendahl had been murdered, but that had not stopped her. Was she going on purpose to meet the killer, believing that he was something else, perhaps? And if so, how had he won her trust? Posing as a sweetheart, a smuggler, a soldier? I shrank from the thought of having to rummage heartlessly through the secret places of another female corpse in search of hidden amber. Yet, everyone seemed determined to help me do it without delay.

'Follow me, sir.'

The young man turned away from the house.

I strode off beside him.

A group of women fell in behind us, holding up lanterns.

Then a man stepped into the light. His goitre seemed to swell and gleam with all the colours of the rainbow. 'May I join you, sir?' he rasped, as if he were a talking toad.

'Herr Pastoris,' I nodded.

'Magistrate Stiffeniis,' he wheezed. 'If only I could say how glad I am to see you here, sir. You'll forgive me if I don't.'

I forgave him without saying a word, and turned back to Adam Ansbach.

'You mentioned a pigsty,' I said.

'It's over this way, sir.'

We had not gone thirty yards before we reached the scrawny, stunted wood of wind-bent trees that I had noticed on my way to Nordcopp that morning. At the time, it had seemed to promise salvation from the desert wastes. I had wondered then what secrets it contained. My nose was quick to identify one of them.

'What smell is that?' I asked.

Adam moved a few yards to the right, then stopped, holding up the lantern.

'The shitting-stile,' he answered bluntly. 'As I told you, sir, the pigs clean it out. But not tonight. Tonight they would not leave the sty.'

It was a simple construction. An open trench, two uprights and a cross-beam made of stout branches. No need to crouch over the filth, no compression of the bowels, no risk of soiling one's boots, or ruining one's trousers, no chance of slipping backwards into the mire. When the latrine is full, they fill in the old trench, dig another one nearby, and reposition the stile. Sometimes such constructions are hidden by a wicket enclosure, sometimes they cover them with a lean-to roof. This drain was open to the night sky, and it was full of excrement. It reminded me unpleasantly of the streets of Lotingen in recent weeks.

'Is the trench old?' I asked him, glancing into it.

'We never fill it in, sir,' Adam said. 'We let the pigs do the dirty work.'

'This is where your family . . .' I hesitated.

'Me and my mother, sir,' he said, 'and the lad who comes from Nordcopp every day to help us. Sometimes women drift across from the Sheds. We never turn them away when their latrine is full. Our pigs make short work of it.'

'These pigs,' I hazarded. 'Do you eat them?'

Adam Ansbach held up his lamp. There was a lopsided grin on his face. 'The pigs go to the French. We sell them bacon, eggs, and vegetables, as well.'

I had not eaten in the French kitchen that morning. No pork bacon had touched my lips, nor would it do so while I remained on Nordcopp shore.

'Very good, we've seen your toilet,' I said shortly. 'I want to see the body.'

I was quivering with tense anticipation.

Adam pointed beyond the stile. 'The pigsty's over there, sir.'

I followed him in a wide half-circle around the stile. Pastoris and his flock of women came hard on my heels. The smell of pigs soon took the place of the fetid latrine, clutching at my throat like a strangling hand. Ancient filth and fresh filth all jumbled up together. I searched in my pocket for a handker-chief. Not finding one, I pinched my nose closed with fingers, and opened my mouth wide.

''Tis worse if you swallow it,' Pastoris warned me. 'You'll taste it on your tongue every time you eat for a week. Breathe in through your nose, Herr Magistrate. You'll get used to it quick enough.'

I did as he said, and let that hateful smell invade every fibre of my body.

The pigsty was a long, low wicker barn in the lantern light.

'How many pigs do you keep in there?' I asked the boy.

'Seven,' Adam Ansbach replied. 'But it's empty now, sir. We closed the pigs in the goat-pen over yonder. When I first went in and I saw what they was doing, I tried to pull them off . . .' He hesitated for an instant. 'They would not leave her, sir. 'Twas like they had all gone mad.'

I looked down at the ground.

The lamplight revealed a great deal of movement, the mulch freshly marked by animal trotters and the slithering of boots.

'But you were able to move them out eventually,' I said.

'I had to call for help, sir. My mother first, then the girls from Nordbarn.'

However many people had been inside to chase the pigs out,

they had certainly obliterated any sign that the killer might have left behind him. There was little use in attempting to draw what I could see on the ground.

'Let's go in, then,' I ordered.

Though the door was open wide, the stench was like a physical barrier. Suddenly, I realised that there were five or six people gathered in the gloom inside. One woman was holding up a night-light. All of them were peering into the darkest corner. In the middle of the group, I recognised the woman that I had seen at the sheds that morning. Hilde Bruckner was clutching a scarf to her mouth and damaged face.

My heart sank even further.

So much for Professor Kant's scientific approach to the collection of data. *Isolate the scene of the crime,* he insisted. *Allow no one in. Record everything, no matter how unimportant it may at first appear.*

I turned sharply on Pastoris.

'Why are your women here?'

The small man stepped closer, wheezed loudly, bent his head and looked in through the low door. 'Adam came by the sheds,' he said, 'thinking that she might be one of my lot. But the girls are all accounted for. I told him where to look for you, Herr Magistrate. I tried to keep my girls away, but it was a dead loss. Two or three came over to help move the pigs. The rest came shortly afterwards. Word got out that one of their old companions from the shore was . . . well. It was difficult to keep them away, sir.'

'Get them out,' I hissed.

Pastoris went in. The dark interior seemed to swallow him whole. The only thing that issued from the sty was the stench. I heard the buzz of voices. Some of them were raised in anger, others were crying bitterly. It was clear to me that Pastoris could do little to control the situation.

I took a deep breath, bent low, then dashed inside. Adam Ansbach followed me. The women were huddled tightly together in the corner like frightened sheep, making a low wailing noise. Were they praying? Pastoris was standing in the centre of the group, murmuring alongside the others.

'Everybody out of here!' I roared through clenched teeth.

The women bobbed their heads and fled. One of them slipped and fell as she turned away. Pastoris pulled the woman to her feet, then shoved her out through the doorway. I could not fathom his power over them. Was he their sheep-dog, or was he the wolf that threatened to tear them to shreds?

'Stay here, Pastoris.' I caught Adam Ansbach by the arm. 'You, too,' I said.

The liquid bath of excremental filth was as deep as my ankles.

'Hold up those lamps,' I ordered.

Buzzing sounded close to my ears. Something touched my eyelids, settled on my face. It was there, it was gone. Then, it was back again. Flies. I waved my hand in front of my face, then covered my nose and mouth, disregarding the advice that Pastoris had given me. Those flies had been feeding on the body. Like the pigs, I thought. Even more voraciously, according to Linnaeus.

The floor was a sea of dark green slime. A dull red sheen glistened on the surface of the puddles near the body like the pattern of an oriental carpet. The victim was in a sitting position in the corner. Slumped against the wall, her head pitched forward, long dark hair bunched and tied at the back, strands dangling free, arms hanging loose, her legs bent at the knees. She might have chosen that unlikely spot to fall asleep, were it not for the fact that her skin no longer looked like human flesh. Nor did her rags resemble the clothing a decent woman might wear. The body and her clothes had been torn to shreds.

Blood and slime, dark red, dark green, clotting to black.

I might have liked to run the way the women had gone, but I took the lantern from the hand of Pastoris, and stepped closer.

Ears, nose, cheeks, lips. All torn off. Not cut, but ripped and shredded. Exposed bone gleamed dull grey between the islands of coagulating blood and the lurid strips of dangling flesh. Her cheeks had been ravished by the pigs. Her teeth and jaws were harshly gritted in a bizarre grin.

Nothing appeared to have been taken away.

The tattered dress exposed her breasts. Two blood-dark circles. Nothing remained. Below was a large blood-encrusted cavern. Intestines and guts had spilled out over her lifeless hands. Her ribs jutted out like the bare struts of a whalebone corset. The legs seemed intact, folded at the knee, apparently demurely covered. I flicked the skirt away with my finger. Slivers of skin and strips of muscle dangled from the left thigh and calf. Her feet were planted squarely in the filth. The shoe had gone from her right foot. And with it, the toes. Below the right knee, there was nothing left but bone.

I found myself communicating silently with that formless mass.

What business brought you here? Whom did you intend to meet? And what did he take away with him before he left the rest to the pigs?

Without thinking, I drew my notebook from my bag, uncapped the graphite-case. Though my hand shook, I tried to record exactly what I saw. It was the most hideous sketch that I had ever made. And as I worked, I spoke over my shoulder.

'Was she like this when you found her, Adam?'

I heard a fearful rattle in the boy's throat. 'I had a hard time shifting the pigs, sir. Like I said. They'd had a taste of flesh and blood . . . Mother and me, we had to prod them with a pitchfork. Chased them out one at a time, more or less.'

'Did you touch the body?'

I heard him shudder.

'Did you move anything?'

'I would not touch her, sir. What good would it do?'

I envisaged the pigs fighting over their unexpected supper, and felt more ill than before. Yet, I had to persist. 'Did you know the girl, Adam? Had she been here on her own before?'

'Herr Pastoris said she wasn't one of his . . .'

Anger erupted from me. 'I am asking *you!*' I growled.

'I'd never met her, sir. Leastways, not as far as I can tell. Now, I mean.'

His reasonableness provoked me. He was calm as the sea on a summer's night. It must have been a horrifying moment, even for a peasant boy who was used to the sights and the smells of the farmyard: slaughtering animals, gutting the carcasses, dead meat, the daily round of maggots and flies, rot and rancid putrefaction. He must have realised that he would be suspected.

'Did you hear that woman scream?'

'I did not hear a thing, sir.'

'Tell me now,' I pressed him. 'The French won't ask you twice, remember. They'll have the answer out of you in no time.'

Rumours were rife that the French tortured prisoners. I hoped that he believed those tales, that he would fear being handed over to them even more than he feared me.

'I heard the row the pigs was making. Didn't think nothing of it, sir. But when they wouldn't come out, I went in to chase them out.'

'You have nothing else to tell me?' I said sternly.

'We've nought to hide,' Pastoris protested. 'This is a catastrophe for us. I hope you understand the danger, sir. The French won't leave us in peace. Wasn't this just what they wanted?'

'The body was found here, Pastoris,' I insisted. 'On this farm. Someone brought her here, or she came of her own free will.' I paused, adding weight to what I wished to say. 'She may have come to meet the man who killed her.'

I expected a reaction, but it surprised me. Adam Ansbach's shoulders began to jerk violently. Loud, gasping sobs burst from his mouth.

Pastoris laid his hand on the boy's shoulder. 'Tell Herr Magistrate that you did not bring her here, Adam. Tell him that you did not plan to meet her. And that you did not even *know* her.'

'It's true, sir.' He was sobbing like a child.

'I have your word alone,' I said.

'You have mine!'

As I turned to meet that angry voice, I raised my lantern. The flames glistened on the boy's wet cheeks, then lit the figure of a woman who was straightening up, having passed with difficulty beneath the low paddock door.

'My son would never mix with them!' she said, stepping up as if to strike me.

The woman was tall, bulky, larger than me. She wore a long black shift, and a black shawl covering her head.

'Who are you?' I asked.

'Magda Ansbach,' the woman replied. 'His mother. This farm is mine.'

At last, I consoled myself sardonically, *a credible witness.*

'Have you been watching this shed all day?' I challenged her. 'And for no better reason than to swear that no member of your family came in here carrying the corpse of a woman?'

'Not all the day,' she replied with dignity. 'I've been busy round and about the farm since dawn. There are the goats and hens to feed, vegetables growing over yonder. I know everything that happens in this place. No one came. At least, that is, I saw no one . . .'

'You must tell a more convincing tale,' I said. 'The evidence here is obvious. An amber-gatherer from the coast is dead in your sty. And with the teeth-marks of your pigs upon her.'

'Who says that she was murdered?' the woman vehemently replied. 'Who says she wasn't drunk? She could have crept in there to sleep it off.'

The woman seemed to crowd in upon me as she continued speaking. She swelled up in front of me like a bantam cock, her broad face seeming to grow ever larger. Before she had had her say, I could see nothing and no one beyond her scowling face. Her wide-set eyes locked into mine as if she never meant to let me go again.

'Those girls are cursed!' she shrieked. 'They spread corruption wherever they go. They pass it round like a disease. You've seen the lot who work for Pastoris here. Not one of them is whole, sir. This one got what was coming to her, I'll be bound.'

'Which disease are you talking of, Frau Ansbach?'

The woman was ugly and aggressive. Her jaw was large and square. When she scrunched her face up into a grimace, the effect was hideous. It was like speaking to a gargoyle.

'Amber,' she snarled, her eyes glinting. 'They gather amber. They know the greed and violence that it unleashes. Just like the horrid insects trapped inside it. The creatures can't break loose, and neither can those girls. It suffocates and crushes them in the end. I know what amber is!'

She was so close. Her breath was fouler than the pigsty.

'I worked on the shore when I was young. I've held a piece of amber in my hands. This size!' She held her closed fist in front of my nose. 'Twenty-seven years ago, it was. We didn't have no Frenchies then, we couldn't scrape by with just the farm. I'd go out searching on the shore, and found that lump of amber in the sea.' She stopped and her eyes peered bleakly into mine. 'There was a bug inside of it, the most peculiar thing I ever saw. Nine months later, I gave birth to a . . . to a *monster*, sir! God was merciful, that poor creature died, but I ain't been down to the sea again. Not once! The Lord gave me Adam four years after. Whole and strong.'

What was she ranting about? Was she trying to tell me that the creature trapped inside the stone had influenced the child inside her womb? Did she believe that physical deformity could be explained away in such a manner?

And yet, she believed it. As if it were an undeniable truth. And I was tempted to believe it, too. I had seen the horrors on that coast. The torn and twisted bodies in the sheds of Nordbarn, the avidity of the men who traded in the amber-market of Nordcopp. Erika Linder. Was it possible that amber, like some cruel witch's potion, could provoke both physical devastation and spiritual deformity?

Suddenly, I thought of Kati Rodendahl. She had hidden amber in her body, and she had been murdered. Had Magda Ansbach done the same, and had her child been deformed as a result of doing so?

I turned away, and faced the corpse of Ilse Bruen.

I was glad that it was night. I was grateful that the pigs had done such damage to the corpse. I was overjoyed that I would not be obliged to search the body, as I knew I must. Tomorrow, I would organise a squad of soldiers, and have the body taken from the sty, together with any clues that the killer might have left behind him.

'I always thought that amber was a gift from God,' I replied. 'For this region, and for the whole of Prussia. Generations of our people have survived and thrived . . .'

'All dead,' she said plaintively. 'All gone.'

At my back I heard the renewed sobs of Adam Ansbach. I was tempted to add my own comforts to those of Pastoris. I wanted to tell the boy that what his mother said in crushing apocalyptic tones was untrue. I heard Pastoris urging him to look up, but Adam was clearly terrified by every word that issued from his mother's mouth. Was his distress the proof of innocence that I sought? If Magda Ansbach could frighten me, she could certainly frighten him. If she told him to avoid those women, would he dare to disobey her?

'Dead. All dead,' she raved. 'Killed for the sake of amber. Those sands out there, sir, didn't you feel the crunch of bones beneath your feet?' She did not wait for my reply, nor seem to expect one. 'Every one of them lost their lives in the search for amber. That is the Baltic, sir. Dry bones, dead bodies.'

Her madness was a litany. She filled the air with hate and dark despair. As she spoke, the corpse of Kati Rodendahl seemed to rear up before me. Kati had lived by amber, died by amber. And what about the wrecked corpse in the corner? Had amber killed her, too? How many more would have to die before the French replaced them with machines?

'Do not try to touch that corpse, do you hear me? Close the sty. Lock the door, Frau Ansbach. That body might infect the farm and every soul that breathes here. Animal or human.'

Even as I spoke, I felt ashamed of myself. I would have said anything to shut her mouth, and I knew that I had chosen the argument correctly. The pigsty would be an inviolable shrine, where the corpse of Ilse Bruen would rest in peace.

At least for that night.

As I went out through the door, the night air was like nectar.

Pastoris came hard on my heels, while Adam Ansbach closed and barred the pigsty wicket. More to keep the evil spirits in, I thought, than to prevent any person from entering. As the son worked feverishly, the mother mumbled darkly, uttering I know not what lugubrious comforts.

'What now, Herr Procurator?' Pastoris asked. 'That corpse is the opportunity that they French have been looking for. A dead Prussian discovered by Prussians in a Prussian pigsty.'

I understood his fear. More: I shared it.

Before I went to bed, I would be obliged to tell les Halles what he longed to hear.

'I'll have to tell them what has happened,' I said.

Pastoris stared at me in silence. Pain was there at first, but then his look hardened, and was as sharp as the blade he used to scrape encrusted amber.

As I returned to the coast that night, the ride seemed endless.

The fog had lifted, but the oppressive silence of the dunes persisted. There were no stars in the sky, the clouds were dark grey, low. No wind at all. My mind was filled with omens. The corpse of Ilse Bruen, the tears of Adam Ansbach, the fears of Pastoris, the dark prophecies of Magda Ansbach.

One thing alone was capable of shifting a little of the weight from off my heavy heart. A song that Helena often sang to the children sometimes. It came into my mind without my bidding, and would not go away.

I started to sing, softly at first, then louder. I was warding off my own fears.

Here comes the sun, here comes the light.
Where is the dark? Where is the night?
Locked in the cupboard, mother. Locked in the cupboard . . .

15

The open door cast a rhomboid of light on the ground.

Stripped to his vest and braces, Colonel les Halles was alone in the cabin.

A bulbous storm-lantern threw ample light onto a large sheet of paper spread out before him. Covered with intricate sketches, this paper absorbed all of his attention. Nothing seemed more important. Not even a spate of murders. The wooden models, which he had been so proud of the night before, were pushed aside like a boy's tin soldiers after the battle.

'Back already, Stiffeniis?' he said, looking up as I knocked on the door-post.

He waved for me to enter, but he did not invite me to sit down. Would I be obliged to stand before him like a school-boy, I wondered, and recite the lesson? I stole a glance at the drawings, and instruments: set-square, compass, dividers. He was reshaping the extending arm of the *coq du mer*, the machine with which he intended to suck up the *blaue Erde*, and the amber that was embedded in it.

'Well, what did you find?' he asked impatiently.

I told him what I had seen at the farm, described the ravaged state of the corpse, mentioned the pigs. I was unable to tell him how the victim had died, of course, but I was relieved to tell him that I had seen no evident signs of mutilation.

'No missing pieces?'

'No, monsieur.'

'Was she carrying amber?' he snorted. 'Amber the killer may have missed . . .'

'I cannot tell you,' I admitted. 'So long as the body remains half buried beneath a sea of sewage, it's impossible to say. I'll go back at daybreak, and make a more thorough examination of the corpse and the sty.'

He continued sketching while I spoke, making minor adjustments to the outlines on the paper. Suddenly, he looked up, his eyes sparkling brightly.

'Sewage, Stiffeniis?'

'The sludge left by pigs,' I said. 'The place has not been cleaned . . .'

'Of what consistency?' he snapped, as if it were the only detail in my report that truly interested him. 'Was this pig-shit runny, semi-solid, solid?'

'A sort of dense liquid mud,' I replied uncertainly.

He raised his forefinger, as if the question appealed to him. 'How deep exactly?'

I made a rapid calculation. Indeed, I took advantage of the expertise I had recently acquired in Lotingen. 'Twenty centimetres of liquid slime, more solid stuff packed hard beneath it.'

'So very deep?' he asked.

'That sty could be a hundred years old. I do not understand your interest . . .'

'It was a grave mistake to let you go alone,' he interrupted, eyes half-closed, his brow creased with deep furrows.

Was he put out because he had made an error of judgement? Or was the necessity of admitting it to a Prussian what humiliated him more? I knew that I would long savour the memory, though I did not understand the nature of the omission. Not then, at any rate.

'A couple of fellows would have been enough,' he murmured.

I thought I knew what he had in mind. 'The people at the farm will help me dig out the body in the morning. I'll question them again more carefully. I hurried straight back here tonight to tell you what I had found.'

It was a lie, but it seemed to please him.

'Did you bring the horse with you?'

'Both of them,' I said.

He smiled for the first time. 'Good. Without horses they can't go far. If anyone attempts to reach Nordcopp on foot, he'll be arrested. I have informed the garrison there. They'll keep a close watch tonight. If any man does try to escape, it will be an admission of guilt.'

'There's no good reason to suspect the people in Nordbarn,' I opposed.

'Is there not?' he challenged. 'We have a body. We have the man who found it. What more do you need?'

Was it all as simple as he suggested?

'I need more time, and better evidence,' I insisted. 'If a Prussian is accused, you know what the consequences might be. Better to have a definite proof before arraigning any man.'

'Which you have not got!'

'Which I have not yet got,' I corrected him.

He groaned with annoyance.

'Very well, sir, you are the magistrate,' he conceded. 'I expect your report tomorrow evening when your enquiries are fully concluded. They will be concluded to my satisfaction, I dare to hope. What was the boy's name again?'

It was an order. He wanted me to arrest Adam Ansbach for the murder of Ilse Bruen.

'Twenty centimetres of liquid slime,' he murmured, his head bent closely over his papers once again. 'You'll need proper footwear for such conditions. That perfume you are wearing cannot hide the stink of your shoes.'

As I began to thank him for his unexpected concern, he cut me off.

'Good night, Herr Stiffeniis.'

Shortly afterwards, I fell down on my cot and tried to sleep.

It was the second time that I had gone to bed fully clothed. The night air clung to my flesh like a cold sweat, and I was seized by a fit of shivering. I folded myself like an unborn child, knees pushed into my stomach, hands beneath my armpits, head bent into my chest. Dorika, the peasant girl who nursed me, alarmed my mother once, telling her how frightened I had been by a nightmare, describing my reaction to it: I curled up like a foetus, eyes closed, hardly breathing, refusing all attempts to comfort me. If I could not see, and did not breathe, I reasoned, then I did not exist. Thus, danger could not harm me.

Would such childish thinking work for me that night?

I hoped that pitch blackness would swallow me whole. I prayed that the things I had seen in the pigsty would not come back to haunt my dreams. I would need a clear head next morning. Les Halles was convinced that I would have no other choice but to arrest Adam Ansbach, take him to Nordcopp, and lock him in the town gaol.

Sleep was slow in coming.

No sooner did my head touch the pillow than the cold tail of my hair insinuated itself like a slithering snake inside my collar. With a grunt, I turned on my side, shook it free. But my hair had a life of its own. The ribbon came loose, and hair fell free across my cheek. I twisted back again, and like a nest of serpents, long hair wriggled between my cheek and the pillow.

I sat up, tied my hair tight, then tried to sleep once more.

It was out of the question. My mind lurched from one possibility to the next. I had prevented les Halles from taking the matter into his own hands for the moment, but how long could I hold him off? Would Adam Ansbach be able to prove his innocence? And if he could not, would General Malaport bend beneath the onslaught of les Halles? For one instant, I was tempted to hope that the colonel was right. If the solution to the killings lay in Nordbarn, and if the murderer were Adam, I would be going home, and sooner than I had thought. Malaport would have to honour his promise. Claudet would be obliged to do what his general told him. The streets of Lotingen would be clean. And I would be at Helena's side when the child was born.

Adam Ansbach's face flashed before my eyes.

He was crying as his mother helped him close the pigsty.

Her words burned in my brain like vitriol.

She hated amber, she hated the women who handled it. Her influence over her son could not be doubted. But how persuasive was she? The boy was young and strong. The mutilated girls who worked for Pastoris might convince him that amber was a curse, that his mother was correct. But what about the ones who passed through Nordbarn from the coast, carrying stolen amber to Nordcopp? They were young, too. *Whole and strong.* Just as Magda Ansbach had described her son. Would a mother's threats and menaces quash the natural instincts of a young man? Or might he find – or have found, indeed – the sensual attractions of the girls a more convincing argument?

I turned on my other flank.

Was that why Kati Rodendahl's corpse was naked? Did the undiscovered piece of amber suggest what had really happened? Had Adam tried to rape her, and failed? Was that why he had killed her? And had he tried again tonight?

Then again, I countered, would Adam rush to make false declarations about a body in his own pigsty if he had actually put it there? If he and his mother had said nothing, who else would ever have discovered the corpse? They could have left it there for the pigs to feast on. To fatten the bacon that the French would feed on afterwards.

I turned to face the wall.

I knew how les Halles would answer me.

'My men would have searched for her,' he'd say. 'They would have checked the farm and sty before the pigs consumed the body. By coming to us, that boy is playing the innocent. He is attempting to lay a trail which leads away from himself.'

I turned again, but could not rest.

The possibilities seemed to multiply endlessly in my mind. Unlike les Halles, I did not even have a working hypothesis. And how could I establish facts and interpret clues, when every witness added his or her own dose of fear and hate to the equation?

Was Magda Ansbach right when she said that amber

corrupted everyone who came into contact with it? I had been on the coast for two nights only, but I had already been seduced by the beauty of it, fascinated by its legends and its mysteries. My head was a jumble of confused thoughts, and unwanted images. I was unable to concentrate on what was essential, incapable of putting aside what was not.

Helena and the children came to visit me, then.

I crushed the image immediately.

I had no desire for sweet distracting thoughts. It was not my family that I ought to be thinking of, but the woman whose body had been thrown to the pigs, abandoned in the slime and the filth. Her ravaged body had become an integral part of the mess. I could smell the vileness on my hands, clothes and hair. Even so, I realised, I had been prepared for it in a way. The same revolting sights and smells were everywhere in Lotingen.

Only the clouds of flies were missing . . .

And yet, there were flies hovering around the body. Despite the salty humidity of the sea air, which ought to have driven them off. In Lotingen that corpse would have attracted flies more quickly than a jar of honey. How many days would it take three flies to consume that human body?

I turned over, facing the wall for the hundredth time, but still I saw the corpse. The dark islands of congealed blood, the holes the ravenous swine had torn in her breasts and stomach, the cruel ripping of the flesh from her face, the bones which gleamed in the lantern light . . .

God give me peace!

I prayed, but I did not ask for the balm of sleep. I begged for the black void of unconsciousness. When the investigation was completed, I would find rest. When the killer had a name. When I had written my final report for Colonel les Halles. For Colonel Claudet. For General Malaport. For Napoleon himself . . .

Revered Emperor, the missive began to write itself in my brain, *your interests in the amber from the Baltic Sea are now entirely safe. In payment for this service, I beg you, sire, to order that the streets of Lotingen be cleaned, the mountains of filth removed, and, with them, the flies which plague our lives, bringing nuisance and epidemics. Do it, sire, as I have done your business, removing with my own hands the stolen French amber hidden in the secret parts of the human corpses which infested the northernmost shores of your vast Baltic . . .*

Our Baltic Sea. *Our* Baltic amber.

Somehow, the tail of my hair had worked its way around my throat like a rope that was intent on strangling me. I pulled my right hand from my left armpit and was about to shift it away—

My wrist was suddenly crushed against my larynx.

Strong fingers pressed flat against my mouth, preventing me from crying out.

I felt hot breath on my ear.

'Do not shout, Herr Magistrate, or they'll find themselves another corpse!'

A shadow hovered over me. Darker than the gloom which reigned in the cabin. Those cold fingers hampered my breathing; that strong wrist was capable of snapping my neck.

'Will you speak quietly? Nod once, and I'll let you up.'

I pushed my head up off the straw mattress.

The pressure began to relax. The fingers slid away from my lips, resting lightly against my cheek. The shadow shifted, as I gasped for air. A little harder, I would have been dead.

'How did Ilse die?'

Had I ever heard such pain in so few words?

'Please, let me sit,' I hissed.

The shadow made no attempt to stop me, and I caught my first glimpse of the assailant. Moonlight or mist had turned the window a dull grey. Perfectly framed by this pale screen, the shadow took on the shape of a human profile skilfully cut with scissors from black paper. It was not the length of her hair, nor the curve of the shoulder, that told me that my attacker was a woman. It was the way in which she retreated as I levered myself onto my elbows. A graceful retreat as I advanced, making room for my legs to slide down from the cot and touch the floor.

'Who are you?' I asked.

The reply was so low, I could hardly hear the words.

'One of those that the killer is hunting. Just tell me what he did this time.'

A great weight seemed to slide from my shoulders as I tried to paint a picture of the revolting compound of human blood and animal filth that I had seen in Nordbarn earlier that night. Indeed, I felt strangely soothed as I shared the horror with another person.

The shadow did not say a word until I had finished.

'But the pigs did not kill her,' she said at last, as if stunned by what I had told her.

'No, it was not the pigs.'

Again, she was silent for some moments.

'Do you know who did it?' she asked.

'I have no idea.'

Time stretched out in heavy silence. On the shore down below, I heard the waves break gently on the pebbles, the slow rattling as the brine drained back to meet the next onslaught. When she spoke again, her voice seemed gentler. A child would be soothed by such a voice as it spun the web of tales intended to hasten sleep. I might have been lulled, were it not for the things that she said.

'What did he rip out this time?'

'I . . . I cannot say,' I whispered helplessly.

'There isn't much you seem to know, sir. How are you going to stop him chopping up the rest of us?'

'What is your name?' I asked.

'Do you want to tell les Halles?'

'God, no! It is only that . . . well, you know who I am.'

'Do you have a candle?' she asked me. 'I want to see your face.'

I remembered the taper that I had stubbed out before coming to bed, and dropped down on my knees, feeling about on the

152

floor with my hands. I brushed against her foot, then found what I was looking for, together with the flint-box.

'If the colonel is up, he may see . . .'

'Light it, sir,' she chided. 'He went to bed as soon as you left him. He's been working like the Devil tonight. His little engine won't do what he wants.'

I heard her giggling in the dark.

How many emotions had swept over her since she entered my cabin? Violence, certainly. I had felt the strength in her arms and fingers, convinced that she was going to smother me. Anxious concern, as she quizzed me about the fate of her friend. Great calm, as she listened to what I had to tell her. Irony, as she revealed that she knew too well the dangers faced by herself and the other women on Nordcopp shore. Now, mirth. The *coq du mer* was playing up.

I struck the stone against the flint, held the candle close to the spark, and the wick caught. I shielded the flame, sat down on the cot, and looked at her. The first thing that struck me was the strange manner of her dress. Above, she wore a vest which exposed her neck and her arms. Below, a pair of trousers cut off below the knee. The two pieces were made of waxed material which was stiff and grey. That plain, drab outfit could not humiliate the body it contained. Everything proclaimed her strength. Well-proportioned breasts, arms and shoulders moulded by the flow of muscle, the ripple of taut sinew. Her thighs and calves were powerful, her hands and fingers long, graceful, expressive. Exposure to the sun had tinged her skin the deep, dark colour of the amber that she fished for on the shore.

I raised the candle. I wanted to see her face, too.

'They eye us up like that at the Round Fort,' she said boldly.

Her head lolled back as if she were about to laugh. Instead, she ran her hand through her hair. In such proximity, I could not help but think of my wife. Helena's curls were wiry and stiff; this girl's tresses were long and gently undulating.

'What is the Round Fort?' I asked.

'It's where they take on girls who want to work on the shore,' she answered.

'You did not tell me your name.'

The softness of my own voice surprised me.

'You just watch your step now, Edviga Lornerssen,' she said, laughing lightly, covering her mouth with her hand, turning her face aside. 'Herr Magistrate means to interrogate you.'

I could see what Magda Ansbach feared. This girl was charged with boundless energy. It was as if the magnetism of the amber that they harvested had rubbed off on her skin. Was it vibrant, gleaming health that made these women seem so dangerous to Adam Ansbach's mother?

'I thought you would have done so sooner,' she added.

'I did intend to question the girls today,' I hedged, wanting to win her confidence. I tried to paint myself as another Prussian oppressed and hindered by the French. 'But Herr Colonel les Halles would not allow it. Only soldiers were admitted to the beach today, as you know.'

She seemed to listen very carefully, still doubting me, perhaps.

'Why don't you sit down?' I invited her.

She glanced at the bed. 'Here?'

I shrugged my shoulders. 'There's nowhere else.'

'I am soaked through,' she said, and crouched cross-legged on the floor.

She had not been beautiful as a child. Her height and the width of her shoulders would have made her seem too boyish. The shaven head that parents impose on girls to fight off lice would not have added to her childish graces either. Nor was she beautiful now. Striking was the word. Her face was well formed, the forehead broad, the cheekbones strongly pronounced. Her eyes were her jewels. They were penetrating pale green studs. In puberty they must have startled many a man who looked at her and saw her truly for the first time. A deep scar sliced her left cheek between the corner of her eye and the angle of her jaw. She had been a beauty once, but not for very long.

'When did you realise that Ilse was missing?' I asked.

'At the roll-call last night.'

She clasped her hands to her mouth. To stop her tears, I thought, but her hand slid down and caressed her throat instead. She was shaken with anguish as she relived that instant.

'Did you know that she had gone to the Ansbach farm?'

Edviga shook her head. 'I knew that she was dead. Wherever she had gone.'

I felt a wave of disappointment: she knew nothing.

'Tell me about Ilse Bruen,' I said.

'I . . .' She hesitated. 'I did not know Ilse well. We have lived in the same hut on and off, that's all. But the other day, they moved me to a different cabin.'

'Why would the French do that?' I asked.

She shrugged. 'They do it all the time, sir. For a hundred reasons. It depends on whether they want to reward you, or punish you. The huts are not all the same down there on the shore. Some are old and damp. Some are newer. I've been put in the very oldest, smelliest one . . .'

'What have you been punished for?'

Edviga raised her knees even higher, hugging them tighter with her arms, pressing her chin against them, rocking backwards and forwards.

'It was for . . . for something that I had done,' she said at last. 'Something that Colonel les Halles didn't like. He wants the bodies, *our bodies*, to be sewn in sacks and thrown into the sea. He says it is for the best. But it isn't, sir. He robs us of eternal peace. He shuts us off from the next world. Why, there are things that have to be done when a body crosses over. There are prayers, rites and rituals to perform. Otherwise, we'd live forever in endless pain. I did what had to be done.'

I remembered the way that Kati Rodendahl's corpse had been laid out: the rough cape of animal skins that covered her nudity, the circle of tiny amber fragments that had been carefully placed around her head. I could almost hear the prayers that Edviga had uttered over her dead body.

'So, you were the one who covered her up.'

'I'd have done the same for Ilse, too,' she went on, 'but there was no getting out of here last night, not once the news was brought from the farm.'

This declaration raised a practical question.

'How do you manage to slip past the guards?' I asked. 'All of you girls, I mean. You were able to enter the cabin where Kati's corpse was kept. Ilse walked at least as far as the Ansbach farm last night. And here you are, in my room now. Do all of the girls go walking when they ought to be in bed?'

She continued to rock slowly, but she did not say a word.

I let her be, listening to the sound of the sea, wondering how long it would be before the camp began to wake up to another day. She needs time, I thought. She is uncertain whether she can trust me.

Still, the silence lasted longer than I expected.

'I am a Prussian magistrate,' I began to say, hoping to persuade her to tell me what I wanted to know.

Edviga Lornerssen let out a sigh, as if regretting what she felt she had to say. 'A Prussian working to a French mandate, as you said yourself, sir. You must report whatever you learn to les Halles.'

'Not everything,' I said. 'Was Ilse seeing someone out there? A lover, perhaps?' I pressed on.

Edviga looked at me, held my gaze, then nodded.

I tensed instinctively, waiting for her to say the name.

Adam Ansbach. . .

But Edviga named no man.

'Who is this lover?' I asked again, though I did it gently.

She rested her chin on her knees again. 'The kindest lover of them all. A prince who brings us royal gifts,' she said at last. Then, she sang a line from what must have been an amber-gathering ditty.

O, the Baltic Sea is my only love.
He is hard, he is cold, but he's fair . . .

'This floor is very cold, too,' she said, nodding towards the bed. 'Can I change my mind, sir?'

I made space for her.

As she sat down close beside me, the straw mattress shifted beneath her weight. I felt intimidated by her presence. The air around her was fresh and clean, damp and salty, as if she had walked or swum through the sea. It was as almost as if she had been formed from the elements around her: the pale light of the moon, white sand, dark sea.

'Amber?' I prompted. 'Is that that the gift you are speaking of?'

She nodded.

'Soon the French will take it all . . .'

'They only want it for the riches it can bring them,' she bridled angrily. 'Like the Prussian lords before them.' After a moment, she added more calmly: 'Like *we* do, I suppose. We keep what we can hide away, and we sell it, too. But we see something different in it.'

There was a simplicity about the girl which I found disarming. Certainly, she had never been educated. No one had ever taken the trouble to refine her thoughts and train her mind, but her sensibility was of an extraordinary sort. She seemed to envisage far more than her words alone could express.

'What do you see in amber, Edviga?' I asked.

Her calves and her feet were bare beneath the knee-length trousers that she wore. She stretched out her legs in front of her, gently massaging the muscles, caressing the skin. Then, she turned her head and looked at me.

'There are creatures locked inside the amber, sir,' she said in a whisper. 'You have seen them, surely. God Himself put them there. He wanted us to see the Garden of Eden as He saw it. That is the greatest gift of the Baltic.'

'Insects,' I murmured. 'Dead ants, dead flies.'

Her eyes flashed wide with anger. 'You are wrong, Herr

Magistrate,' she hissed vehemently, as if she did not wish to hear such sentiments as I had expressed. 'They are no longer insects. They are much, much more. Would people pay so much for insects? Would they do *anything* at all just to possess them?'

Her voice faded into silence.

Edviga, too, had her superstitions. But they were of a different order from those of Magda Ansbach. I heard enchantment, admiration, awe. For God, the Baltic Sea, and the amber that it showered upon them. There was nothing dark or ominous in what Edviga said. And yet, something struck a discordant note in my head.

'There are men who would do anything to get those pieces,' I said. I spoke calmly. I had no wish to frighten her. 'You said so yourself. Do you think that there are men – one man, perhaps – who would kill for amber?'

'Two girls have died, have they not? Kati and Ilse are not the only ones. Other girls have disappeared before,' she protested.

It was not the first time that I had heard that story, but perhaps this girl knew more than anyone else.

'Do you know how many girls have disappeared?' I asked.

As she shook her head, her hair swished softly.

'Many.'

The word hung in the air like a phantom.

'When did it start, do you think?'

'This terror?' she said offhandedly. 'Months ago. A year, perhaps. Names were called, and no one answered.'

'But only two bodies have been found,' I opposed.

'The others may have run away,' she conceded, just as Pastoris had done. He had begun to tell me what he thought, but then had watered it down for fear of me, for fear of my dependence on the French. Would I learn no more from her than the little I had learnt from him?

'Is it so easy to escape?' I asked.

'It never used to be,' she said. 'When the French first came they were very strict. They wouldn't let us out without a thorough search. But then . . . something changed . . .'

I could understand her prudence – she would speak, then clam up a moment later – though I found it frustrating. I could almost see the question racing though her mind. It had hampered the tongue of Pastoris, and every other Prussian that I had spoken with.

If I speak, am I putting myself in danger?

'What changed, Edviga?' I asked lightly.

'The machines . . .' she said quietly. 'They said that they would use machines to dig up amber. They said they'd have no further use for us. And now the machines are here. How long do you think we've got before they send us on our way, Herr Magistrate? Now, there is only one thing in our heads: find it while you can! Take the gift the Baltic gives. Keep those bits that are rare, or beautiful. Sell them to the highest bidder.'

'Who offers the best prices?' I asked.

She lowered her head, shook it slowly.

'Don't you want the killer to be caught, Edviga? He murdered Kati and Ilse. He'll kill again, unless he can be stopped.'

She stared at me intently. Her eyes were mysterious liquid pools reflecting light. Her beauty was unmarred. Even by the scar on her cheek. In that instant, I would have said that such a scar was the sort of ornament every girl should have. I had seen a number of printed pictures of natives from the Pacific Ocean. It was tribal practice there, they said, to mark their women with ritual scarring to enhance their natural beauty.

'Amber drives them out of their minds,' she whispered. 'Especially . . . especially when it contains something unusual. There are many buyers . . . Every man is looking for those pieces . . .'

Suddenly, she changed direction.

'You asked me how we come and go,' she said, and gently laughed. 'You spoke of French patrols, French guards. They know we are smuggling amber out, and they pretend to control us, but they profit from it. The soldiers will let us through, if we pay the toll. If we smuggle, they hoard. We're like hens outside the henhouse, while wolves are waiting in Nordcopp. Now, one of them is killing.'

'Are you saying that the killer is a Frenchman?'

'I did not say that,' she answered brusquely. 'If the girls were killed inside the compound, any magistrate would know who to blame. There are only Frenchmen here, sir. But outside, it could be any man.'

While she was speaking, I was fingering the piece of amber in my pocket.

'Kati Rodendahl had this,' I said pulling it out, opening my hand, showing her. 'It was found . . . hidden deep inside her body.'

Edviga took the nugget, turning it over and over. 'Inside . . . herself?'

'You know what I am saying,' I said, sounding less patient than I intended.

She closed her fist around it, opened it, held the amber up to the light. 'This is worth a fortune, sir. She must have considered herself very lucky when she found such a beauty,' she said. She shook her head, then added: 'Isn't it sad? Instead of riches, she found death.'

'Was she intending to sell it in Nordcopp, do you think?'

She sat in silence, gazing at the amber. 'Maybe. Maybe not,' she said after a while. 'There could have been another reason why she had it in *that* place.'

'What other reason could there be?' I asked.

'She may have learnt that she was carrying a child,' she said. 'A child she did not want. She could have put this piece inside herself, hoping that the monster would eat the baby up.'

I felt a surge of revulsion. Since coming to the coast I had heard many disquieting and unpleasant things where amber was concerned. The borderline between humanity and bestiality was very fine. Often, the two worlds overlapped. Magda Ansbach had mentioned legends of the sort. Now, Edviga offered her own view. Could the women on the coast believe such horrendous tales?

'I have a question to ask you, sir. And a favour, too. Can I?' I nodded.

'They say that you are married.' Her voice was so soft, I could hardly hear it. 'May I know the name of Frau Stiffeniis?'

This was the final impression Edviga Lornerssen left behind. Shy, inquisitive, very vulnerable.

'Helena,' I said. But then, something prompted me to tell her more. 'My wife is waiting for me at home. She is expecting a child very soon.'

'Helena,' she repeated, as if the name were, somehow, magical. 'And what is this favour that you wish to ask?'

16

I gave Edviga plenty of time to escape.

Then, I followed her out into the pale grey light of dawn.

A pair of brown *Gaulisches* were standing on the top step of the hut.

My heart beat violently, my legs gave way, and I sat down heavily. Colonel les Halles had spoken of the overshoes the night before. Had he delivered them in person to my hut? Had he overheard me talking with Edviga? Had he seen her creeping from my room at dawn?

My discomfiture did not last long. Would les Halles deny himself the pleasure of breaking in on such an intimate *tête-à-tête*? Of course he wouldn't. Our secret was safe. I picked up the *Gaulisches*, slipped them on over my shoes, pulling the straps to tighten the leggings around my ankles and calves. Made of rough leather stitched to a thick wooden sole, they were generally worn by engineers engaged in siege warfare. They would save my shoes if I had to wade through the sewage of the pigsty, and I expected to spend the day in that unenviable condition.

I took a few trial clomping steps, and looked out to sea.

The air was a shimmering translucent haze, quite unlike the dense fog of the day before. The vast banks of pebbles were dark and wet. The tide was at its lowest. The sea purled and lapped inside the *haf* like an old man over his pap. And floating on this tranquil pond, I caught my first glimpse of the *coq du mer*, of which les Halles was so proud. It was an exotic name for a flat-bottomed barge with a tall derrick reaching upwards.

And in the smoke-like haze, I could just make out the figures of men who were working her. One of them was managing a long rudder; two more were manoeuvring a heavy anchor. As it fell with a splash, the noise echoed over the placid water.

Was les Halles himself out there?

At such a distance, it was hard to say. I strained to identify him, hoping that he was stranded in the middle of the sea. I had no wish to speak to him that morning. The colonel had already formed an opinion. A female corpse had been found in the Ansbach pigsty. Adam had murdered her. And if he had killed Ilse Bruen, he had murdered Kati Rodendahl, as well. Adam was a Prussian. It was all clear and simple, in his opinion.

A shrill trumpet sounded.

A procession was moving slowly along the beach.

I blinked, and peered harder in the weak morning light, remembering a picture in an ancient copy of Hartmann's *Succini Prussici* in our family library. As a child, I had been puzzled by the bizarre illustrations in that book.

'Can lobsters really walk on their tails, Papa?' I asked.

I knew what a lobster was. We had a Dutch still life of fish on the wall in the dining-room. Our lobster was a big, black creature with long, twitching feelers.

'Those are people,' my father laughed. 'Though it might be better for them if they were lobsters. They work in the Baltic Sea, and the water is always cold – summer or winter. Lobsters love cold water.'

The 'lobsters' down on the beach below were tall, strong creatures. They strutted along the pebbled shore in stiff leather uniforms which hampered their every movement. Leather breeches, thigh-high leather waders, a stout leather jerkin with a pouch in the front, and a large leather cap. Some of them were armed with spears; others with nets attached to long poles.

At the second trumpet blast, they waded out into the water.

The 'prodders' began pricking at the sea-bed with their spears, the 'catchers' swept their nets in the waves, throwing away the weeds and rubbish, keeping any amber that they happened to find, storing it in the pouches of their waterproof clothing. Bubbles of air trapped inside the amber make it relatively buoyant in water, Hartmann wrote. The more air, he said, the better it floats. Yet the quantity of air is in inverse proportion to its commercial value. The finest-quality amber – denser material than the amber-gatherers would find – lies buried deep beneath the shingle.

Colonel les Halles intended to dig for it with his machines.

I glanced from the workers to the French barge.

Here it was, then, a vision of the industrial future in the form of the *coq du mer*; and material evidence of Prussia's disappearing past in the shape of the amber-girls. The amber-fishers described and drawn by Hartmann were mainly men, but in more recent times, it had become a job exclusively for women. They asked for, or accepted, less, I suppose. I watched them for some time, thinking now and then to catch a glimpse of Edviga Lornerssen. It was impossible to distinguish one girl from her neighbour. In their leather uniforms and sou'westers, any one of them could have been Edviga.

And any one of them could be the next victim.

I turned away, praying to the Lord to keep a watchful eye on those women, as I went to breakfast. To my surprise the officers' mess was empty. Where were the French? Were they all down on the shore already? Les Halles had promised to work them hard, after all. I helped myself to a piece of bread, and a lukewarm cup of toasted corn. Five minutes later, I hurried to the gate, intending to requisition a horse and return to the Ansbach farm.

A French soldier was repairing a broken saddle beside an empty stall.

'All gone,' he grunted, forcing a stout needle into the leather. 'Something important's going on this morning. There's not one left.'

His flat nose, the bridge collapsed, the nostrils wide and fuming, spoke all too clearly of some ravaging venereal illness.

I tied my heavy *Gaulisches* together by the laces, hung them around my neck, and began to walk along the path to Nordbarn. The weather was not so stiflingly hot as the previous day, thank God. I did not try to take the route that I had ridden the night before with Adam Ansbach as my guide. So long as I followed the rutted track, I knew that I would get there in one piece.

Eventually, I caught sight of Nordbarn.

The workshop of Pastoris was strangely silent. No whirring grindstones could be heard that morning. Had the bees abandoned the hive? As if in answer to my question, the door opened and Pastoris himself appeared on the threshold.

I stopped, waiting for him to come across and join me. If his people were up at the farm, I thought, surely he intended to join them there. He settled himself against the door-frame, instead, as if expecting me to go to him.

I raised my hand and waved.

He did not shift or reply. Even at that distance, his goitre rested on his chest like a second head. Remembering his cataracts, I wondered whether he had failed to recognise me. I took a step in his direction, intending to tell him that I would welcome his presence when the time came to interrogate Adam and Magda Ansbach. Surely, they would think of him as a reassuring old friend.

The 'old friend' withdrew inside his door.

I heard it slam, then the harsh rasp of metal bolts being drawn.

I recalled his protectiveness towards his employees the night before. Did he wish to shield the women from what was happening up at the farm? If he wanted to restore peace in his workshop, my presence would only remind them all of the body in the pigsty.

I turned back to the path, my mind racing ahead to the task which awaited me.

This morning, I would be obliged to make a thorough examination of the corpse. I would have to establish precisely how the girl had been murdered. And I would need to sift through the pig-slime in search of the probable presence of a piece of amber, or some other clue.

If I did find amber, what would it signify? That both the girls were thieves? That both of them were pregnant and had attempted to rid themselves of an unwanted child by provoking a spontaneous evacuation of the foetus?

And what if I found nothing?

What if the pigs had swallowed the amber as greedily as human flesh?

I veered to the left and walked through the rough grass towards the stunted trees which marked the perimeter of the Ansbach farm. As I left the silence of the Pastoris workshop behind me, I began to distinguish a different noise, a noise that I recognised, though I was still a quarter of a mile from my destination.

Was someone doing the washing?

I might have been at home. Every Tuesday morning, Lotte piles the dirty linen into a large barrel in the kitchen by the water-pump. A layer of stockings and hose on the bottom, then a generous sprinkling of grey ashes and lye made from crushed cinders. A layer of undergarments after that, then more lye and ashes. Shirts, blouses, bed-sheets, each layer separated by ashes and lye. When the barrel is filled with water, Lotte presses down hard on a paddle that enters through a hole in the lid. Manni and Süzi often watch her as she labours. The harder she presses, the ruddier her large face grows. Which will burst first, Lotte's cheeks or the ribs of the barrel? But what delights the children most is the sound the washing makes. Air gets trapped inside the sheets and the clothes. As she pushes downwards, it comes bursting out in an endless succession of rude noises. 'Big farts', as Manni learnt to call them, from Lotte herself, who laughs out loud whenever she – that is, the washing-tub – produces them.

As I approached the Ansbach farm, the noise grew louder.

I passed the house, and marched towards the pigsty. The noise was coming from there.

While still at a distance, I saw a strange tableau before the door of the pig-sty. Colonel les Halles was not on board the *coq du mer*. He was there at the Ansbach farm, standing in the very centre of the group, directing operations of some sort. A man was seated nearby on a camp-stool, writing notes as les Halles dictated them. Soldiers in rolled-up shirt-sleeves were working the handles of a very large pump. Two men pressed down on one side, two more pulled up on the other side, and with a loud organic eruption the contents of the pigsty began to spout out in a shower from a pipe that a fifth man was obliged to hold in his hands, his face distorted by a grimace of revulsion. Beside him, another soldier was standing with a bucket in his hands.

They were evacuating the pigsty.

My heart, lungs and brain seemed to seethe and gush in syncopated rhythm with the pump. I began to run towards them. I should have guessed when I spotted Hans Pastoris so surly. He had known what was going on. He must have thought that I was a party to it, and that it was the proof that I was in league with the French. Probably he believed it was all my idea.

I stopped before the pigsty.

If the curious onlookers had eliminated all signs of entrance and exit from the building the night before, les Halles was literally destroying whatever hope I had of finding anything useful in that sludge.

'Colonel les Halles.' I shouted, preparing myself for a confrontation.

He did not deign to look at me, but carried on dictating. 'One hundred per cent effective. Six downward strokes for compression. Water to cleanse the nozzle. Eighty per cent immersion of the suction tube. Twenty per cent air content facilitates the degree of evacuation . . .' He turned to me and said: 'Oh, you are here, then.' It was not a greeting, it was a statement of fact. He turned again to his amanuensis. 'Cancel the last sentence,' he snapped.

'I am the magistrate in this case,' I said, equally sharply. 'You are interfering with the scene of a crime. Indeed, you've managed to spray away whatever signs the murderer may have left behind him, and cover half of the farm with it.'

He smiled at this rebuke.

'You needed to free the corpse from the sludge, did you not? I wanted to calibrate the aperture of the tube which will suck up material of similar consistency from the sea-bed. I'd call it co-operation. This experiment provided the opportunity to solve a problem of dynamics which dogged my efforts yesterday. On the other hand, you'd have been here for hours with buckets and shovels. I've saved you the trouble. You ought to thank me.'

My anger mounted.

'That body could have been easily moved, if that was what I wanted,' I replied. 'But that was not my only aim. I intended to search the place for any clue which might indicate a link between the murdered women. Amber, for example. Remember the piece that we found in the corpse of Kati Rodendahl? You didn't think of that! I'll be obliged to mention this fact in my report to the general . . .'

'Before you waste more breath,' he interrupted, 'you will be pleased to learn that I have found something. It will interest you, I am certain of it.'

He placed his hand on his hip, and stared at me, smiling broadly. Then, he turned to the man holding the tube: 'Show him what you found in the filter, Blanc.'

Private Blanc dropped his hose, and picked up a large, deep jute sack. He brought it to me, and held the bag open, inviting me to reach inside it, which I did. Finding nothing, I was obliged to reach in further. And further again, before my finger was pricked by something cold and damp at the very bottom. I closed my fist around the objects, then quickly pulled my hand from the fetid sack.

'Fragments of bone,' les Halles spoke out.

I opened my palm, and examined the slime-stained slivers and splinters.

'We found a lot of them,' he said. 'They certainly don't belong to the corpse in there. Other bodies have been buried here less recently. Clearly, this was a private burial ground, Herr Magistrate. I bet we'll find the remains of all the other girls who have gone missing.'

Again, he did not give me the opportunity to speak.

'I am satisfied,' he roared on boldly. 'They are the equivalent of amber. My engine sucked them up and spat them out. If we do half so well on the coast, the *coq du mer* will be a great success.'

'Colonel,' I interrupted him, 'these finds might well have been important. Now, however, they are useless. We do not know precisely *where* they were located inside the pigsty. Nor can we say how deeply they were buried in the slime. They could be chicken wings, or dead pigs. There may even be some human bones, as well. But any fragments of clothing or flesh that had not already decomposed have been destroyed thanks to you and your "well-calibrated" pump.'

He stared at me, and a frown of annoyance scarred his brow.

'You have your bones, what more do you want?' he said.

'I want to question the Ansbachs,' I said.

His confidence returned as he considered this request.

'They're in Nordcopp,' he said offhandedly. 'You'll have to go there if you want to interrogate them. I had them taken into custody this morning. They are being held in the town gaol . . .'

'In gaol?' I said, as if the word were new to me. 'On what charge? On the basis of what proof?'

'Murder. That's the charge,' he said, as if the judgement were a foregone conclusion. 'I'll leave you to find the proof, and tie up loose ends. Things will soon return to normal here, mark my words! There'll be no danger of a repetition of the crime. Indeed, as a direct result of this successful trial run with the pumping engine, I expect to send the women on their way in a week or two. They'll be out of harm's way. If any danger still remains, that is. The amber mining industry will be supervised by men. My own.'

He seemed to have satisfied himself that the case was closed. Of course, a report would have to be sent to General Malaport. He would sign it with a flourish, I would countersign it in much smaller letters at the bottom of the page, and that would be the end of the story. He had found the Prussian scapegoat he was looking for, but that is not the same thing as arresting the perpetrator. There was no incontrovertible evidence, much less an open admission, that Adam Ansbach had been trafficking with the girls from the coast, let alone murdering them.

I took the *Gaulisches* from around my neck, set them down on the ground, slipped my shoes inside, then pulled the leather straps tight. I had been carrying them for over an hour. It was time to put them to good use. Les Halles watched what I did, but I did not say a word to him.

'Do you intend to examine the corpse, monsieur?' he enquired.

Again, I did not answer him, but made straight for the pigsty.

I heard him tell his men to leave off pumping. Then, he strode across to me. 'Shall I tell the men to come in with us?' he asked, puffing as he struggled to keep pace with me.

'Enough damage has been done,' I muttered to myself.

He nodded, but there was a hint of irony in his voice. 'Just you and I, then?'

'You and I,' I replied, bending low, ducking beneath the door.

The sea of sludge had been entirely removed, stripped away. Indeed, as I stepped inside, I plummeted down a sharp slope. The slime had been sucked out, together with a great deal of the dark, stained, underlying soil. The smell was strong, but it was different from before. The musty smell clogged the air. The roof had been ripped away on one side of the sty to let in light.

Only the body seemed immune to change.

She was sitting in the far corner of the sty, her head hanging down, her chin resting heavily on her breast, exactly as I had left her the night before.

She might have been waiting for me.

'Don't you want the body carried outside?' les Halles asked at my back.

'Not yet,' I said. 'She needs to be examined inch by inch before she is moved.'

'Get on with it, then!' he groaned.

As I bent to look at her, I heard his voice outside the pigsty, ordering his men to start packing up their equipment and get it loaded onto the carts, ready for its immediate return to the coast. I was glad that he was gone, though not comfortable to be alone with the corpse. The exposed skin of the arms, the bloody circles where her breasts had once been, the dark cavern of the ravaged stomach, had altered since the night before. She was now entirely black, her skin spotted with drops of dried mud and yellow slime.

I reached out a finger and laid it on her forehead.

It was warmer than I expected. It might have been an effect of the interminable organic decomposition of the slime in the sty, though I could not be sure. I slid my hand beneath hers, and lifted. Her stiff left arm came up. I repeated the operation with the right arm with the same result. Nothing was broken there.

I felt for the bones in her legs, squeezing the rigid muscles between my thumb and forefinger. The bones of both legs were intact, though the pigs had caused great damage to the soft tissue of the calves and the lower legs.

I closed my eyes for a moment and silently asked forgiveness to her, placing my hands flat against her blood-caked breast, pressing hard against the ribcage. Nothing cracked, nothing gave, which seemed to suggest that there was no internal damage to her upper body.

I lifted her dress and looked up between her parted legs, moving my head left and right to take advantage of the light, searching in vain for amber hidden in that mass of meat and blood and innards. I did not have the courage to search with my fingers. If anything were amiss, it might be the work of man or swine. It was hard to imagine which was worse.

I dropped the skirt-hem quickly.

'What killed her?'

Les Halles was standing behind me once again.

'It is hard to say,' I admitted.

Her scalp was marked, despite the filth, by a clear line of division where her hair was parted in the centre.

I lifted a lank, filthy curtain of hair away from her left cheek, bent down beside her, my face inches away from hers. She did not smell like any person I have ever met; no individual human odour could match the stench in that place. I examined her left ear and temple and felt her skull with my fingers.

'No sign of cutting here,' I said.

I doubt that anyone who had known her would have recognised her face. The skin was mottled black and blue, swollen around her eyes, the lips, nose and cheeks shredded and torn. I could only say, as her hair fell back into place, that it had been blonde before she entered the pigsty.

'What about the other side?'

There was something blunt, practical, inhuman about the Frenchman. In that instant, I abhorred the sound of his voice, resented his interference, though he suggested no more than I would have done without his help.

My hand grazed her cheek as I lifted the filthy, heavy hair away. My fingers trembled as I bent close. Dead flesh has a texture like no other. It was as if the life had evaporated out of her, leaving something behind which was human in shape alone.

'Impossible to say what has happened . . .' I said.

'Adam Ansbach will tell you.' Les Halles was burbling at my back like a brook in spring flood. 'And if he does not, well . . . he will . . . But what do you think he wanted from her? And from the other girl, too, of course. Amber? Sex?'

That was not the end, but I stopped listening.

'She will need to be turned over,' I said. 'He may have stabbed her from behind . . .'

Words failed me. So did my strength. I gathered just enough. It was concentrated in the tips of my fingers as I placed them on the point of her jaw and tried to lift the head up, pushing it backwards with all the force that I could manage.

As the head lolled back against the meeting of the walls, I believe I may have cried out. Certainly, I fell backwards, and I felt the cold dampness soak quickly through the seat of my trousers.

Her chin had been covering her throat, protecting it from the assault of the pigs, from the sludge and the slime as the draining of the sty was carried out by the suction pump of les Halles and his intrusive team of labourers. The skin beneath her throat was surprisingly white, starkly contrasting with all the rest. It was like a white picture-frame enclosing a surgical drawing that had been made by an expert medical illustrator. Three neat cuts made a neat triangle, the horizontal upper line shorter than the two downward strokes which met at a point where her Adam's apple had once been. All was red and fresh within. Maggots wriggled where an entire section of her gullet had been removed.

'He has stolen the larynx,' I remember saying.

I came to, lying on my back in the open air, gazing up at the sky.

A soldier had just poured a bucket of water in my face.

17

'*Beyond – your – jurisdiction.*'

His fleshy lips made a sucking sound as he read the words out slowly.

I had seen the sergeant sleeping in the guard-room the day before when I went there to enquire where the doctor might be found. Now, he was wide awake, his piercing black eyes bold and challenging. It was hard to say how old he was. Two deep wrinkles scarred his puffy cheeks; blond curls worthy of Apollo framed his chubby pink face. His blue tunic was pulled as tight across his broad chest as if he had donned his younger brother's jacket by mistake. Tiny eruptions sprouted from the cloth where buttons had been shifted to accommodate his bulk. The company tailor had had to labour hard to fit him into that uniform, but his authority was in no way diminished. His epaulettes and buckles gleamed, his belt and cross-belts as black and shiny as a quivering blancmange. They might have come from the tanner's workshop five minutes before.

'The prisoners are your concern no longer, monsieur,' he insisted.

Jean Tessier, Sergeant of the Guard, sat behind his desk in the North Tower, balancing the conflicting papers in either hand, while I looked down on him. It was less humiliating to stand than sit: the stool he had offered me was lower than the table which separated us.

'My authority is signed by General Malaport,' I challenged. 'He ordered me to investigate what is happening here. The persons taken into custody are my responsibility. I have not yet finished questioning them.'

He let out a sigh.

'Adam Ansbach is twice accused of murder,' he replied, holding up the document in his right hand. 'The woman is listed as his accomplice.'

I could not accuse him of failing to co-operate. Still, I felt humiliated, imagining what had been said when the soldiers of les Halles brought the prisoners in that morning: *The colonel says to humour the Prussian magistrate. He's Malaport's man, so he's bound to kick up a fuss. It's a bureaucratic question, Tessier. Nothing more. His task is over once the guilty parties are found. He's the investigator, not the judge. Tell him that, then send him on his way.*

Les Halles did not contradict General Malaport, he simply brought him up to date on the latest developments. Tessier had let me see the colonel's note the instant I walked into the room. I had read it through a couple of times, searching for a loop-hole which would open the door to the cell where Adam Ansbach was being held.

The persons under arrest are accused of complicity in the murders of Katiuscka Rodendahl and Ilse Bruen, registered amber-gatherers. The corpse of the latter was discovered in the pigsty of the Ansbach family; the former was found on the beach adjacent to Military Post 67, Nordcopp Installation, three miles from their farm.

Prussian magistrate Hanno Stiffeniis, on the direct authority of General Malaport, successfully conducted the groundwork for the investigation, and he will now continue to pursue the matter in Nordcopp.

As military commander of the zone, I, the undersigned, on this day, 15th August 1808, declare that further interrogation should be carried out by the competent military authorities, as per Reg. 176.b/1804, and that trial and execution of the

*sentence should be passed to the relevant judicial authority
for the governance of East Prussia.*

The Ansbachs were being sent to Königsberg.

As Sergeant Tessier explained it, the order issued by General
Malaport limited my duty and my authority to Nordcopp alone.

'Nothing could be simpler, monsieur,' he said, dropping the
paper on the table, looking up to meet my gaze. 'As Colonel les
Halles mentions here, your task has been successfully accomplished.' He ran his fingernail along the pertinent line. 'Here's
the word. *Groundwork.* A military judge in Königsberg will be
appointed to complete the procedure and pronounce sentence.
Surely, you have discussed the matter with the colonel?'

He smiled at me in the mild manner one might employ to
calm a lunatic.

'In your opinion, Sergeant, how am I to do what Colonel les
Halles suggests,' I paused before using the verb which indicated
my new role, 'and pursue the matter here in Nordcopp?'

He shrugged his shoulders, threatening to burst his jacket
seams. 'The soldiers who brought these orders told me that
Colonel les Halles is convinced that other women have been
murdered. Not these two alone. Perhaps you ought to go and
look for the corpses?'

Was that the bone I had been thrown?

Only General Malaport could relieve me of the investigation.
Until he did, I must remain in Nordcopp and try to ascertain
precisely how many amber-workers had been killed. Those two
girls alone? More?

For an instant, I was tempted to lean over the table, take
hold of Tessier's cross-belts, wrap them around his neck, and
pull with all my might. If luck were with me, I might be thrown
into the same cell with Adam Ansbach and his mother. There
could hardly be more than one cell in that cramped tower,
which was as spacious as a privy.

'I demand to see them,' I said, struggling to control my
anger.

'That is impossible, sir.' Tessier looked down and began to rifle through the papers on his desk. Finding nothing there, he looked at the grey-green stains of mould and the blocked-up cannon-holes in the ancient plaster wall. Then he murmured: 'They were taken away an hour ago. They'll be on the high road to Königsberg by now. Is there anything else?'

The door was narrow, very low. I had to bow my head – it might have been a ritual obeisance to the power of France – as I ducked outside. In the narrow alley, I took a deep breath. The air was foul, but fresher than in the confined space of the gaol, where Tessier and I had each breathed in what the other breathed out.

Nordcopp seemed empty. It made a contrast with the frenzied activity of the day before. Entering the town half an hour before, the guard on the gate had warned me: 'It's a public holiday today, monsieur. The shops are closed in honour of some . . . well, I don't know. Do Lutherans *have* saints?'

I was angry and uncertain.

What next? Where now?

I did not intend to walk back to the coast. I had no wish to write a report for les Halles, and wished even less to speak with him. I had had my fill of eating cinder and ashes for one day. As I came to the end of the alley and turned right, I saw the high walls of the Pietist church, and all my hesitation dissolved away. I suddenly remembered the letter in my pocket. Corporal Grillet had delivered it into my hands the evening before, and I had ripped it open thinking it had come from Helena, afraid that something had happened to her, or to one of the children. I had been so anxious, I did not stop to examine the handwritten address.

It was not a note from home, I was relieved to see.

Most honoured Sir,

I have been instructed to report to you without delay, having come with letters of introduction from the High Court in Potsdam. Given the situation on the coast, where I

was refused access to your person yester-night, I will await
your pleasure at the Pietist guest-house in Nordcopp. You
may find me by asking for,
    Yours, most obsequiously,
    Johannes Gurten.

The name was like a rope thrown to a drowning man. He
was Prussian. From the elegance of his calligraphy, I judged
him to be a man of letters, and, possibly, of breeding. The
tone of his note suggested that it was a bureaucratic matter,
some urgent communication from the court in Potsdam
which Gurten had been entrusted to deliver. If the messenger
had been obliged to travel so far, it was my duty to meet with
him at the earliest possible moment. With the finding of the
corpse of Ilse Bruen the previous evening, the confrontation
with les Halles that morning, and the discovery that the girl's
body had been mutilated, I had forgotten all about Johannes
Gurten.

I would search him out and see what he wanted.

The Pietist meeting-house was the largest edifice in
Nordcopp, though not so grand as the Pietist church in
Lotingen where I had held court just three days before. Even
so, as I stood before the large double door, I had the impression that the Pietist church and the attached convent were
large enough to contain the rest of Nordcopp. I had seen
the church the day before while looking for the house of
Dr Heinrich, but I had had no other impression of the convent
than of a blank grey wall at the very end of a lane, where the
scurrying crowd who rushed from one shop to the next were
obliged to turn right.

I lifted the latch, and entered.

The act of entering a Prussian church always moves me. I do
not feel the same emotion when I enter a Catholic cathedral,
though I have visited many such temples in Italy, and seen the
frescoes and the paintings that they contain. The armies of
saints – Gerolamo bent over his books, a tame lion seated at

his feet; Sebastian, looking like a pin-cushion; the host of Madonnas and long-haired Magdalens – distract me from prayer, and seem out of place in the House of God.

In a Pietist chapel, everything is as it ought to be.

Silence reigns. The perfume of incense scents the air. An atmosphere of rarefied sanctity is tangible. No idols based on human models prance upon the walls. The mystery of godliness remains undefiled. A simple wooden cross reminds the visitor of Christ's sacrifice: no futile attempt is made to represent His endless suffering. The cold is penetrating; it provokes shivers. And yet, it is not the cold alone, it is a sense of the abiding presence of God which calls forth goose-pimples. I remembered the cavernous nave of the family chapel in Ruisling on a Sunday, as I took my little brother, Stefan, by the hand and led him into the darkness that he feared so much. I have seen some of the greatest spectacles in Nature – the soaring mountains and sweeping glaciers of Switzerland, the thundering cascade of the Marmore cataract on the River Nera in Italy – yet my experience of the Infinite was formed in Pietist chapels. What are fury and exaltation in comparison with silence and immobility?

As I pushed the door and stepped inside the Church of Christ the Saviour, I left my rage and stinging sense of humiliation outside. I knew that Johannes Gurten would be waiting there for me. A Pietist promise is not like any other.

The silence and the chill embraced me like a familiar cloak.

The air was scented with all the essences of a lifetime: damp earth, sweet myrrh, melted wax. The nave was long, the hammer-beam roof high, the aisles on either side divided by matching rows of slender columns. I made my way towards the altar-table, closed my eyes and turned my thoughts to God. I begged Him to illuminate me, to help me see the way ahead, to sanction my decisions and guide my thoughts.

One thing above all others concerned me. I prayed that Johannes Gurten would help, not hinder me. I hoped that he would not heap more problems upon me. I stood in silence for some minutes, head down, eyes closed, listening for the Voice of the Lord inside myself.

The perfume of the place grew so intense, it seemed to possess me.

I opened my eyes. The candle on the altar-table sputtered, guttered, went out, then lit up again, though no door was opened, no one came.

Was this a sign from God? And if so, a sign of what?

An ogive arch and a wooden door at the end of the left aisle caught my eye. I read the sign: GUEST-HOUSE. I lifted the latch and found myself in a small courtyard formed by the church itself, a low building across the way, and the ancient city walls of Nordcopp. Once, it might have been a garden, but there was not much light, and the garden had been paved over, leaving only a single apple tree in the centre of the courtyard.

On the far side of the space, I saw the sign again. GUEST-HOUSE. Another ogive arch, another narrow wooden door. I listened carefully before pushing the door and entering. As quiet as a forgotten tomb, the flagged corridor was barely illuminated by a single lantern. A paper hanging from a pin on a wooden board shifted in the draught. I lifted it up, and turned the paper towards the light.

Regulations of the community.

5.00 Bible reading; 6.00 Cleansing of the house; 7.00 Breakfast duties; 8.00 Tending the sick; 9.00–12.00 Biblical instruction to the children of the poor; 12.00 Cleansing of the church; 13.00 Luncheon; 14.00–17.00 Private study.

There was more of the same, but I did not read it all. A second sheet listed the names of the guests. I was interested in one alone: Johannes Gurten. It was at the foot of the list, and next to it the number VII was inscribed in Latin numerals.

I glanced along the corridor and counted seven doors. Over each lintel was a number, together with a Biblical quotation.

I made my way to the last door in the row, at the farthest, darkest end, and read the inscription above the door: *Only knock, and ye shall enter*. Leaning close, my voice low, I called out: 'Herr Gurten?'

No answer came.

With the heel of my hand, I knocked three times very gently. Silence.

I waited a few moments, then called out: 'Herr Gurten?'

As I lowered my hand, preparing to turn away, my sleeve caught on the handle, and the door swung slowly open on the wings of gravity and faulty carpentry.

There was a man inside.

He was naked, sitting on the cold floor, legs crossed, ankles hooked over his hips. His eyes were large, the irises bright blue, his arms were raised, the thumbs and forefingers meeting in front of his face to form an oval. His hair was blond and cut very short, showing off the planes of his skull. A candle burned on a saucer in front of him, casting a pale golden light over his rippling muscles. He had made no attempt to cover his sex, which rested limply on the tiles. His mouth distended in a tranquil smile.

Had I disturbed some mysterious and intimate rite?

'Do not desert me, sir,' he said quietly, moving only the muscles of his mouth. 'Give me a moment to complete my meditation.'

I took a step forward.

'Please, close the door.'

I did so, then turned to him again.

His eyes flashed open. They were large, the pupils blue. He unfolded his legs, and stood up with surprising alacrity.

'This is no Himalayan temple, sir. You are still in the convent of *Christ the Saviour*,' he laughed, holding out his hand in welcome, totally oblivious, it seemed, of the fact that he was as naked as a Greek god. Though slightly shorter of stature than myself, he projected a self-confidence that I could hardly have matched in my judge's cap and toga.

I am not used to nudity. Not even my own. While still at university in Halle, sharing a room with three other students, I was obliged to have my monthly bath in the stone tub in the basement of my lodgings, taking my turn with the water and the soap. I made a point of scrubbing my body as quickly as I could – summer or winter, the water was always cold – then drying myself off, and dressing as rapidly as possible. And even where my wife and my duties as a husband are concerned, there is a great deal of natural reserve. More on my part than on Helena's, I admit.

I took his hand and pressed it.

'I was . . . was looking . . . for . . .' I stuttered.

'Johannes Gurten,' he smiled and bowed, laying his right hand on his heart as if swearing an oath. On his middle finger he wore a ring with an inscribed cornelian. 'You received my message, Herr Stiffeniis. I was beginning to wonder if it had gone astray. The French could have . . . Please excuse my state of undress. You may not believe it, but I am a trainee magistrate. And I have been ordered to continue my apprenticeship under your tutelage.'

His statement surprised me more than his nudity.

'I will tell you everything in a moment, sir, though it might be better if I dress first. My hour of meditation was almost done, in any case.'

He brought the only chair and set it out for me. There was no other furniture except for a narrow bed. The room was austere, cramped, damp and bare, except for a cross hanging from a nail on the grey wall above the bed. Ventilation was provided by a window no larger than a playing-card. To see outside one would have had to peep out, one eye at a time, like looking through a telescope.

Gurten threw on his stockings, linen and trousers, then searched in his bag for a letter. Sealed with wax, it was addressed to me. He handed it over with a bow, then continued dressing with nonchalant elegance. A cambric shirt, a yellow waistcoat finely embroidered with rosebuds. He slipped effortlessly into riding-boots, which were new and costly.

I had never seen a man so sure of himself – with, or without, clothes. There was nothing bold or reckless about him. He seemed to match exactly the measure I had taken of him when I read his note the night before: confident, but respectful at one and the same time.

I broke the wax, and opened the letter.

Honourable Magistrate Hanno Stiffeniis of Lotingen,

The most urgent requirement in the formation of a judge is practical experience, as you well know. In response to the request made by the bearer of this missive, Johannes Gurten, trainee magistrate, has been assigned to your care for a period of two months with precise instructions to assist you in your daily round, and question you in regard to your administration of Civil Law.

On completion of his probation, please submit a detailed report to,

Your most humble servant,
Gregor von Gernshorn,
Senior Magistrate in the City of Potsdam

I closed the envelope and handed it back.

'I'm afraid you'll have to postpone your training, Gurten. I cannot say when I shall return to Lotingen and my duties . . .'

'Lotingen is not the point, sir,' Gurten said politely, slipping effortlessly into the space that I left him as I drew a deep breath. '*You* are the point, Herr Stiffeniis.'

He sat on the bed, back straight, hands on knees, blue eyes focused on mine, like a prisoner waiting for me to pronounce sentence.

'I asked specifically to be assigned to you, sir,' he added. 'It was not so easy to achieve in Potsdam, you can imagine. They wanted to send me to Berlin. Magistrate Otto von Rautigan's name was mentioned. You've heard of him, I shouldn't wonder.'

I knew von Rautigan as the author of a shelf of standard works of reference in any decent School of Law. Now, I supposed, he would be nearing the end of his working life. Still, any young graduate would have given the world for the opportunity to work in his office. I most certainly would have.

'I do not wish to sound like a flatterer, sir,' Gurten continued, 'but I should have been disappointed had they sent me to work in the offices of Minister von Arnim himself.'

'I am certainly flattered,' I said, and I was telling the truth. Another thought occurred to me. Out in the church, I had asked God to spare me further problems. Had God sent me help, instead, in the person of this young man? 'What advantages do I offer that von Rautigen cannot surpass?'

Gurten bounced on the bed, and answered quickly. 'Herr Stiffeniis, were it not for the serious expression on your face, I would think that you are making fun of me. Not one of the greatest magistrates in all of Prussia possesses what you possess, sir.'

Was he making fun of me? His seriousness suggested that he was not.

'I do not understand you.'

'Kant, sir. Immanuel Kant.' He raised his hands and joined his palms together as if he meant to pray to the soul of the philosopher. 'Four years ago, you went to him in Königsberg. Kant has always been my spiritual north . . .'

'I thought your spiritual north was east,' I quipped, looking at the spot on the pavement where I had found him lost in meditation five minutes before. 'Are you not a praying Buddhist, sir?'

He smiled. 'Buddhists have no god and do not pray. I use their technique of meditation to enter into closer contact with the spirit of Christ. There is no better place than a Pietist church to ponder on the mystery of God's essence, sir.'

Had anyone asked me why I had been praying in that Pietist chapel five minutes before, I would given the same answer.

'You find me in a difficult situation, Gurten,' I explained. 'The investigation in which I am engaged has nothing to do

184

with our Prussian authorities. I would like to help you, but I cannot.'

His eyebrows arched. 'Are not *you* the legal representative of Prussian interests in this case?'

'Do you know what is happening here?'

'I know something,' he said. 'I called on you in Lotingen yesterday. Your office was closed, but a note was pinned to the door, saying that you had been sent to Nordcopp on an urgent mission. It was signed by a certain Colonel Claudet.'

Despite myself, I let out a loud sigh. No man in Prussia would read such a note without assuming that I had sold my soul to the French. That I had chosen to further my career by serving them. Would anyone in Lotingen believe that I was interested only in removing the putrefying waste from our streets?

'Did you see the state of the town?' I asked him, anxious for news.

Gurten wrinkled his aquiline nose. 'I've never seen such filth, sir. Only flies and other insects prosper in Lotingen, I think.'

I had left Helena and my children in that stinking mire, and I continually chastised myself as I went about my business on the coast.

'The French don't seem to care,' he muttered.

Our eyes met. Shared resentment flashed between us. He did not say a word against them, but it was clear that he had no time for our foreign overlords.

'I must show you something,' he said, standing up, opening his bag, taking out a roll of papers. 'I gathered these in Lotingen, sir. Before the dust had settled behind your coach, these were already floating in the air.'

He handed over two broadsheets – one of fair quality paper, the other a rough rag.

The *Bulletin militaire* announced that '*Prussian magistrate Hanno Stiffeniis of Lotingen has been appointed to investigate a murder in Nordcopp.*' The writer underlined the fact that I had accepted the task of helping the French without hesitation, pointing out that '*such willing collaboration is rare among the native populace*'. Before the end, he casually mentioned the fact that I had left an eight-months-pregnant wife and three small children behind without a second thought.

'It puts my family and me at risk,' I said, and felt my cheeks burn brightly.

Gurten sighed and turned his head aside, as if to spare my shame.

L'Ami des peuples was a blatant copy of the Parisian broadsheet with which the monster Marat incited the crowd before the victims of his ire went to meet the guillotine blade. The news reported was the same, except for a rough silhouette of a tall, thin man striding away, while a large-bellied woman with three small children in tow waved him goodbye.

'May I keep these?' I asked.

'I'd rather burn them,' Gurten replied.

I quickly folded up the papers, and put them in my shoulder-bag.

'Your wife must be exceptionally brave,' he added quietly.

'Did you see her, by any chance?' I asked.

'It would have pleased me greatly,' he replied. 'But I didn't stop half an hour in town. I jumped on board the coach again, and dashed here after you, sir. In the future, perhaps, I may have the opportunity to make her closer acquaintance.'

'My wife is everything that a man . . .' I began to say, but then I faltered.

I had never revealed such sentiments to a stranger. Why was I doing so with Johannes Gurten? He claimed to be a trainee magistrate. He insisted that he had chosen me as his tutor. Was he telling the truth? How many powerful men in Berlin – the king, or Minister von Arnim himself – would want to set a hound on my heels? A man who would ingratiate himself with me. A spy, in other words.

'Have you been sent to watch me?' I asked him flatly.

The laughter which erupted from his lips was the loudest thing I had heard since entering the chapel confines. 'You must excuse me, sir,' he said, shaking his head. 'I wondered how long it would take before you asked me. After all, here am I, an acolyte, who turns up out of the blue. And there are you, a magistrate depicted as a traitor to his nation. It was a natural supposition on your part, but there's no truth in it. I cannot prove to you that I am not what I am not, but there is one thing that I can do. Let me serve you, sir. Let me learn what you have learnt from Professor Kant. I swear to you in *his* name that I am not a spy.'

I shook my head, though he had in part convinced me of his good faith. It was the name of Kant that did it. I had believed as fervently in Kant when I was Gurten's age. 'I am quartered inside the French camp,' I explained. 'That is where the victims lived. And General Malaport alone has the power to open the gates and let you in. I can see no way around the difficulty. The commander is eager to be rid of me. He will not welcome my assistant.' A bitter laugh escaped from my lips. 'Today, he believes that he has got rid of me!'

'Does he really, sir?'

It was the expression on his face that finally won my confidence. I did not feel as though I were talking to a stranger. Instinctively, I felt inclined to trust him. Something similar had happened four years before, when Amadeus Koch had come to carry me off to Königsberg and Immanuel Kant. Irksome incomprehension had quickly given way to abiding friendship, while all around us the city was plunged into chaos. I had not felt alone. Now, I was drawn to Gurten by the thought that he would listen and respond to me in a language that was native to us both.

The young man pressed his fingers to the bridge of his nose, a gesture I would soon know well. 'The victims lived in the French camp,' he murmured. 'Yet, they managed to elude the guards and reach Nordcopp. Surely they were trafficking in stolen amber?'

'Perhaps,' I countered.

'What other reason could there be to murder amber-gatherers?'

'Colonel les Halles has arrested a man named Adam Ansbach,' I replied. 'The Frenchman believes that sex is the motive.'

He edged closer, and frowned. 'Is this man a Prussian?'

I nodded, curious to know where his reasoning would lead him.

'And he is accused of murder by the French,' he said with a grimace. 'Nothing happens here on the coast, but amber is the cause. And especially now that it is in their hands.'

'But I have found nothing to contradict the accusation,' I said. 'So far, at least.'

Gurten stretched out his hand, as if to lay it on my arm. He stopped short, his hand in mid-air, smiling awkwardly, embarrassed by his own impulsiveness, perhaps.

'Procurator Stiffeniis, you will need a spy in Nordcopp,' he said. 'Someone to act as your eyes and ears. A man who is not known in the French camp. A Prussian who can move with ease among our own people.'

I had to smile. He seemed to contradict my fears, generously offering to do for me what I suspected him of doing already.

'I am that man, sir.' He paused, looked up eagerly. 'As a child I travelled with my father in this region. He was a comptroller for the old Baltic Trading Company. Fish and furs for the most part, but they also dealt in amber.' He edged closer. 'When I learnt that you'd been sent out here on a case involving amber, it seemed to be a potent sign of my destiny, sir.'

His mysticism took strange and unexpected paths, I realised.

'Did you see a sign before you asked to be seconded to my office?'

I found it hard to keep the sarcasm from my voice, but he did not react to it.

Instead, he laughed, and said: 'That's not the half of it, sir! When I discovered that you'd been sent to the amber coast, I thought to myself: this was meant to happen. I may be able to help the man who learnt his trade from the great Immanuel Kant. By helping you, Herr Stiffeniis, I may be able to help my country.'

A sort of growl erupted from my throat. 'Judging by those papers that you brought from Lotingen, you seem to be one of those rare Prussians who thinks that I am acting in the national interest.'

He shook his head, held up his hands. 'I should not have shown them to you.'

'You did the right thing,' I said.

'I may do another, yet,' he said. 'At five o'clock this morning, sir, I opened my Bible, and began to read the first passage that came to hand. You'll never guess what it was!'

'It is possible to find everything in the Bible,' I replied dismissively.

Would he use the Holy Book in his attempt to make me take him as my pupil?

'I read the page where Moses leads his people through the Red Sea,' he rushed on. 'The waters close again on the heads of the Pharoah's army, and drown them all. And as I read it, I was thinking of the French . . .'

The image of les Halles being swallowed up by the Baltic Sea was a pleasing one.

'And there's something else, sir,' he pushed on quickly. 'Something inside this convent that you ought to see. I have been here with my father many times, the pastor knows me well. Yesterday, I had just arrived, he told me something he would not have told to you, or anyone else. It may be helpful to your investigation.'

I had prayed to God for help when I entered that convent.

Had my prayer been answered?

18

Johannes Gurten led me down a dark corridor.

A row of identical wooden doors was set into the right-hand wall, a different inscription carved in Latin in the lintel above each one. At regular intervals along the opposite wall, a narrow unglazed slit let in a sliver of light.

'They live according to the rule of Jakob Spener here,' Gurten explained.

I had been brought up in a Pietist family, and had no need to ask what he meant.

'Unfortunately, the convent is built like a rabbit warren,' he added.

He paused for an instant in front of one of the doors, then entered without troubling to knock. I followed him into a small room which was dimly lit by a single tiny window. A score of people were huddling in the gloom, adults and children, seated all together on a narrow bench along the far wall. A man held up a large Bible; a woman read from it. Her words were echoed in a whisper by the assembly; they seemed to know the text by heart, reciting something concerning 'unfaithful shepherds who abandon their flocks'.

A man was waving his hand in time to the chanting, like a *kappelmeister*.

'With your permission, Pastor Bartosik?'

One might have expected resentment at this interruption of their Bible studies, so I was surprised by the way in which the people, most of all, the children, smiled and nodded, as if they were overjoyed to see Gurten.

'Would you care to join us?' Herr Bartosik enquired.

'Later, perhaps,' Gurten smiled. 'We are going to see Pastor Bylsma.'

'He is preparing for the exposition,' Bartosik replied.

'Today is Spener's memorial day,' Gurten added for my benefit.

As we left by a door on the far side of the room, the hands of the people came up and waved to us, as if they, or we, were setting off to sea on a long voyage.

'God bless!' called Gurten.

'I thought the place was empty,' I whispered, as we crossed the threshold into a dark corridor.

Gurten looked at me, an expression of severity on his face. 'The shops are closed in Nordcopp for the day. True Christians take comfort in the words of the Lord.'

He crossed the corridor and knocked on another door. Above it, there was another inscription. GOOD WORKS.

A voice called out, and we entered.

The room was almost bare, though larger than the last. Oddly, there were only two men in the room. One was stretched out on a sort of chaise longue. The other man stood over him, his legs straddling either side of the couch. The latter was wearing a long white shift that might have been freshly laundered and ironed, while the patched and ragged trousers of the reclining man gave the impression of having never been washed or cleaned in their existence. Neither man turned to look over at us. There was a strong smell of disinfectant in the air. As if to excuse himself, the man in white held up his hand.

He was gripping a very large pair of black pincers.

'One moment,' he said. 'A few more tweaks, and it will come out.'

I stepped to the side, glanced at the reclining patient, saw a cheek and jaw so swollen that the man's left eye had closed entirely. I had never seen such a frightful abscess. It must have been dreadfully painful, as must the operation, yet not a sound was heard.

'Don't disturb yourself, Pastor Praetorius,' Gurten said. 'We are passing through.'

'Is it you, Herr Gurten?'

He did not turn around. The pincer had taken hold and he was pulling and twisting so hard that his voice came hissing out from between his teeth. Suddenly, his arm jerked upwards, the troublesome tooth trapped in the maw of his pincers. The sufferer hardly made a sound. A long, low groan, but nothing worse.

'Spit,' ordered Pastor Praetorius.

A gob of blood flew into a pewter dish that was resting on the floor.

'Did you feel any pain?' the dentist asked, letting the tooth – a huge, hooked mass of black roots – fall with a loud clatter into the same bloody bowl.

'God bless you, no, sir. That vinegar of yours is a miracle.' The man's voice was as bright as that of a child who has just received an unexpected gift.

Gurten called back: 'God guide your hand, sir.'

We walked together into another passage, stopping in the gloom outside a door over which was carved the inscription: ZEAL IN STUDIES, AND A DEVOUT LIFE.

'The fifth rule of Jakob Spener,' Gurten intoned in a low voice. 'We have reached our destination.'

Whatever he was about to show me, I knew that I would see it in absolute silence, and that the lighting would be poor. Severity and parsimony were the essential elements of Pietist practice. In effect, this translated in the Convent of the Saviour into silence and darkness, a detached atmosphere in which mystic fervour could flourish.

As Gurten opened the door, my hands flew up to cover my eyes.

How many candles had been lit in there? At least a hundred. Perhaps more. There was not a shadowy corner in the large room. The air was pleasantly warm from the heat of the flames, delicately scented with the perfume of the melting wax.

It was so bright in there, it made the rest of the convent seem as dark as a cave.

'Lord above, Pastor Bylsma!' Gurten exclaimed. 'Is this the waiting-room of Paradise?'

I glanced around, noting two large cabinets containing ancient leather-bound volumes and paper scrolls arranged like a honeycomb. A long table occupied the middle ground of the room. Open books were laid out on lecterns, as in a medieval scriptorium. But the main feature was a large portrait on the wall opposite the door. Painted over a rich Prussian-blue background, I recognised the hollow cheeks and long curly locks of the founder father of Pietism, Philipp Jakob Spener. Beneath the picture, a mosaic of amber fragments of different colours formed his name, together with the dates of his birth and death, 1635–1705.

'Congratulations, sir,' Gurten enthused. 'The people of Nordcopp will remember this day for a long time to come.'

Pastor Bylsma was dressed in the same outmoded fashion as the man in the painting. He wore a large winged linen collar and a dark padded jacket with high shoulders, and his hair (or was it a elaborate wig?) had been set in a fair imitation of the founder's curls. Even so, I thought, Herr Bylsma failed to capture the mysticism and severity of expression which dominated the portrait of the father of German Pietism. And Gurten's compliments made no impression on his melancholy face.

'Who is this?' he asked, making no attempt to hide his animosity.

I was surprised. Pietism welcomes converts and the curious as a matter of faith.

'Allow me to present Magistrate Stiffeniis,' Gurten replied quickly. 'He has been sent here to investigate the recent murders on the coast.'

I bowed.

'The magistrate who is working for the French?' said Bylsma, frowning. 'What brings you to our convent, sir?'

I glanced questioningly at Gurten.

'Pastor Bylsma is the custodian of the Jakob Spener library,' Gurten explained. 'This chapel contains relics which once belonged to the great Reformer. There are even locks of his hair in a box.'

'True hair,' Pastor Bylsma insisted. 'From his own head, sir.' 'Celestial!' Gurten exclaimed. On his face I observed the same expression of ecstasy which had possessed him while he meditated naked on the cold tiles of his cell. 'I was more violently moved when I examined those grey curls last night', he went on, 'than when I stood beneath the painted ceiling of the Sistine Chapel. Great art may inspire us for a moment, but sanctity is eternal. Professor Kant understood this concept.'

His piety seemed genuine enough, though I wondered whether this inclination towards the mystical might induce him to view material things with less cold realism than they merited. If I did decide to employ him, I thought, I would need to beware of his facile enthusiasm. A different aspect of the question occurred to me. Our Reformation was fired by a healthy disrespect for relics. And yet, they were venerating those grey curls from the head of Philipp Jakob Spener as if they were sacred. Nordcopp Church seemed more pagan than a Catholic temple. And yet, that aspect did not disturb Johannes Gurten. Rather, it seemed to excite him all the more.

I wondered what Pastor Bylsma knew that might be useful to me. Why had Gurten led me there?

Johannes Gurten might have read my mind.

'Pastor Bylsma,' he entreated, 'would you care to tell Herr Procurator Stiffeniis what Nordcopp is celebrating today, and explain the part that this particular room and you, of course, will play in the ceremony?'

Bylsma frowned again, and glanced reproachfully at Gurten. 'Step up to the altar, sirs,' he said.

A row of candles had been placed along the front edge of the altar-table, which was at the far end of the room. A plain wooden cross hung darkly symbolic on the wall behind. Bylsma bowed his head and whispered hoarsely in a voice not his own. I heard some words of prayer in Latin, '*Cum dederit dilectis suis summum . . .*'

He seemed to change before my eyes into a different man. Fervent intensity blazed brightly in his eyes, his tiny figure seemed to swell and grow. Of a sudden, he twirled around and began to speak about himself, but not in the person of Pastor Anton Bylsma of Nordcopp. His speech was measured, formal, distinctly archaic. He had become the long-dead founder of the Pietist Order in Germany.

'It all came about in 1691, you see. I happened to be dwelling in the palace of Dresden at that time. I was employed as private chaplain to the Grand Elector of Saxony. But then, the Elector of Brandenburg – he soon became King Frederick I of Prussia, as you know – well, *he* proposed that I should go to Halle to select the teachers for the new Faculty of Theology at the university. I accepted the task, as I was bound to do, and so I took the opportunity to extend my absence and visit a friend, who was living here in Nordcopp. I stayed with him for – oh, two months, it must have been. Slightly longer, I suppose. Indeed, it was I, *Philipp Jakob Spener*, who founded the chapel and convent of the Holy Saviour . . .'

That first-person 'I' was disquieting; I had never spoken to a dead man before.

'In this very room, sir!' he thundered, spreading his hands wide. 'And why did I stay so long in Nordcopp? My works will tell you,' he said, pointing to the manuscripts and the scrolls on the table and the shelves. 'My unpublished works, I should add. Take a look at those two pages on the table. Look at them, I say!'

I glanced uncertainly at Gurten.

He smiled back at me, and raised his finger to touch the side of his nose.

Wait, that gesture seemed to say.

Reluctantly, I did as I was told. I was expecting to find some obscure religious tract. Instead, the papers appeared to be rough notes of a scientific nature. There were diagrams and sketches of no artistic quality, yet what those drawings portrayed was clear enough. They depicted pieces of amber, some large, some small, but all containing insects.

'It was here in Nordcopp', the pastor continued, 'that my reflections led me to propound the True Faith in the Germanic lands. It was here that I, Philipp Jakob Spener, founded the spiritual roots of our national history.'

Bylsma paused.

Was he waiting for me to share his enthusiasm?

'I am aware of the greatness of the man,' I said, glancing uncertainly at Gurten. 'You do not need to convince me, sir. At the same time, I do not wish to interrupt your preparations for the feast. Indeed, I have . . .'

'Pastor Bylsma was referring to what Spener discovered while he was here, Herr Procurator,' Gurten said quickly, holding my gaze longer than was necessary. *There is more that you should know*, he seemed to be saying.

He turned back to the priest. 'I was hoping, sir, that you would speak particularly of the Venerable Spener's interest in amber.'

'He was alluding to that fact, to amber, I mean, when he mentioned that he had uncovered the roots of German history and culture here in Nordcopp,' Pastor Bylsma added somewhat huffily.

The first person singular had been replaced by the third. I felt relieved.

'I was fortunate to find his written notes on the subject,' the priest added more meekly. 'Spener passed a great deal of his time on the seashore, drawing what the people found there. It was Prussian territory then and Baltic gold fascinated his mind. He spoke of amber as the heart of Prussia in the text that I discovered.'

'Spener collected amber,' Gurten put in, as if afraid the detail might be lost.

'He left a veritable treasure,' agreed Pastor Bylsma, lowering his voice.

'What kind of treasure?' I asked with less enthusiasm.

Is there a village in the continent of Europe that does not have its tale of hidden treasure of inestimable worth? Was this what my would-be pupil, Johannes Gurten, wanted me to hear? A half-witted priest recalling the short visit of a notable theologian to the area, his passing interest in natural amber, the fact that he had collected a piece or two while visiting his friend in the town two centuries earlier?

My mind flew back to the corpse of Ilse Bruen. The triangle carved in her gullet. The fact that Adam Ansbach and his mother were already locked up in the darkest dungeon of Königsberg Castle. I had allowed myself to be distracted by an over-excited youth who wished to practise law under my tutelage.

'I am sure it says a great deal for the honour of Spener and Nordcopp,' I said, preparing to make my excuses and leave them to it.

'Great mysteries surround the greatest names in our national history . . .'

'Pastor Bylsma,' Gurten interrupted him brusquely, 'please show Herr Stiffeniis what you showed to me last night.'

The pastor's mouth fell open. 'You are a devout Pietist . . .'

'So is Procurator Stiffeniis,' Gurten fired back. 'He is a Prussian, and he is trying to help our countrymen. Help *him*, sir!'

There was a fever of passion and anxiety in this exchange.

'I thought . . . that is . . .' Pastor Bylsma burbled. 'I believed it was the *French* who were to benefit in this case from the magistrate's assistance.'

I heard the note of sarcasm in his voice.

'Herr Bylsma, whatever you intend to show me,' I paused for a moment, afraid to add my own rhetoric to theirs, 'show me quickly. Herr Gurten is right. I have seen two corpses in three days. Prussian lives are at stake. My only aim is to save them.'

Bylsma fixed me with a watery stare. Then, he nodded. Turning to the altar, he bowed to the cross and stretched out his arms, resting his hands on either edge of the table. Was he praying to the founder again? A loud mechanical click broke the silence, and a narrow drawer slid out from beneath the altar-table.

'Come up,' he said.

I stood on one side, Gurten took his place on the other.

A vivid scarlet cloth hid from view whatever the drawer might contain.

Bylsma turned his face to mine. His eyes were bright, his cheeks seemed to swell, as if he wanted to speak, but feared to do so.

What was he afraid of?

'What you are about to see,' he warned me, his voice a tremor, 'has survived the greed of Russians, Lithuanians and Poles. Unscrupulous Prussians have tried to lay their hands upon it, too. With the arrival of the French, the time-honoured rules of prudence have been doubly reinforced. They would certainly remove it from this holy place. I am hesitant to . . .'

'Show Herr Stiffeniis what you showed to me.' Gurten's voice was imperative.

Bylsma nodded, caught hold of the edge of the scarlet cloth, and threw it back.

'The collection of Philipp Jakob Spener,' he announced.

The drawer had been divided into compartments of various sizes, lined with the same bright scarlet material, though it was irregular and puffy like a well-worn cushion. Fifteen or sixteen pieces of amber rested on top of the cloth, though there was room for more. Vague, impressed outlines seemed to suggest that certain pieces had been recently removed. Some were dark in colour, others a rich, bright yellow; some were large, others smaller. Some of these objects had been carved into forms which were recognisable: a figurine of a woman with a distended belly; a head of a wolf, its tongue protruding from its jaws. The largest piece of all was a crucifix made of red amber; the body of Christ had been cut in a paler yellow. All of the pieces had been polished to highlight their natural beauty. And yet, there was a blasphemous, pagan element in every one. They contained a fly, a beetle, or some other insect form which was entirely new to me.

'The treasure of Jakob Spener,' Gurten whispered passionately.

We studied the collection in silence, each man lost in his own thoughts.

'Spener was strongly attracted to amber,' Gurten explained, his eyes fixed on the display. 'He found great religious significance in it. Clearly, he was influenced by the likes of Nettesheim and Paracelsus. If amber had survived, together with the creatures that it contained, Spener said, then there must be a reason. It was God's will, His gift. On the other side, Spener was intrigued by the strange physical properties of the material, in particular the crackling force that it gives off when rubbed with a dry cloth. The ancient Greeks were equally fascinated, and had a name for it. *Elektron* . . . Why, Spener asked himself, was there such a vast quantity of amber in the Baltic Sea? What place was this in those lost days before the Prophets? What unknown world was being revealed, piece by piece, by the action of the erosive sea? Pastor Bylsma was telling me just last night that Spener wrote many beautiful pages on the mystery of amber.'

I thought of Edviga Lornerssen. She, too, had spoken of amber as a gift from the Baltic. Yet she sold amber, and she had told me something of the unscrupulous passion with which men searched for it.

I pointed with my finger at the empty spaces.

'Was he planning to add other pieces here?' I asked.

Pastor Bylsma looked gravely at me. 'The reliquary has been violated,' he said. 'These three pieces were the finest in the whole collection.'

Tears stood out in his grey eyes.

'What happened to them?' I asked.

'Robbed.'

'Four or five months ago, sir,' Gurten specified.

'They've been here since 1687!' Bylsma cried, appealing to me as a magistrate. 'Here! In this secret drawer. My custodial position requires me to examine the collection. I have to remove the dust, and make certain that damp does not invade the reliquary and damage the contents. To reduce the danger of cracking, I polish them twice a year with fish oil.' He sobbed, and raised his sleeve to his eyes. 'Last month, I came to clean them, sir. Today is the memorial day, you see. Once a year this treasure is shown to the faithful of Nordcopp. They'll come in through that door at four o'clock this afternoon to pray before the relics. Oh, the shame of it! Nothing has ever been stolen before. It is a sacrilege . . .'

Again, Gurten cut him off.

'You know who did it, do you not?'

If a witness was being questioned, Gurten was leading the enquiry.

'I would not wish to put the blame on any person,' Bylsma whined. 'It's just that . . . well, as I mentioned to Herr Gurten, there is a certain . . . well, a *coincidence* that cannot be ignored. Nothing more . . .'

He glanced at me as if he wished to be reassured.

'Whatever you tell me will remain between the three of us,' I forced myself to say.

'Two Prussian girls came here seeking sanctuary, sir,' he admitted. He might have been spitting out needles. 'They said that they had run away from the French camp on the coast.'

'This was in the month of March, Herr Stiffeniis,' Gurten added.

Gurten knew the story, but he wanted me to hear it from the lips of Pastor Bylsma. Indeed, he added details that the clergyman forgot or glossed, details which Gurten clearly thought were important. I was impressed with the young man's discreet manner of going about things. He was intuitive, relentless. I knew that I would make a magistrate of him.

'It wasn't the first time we've had fugitives,' the pastor explained. 'Most of them have no place to go. They are girls doing men's work, foreign conquerors watching over them like hawks. No law protects them inside the French camp.'

I thought of Edviga. The girl was tall, and strong. A woman doing the work of a man. The French were certainly watching her. Colonel les Halles was digging for the opportunity to punish and demean her. *Foreign conquerors*. Bylsma had summed up the situation well. But Edviga had spoken only of cabins that were cold and damp. How far did the French idea of punishment extend? Long ago, as every Prussian knows, the Teutonic Order punished amber theft with death by hanging on the seashore.

'They said they were afraid for their lives,' the pastor continued.

'Did the French come looking for them here?' I insisted.

Pastor Bylsma shook his head.

'Perhaps they had no need to look, sir,' Gurten observed.

'I do not understand your argument,' I said to him.

'Maybe the French *knew* that the girls were here,' Gurten continued with a wry smile. 'The French may have sent them, commissioned them, so to speak, told them exactly what to steal.'

'How did those women know where the treasure was?' I asked.

Bylsma's cheeks began to colour. 'I . . . Well, that is, I got them to wash all the windows. Not just in the church. In here, as well.' He paused for a beat, looked away, and caught the eye of Gurten. 'Like I told you, Herr Gurten. They were very . . . well, it was very difficult to say no . . . diabolical, I suppose . . .'

Gurten stepped into Bylsma's shoes. 'They won his trust, sir. He let them come in here to wash the windows and dust off the books in Jakob Spener's library.'

Magda Ansbach swore that the amber-girls were a danger to celibate men. And chastity played no part in the rules that Spener had laid down for his followers. How easily might two handsome temptresses have played upon the weaknesses of a middle-aged priest like Bylsma? If the girls had come intent on theft and seduction, I did not doubt that they had succeeded in their ploy.

Were they Kati Rodendahl and Ilse Bruen?

'They stayed for two days only,' Bylsma mumbled on. 'They helped with meals, cleaned the church, worked in the kitchen. Then, suddenly they disappeared without a trace. I did not understand it then. But the next time I came to open up the relic-box, I found those pieces missing.'

He halted suddenly, as if the tale had robbed him of his energy.

'What could I do, sir? Could I tell the French? If the soldiers had seen the treasure, they'd have seized the rest of it. And then, some days ago, a girl was murdered down on Nordcopp shore. Another one died just yesterday.' He shook his head, and peered at me uncertainly. 'Could the victims be the same two girls who stayed here in the convent?'

'What names did your visitors give?'

'Annalise and Megrete, sir.'

'Those are not the names of the dead women,' I said.

'They may have given false ones,' Gurten quickly interposed.

'Can you describe them?' I asked.

The small man raised his shoulders, as if to suggest that he had not paid much attention. But his pale cheeks began to flush very red. 'Very tall girls, sir. Big, strong, healthy girls with callused hands. Working girls with long blonde hair . . . that is, I noticed the fact, though they were always wearing scarves.'

'You told me last night that they were both very beautiful, Herr Pastor.'

Gurten spoke as if to add a forgotten detail, but he sought my eyes out, and he held my gaze. He glanced at the priest, who was agitating his hands, rubbing them nervously together. He was clearly in a state of acute embarrassment, thinking of his recent guests. I might have blushed myself, I thought, remembering Edviga as she sat beside me on the bed the night before.

'Can you describe the missing pieces of amber?' I asked the priest.

Bylsma bent his head very low over the reliquary. 'They didn't take the oldest pieces, the ones that are elaborately carved,' he said. 'They took three pieces only, but they were large ones, each containing an insect. Big, black bugs. The largest insects in the collection. The amber was the colour of gold, and incredibly beautiful.'

'And you've no idea where those women went afterwards?' I insisted.

Pastor Bylsma pressed his hand to his mouth and shook his head, but Gurten had an answer.

'They may have gone back where they came from,' he said. 'If that was the game, whoever sent them would have welcomed back the thieves with open arms. Until they'd laid their hands on what the girls had stolen, that is. At that point, they could be dispensed with.'

'If the French sent the girls to steal Spener's treasure,' I countered, seeing the holes in his argument, 'why content themselves with three pieces? They could have stormed in here with a troop of soldiers and seized the lot. Still, there is a way to settle the business,' I said, taking Kati Rodendahl's piece of amber out of my pocket. 'Pastor Bylsma, is this specimen one of the stolen pieces?'

Gurten's hand shot out. Instinctively, I closed my fist around it.

'I . . . I thought it was about to fall, sir,' Gurten said apologetically.

'Pastor Bylsma,' I said again, turning to him, indicating that he should open his palm and stretch it out. As he did so, I placed the nugget in his hand.

Gurten leant forward and peered at the amber.

'A wasp . . . a bee of some sort, sir,' he said. 'But absolutely enormous.'

If eyes had hands, I thought, that gaze of his would have carried the prize away.

Bylsma shook his head. 'The size is right, it's pretty enough,' he said, obviously caring little for amber that had not belonged to Jakob Spener, 'but this is not one of the pieces missing from the reliquary.'

'Where did you find a piece of that quality, sir?' Gurten asked.

I picked the amber up between my thumb and forefinger, and put it safely away in my pocket. 'On the body of the girl who was murdered three days ago,' I told him. 'The killer did not find it. If he was looking, that is.'

Bylsma made a rapid sign of the cross.

'Pastor Bylsma,' I said, 'I need your help, sir. Would you direct me to the office in Nordcopp where the amber-gatherers are recruited. I believe it is called the Round Fort.'

Edviga had mentioned the place the night before.

I intended to see it for myself.

19

'It's out along the coast road, going east, sir.'

Pastor Bylsma turned to me with an approving smile. 'You have chosen well, Herr Procurator,' he said. 'This assistant of yours knows the area better than many of the local inhabitants. No one goes to the Round Fort very much these days.'

'I went there with my father several times for the fur-trading,' Gurtan explained.

Bylsma's words rang in my ears as we left the convent. Had I chosen Gurten, or had he chosen me? As for whether I would allow him to assist me in the investigation, the question was still unresolved in my own mind.

We left town by the South Gate, where four French soldiers were on guard.

'Had your fill of praying, then?' one of them barked at me.

I did not reply, as we hurried out onto the dusty Königsberg turnpike. Johannes Gurten wore a stylish dark brown corduroy riding-jacket. An unstoppable fountain of news and information all morning, now he walked in brooding silence at my side. His eyes were fixed on the road, his brow was dark, and he had nothing at all to say for himself.

'Is something troubling you?' I asked him.

'The French, sir!' he said through gritted teeth. 'They care nothing for our traditions.'

'You'll have to get used to them if you hope to work for me,' I warned him.

'Our religion means nothing to them,' he burst out.

'The less they know about Jakob Spener and his treasure,' I replied, 'the better.'

Gurten stopped short and stared at me.

'Surely they must learn to respect Pietism?' he challenged.

I thought for a moment of sending him back to where he had come from. I had trouble enough with the French. I did not need a Prussian *provocateur* at my side to make matters worse.

'Listen to me,' I said sharply. 'I'm not employed to teach the French our history and traditions. Don't you understand my position? The French authorities ordered me to come here. I must give a good account of myself to them. There is a murderer in Nordcopp, and he will not be caught without their help. This is a criminal case. You said this morning that you chose me as your tutor. Let me offer you another choice. Stay here and help me, or take the next coach to Berlin. I'm sure they can still find a place for you in the offices of Otto von Rautigan!'

Gurten looked up sharply.

'I would not wish to make your task more onerous than it is, Herr Stiffeniis,' he said. 'But my heart ran away with my tongue. I can never forget that you were once the confidant of Herr Professor Kant. He recognised your qualities. Indeed, sir, I believe that he saw talents in you that no lesser man would ever have guessed at.'

He spread his hands wide as if to display the sincerity of his sentiments.

'That's why I wish to become a magistrate, sir. That is why I hoped to serve you, to learn from you what you had learnt from Professor Kant. Why, even now I feel as though he is listening to our conversation!'

I hoped that Kant was deaf to all living voices. As deaf as he was dead. My only wish was to cancel from my memory the days that I had spent in Königsberg. I wanted to forget that Kant had ever chosen me to work at his side. Instead, Gurten threw the fact in my face, expecting me to boast proudly of all that I had learnt under the tutelage of the philosopher whom he admired without reserve. If I had one desire, one ardent wish that I did not dare confess – I hardly dared admit it to myself – it was that the French would extirpate the name of Immanuel Kant from the history of Prussia.

'You know much of me, Gurten,' I admitted. 'But I know nothing of you. If I do decide to tutor you, I would like to know more.'

The dark cloud shifted from the young man's face.

He chatted amiably, telling me stories from his family life, his schooling, and, most especially, his time at the University of Dresden. He had begun by studying medicine for a year or two, but then he had visited Königsberg, paying homage at the tomb of Immanuel Kant. He had read a newspaper account of Immanuel Kant's last days – my name was mentioned in the article, he said – where much was made of our hunt for a murderer who was terrorising the city.

'As a consequence, I decided to change to jurisprudence,' he concluded. 'Just as you did, sir.'

What would Gurten have thought if he had known the real motive which had induced me to become a magistrate? Would he still have held me up as a paragon to admire and follow?

We did not have to walk very far, which was fortunate, given the persisting heat. The Round Fort was not a mile from Nordcopp. Before the French arrived, Pastor Bylsma said, the building had been used for centuries as a stronghold repository by the margraves of Marlbork. The aristocratic family had held the royal mandate for the amber-working on that stretch coast for generations, until the French invaders seized possession of their monopoly. Now, the Round Fort was a local labour station for the French administration. Each Monday morning, new girls were taken on to replace the ones who had run away of their own accord, often without collecting their pay, or to replace others who had decided to leave the employment for some reason known only to themselves, but with money due to them in their hands.

Naturally, I thought, Colonel les Halles would close the place at his earliest convenience.

'Bylsma did not say that the place was falling down,' I observed, as we caught our first sight of the tower. Nor had he said how old the building was.

Thirty feet high, and almost twice as wide, the Round Fort squatted on the crown of the hill like a well-fitting hat. Its walls were a dense mosaic of grey and black stones set in a muted green overcoat of moss. Round and smooth, of every size from very large to very small, those stones had not come from the local seashore. Somebody had gone to a deal of trouble to import the materials and build that stronghold. A crumbling curtain-wall on top of the fort was castellated to aid defence. Angled arrow-slits had been cut in the wall to allow the defenders to fire obliquely on anyone trying to undermine or storm it. I was impressed by the strategic position of the edifice.

Equally, I was impressed by something that Johannes Gurten had just said.

'Just think, sir, the Teutonic Order controlled the amber trade for several hundred years,' he said, his voice bubbling with ardour. 'Can you imagine the riches that must have passed through their hands?'

'All gone,' I murmured. '*Mutatis mutandis.*'

'Are you certain about that, sir?' Gurten challenged. 'Can six hundred years of valiant history be wiped out by a single battle, and a temporary subjection to a foreign power? Is Prussia dead? A man may wear his heart upon his sleeve, but he will hide his truest feelings deep within his soul if he is wise. We share that sentiment, I do believe. Professor Kant has shown that thought and action are not invariably consistent.'

He might have been waiting for me to agree with him.

When I said nothing, he added passionately, 'Prussia is crushed, but for the moment only. The Prussian eagle will soar again.'

From the look of the Round Fort, I thought, Prussia had been crushed for Eternity.

We reached the top of the hill, and stopped before the entrance to catch our breath. A dry ditch ran around the building, twenty feet deep, and wider still. Access to the only door in the squat tower was provided by a narrow bridge constructed of the same heavy stone. As we walked across it, Johannes Gurten read out a date that was carved above the door. 'Thirteen hundred and two,' he intoned, as if the numbers were some magical code from the Kabbalah.

Above the arch, an ancient inscription had been recently chipped and chiselled at. Someone had tried to obliterate the Gothic lettering, though it had proved no easy matter to dent the granite slab so deeply set in the wall.

Teutonic Order

'Do you see, sir?' he said, pointing up. 'We cannot be so easily cancelled out.'

'If I were you,' I advised him, 'I'd be more guarded in my speech. We do not know who runs this place. Perhaps the French themselves. At the very least, they finance it. This is where they find replacement labour. A magistrate must listen first, and only judge when he has heard all sides of a case.'

If I sounded overly pedantic, I made no attempt to soften the lesson.

'Better a reprimand now than a year in a French labour camp,' I warned him.

'I'll watch what I say,' he promised with an apologetic smile.

His loose tongue was the best proof of his ingenuous nature, I thought to myself. Even so, I was not so foolish as to trust him entirely. Wouldn't a spy speak in the most enthusiastic terms of his nationalist sympathies if he wished to sound out my opinions on the same subject?

There was no need to knock on the squat fortified door. It hung loose from the upper hinge, and was so heavy that a team of labourers would have been required to set it straight again. The wood was leached grey with age, damp, and salty encrustations. And so, with no undue hindrance, Gurten and I invaded and took the citadel.

The place appeared to be deserted.

'Is anybody here?' I called.

My voice echoed around the large circular stone chamber.

It was dark and chill, almost impossible to see the perimeter wall on the far side of the room. Motes of dust jigged and danced in the beam of sunlight coming in through the door. There was no other source of illumination.

I heard the scrape of a boot on the stone floor, then a man of middle height and great age stepped out of the shadows.

'What can I do for you, sirs?'

I identified myself and Johannes Gurten – it was, I recall, the first occasion on which I chose to describe him as my assistant – then I asked the old man who he was.

'Benedikt Tanzig, Herr Procurator. At your service.'

'And you are . . . ?'

'The archivist, sir. Now, I am more of a caretaker. Paid by the Margrave of Marlbork to maintain his fortress and his records. In the interests of neighbourliness, I also do the picking on a Monday for the French gentlemen. They're supposed to take on women for the amber-workings,' he explained. Then, he sneered: '*I* know what they should be looking for. In the way of fit women, if you know what I mean.'

I hid a smile by coughing into my hand. Herr Tanzig could not have been less than seventy years of age. *Sans* hair, *sans* teeth, *sans* who knew what else!

'When they bother to come,' he rumbled on. 'The girls, I mean, sir. There aren't so many these days looking for this sort of work. Won't be any before too long from what I be hearing.'

'How many girls were taken on by the French last Monday?' I asked him.

Tanzig raised his hand, crushed his gnarled fist to his bare gums, blew hard, and let out a curious popping sound. 'Not a one, sir,' he answered. 'And no one came up from the camp either. Usually they send an officer. No hiring officer, no hands to hire. There are always accidents, girls running off . . .'

'Or being murdered,' I put in.

He sniffed, wiped his nose on his sleeve. 'Makes no difference to *them*, does it?'

Clearly, he was talking about Colonel les Halles and his
officers.

'Amber isn't what it used to be, Herr Procurator. I been here
close on fifty years. There were men here then, as well. But
the great King Frederick turned the country into a barracks.
All men had to serve in the army. Which left the women in
the water. When the margrave had the diggings, we'd have
twenty, thirty, forty comely wenches lining up, depending on
the season.'

'What difference does the season make?' Gurten had taken a
step forward.

'Very few in winter, sir. Count 'em on one hand. Them's the
desperate ones – work, or starve! Spring's the very best time.
That's when the pick o' the crop turn up in droves. Big, strong,
healthy wenches, thighs like tree-trunks!' he exclaimed with a
toothless leer. 'When harvesting comes around, that lot go off
to do a bit of reaping out in the fields, sir. Get free ale, bread
and cheese, and a lark about in the hay with the workmen.
Them girls, they . . .'

'What about the summer?' I interrupted him. 'What
happens when the weather's very hot, like it is today?'

'Generally good. But times are changing, sir,' he said,
and rubbed his hands. 'As I told you, Monday last there
wasn't one.'

'Which archives do you keep?' I enquired.

He made that popping sound again with his gums. 'Archives
keeps themselves as a rule. In the old days', he went on, 'we
used to weigh and add the totals for all the amber that was
being brought in daily. Herr Margrave had three collection
centres down along the coast. Every night they'd bring it up
here for safe-keeping. Six armed guards, there were. The
roundhouse is impregnable when the door . . . that is, when
the door *was* locked! Now, the French make their own
arrangements. Have to fix the door again once they're gone,'

he said dismissively. 'I keep the paperwork here. Try to keep the place in order . . .'

'Can I see these records?' I interrupted brusquely.

Herr Tanzig sniffed, then shook his head. 'Without permission, sir, I couldn't do that,' he said.

'Permission from the French?' I queried.

'No, sir,' he chuckled quietly. 'Not them. They don't give a toss one way or the other. The margrave, sir. The Margrave of Marlbork, my master.'

'And where may he be found?' I asked. My patience was running thin. The French were bad enough, but this decrepit Prussian book-keeper was worse.

'I would not know precisely, sir,' he said. 'He may be on the Marlbork estate, that's twenty miles t'other side of Lotingen, or he may be off someplace else. It's more than a year since I had a reply to one of my despatches. You'll have to go . . .'

Gurten took a brisk step forward, and clasped hold of Tanzig's hand.

For a moment, I thought that he was about to ask my permission to whip the man. In the days of Frederick the Great, a superior official would often whip an underling, or order him to be whipped. Instead, he began to drop coins into Tanzig's palm. Having counted out five, he twisted the archivist by the wrist, and brought his shoulder low. He gazed down into the old man's face, and said: 'I hardly think we need to trouble the margrave, do you?'

Tanzig nodded, and Gurten let him go.

'Now,' he said, while the old man pocketed the coins and made a fuss of rubbing his wrist, 'I believe Herr Procurator Stiffeniis would like to visit this archive of yours without further delay.'

A stone staircase hidden in the deepest shadows curved up along the wall.

Herr Tanzig led us to the floor above without a word.

All was blinding light up there.

The circular room was slightly smaller than the one below on account of the dictates of military architecture. Sloping castle walls are harder to climb, and easier to defend, Leonardo da Vinci once declared, and no one had ever dared to challenge his wisdom. But the upstairs chamber had not been used as a military keep in a long time. Indeed, where once a round hole in the stone roof had let in rain – the only source of water in that barren land – the aperture had been domed with panes of glass to let in light alone. The sun shining strongly through it spread the pattern of the leaded window-frame like the legs of a spider which seemed to hold the room in its embrace.

I peered at the custom-made arrangement of ancient shelves and cubby-holes that had been constructed all around the walls. It might have been a pigeon-loft, but there were no pigeons. Each dusty hole was stuffed with a ledger or a bulging folder containing a sheaf of papers.

'How many ledgers are there?' I mused aloud. I looked around and began to calculate: from 1306 to the present day. That was 502 years. Multiply it by fifty-two . . . I began to multiply by fifty instead, thinking it was easier. Then I would add 1004 to my total.

'Twenty-six thousand, one hundred and four,' said Gurten instantly.

'Impossible!' I said, looking around me. There were certainly many hundreds of spaces in the wooden honeycomb, perhaps a thousand books and bundles of paper, but hardly so many thousands. And some of the holes along the right-hand side were empty, still waiting to be used.

Benedikt Tanzig regarded us as if we were a pair of idiots.

'Keeping track of names and numbers is what my job is all about. When we're short of room,' he said, 'we take the oldest ones out and burn them. We . . . I'm the only one left here now. Every year I have a bonfire. Today's the day, as it happens. Feast of the Venerable Jakob Spener. My way of celebrating. I was about to make a start when you gentlemen arrived. An entire shelf will be going up in smoke very shortly.'

Would someone do the same thing to my own archive in Lotingen one day? Burn all the notes and drawings that I had made so carefully while preparing for the trials that had occupied my working days? The case in Königsberg with Kant? Last year's investigation of the Gottewald family massacre? All the other less memorable proceedings, including the one that I had left unresolved just a few days before in Lotingen?

'Which ones are you planning to burn?' I asked him.

Tanzig pointed to a stack of files and thick leather ledgers lying on a desk in the centre of the room beneath the skylight. '1700 to 1720,' he said. 'I'll rip the covers off, of course – all the leather goes back to the margrave's factor – but the paper is no use to anyone. Who wants to read the names and the dates of a million dead amber-workers?'

'A million?' I queried.

Tanzig turned to Gurten with a toothless smirk.

'You're the one that's good at counting,' he said. 'I'm asking *you*, sir. How many men, women and girls have passed through them doors down there at the rate of . . . say, forty a week – averaging them out, of course, good times and bad times taken altogether – over a period of five hundred years?'

Gurten smiled and said: 'One million.'

'Exactly,' the archivist smiled back.

'But you do still have the recent records,' I insisted.

'Of course, sir.'

'Let's start with those,' I said.

'If I may make a suggestion, Herr Stiffeniis,' Gurten intervened, 'perhaps we ought to look at the records for the year 1805, that is, the year *before* the French arrived. Just for the sake of comparison.'

It was a sensible proposal. 'Herr Tanzig?' I said, turning to him.

'I have to warn you,' he replied. 'I shall be obliged to inform the margrave.'

'Do as you must,' I said.

Tanzig went across and took a ledger out from the stack. It was as large as a slab of black bread, but twice as thick, a heavy studded volume with dark brown leather covers. As he dropped it onto the desk, a storm of dust flew out from between the pages, dancing and floating in the sunlight. 'Here you are, sir. This one runs from 1804 'til the day that we were ousted. We used to keep the records proper back in them days. Without a birth certificate, no girl could be employed. Prussian law was strict . . .'

I opened the book near the middle, took out a sheaf of loose papers that divided the pages, and set them to one side on the desk. The top sheet was a fading copy of an edict. The title caught my eye: *Amber Edict & Convention – France & Prussia*. Two paragraphs had been ringed in ink:

Commercial amber, that is to say, amber of any quality, type or size (from the finest powder to the largest block), and for any general purpose (medicinal, chemical, decorative, etc.) will be consigned to the nearest French Office.

All amber of a scientific nature, that is to say, amber containing objects, animals, plants, or any other unusual 'insertion', will be consigned to the Round Fort, in the person of Benedikt Tanzig, Archivist to the Margrave of Marlbork, who will despatch the said consignment to the Royal Academy of Science, Berlin, for immediate examination and classification . . .

I had just such a piece of amber in my pocket. It had belonged to Kati Rodendahl. That is, I corrected myself, it belonged to the Royal Academy of Science, and it ought to have been consigned into the safe-keeping of Herr Tanzig.

'Do you send many pieces to Berlin?' I asked him, waving the edict in the air.

'Haven't seen one in the last uh . . . ten or twelve months,' he said. 'The other papers in that pile are official receipts for pieces sent, which I retain for the margrave's inspection.

I have, of course, written to inform him that somebody is robbing him. That's his only income now from the coast. Today, of course, I'll add the thalers that your young assistant has given me.'

So, that's where the money would end up, I thought. Not in beer, or food, or a new pair of stockings, but, as tradition required, those coins would go to fill the coffers of the Margrave of Marlbork, wherever he was surviving after the deluge that had swept away the remnants of ancient Prussia.

'Are you suggesting that the French are holding back amber?' Gurten asked. 'And that they are not respecting the agreement?'

' 'Tain't my job to suspect no one, sir,' Tanzig replied gruffly. 'Let the margrave suspect, if that's what he wants to do! Still, I reckon it is the French. They don't bring it here, which doesn't mean that they don't send it someplace else!'

Tanzig suspected the French. The French, of course, accused the Prussians of wholesale theft. Only the verb differentiated them: Prussians were not permitted the luxury of accusing anyone.

I turned my attention to the ledger, and began my search for Annalise and Megrete.

1. *Anna Strudel, 26, of Ostróda, 24th April 1804–6th May 1806.*
2. *Mabel Bartold, 25, of Elbing, 24th April 1804–1st September 1804.*
3. *Krista Wiecwinski, 19, of Warsaw, 24th April 1804– 11th June 1804 – lost a hand (compensation – 150 thalers).*
4. *Angeljka Cord, 30, of Lotingen . . .*

I had lived in Lotingen for fifteen years, but I had never heard that name.

I picked up the separate bundle of papers and began to search through the leaves until I found the yellow registration certificate of Angeljka Cord. Born in the Roederstrasse district of our town in 1771, the girl had been raised inside a Pietist community for destitute female orphans. From this scant information, I guessed that she might have been the illegitimate daughter of a prostitute. Where was she now, I wondered. Above, or below ground? The last recorded date of her existence was written in the ledger as *7th November 1807*. She had worked on the coast for two and a half years, then left as suddenly as she had arrived.

'Is this your handwriting?' I asked the archivist, who had seated himself on the chair behind the desk.

He pulled a glass from his pocket, and lowered his nose until it grazed the page. 'It is,' he said, glancing up.

'I don't suppose you remember this girl?'

'Don't remember any of them precisely,' he said. 'They're here one minute, gone the next. They drift from place to place in search of work. She was in one piece when she left here, otherwise there'd be a note of injury. My records were a miracle of precision 'til the French took over. Date of arrival, date of departure . . .'

When had Edviga Lornerssen appeared in Nordcopp?

I ran my eyes over the pages ranging up and down the lists with my forefinger. Ostensibly, I was looking for the names Annalise and Megrete, but my finger jolted to a halt as I read the name *Edviga*. It was not the entry I was looking for, however. Edviga Brandt had arrived from Danzig in April 1806, and she had disappeared in June of the same year. *Swept out to sea by a storm*, the note read, as if that storm had come for her, and no one else.

What would Edviga Lornerssen make of that? A girl adrift in the after-life without a piece of amber to protect her.

'Can I see the records kept since the arrival of the French?' I asked.

Tanzig began to cough and splutter violently. He was laughing, I realised.

'The French don't bother with formality,' he said. 'If a girl looks fit, they take her on. If not, away with ye!'

'Surely you have a copy of their lists? For the margrave, I mean. Surely he would want to know the names of those who left the shore,' I said. 'And who was taken on to replace them.'

Herr Tanzig shook his head. 'None of my business, the Frenchmen said. I wrote to the margrave, of course . . .'

'So, there's no way of knowing who is working on the shore at present,' Gurten concluded.

'They may keep a roster down on the beach,' the old man replied.

I could verify that fact from personal knowledge. I had heard the roll being called before I went with Adam Ansbach to examine the corpse that he had found in his pigsty. I had been hoping that the Round Fort records would verify whether the girls that Pastor Bylsma accused of theft were registered as amber-gatherers. Now, I would need to check the French lists instead, and convince Colonel les Halles that it was not Prussian intrusion in French military affairs.

'What else can we do here, sir?' Gurten asked softly.

'Nothing,' I admitted.

Downstairs in the entrance hall, I was just about to leave when the archivist called me back. 'Herr Procurator,' he said, 'you asked me before if I remembered a particular girl.'

'Angeljka Cord,' I reminded him.

'That's right, sir. And I told you that I didn't. Well now, there is somebody who might know.'

I clutched at this straw. 'There is?'

'There is, indeed, sir. I may have mentioned it, in fact. She's been hanging around here, off and on, for a couple of years, I'd say. She pesters the girls when they're coming in. Or she chases after them on the way out.'

'She?' I asked surprised.

Herr Tanzig began to chortle, as if he were seeing something very funny in his mind's eye. 'A strange little creature, sir. The contrast is quite hideous. Just imagine, all them big, fine strapping maids – beautiful, all of them – and this little imp in a skirt that skips and limps at their heels, telling them God knows what. If you could find her, sir, she might have a better memory for names than me. She'll know them. She speaks to every one without exception. She was hanging about outside last Monday, too, come to think of it. When no one came, she sat herself down on the bridge, dangling her legs over the ditch, and waited for a couple of hours. Next thing I looked, she must have realised nobody was coming, she'd taken off. I wouldn't be surprised if she comes back next Monday, though. Never misses a day, she doesn't.'

As Gurten and I began to retrace the dusty road to Nordcopp, the image of Erika Linder would not leave me alone.

Did Erika know what the Round Fort register could not tell me?

20

Everything was grey as the rowing-boat pushed off.

The sea, the sky, everything in between. Only the stark out-line of the *coq du mer* stood out in the gloomy light of dawn. The derrick hung over the water like a gallows painted black. The sky pressed down like a sheet of basalt on the molten lead of the sea. The boatman groaned and grunted at his labour, each dip of his oars producing an oily swirl in the water, yet we barely seemed to advance an inch. Rippling reflections grazed the flanks of the boat, fanning out in a wide chevron behind us. He was carrying me to the barge where les Halles had been labouring all night. There was no one left to whom I could turn for help. But would he help me? Was there one single reason why he should?

Inside my head a dull heaviness reigned.

The day before had been a total failure.

The Round Fort in the morning. Nordcopp in the after-noon. Gurten and I, looking everywhere for Erika Linder. The cellar was empty, as if a magician had waved his wand and caused every single thing to disappear: Erika, her mother, the tables and benches, the cauldrons of amber and fish soup. Only the smell of fish confirmed the fact that I had not been dreaming.

I had turned for help to the French.

Sergeant Tessier was not on duty. The soldier who was pretended not to understand my French until the name of Colonel les Halles brought him to his senses. He admitted that a girl answering to the description of Erika was often seen around town, but neither her name nor her mother's was registered with them. As for the cellar, he explained, it was rented out on a daily basis. One day someone might be brewing beer down there, the next it could be used as a tavern. Sometimes no one rented it. In Nordcopp, anything could happen when the streets were full of amber-traders.

As the sun began to sink, Erika was nowhere to be found.

Gurten invited me to spend the night in the guest-house of the convent.

'I need to speak to les Halles,' I said.

'Well, you . . . you know where you can always find me, Herr Stiffeniis,' Gurten said, an expression of uncertainty on his face.

I knew what puzzled him, and I had no reason to prolong his uncertainty. Could I deny that he had set me on a new track? Adam Ansbach was no longer the only suspect. That was the news that I would be carrying back to les Halles.

I nodded, smiled, and said: 'It is important for a magistrate to know where his assistant may be found.'

Assistant.

Gurten's face lit up at the word. And I was glad to have him at my side.

I no longer felt like a total stranger in my own country.

I had to pass through Nordbarn going back towards the coast. Pastoris was next on my list of things to do. But as I approached the settlement, I saw French uniforms milling around outside the workshop.

I ran, expecting the worst.

They had found another corpse.

But as I drew near, I saw no signs of alarm on the soldiers' faces. I showed my papers to an officer who was holding a black cheroot in the doorway of the workshop. He blew a puff of aromatic smoke in my face.

'I know you,' he quipped. 'The Prussian magistrate in our camp!'

'Has something happened?' I asked him.

'Nothing,' he said, flicking away the stump of his cheroot. 'We marched here this morning with Colonel les Halles. When he left for the coast with his steam-pump, he told us to stay put. Up at the farm, and here.'

The Ansbach property would be run by four men who had worked on farms before being drafted into the army. The soldiers would look after the pigs, cows and hens, and make sure that the supply of food and milk to the camp on the coast was regular. The Ansbach family would not be coming back, the officer said, sounding ominously like Magda Ansbach herself.

'The corpse?' I asked him, wondering whether les Halles had had it carried back to the coast.

The officer shrugged. 'Fish food by now, I reckon.'

The night before, Edviga Lornerssen had asked a favour of me. She had given me a chip of amber, telling me to place it under the tongue of Ilse Bruen before her body was thrown into the Baltic Sea. That bit of amber was still in my pocket. I had fainted when I saw the body. And now, it was too late. I would never be able to fulfil my promise to Edviga.

'What's happening here at the workshop?' I asked him.

His name was Ducros, and he was a second lieutenant. There would be seven soldiers under his command, he said, two for each room, plus one to guard the door and search each person passing through it. All the rough amber coming in from the coast, and all of the polished amber going out to Nordcopp, would pass through his hands.

'Herr Pastoris will translate my orders for as long as I need him,' he said.

I looked across at the master grinder, but Pastoris looked the other way.

'My men will learn to handle these grinding wheels easily,' Ducros confided. 'I mean to say, French soldiers with two hands can do what a Prussian cripple manages with one. Don't you agree?'

There is a legend on the coast. Some folk even claim to have seen such phenomena. Monster waves which sweep down from the North Pole, pushed by the winds, gathering momentum as they race across the Baltic Sea, where they crash at last upon the Prussian shore, then flood the hinterland, bringing choking mud and wholesale destruction. Ilse Bruen had had the same effect on Nordbarn. The discovery of her body in the neighbourhood had swept away everything, destroying the lives of all the other people who were living there.

Pastoris refused to meet my eye.

He sat at his place, giving orders to his women in short sharp barks, showing the French soldiers by eloquent mime and gesture how to use the treadle, how to bring rough amber into contact with the whirring grindstone. He taught them to chip away marine deposits, turning the amber all the while, insisting that they keep it soaked with grease, and avoid overworking the parts where air-bubbles were present.

The Frenchmen watched the women work.

Now and then, the girls looked up, studying the concentrated expressions on the foreign faces, glancing back at their grinding-wheels as fear got the better of them. One question was written openly on their features.

What will happen next?

Only Hilde Bruckner worked alone. No Frenchman wanted to get too close to her. Pastoris busied himself about everything, explaining something to the French, chivvying the sad-faced women, making sure that all the amber went back into the sack that it had come from. He was purposely avoiding me, I decided. But sooner or later, I thought, he would be obliged to speak to me. A storm was coming on, the sky outside was the colour of sand. The air inside the hut was hot and heavy. The overcrowded, festering, unwashed bodies, the unremitting concentration which Hans Pastoris forced on the French, the intensity of the labour which was new to them, could not last forever. The soldiers would wish to stop, sooner or later. They would want to smoke and relax. I was waiting for this moment, and I meant to take advantage of it. Pastoris kept them at it for an hour, or more, but then Officer Ducros spoke out.

'My men need a break,' he said.

Hans Pastoris could only nod. The wheels stopped spinning. The soldiers trooped outside, and Ducros followed them. I took advantage of the interruption, walked across and cornered Pastoris. The ugly scrofula beneath his chin was physically trembling.

'What will become of us, now?' he hissed at me, before I could speak.

'You knew les Halles was coming,' I said. 'It was only a question of when.'

'You gave him the excuse,' he snarled. 'They wanted a Prussian, and that is what they got! Now, we'll all be given the push. And a Prussian magistrate will sign the order!'

The women studied our lips, trying to make sense of what we were saying. No one left her place, fearing that she might never be allowed to return to it, perhaps. All eyes were on Pastoris. They were waiting for a word from their master which would signal the hope of survival, or the beginning of a painful exodus.

'I did not order Adam's arrest,' I insisted. 'The corpse of Ilse Bruen was found at the farm, together with a pile of bones that no one has been able to identify. Adam Ansbach was there, and les Halles refuses to look any further. He ordered the boy's arrest.' I lowered my voice. 'But all is not yet lost. There might be an alternative solution. A plausible one, which would set Adam free. You must help me, Pastoris.'

The man looked up at me. 'What are you talking about?'

'Amber was stolen from the church in Nordcopp some months ago. Two women, posing as runaway amber-gatherers, gave their names as Annalise and Megrete. I've been to the Round Fort, but I found no trace of them in the registers.'

Pastoris peered at me attentively.

'What has a theft to do with the murders of Kati and Ilse, Herr Procurator?'

His sharp breath blew into my face. I had to resist the temptation to pull back.

'What if those names were false?' I said.

'Kati and Ilse? Is that what you're saying? You think that they stole the amber?'

'Tanzig at the Round Fort says he's seen no amber with insertions in a long time. Yet that is the amber that everyone wants. The girls know it. They must be smuggling lots of it out. But no one seems to know who comes, who goes. I'm going back to check the lists the French keep on the coast.'

I paused, expecting his reaction, but Pastoris did not say a word.

'You were right,' I went on, 'the French *do* know what's going on. The guards are a party to the smuggling. If Kati and Ilse went to Nordcopp using false names, then that is the end of it. But if they did not, Annalise and Megrete could be two more girls who have vanished, possibly murdered. Have you ever heard those names pronounced by your workers, Pastoris? I need to know it before I speak to Colonel les Halles.'

'Is that your game, Herr Stiffeniis?' The words bubbled angrily up from his throat. 'See if you can get Pastoris into the shit, as well? Whose idea was this? The colonel's? I'll give you Adam, if you give me Pastoris. Is that what he told you?' His face was bright red. Veins stood out on his forehead. The swollen sac throbbed and pulsed beneath his chin with rage. 'There's not one drop of Prussian blood left in you,' he said. 'Can't you see how low you've sunk, working for *them*?'

He spun away before I could reply, advancing on the women.

'Back to work!' he shouted. 'This pause has lasted long enough.'

Ducros came in as these words were spoken.

'You'd do well to stay, monsieur,' the French lieutenant called from the door, inviting me to take note of the sky. A forbidding, black barrier masked the horizon. 'A storm is brewing,' he said.

I tried to sleep on a hard wooden bench, and set off for the coast before daybreak.

Without managing to speak to Pastoris again.

* * *

The boat was halfway to the barge.

The sky was growing darker by the moment.

The sea was a black mirror, which reflected my pessimism.

'What time did the colonel come out this morning?' I asked the boatman.

'Been here all night, monsieur,' he replied.

'Problems?' I asked warily.

'There's nothing wrong with the *coq*,' the boatman said. He thought on that for a while, then he added, 'It's the pump. Something must have blocked the suction pipe.'

The pump had drained the slime in the Ansbach pigsty perfectly, according to les Halles. Now, it was broken. I took a deep breath. Les Halles would not be in any sort of a mood to speak to me.

And yet, I had to face him.

I looked down at the register on my knees. It had cost me a great deal of effort to lay my hands on it. I had arrived at the gate an hour before, plastered with sand and mud. It had showered on and off all the way from Nordbarn. The muscles in my legs were taut and aching. I had to speak with les Halles, I announced. The guards on the gate had told me that it was out of the question. I threatened to report them to General Malaport. They looked at each other and decided that les Halles was a greater threat.

Impossible, monsieur!

Desperation led to inspiration. 'I have news of a potential rebel attack on the *coq du mer*,' I announced. 'Try telling Colonel les Halles that you refused to let me through, if anything should happen!'

In fifteen minutes, I had got what I wanted. A rowing-boat to take me out to the barge. And a list of all the people who were present in the French camp: French soldiers and Prussian workers.

I glanced again at the lists.

That rowing-boat seemed fixed for eternity on the same spot. The water rolled against the clinkered boards as heavy as liquid quicksilver. No sound came from it.

I had made a promise to Spener as I opened that book and scanned the names. If I found the names of Annalise and Megrete in the French register, I would donate Kati Rodendahl's amber to the church in Nordcopp to make up the loss which their theft had caused. I realised how ridiculous I had become. I was asking God to intercede for something that I wanted. Was I becoming Catholic in my desperation?

On the first page were the names of Colonel les Halles, his officers and men.

Then, a longer list of all the women who were currently employed on the shore.

My name, and those of the French technicians, completed the roll.

I ran my finger down the women's names.

No Annalise. No Megrete.

Next to the name of Kati Rodendahl someone had written the briefest of annotations. *Tuée*. There was no reference to the date, place or manner of her murder. And as for Ilse Bruen, according to the French list, she was still alive.

Next to some of the names was a note to the effect that the girl had run away. In several cases, the list had been updated when the runaway had returned. No such information was reported in the case of Kati Rodendahl. The name of Edviga Lornerssen caught my eye. She had 'run away' twice, and 'come back' on both occasions. No details were provided of where she had gone, or why she had returned.

The list was a slipshod, hit-or-miss affair.

Did the absence of Annalise and Megrete signify that the names were false? Were Ilse Bruen and Kati Rodendahl the girls who had entered the church and committed the crime? And if they had stolen Spener's amber, what had they done with it?

The boatman docked his oars.

The rowing-boat bumped gently against the side of the *coq du mer*.

Les Halles leant out over the side. 'I was about to send out a search-party,' he muttered. His voice was a harsh growl. It was the voice of a man who had worked all night, shouting orders into the face of a raging storm. And yet, I knew that he would find the strength to spit poison in my direction if he needed to.

'You've brought your report about the killer, I suppose?'

I gripped the slimy rope-ladder and began to climb.

The colonel stood back at the last moment and let me board.

He was not alone. Two of the engineers who had travelled up with me from Lotingen were resting on the taff-rail. They were as haggard and pale as ghosts. Their eyes sparkled like frightened children. He had worked them hard, that was obvious. But les Halles himself made the greatest impression on me. A bib and trousers cut in one piece hung from his shoulders. His chest was bare, his pale arms naked. On his head he wore a woollen bonnet that had taken on a strange dangling shape from all the rain it had absorbed during the night. In that rig he looked like a common labourer, a drudge who followed orders, rather than giving them.

Our eyes met.

He read my thoughts, I think.

And I caught a glimmer of something else. He did not wish me to see him in that state. His cheeks and forehead were streaked and black with oil, smoke and filth. His eyes were hollow red rings of exhaustion.

Defeat, I thought. There was defeat in his eyes.

As combatants, we were well-matched. I had not slept, I was equally filthy, my own eyes would betray my tiredness. But I was the stronger. Whatever my defeats had been, his failures had been worse. The silence aboard the barge was eloquent. I felt my heart lift.

He saw it, and his eyes flashed away from mine.

'I have written no report,' I said. 'Nor will I do so until I have heard your explanations.'

'Explain myself to *you*?' he asked, his eyes flashing angrily.

Again, I saw a trace of something unexpected.

Fear . . .

What fear could I inspire in Richard les Halles?

'There are many questions regarding the running of this camp . . .'

'Give over with your nonsense,' he snapped, failing to hold my gaze. His eyes slid away to the top of the derrick, then glanced at the chimney of the steam machine. 'A minor incident, but it can be resolved. The sea-bed here is not . . . *exactly* as I thought. The *coq* handles silt and pebbles well, but there are larger obstructions down there. They are the problem. She sucked up everything for three hours, more. The amount of amber – quality amber – was quite prodigious . . .'

'Then something went wrong,' I reminded him.

'A minor hitch,' he replied, wiping the back of his hand across his brow. 'The angle of inclination, perhaps. The rapidity of aspiration. The variable density of the silt. The size of the stones . . .'

He outlined the problems, and proposed possible solutions in a strange concoction of bold defiance, simmering anger and perplexed uncertainty. Was he telling me how he did his job? Was he trying to defend himself against accusations of incompetence which nobody, especially myself, had made against him?

'It worked well enough in the pigsty,' I conceded.

He took off his woollen hat, shaking it out, resetting it on his head again.

'The pump was the quickest way . . .' He did not finish the sentence, but shook his head, instead. Perhaps he thought that I had come to accuse him of destroying the scene of the crime again.

'Nothing is what it seems in this foul country of yours, monsieur,' he said. 'The local soundings suggest that everything is sand down there. No one mentioned finding rocks and slate-like conformations. Of course, if I had been allowed to do the surveys for myself . . . I hope you'll mention this fact to General Malaport?'

I thought I had misheard him.

Did he believe that I could be used to explain to General Malaport why the steam-pump had failed to function?

'My report will speak of different things,' I specified.

'I'm sure it will,' he said quietly, his eyes on the invisible horizon, as if he expected a British fleet to sail into sight at any moment. 'Isn't that why Malaport sent you here?'

'I was sent to investigate a murder. Two, or four, as now seems probable,' I said, wondering whether he had exhausted himself with relentless ambition.

'Oh yes, murder!' he exclaimed sarcastically.

Suddenly, he turned on his men. 'We will pause until noon,' he ordered. 'I wish to speak with Procurator Stiffeniis alone. The boat is waiting. Go ashore, get yourselves some breakfast, and a few hours' sleep.'

The two men looked at each other, surprised at the generosity of this offer, then saluted and scrambled down into the waiting rowing-boat. They made no attempt to hide their haste to be away.

'I'll ring the bell when I need you,' he called after them.

Then, he turned to me again.

'I knew I'd have to keep a careful eye on you, monsieur,' he said with undisguised acidity. 'The murders needed solving. They sent a Prussian magistrate. What better way to keep a careful eye on *me*!'

The barge creaked and groaned as it rose and fell on the gentle swell of the sea.

'What makes you think that I would accept such a task?'

'Use your head, Stiffeniis. I built the naval dockyard in Boulogne. I planned the undermining of the Spanish forts. No Frenchman would ever dare to spy on me. But a Prussian who has worked for the French would. A magistrate that even the great Serge Lavedrine approves of. A man without scruples, who would sell his country to a foreign power. A man of talent. A man like you! A man who could write not *one* report, but *two*. The first about the murders, the second concerning my success here on the coast. Or lack of it. The emperor likes to know exactly who is doing what. That's the way it works in France.'

I opened my mouth to speak, but he held up his hand.

'Six months ago I spoke to the emperor about my project. I spoke to him in person.' He smiled as he told me, but he did not look remotely happy. 'Not a day passes but I get a despatch from Bonaparte's aides inviting me to speed the business up. Inside twelve months, I promised him, but continents can change in such a short time. Indeed, they have already changed. The treasury wants more amber and wants it fast. They want it more than I do. The emperor wants to see a hundred *coqs du mer* strung out along the Baltic coast. Spain is costing a fortune. But down there . . .' He pointed his finger at the sea. 'Under those grey waters, there's amber enough to finance a hundred campaigning seasons in Spain, a long-term invasion of Russia. There's more wealth in this sea than you Prussians have pulled out in the whole of your history.'

'Your steam-pump is of no interest to me, Colonel les Halles,' I said carefully.

I did not deny what he said. I meant to ease his fear and reassure him, but, equally, I intended to profit from his misunderstanding of my situation. If he believed that I was a spy, the gods had decided to assist me. 'My only concern is to identify the killer of the women. The true killer. Not the first poor Prussian soul who happens to cross your path.'

Les Halles sat heavily on the stern-rail. From a distance, we must have looked like two old friends. 'You are not convinced that Adam Ansbach killed the women, then?' he asked.

'I have found out something in Nordcopp which makes me doubt that he is guilty,' I replied. 'I am convinced . . .'

'That corpse was in his pigsty,' he objected. 'A mass of other bones, too.'

I remembered touching those damp splinters of bone with the tips of my fingers.

'According to Dr Heinrich, bones are spread all over this area. He collects them, and is an expert palaeontologist in his own opinion. If you ask him, sir, he will tell you . . .'

Les Halles nodded, interrupting me. 'I sent the sack of bones from the farm to Dr Heinrich. You'll trust his opinion of them, I hope? He is a Prussian, like yourself, after all.'

'And like me, he works for the French.'

'We'll see what he has to say,' he fired back sharply. 'What strange things to collect! I have never understood the value of anything that is dug up from the ground. Apart from turnips and potatoes. If it cannot be eaten, what use is it? Gold and silver have their uses, but old bones . . . Even amber. It is hard to see why people pay so much for it.'

'Even harder to imagine why they would kill for it, then?'

He shook his finger sternly at me. 'You still believe that smuggling is the cause of those deaths. So how do you explain the mutilations?'

I did not answer him at once. I wanted him to take careful note of what I was about to say. 'I know that the women come and go from your camp with great ease, Colonel les Halles. The guards are slack. Complicit is the word that I would use. Your men and those women are working hand in hand to smuggle amber that they hide from *you*, sir. Now, what would General Malaport, or the emperor Napoleon, have to say about that?'

He sat in silence, his hands clasping the wooden rail so tightly that his knuckles stood out stark white on his filthy hands.

'Is that a threat?'

I did not reply. I had no need to answer him. He thought I was his watchdog.

'What do you want to know?'

He spoke as if the words had been torn from his throat.

'I went to the old recruiting station yesterday. The records there have not been updated. That information should have come from you,' I said, and I made no attempt to soften the accusation. 'The lists kept by your own men are a shambles. It is impossible to say with certainty who is working here at this moment. Women come, women go, they disappear and sometimes they die. And no record is kept of their vicissitudes. To cite one glaring instance, Ilse Bruen, the girl whose corpse you dug out of the pigsty yesterday, is apparently alive and well and working on the shore at this very moment.'

Les Halles crossed his arms. 'What use are lists to us?' he said defiantly. 'Soon they will be swept away. When a hundred *coqs* are strung out along the coastline, there'll be no work for the women. Three Frenchmen on board each rig will handle every task. Registration, lists, documents . . . I am not here to drag archaic Prussia into the nineteenth century, Herr Procurator. I am here to strangle that outmoded system. And I will do it quickly.'

'A killer is preventing you. General Malaport knows it. The murders of the amber-workers, and the slower death that your machines will bring to everyone on this coast, are dangerous. The Prussian people are not prepared for such dramatic events. They might rise up. They might revolt. Unless we find the killer. The true killer, that is.'

'What can I tell you that the old and new lists cannot?' he said angrily, springing to his feet.

I had hooked my fish.

'You can tell me nothing,' I replied. 'But someone can. I want to speak with the amber-gatherers. The girls who work here on the shore. You have kept me well away from them. Now, I want to talk to them freely.'

Les Halles watched me for some moments. Still in silence, he walked over to the derrick, picked up a wooden mallet, and hit the bell three times very hard. He stood by the side, looking out over the water as the boat pushed off from the shore and began to glide across the mercury pond towards the *coq du mer*.

Suddenly, he turned to me.

'You might think of it as a diplomatic exchange,' he said. 'I prefer to consider it a swapping of favours.'

He said no more until the boat drew alongside.

As the men climbed aboard, les Halles leant over the water. 'Robert,' he called. 'Row the magistrate back to the beach.

Make sure that he is permitted to speak with the women. He can question whoever he pleases, and go wherever he wishes to go inside the camp today.'

He turned to me, his eyes bright. 'Now, it is your turn, Stiffeniis.'

'My turn for what?'

'To give me something in exchange. Your report to the general. I mean to read it.'

The trumpet shall sound,
  And the dead shall be raised . . .

Bodies lying prone and apparently lifeless on the shore suddenly began to stir and rise up. It was like the vision of the Day of Judgement in Corinthians.

'That first blast sounds the *reveille*,' Robert explained, more loquacious now that Colonel les Halles had sanctioned fraternisation with the Prussian. 'When it blows again, the women must enter the sea. It'll be hard to know exactly where each one is. Do you have any names in mind, monsieur?'

The girls were spreading out along the shore. In their gleaming leather garments, each one holding up a spear or net on a long pole, they looked like insects, their antennae twitching defensively as if they feared to be attacked. Glancing down the line, I searched for the girl. The women's faces were invisible inside their leather hoods, so I was obliged to name her.

'Only that one, monsieur?'

'For the moment,' I nodded.

The boat beached on the pebbles some way from the women. As we dragged the boat out of the water, I looked back over the sea that we had crossed. Sitting low on the eastern horizon was a burnished silvery plate, looking more like a pale moon than the sun of a new day. It cast a blue metallic light on the sea, the sky and the distant barge.

Another squall was coming on.

For a moment I imagined the *coq du mer* swept away.

But then again, the women would be carried off, as well.

'Find her quickly, Robert,' I incited him, struggling forward on the shifting pebbles. I had to stop her from entering the water, keep her safe by speaking to me until the storm had passed.

'Wait over there, monsieur.' He pointed to a group of huts raised on stilts above the sea. 'I'll send her to you.'

He sounded like a pimp, and this unpleasant impression was reinforced, as I made my way towards the huts. 'Hang on a minute,' I heard him call across to the trumpeter. 'The Prussian magistrate's got his eye on one of the lasses.'

Vulgarities followed on, but the trumpet did not blow.

I swallowed my pride as I stepped onto the narrow wooden gang-plank which connected the shore and the compound where the women lived. The place was deserted. Six wooden huts protected from the worst of the sea by a small bay and a curving shingle *haf* a mile from the shore. I stuck my head inside the first cabin, quickly pulled it out again. The air was stale and salty, rotten with the mouldy smell of warm bodies and damp clothes. Like seaweed-covered rocks at low tide.

The hut was tiny, yet it contained six narrow pallets, one along each wall, two more in the centre. Each head would be very close to someone else's feet. What little space remained was taken up by a makeshift table and two wobbly chairs. The walls were hung with grotesque souvenirs of the deep: knotted tangles of wood like arthritic hands, the skeleton of a tope, a collection of dried-out crab-cases. Large sea-shells dangled from the ceiling, tinkling like bells as I touched them. It would be a crashing symphony when a wind rushed through the room. In the corner, a covered pan stood on a tiny cast-iron stove. The odour of recently fried fish hung heavily in the air. A small wooden shutter had been thrown open to expose a tiny hole in the wall, though it could not improve the circulation of air.

'Where were you last night, Herr Stiffeniis?'

Edviga Lornerssen seemed taller, even more statuesque, than I remembered.

'Is the baby born?' she asked me eagerly.

'I've not been home,' I replied defensively. 'I stayed in Nordbarn, sheltering from the weather.'

What was I doing? Justifying the fact that I had not been in the camp last night?

She came towards me slowly, shrugging off her leather hood, shaking out her hair like a hunting-dog after a ducking. Droplets of dew glistened in her hair. With a sudden sweep of her hands she pulled back her tresses, revealing her ears and the fullness of her face. Two points of colour hung from her lobes. Amber suspended on knotted thread. Tiny pink eggs, glazed and polished to perfection. The Botticelli *Venus* flashed into my mind. I had seen it once in Florence. Only the pale nudity was missing and the sea-shell on which the *dea* floated. Edviga had not emerged from some azure southern sea, but from our own murky northern pond. She was taking a risk, showing herself to the world with amber hanging from her ears.

'Were you looking for me again last night, Edviga?'

Was she wearing amber the night before, as well? For me to see?

'I was,' she said. 'I came in the dark so nobody could see me.'

She looked around the hut to check that there was no one else. She was reproaching me, I realised. Meeting her alone like this was dangerous for her. Everybody in the camp might suspect that she was telling me things that were better left unsaid. Her friends, the friends of those friends, might believe it was best if she did not speak to me at all. I was, and always would be, the Prussian working for the French.

We stood in silence, face to face.

'What do you want from me?' she asked.

I saw her nervousness, and felt the ambiguity of the situation.

'You must help me,' I said, my voice harsher than I intended.

'First let me out of this restrictive cage,' she said, her fingers running like quick spiders over the thick laces of her bulky leather uniform. She slipped the upper half of the heavy costume off from her shoulders. Beneath, she wore a thin white singlet. As she sat herself down on the nearest bed, she wrinkled her nose. 'Last night was dreadful, the sea was wild and cruel. It isn't over yet,' she said, looking towards the door.

Black clouds were gathering on the horizon, swallowing up the grey.

'If you are here,' I said, 'you'll not be in the water . . .'

'That's not what I'm afraid of, sir,' she said, staring fixedly at me. 'I was thinking of poor Ilse. They threw her body in the sea last night. You kept your promise, didn't you? I mean, you know, the bit of amber . . .'

A lie may damn one's soul, yet ease the suffering of someone else's.

'I placed it where you said. Beneath her tongue.'

'Thank God for that,' she said in a whisper.

Outside, the trumpet sounded. Muted cries were heard. Women crying to their neighbours to 'stand further off' or 'go more to the left'. The language was strong in tone, the vocabulary rich, but the racket soon died down, and the soothing flow of the waves lapping gently on the shore took its place.

'Kati and Ilse may have gone to Nordcopp,' I began. 'Some months ago.'

Edviga looked up sharply.

'Two girls took refuge in the Church of the Saviour. They stole amber relics from the sacristy when they left. Did all of the women know that there was precious amber in the church?'

Edviga shrugged her shoulders. 'There has always been chatter.'

'Did Kati and Ilse do the chattering?' I asked.

'We all tell tales,' she laughed carelessly, 'but we are a bunch of seasoned liars. Whores, thieves, *and* liars, as the French would say. And the folk in Nordcopp agree with them.' She was silent for a moment. 'The amber in Nordcopp Church was not a fairy tale, then? And Kati had one of those pieces?'

'It was very similar,' I said. 'It is possible, therefore, that they might have known someone who was buying amber of that quality, whether found or stolen. I was hoping that you could tell me something more.'

'Why should I know anything?' she asked, rubbing her cheeks with her hands, causing those amber earrings to dance again.

'Because you knew Kati and Ilse. And if they did not steal from the church, who did? Are there only two victims, or are other girls missing, as well?'

She stared at me, but did not say a word.

'You told me that many girls had disappeared.'

'Last month, a soldier told me that a girl had run away to Russia.' She shrugged. 'Was it true? He said the colonel would hang her if he caught her, but maybe that soldier was trying to scare *me*. They threaten us all the time. It's amber that they want, sir. I did not note that anyone was missing, but I know for sure that many other women have gone. Some came back, others didn't.'

I decided to come at the question in a different way.

'Where do you go, Edviga, when you leave the camp?'

'Nordcopp, sir,' she answered quickly. 'Sometimes further.'

'Carrying amber with insertions?'

'Those are rare,' was all that she would say.

'And dangerous, too,' I added.

'We all go out. Kati, Ilse, and all the others. Sometimes we go alone, sometimes we go together. Usually we come back for more. Is that what you want to know?'

'Did Ilse ever mention the Church of the Saviour when you were sharing the hut?'

'We don't speak much of where we go, or what we do. If you find a good piece, you don't breathe a word to anyone. And as for robbing the church, sir, who'd dare speak of that? We may be friends, but amber is amber.'

Should I believe her?

Edviga had taken risks to honour her dead friends. Did that not mean that she felt strong ties with her companions? And weren't those ties even stronger than her greed for amber? Or did she fear the ugly destiny that had befallen them; was she afraid to end her own days in the dark, cold depths of the Baltic Sea?

'The girls who robbed the church told Pastor Bylsma that their names were Annalise and Megrete. But I can find no record of those names in the camp register . . .'

'And so you thought that they were Ilse and Kati?' Edviga interrupted.

I nodded. 'Unless you know those girls by name. Annalise, Megrete. Have you ever heard of them?'

She was silent for a moment. 'Names don't mean a great deal here,' she said. 'I know the girls by sight, but only three or four by name. The camp is a sort of limbo, sir. In the real world, a name marks you out from others. Out there, you meet a person, and if you want to see him again, you give him your name. But here, what use are names? Why bother to learn them? Will I go looking for them, or they for me, when we get clear of this place?'

She was talking, but she had not told me much. Who did the girls sell amber to? Who might have stolen the amber from the church? Were Ilse and Kati Megrete and Annalise? Were there really two more victims than the French records showed?

Again, I changed tack.

'You say you go to Nordcopp to sell amber,' I began. 'Tell me, Edviga, how would you find a buyer? Or do you go to one person alone?'

'Me?' She was looking down at her hands. Strong, dark with the sun, they rested elegantly joined in her lap. She looked up, held my gaze, and an expression of amused curiosity lit her face. 'I go where the money is.'

'Would you tell the buyer what you do, where you work?'

'Never that!' she countered. 'Not until I know who I am talking to.' She tilted her face at me. 'I pretend to look for a bauble for a sister, say, who's getting married. Amber is cheaper here than in Königsberg. That's why I've come, I'd say. If they see me again and again, they'd think that I am a regular customer. Instead, I sell it to the right person,' she said with convincing vivacity. 'But only when I'm sure it's safe.'

'What about Erika Linder? Erika knows you all . . .'

'Erika?' she said, and smiled, turning her head away. 'I've sold her things, of course. She is obsessed by amber more than anyone else in Nordcopp. She knows us all. She is attracted to the amber-girls. She clings to us, and wants to feel the strength in our arms and hands . . . You should see her, sir! I almost think that she is . . . well, that she is physically attracted to the amber-girls.'

This statement caused me to shiver.

'She's a strange little creature. Like the gnomes that roam the woods. She would not harm us, sir. She is in awe of us. We could snap her neck in an instant, if we wanted. She thinks that amber makes us beautiful. She thinks that it will make her beautiful and strong, as well, when she has gathered enough of it.'

'Do you know where she lives in Nordcopp?'

She seemed less reticent now. She laughed and shook her hair out. It fell upon her shoulders, taking on a strange blonde reddishness. In that instant, Edviga herself looked like a super-natural creature from some other world. 'I see her dwelling in an abandoned cellar like a bat,' she said, 'or nesting high in the trees with sparrowhawks. Or in a deep, dark hole dug by moles in the ground.'

'That is precisely where I met her,' I said with gravity.

Edviga laughed.

So, the girls could move about the town without being recognised, or challenged. And anyone who knew them would say nothing, so long as it suited them.

'What about the French in town?' I asked. 'Wouldn't they be on the look-out?'

Her eyes flashed wide. 'We pay them, sir.'

I swallowed hard. 'How do you pay them? Amber? Money?'

'One or both, or something else,' she replied without flinch-ing. 'They let us in, they let us out again.'

I looked away. That thought disturbed me.

There was nothing feminine about the leather breeches and the heavy laced-up boots that Edviga was wearing. Instead, I imagined her in pink hessian pumps, a matching summer gown of fine silk muslin. And dangling from her ears, two sparkling baroque pearls in the place of those bits of amber.

It was a blinding vision.

'And yet,' she said, throwing a glance in my direction, 'if I had gone to Nordcopp Church really seeking a safe refuge, I would have told the pastor who I was, and where I had come from. They know how difficult our lives can be. The French soldiers . . .'

She did not finish. What more was there to be explained?

'But if I went to steal from the Church, I would give no name at all.'

Edviga stopped abruptly, and looked down. Was she trying to tell me something?

'What would you do?' I encouraged.

'I'd go about the business in a different way. To make sure no one there would be in a position to report the theft.'

'How would you do that?'

'There are things that no respectable priest wants the world to know.'

Gurten was right, then. Here was an explanation for the red cheeks of Pastor Bylsma. It explained the ease with which those amber relics had been taken from his charge. A diabolic sensuality emanated from those women, a sensuality no man could easily resist, according to Magda Ansbach. Not even a man of God, I thought.

'Is that what Ilse and Kati would have done?'

'It's what Megrete and Annalise *have* done,' she laughed. 'Whoever they may be.'

One pace forward, two steps back. She might have been toying with me. It was not the first time she had done so. Beyond her shoulder, I caught a glimpse of the women working in the sea. The grey water reached their armpits. They prodded beneath the waves, swept the surface with their nets. Stark black outlines against a uniform grey backdrop of the sky, the sun casting a weak, slanting light across the scene.

'How would you get in and out of the camp, Edviga?'

She clenched and unclenched her fingers, uncertain whether to answer me at all.

'We walk upon the water,' she said impulsively. 'What else?'

She seemed to enjoy the ease with which she could perplex me.

'Not like Jesus on the Sea of Galilee,' she said. 'We know the secrets of the coast. Out there, not far from the end of this enclosure, there is a level outcrop of solid rock. It's three feet wide, a few feet below the surface of the sea. There was an ancient harbour here, they say. It runs due east for a quarter of a mile.' She drew a line in the air with her finger. 'You can walk along that wall at night without the risk of drowning in the sea. At that end of the beach, there is a guard-post. You must watch and wait, take your chance when it comes. Sometimes you manage to slip through. But other times, they catch you, and you have to pay.'

The naked corpse of Kati Rodendahl had been found down there.

'You'd be soaked,' I said incredulously. 'How could you escape attention in that condition in Nordcopp? Quite apart from those clothes you are wearing. Anyone would guess where you come from, if . . .'

'We don't wear these,' she smiled demurely. 'We carry a dress and shoes in a bundle on our heads, the way a peasant woman carries a basket. Even in the winter. The water's not so cold as you might think. If the bundle falls into the water, the game's up, of course.' Suddenly, her face clouded over. 'Few of us can swim. One foot wrong, a wave that's bigger than most, and you'll be swimming in the dark for all Eternity.'

Had Kati Rodendahl lost her clothes in the sea? Had the killer met her naked on the beach? Ilse had been wearing a light summer gown when she reached the pigsty. Had she been carrying a piece of amber hidden in her sex, as Kati was?

'You took a great risk last night in such a storm,' I said softly.

'I had to,' she replied even more softly.

We were murmuring like lovers. My cheeks were hot. Just like Pastor Bylsma's.

'Why did you have to come?'

'I remembered something,' she said. 'Something Ilse spoke of. We were resting on the beach between one shift and the other. This was weeks ago, when we were sharing the same hut. She said she had received a strange proposal.'

'Regarding amber?'

Edviga shook her head vigorously. 'Regarding herself. Ilse said that someone wanted to draw her.'

'Draw her?' I echoed, astounded.

Edviga nodded, as if she found the idea equally surprising.

'Who was this artist?'

Edviga shrugged. 'She did not say, sir.'

'What did she say, then?'

'She said she'd met a man in Nordcopp. And that he had made a picture of her. I thought that she was mad to tell such a tale.'

'Did you see the picture?'

'No, I didn't. There, that's the trouble, sir. I didn't know if she was telling the truth. We are like the squid in the sea,' she laughed. 'They spit out a cloud of ink. We hide behind our storytelling.'

She pointed her finger at me, assuming a stern attitude. 'I do it better than most,' she added. 'But that was Ilse's story that day. The others made a mock of her because she took herself so seriously. Apart from one girl.'

'You?' I asked.

'Kati Rodendahl.'

I sat up straight, and bent towards her.

'You told me that you don't know names. You said you hardly know each other . . .'

'I knew those two. And then again, it's strange the things you have in your head, the things that you forget about. They pop up, just like that!' she said, and snapped her fingers. 'Yesterday, while working in the water, I was thinking back on things that you might want to hear. Things that you'd find useful, sir. That's when I remembered. We were on the beach, the three of us. Kati, Ilse and me, and Ilse told us that strange story. About the man who wished to draw her . . .'

Had Edviga dreamt it up, I asked myself, *as an excuse to return to my cabin at dead of night?* And what might have happened, I wondered, if I had been there, and not asleep on a hard wooden bench in Nordbarn?

'Why would Kati believe Ilse?'

'Kati said that he had drawn her already. And Ilse was jealous. She was even more jealous when Kati told her that he wanted to draw another girl, as well.' She slapped her hands down hard on her thighs. 'And guess who that girl was?'

'Who?'

'Me, sir!'

The blood in my veins might have turned to ice.

'Where had he seen you?' I asked. 'All three of you, I mean.'

Edviga shrugged her shoulders. 'In Nordcopp, I suppose.' She shook her head. 'But here's the point, sir. Were they lying? Both of them? Or was Ilse telling the truth, while Kati chose to pull her leg, and drag me into it, too?' Her face took on a melancholy expression, and she sat in silence for some moments. 'Is it not strange, Herr Stiffeniis, that both of them were murdered?'

'Did either girl ever name this phantom artist?' I asked.

'No, sir, they did not. But Ilse did mention something that might help you. Not who, but *what* he proposed.'

'What was that?' I asked .

'He did not want to draw her face,' she said in a low voice.

'What did he draw, then?'

'She was most mysterious on that point, sir,' she added with a grimace. 'And yet she did say that it was something very particular. A detail that fascinated him. Not her face, but a part of her body . . . We made some filthy suggestions, of course. That's why I thought they were inventing the story. Both of them. Just to attract attention to themselves.'

Kati, Ilse, Edviga, and someone proposing to draw them.

'Were Ilse and Kati beautiful?' I asked her.

'Someone thought them pretty enough to draw,' she replied. She smiled a strange, shy smile. 'If this artist is real,' she said, 'and if he asks to make my picture, I'll tell him yes. And straight away!'

Edviga was striking in her looks. Any artist would jump at the opportunity to sketch her. And if this artist really did exist, and if he used his art to approach girls like Ilse and Kati, he could do the same with Edviga.

'I shall draw you,' I announced.

Edviga's expression froze in a stupor, then suddenly flushed the colour of the amber dangling from her ears. She did not speak. I think she had lost her tongue, watching as I opened my bag and took out my drawing album and graphite-holder.

'Stay quite still,' I ordered. With gentle pressure, I turned her face towards me, revealing the scar on her cheek. She stiffened for an instant. Then, almost imperceptibly, she began to move her head up and down, gently caressing my fingertips.

I pulled away my hand as if she were a burning flame.

'Do not change expression,' I commanded.

I began to trace the general outline of her face. High cheekbones, large green eyes, the delicate structure of an aquiline nose. The tapering line of her jaw and chin. The fine delicate bow of her lips, and, finally, the slanting slice of that narrow scar which ran from the corner of her left eye to the dimple at the left-hand corner of her mouth. I began to work the graphite into the paper with my thumb, smoothing and polishing the surface of her skin here and there. The bated breathing of the girl, the swell of the sea which seemed to grow heavier, the distant voices of the women working out in the water were

the only audible noises. When I had finished, I turned the book, and showed her what I had done.

'Do you recognise yourself?'

As if touching were believing, her fingertips stretched to caress the paper.

'My own face!' she murmured incredulously. She remained there contemplating her portrait for a minute or two.

'Show me the face of Frau Stiffeniis,' she said suddenly.

I smiled, turning away as I flicked back past the sketches of the corpses of Kati and Ilse, until I found the page that she wanted to see. I held up the album, and showed her my portrait of Helena. She looked at it for some moments.

'Did she know that you were drawing her?' Edviga asked.

I had drawn that picture one evening, several weeks before, while she was musing in the kitchen. Taken up with her own thoughts, Helena did not realise what I was doing until it was done.

'No, she didn't,' I said.

'Perhaps that's why she did not try to hide her fears.'

I looked more carefully at the picture I had drawn of Helena. She was frowning, her eyebrows almost meeting. And her eyes were wider than was normal. I had thought that she was tired. But now, I wondered. *Had Edviga seen what I had failed to see?*

'A pregnant woman is always a little afraid. I know the feeling, because I . . .' As she spoke her right hand came to rest gently over her womb. 'The freezing waters of the Baltic Sea are dangerous if you are pregnant.'

The thought flashed through my mind.

Was she expecting a child?

She looked at me. 'Did you draw that picture, sir, to protect me from him?'

'From who?' I asked in a state of mental confusion.

'The artist who kills his models,' she said.

I tried to laugh. 'As you said yourself, he may not exist.'

'But if he does, and if he asks to draw me, I can say that someone else has done it, and I'll be safe.'

I did not hesitate. I turned the album, intending to tear out the page and give it to her. But her hand reached out and stopped me. Her palm was warm on the back of my hand.

'Keep it there with Helena,' she said.

A shadow darkened the door.

'*Excusez-moi, monsieur*,' Robert called out, rapping loudly on the door-post without showing himself, as if unwilling to interrupt my tête-à-tête with the amber-girl.

He waved a piece of paper in the air, though he did not enter the hut.

'A courier brought this for you, monsieur.'

I stood up quickly, took the paper from his hand.

'Is it from your wife, sir?' Edviga asked anxiously.

'No, it's not from Helena,' I said with a smile. I had recognised the handwriting immediately. The tension on her face dissolved away. That note was signed by Johannes Gurten.

Three words only: *Erika is here.*

22

I spotted him near the North Tower in Nordcopp.

Sitting cross-legged on the ground beneath an overhanging roof, naked from the waist up, with his hands stretched out before him, his palms turned upwards like those of a beggar. A *blind* beggar, I corrected myself. Head tilted back, chin pointing up at the sky, his eyes were half-open, the pupils invisible, as if they had turned upwards in their sockets. His complexion was as white as a bowl of milk.

'Herr Gurten,' I called.

His eyes snapped open.

'Forgive me, sir,' he cried, jumping to his feet, and pulling on his shirt. 'I've been trying to make good use of the time.'

'How long have you been sitting here?' I asked him.

'Steady rain is a perfect *mantra*, you know. Its rhythm leads us to the core of our Being.' I suppose he must have seen perplexity on my face. 'If you concentrate on nothing,' he explained, 'hours pass away in a moment. I have heard the clock strike twice.'

'Two hours,' I said with glum scepticism.

'I tried to reach you on the coast first thing this morning,' he said. 'But they would not let me go beyond Nordbarn. The village is full of French soldiers. "Another bit of old Prussia lost" was how Hans Pastoris described it.'

'Pastoris?' I was surprised. 'Did he speak with you?'

'Oh yes, sir,' he replied at once. 'He seemed glad to speak with someone Prussian. He has been dispossessed by the French, he complained. They are taking the place of his workers. He'll be driven out, and the women will be driven off. God knows where they'll go.'

'No doubt, he blamed me for his troubles,' I muttered.

Gurten buttoned his jacket. 'He did not speak of you at all, Herr Stiffeniis.'

Pastoris had said nothing to Gurten about the fact that we had met. He seemed to deny that he had spoken anything but French for a day and a night. One thing was plain. Pastoris no longer thought of me as a Prussian. I was one of the enemy.

'What's all this about?' I asked, pulling the note from my pocket.

'Erika is being held in there, sir,' he said, nodding towards the tower.

'How did you track her down?' I asked, feeling a tiny sting of envy.

Gurten's eyes were ablaze with enthusiasm. 'A stroke of luck, really. I was on my feet before dawn. Pastor Bylsma had invited me to attend the ceremony which concludes the annual Spenerian feast. I went to the Founder's Cell before sunrise, as he had instructed me, but I found it empty. That is, the cell was dark, there was not a candle. But then, lightning flashed, and I saw a figure standing at the window. It was Pastor Bylsma. He was in such a state that I thought the church had been robbed again. He was trembling. "Today of all days!" he hissed with anger. "No one is arrested in Nordcopp on Founder's Day!" I reminded him that the feast day was almost over, but he would not be calmed. We watched together from the window. The French were bringing in three smugglers. Two Russians, as I discovered later. And a little girl was with them . . .'

His voice gave out with emotion and the fury of the telling.

'Erika?'

'Soaked to the skin, sir, worn out, and in chains. Pastor Bylsma was right, sir. Arresting them was an offence against Pietism, against all Christian religion, an insult to our nation. And yet – now *this* was strange! – in the same instant, I was

250

overwhelmed by a sense of peace. A revelation, I suppose you'd call it, an insight of such powerful intensity that it robbed me of my breath.'

'What was this revelation?' I asked.

Johannes Gurten smiled. 'I was witnessing the fruits of our lawful labours. Yours and mine, sir. Yours above all, Herr Procurator.'

The mysticism of my assistant – his effortless transition from Buddhist to Pietist, and back again – was beginning to wear on my nerves. I would have told him, too, but he expressed himself with such natural, unaffected candour.

'Is it not incredible, sir?' he continued joyfully. 'You need Erika Linder to help you find a killer that the French believe they have already found. And the French deliver her into your hands! They even went to the trouble of bringing her back to Nordcopp for you to question!'

His pale face seemed to shine with excitement.

'I doubt the French had that in mind,' I replied sardonically.

'I only mean to suggest that it is evidence of their *karma*,' he replied. 'Their destiny, that is. As the sacred texts of the *Vedanta* tells us, no human action is without a consequence. The outcome is always what we deserve. The French arrested her for stealing amber. The mother escaped, by the way, so I was told, while the daughter could not, on account of her physique. I saw how badly she was limping.'

'Have you nothing to say regarding my own *karma*?' I added slyly.

'You will interrogate her, and find the true killer,' he rushed on. 'Not the innocent that Colonel les Halles has sent to Königsberg. It will be a personal victory for you, sir. A battle lost for them!'

I thought of that devilish little sprite, and wondered whether his prophecy would be fulfilled as easily as he thought. Gurten did not know Erika Linder. He had no idea what I was up against, the difficulty that I had found in trying to extract useful information from the Prussians on the coast.

Sergeant Jean Tessier was on duty again in the North Tower. His blond curls appeared to have been recently puffed up, his cheeks smooth and shining, as if he had visited the regimental barber that morning. He glanced up and recognition flashed in his eyes.

'*Oui?*' he said, drawing out the vowels into a question.

'I am sure you remember me,' I replied. 'Magistrate Stiffeniis.'

'Still here, sir? Haven't you counted all the victims yet?'

I ignored this provocation.

'You are holding a prisoner,' I snapped. 'Erika Linder. I want to speak with her.'

I said no more, but I did not take my eyes from his face.

'Have you informed Colonel les Halles?' he protested.

'You may inform him, if that is what you wish to do,' I replied. 'Erika Linder is a Prussian thief, as I think you know. She is of interest to me alone. Colonel les Halles may resent your wasting his time. Still, that is for you to decide, Tessier.'

Sergeant Tessier appeared to consider his options. Clearly, he had received no instructions from les Halles. And why should he? Erika Linder was an insignificant cog in the mechanical world of Colonel les Halles. She had no name, no face.

'*Très bien, monsieur,*' Tessier replied at last, and his fleshy lips made that unpleasant sucking sound that I remembered from my last visit to the prison. He stood up, went over to the door, called for one of his men, told him what to do. The soldier was to take us down to the cells, wait by the door, report immediately if anything aroused his suspicions. 'I hope I will not live to regret this decision,' Tessier added, as he stepped aside to wave us out.

'*Au contraire,*' I assured him.

The North Tower consists of four floors above the ground, and one below which might have corresponded to a cellar or a basement. As Gurten and I followed the soldier down the steep stone ramp to the underground floor, I realised how cramped the ancient tower really was, how complex the warren beneath the streets of Nordcopp. We found ourselves in a confined square space, similar in size to the chamber above it, which was filled by Sergeant Tessier and his desk, though the ceiling was lower. Each wall was no more than thirty feet long. Into this small area were crammed a dozen rusty iron pens on either side of the ramp. Just tall enough to stand up in, these cages were hardly wide enough to allow the prisoner to turn around. Three of them were occupied: two men, and Erika Linder.

Pointing her out, the soldier laughed: 'Given her size, ain't *she* the lucky one!'

'What will happen to the child?' I asked.

'That child steals amber, monsieur,' he replied sternly.

Before I could stop him, Gurten bowed close and spoke to her.

'Have they treated you badly?'

Erika lifted her head to a German voice. Her long matted hair fell away from her face. She was filthy. Filthy and bruised, I corrected myself. Sweat had gathered in the wrinkled folds of her skin, then evaporated away in the sweltering heat of the dungeon, leaving a residue of grime in clinging black lines.

'Have you come to help me, sir?' she asked.

Gurten reached through the bars and took her hand. The gesture made her gasp. Then, tears trickled down her sooty cheeks, leaving channels of white skin which converged at the point of her chin. Her bloodshot eyes fixed on his like two tiny balls of opaque glass. Her expression was a contorted mixture of hope and terror.

'What . . . what will happen to me?'

'They may decide to hang you,' he breathed in a soothing undertone.

His cruelty robbed me of breath. And yet, I realised what he was doing. Erika was a gift of Destiny. We had to use her fear of mortal punishment to our own advantage.

'You were carrying amber when they caught you,' I said, stepping close to the bars. 'The French will make an example of you to warn off the others. And yet,' I added, as if it were an afterthought, 'I may just be able to loose the hangman's rope from round your neck.'

No female has been hanged for illegal possession of amber since the days of Frederick the Great, though there are still gallows set at regular intervals along the coast, and the coast road, to remind potential thieves of the seriousness of the offence. The great King Frederick would have hanged a child. The French would not.

But Erika did not know that.

She looked up. A fountain of terror seemed to surge through her soul. She was unable to speak. A whimper, a shudder, a burst of silent tears – she was not capable of anything else.

'How much amber were you carrying?' I asked, waiting for the storm to subside.

'Just a few bits,' she replied between sobs. Her eyes blazed suddenly into mine. 'Not so big as the piece that *you* had, sir!'

I reached into my pocket, pulled out Kati Rodendahl's piece of amber, and held it up to Erika. I remembered her frenzy in the tunnel, the first time that I met her. 'This one, you mean?'

The child's hand shot out between the bars and tried to grab it from me. Despite the fact that she was in a cage, that piece still had a strong power over her.

'Not so fast,' I said, pulling back, playing lightly with the amber, throwing it up and down, catching it in my palm. 'Now, if you were to tell me what I want to know . . .'

Who was crueller, Gurten, who had let her believe that the French would hang her, or myself, pretending to offer her what she was obsessed with?

She sobbed no more, waiting to hear what I would say.

'You told me that you knew Kati Rodendahl,' I began. 'What about Ilse Bruen? A girl named Annalise? Or Megrete? Did you know them, as well?'

'I knew the name of Kati. You told me she was dead,' the girl replied. 'I may well know them all, but I don't know names. I never ask them what they call themselves. They don't tell me neither. I just do business with them . . .'

She looked up, eyes wide with alarm. 'Are they all dead, sir?'

I ignored her question.

'Which business are you talking of?' I asked.

Despite being locked in a cage, the child had not lost her spirit.

'Don't play the innocent with me, sir,' she snapped. 'You know what those girls do. And what I do, too. I am always looking for girls who are strong and tall.'

'Why them?'

I tossed the nugget in the air again.

'They work far out from the shore, sir. That's where the best amber lies these days. The amber that I need . . .'

'What do you mean?' I interrupted.

'Large lumps of purest amber with big insects in them. Like that one in your hand.'

I held the amber up to the light, saying as matter-of-factly as I could, 'I asked you once. Now, I ask you again. Would those girls bring pieces like this one to you?'

'They might,' she said.

'Two girls stole relics from the Church of the Saviour,' I pressed on. 'Amber relics. The sort of amber you said you need. What can you tell me about that theft?'

The lines in her face seemed to harden, her eyes seemed to drift out of focus.

'Someone finally did it!' she exclaimed, but then the smile froze stiff on her lips. 'You are not accusing me, sir, are you? I know nothing about that robbery. I did not have a thing to do with it.'

'But you knew about the treasure,' Gurten put in.

'Everyone in Nordcopp knows about Spener's amber. I have seen those pieces. Before the French came here. They are similar to that one, there,' she said and pointed to the amber in my hand. 'Full to bursting with big, fat insects. The sort of piece that everyone is looking for. Anyone could have stolen those relics. But I don't know the names, I swear it, sir!'

'Anyone?' I muttered to myself.

Ilse? Kati? Annalise? Megrete? Which two were the thieves? Had two women been killed, or were the victims four?

'Let's see how much you really know,' I said, shrugging my bag from my shoulder, unlatching the strap which held it closed, taking out my sketch-book. I flicked through the pages looking for a drawing I had made of Kati Rodendahl. Not the detailed sketch I had made of her mutilated face, but a fanciful reconstruction based on guessing at the shape and form of the skin and fat which might have overlain the bone structure of her face. I had learnt this skill from Aaron Jacob, a Jewish scholar living in Lotingen, who had helped me to reassemble a crushed skeleton during the Gottewald investigation. This time, of course, I had based the drawing on my own unaided intuition.

I held the album close to the bars.

'Have you ever seen this girl before?' I asked her.

Erika nodded twice. 'A familiar face,' she said. 'I've seen her in town any number of times. She sold amber. But not to me alone.'

I wondered what she would make of the gutted remains I had examined on the table in the company of Colonel les Halles.

'I repeat. Have you ever heard her called by the name of Annalise or Megrete?'

Erika shook her head. 'You still don't believe me, sir? I don't know what she was called,' she said flatly. I had the feeling that she would have liked to help me. By helping me, she would be doing herself a favour, after all.

I turned some more leaves, skipping over the pages showing what the killer and the pigs had done to Ilse Bruen, then I held my album up again. In this sketch, Ilse's face was relatively intact, though her throat was not. I was careful to cover the bottom third of the page with my hand before I showed it to Erika.

'What about this one?'

She nodded again.

'She brought me one or two good pieces.'

'No names, I imagine, while you were dealing with her?'

'I cannot help you,' the child replied. 'But tell me, sir,' she whispered excitedly, her eyes sparkling at the thought of such a heist. 'Did the thieves get all of Spener's collection?'

'Three pieces at the most,' I said.

'And they did not bring them to me,' she muttered. There was anger in her voice, as if those pieces should have been hers by right.

'If not you,' said Gurten, stepping forward, 'who would buy such items?'

'Someone who would cure me if I brought him amber of such quality . . .'

Her voice ran down like a clockwork automaton. Perhaps she saw the smile on my face, and realised that she had led me unwittingly where I wanted to go.

'Who is that person, Erika?' I asked.

Frau Hummel opened the front door at the second knock.

This time, she made no attempt to hinder my entrance. Instead, she glanced at Gurten enquiringly, as if to ask him who he was, or what he wanted. Obviously, she ought to have remembered me. And yet, it was to Gurten that she spoke. As if he were the magistrate, and I were his junior.

'What's your business with the doctor?' she asked.

'*I* have come to speak with him,' I said.

Frau Hummel continued to stare at Gurten. She might have been mutely asking his advice. Should she answer me, or not? I was not surprised by this attitude. Hans Pastoris, Bylsma, and now the doctor's helper. All the Prussians in Nordcopp seemed to view me as a threat, while clearly Johannes Gurten was not. I was the one that they could not trust. If they could avoid speaking to me directly, they did so.

Dr Heinrich was not amputating legs that day.

He looked up from a large blue bowl in which his arms were fully immersed. A white linen handkerchief covered his nose, so that only his eyes were visible. The smell which issued from the jar was so very strong, it filled the whole house. I had felt it washing over me, the instant the housekeeper opened the door, and I recalled it from my previous visit, though it had not been so pervasive on that occasion. Now, it stuck in my throat like a piece of bread that was too stale to swallow.

'I am making casts,' he growled, as Frau Hummel led us into the room.

Seeing that she was not alone, he stood up and immediately clamped the lid onto the bowl. He slipped the mask from his face, wiped his hands on his brown apron, and came to meet us. His behaviour, however, was the exact opposite of the lady's. Dr Heinrich spoke to me, and me alone, as if Johannes Gurten were suddenly invisible.

And Gurten, in his turn, ignored the doctor.

Drawn like a moth to a flame, my assistant fluttered to the wall at the far end of the room, where half a dozen plaster casts had been hung up to dry in the bright sunlight which entered from the rear garden.

'Do you cure your patients' ills with these?' he asked.

The tone of his voice was sharp and rude. I was even more surprised by it, I think, than Dr Heinrich was.

Heinrich turned in his direction, a bellicose expression on his face.

I stepped between them.

'The question to be answered is more precise, Dr Heinrich,' I said.

He stared at me for a moment.

'Which question is that?' he asked.

'I want to know the name of the illness for which you are treating Erika Linder.'

23

'The Italians have a name for what you have just described. They call them *stravaganze*,' Gurten sneered.

The two men had taken an instant dislike to one another, but I made no attempt to curb Gurten's rudeness. When fighting cocks set to, they often show their true colours. If Gurten could do what I had failed to do, that is, draw blood, and provoke Dr Heinrich into speaking his mind, then I would benefit from the fracas.

What I could not understand was the reason for their animosity.

Heinrich seemed to be the only man in Nordcopp who found Johannes Gurten irritating. While the physician was attempting to explain what was wrong with Erika, Gurten interrupted him on several occasions.

His questions were rude, his tone impatient, but still I did not intervene.

'That is not a scientific definition,' Dr Heinrich replied. His voice was mild, but his meaning was not. 'Your words reek of travelling circuses, bears in chains, the public exhibition of what is rare or unusual in Nature. Certainly, Erika Linder would find employment in such a place, but as I am a doctor, I view her situation differently. I aim to study her. In medical circles, we speak of such beings as *lusus naturae*, from whom a great deal may be learnt.'

'What exactly are you talking of?' I asked him.

'Erika Linder is a rare medical phenomenon,' he explained, turning to face me, showing his back to Gurten. 'I have examined her many times. When she first appeared in Nordcopp, I could not believe my luck. She was ten years old at the time, but she had already stopped growing.' Heinrich looked me straight in the eye. 'That was all of twelve years ago.'

For an instant, I thought that he was joking at my expense.

'Not a child?' I murmured, glancing from the serious expression on Heinrich's face to Gurten's even sterner mask.

'A twenty-two-year-old child, if you like,' Dr Heinrich went on. 'That is her chronological age. Physically, she would be classified as a dwarf, but that is not the end of her medical condition.' He sighed out loud, as if it caused him pain. 'Her skin, as you may have noticed, is folded and wrinkled. The bones of her spine and legs are bowed and brittle. Were it not for her undeveloped face and diminutive size, I'd have said that she was in her late sixties.'

He passed his hand across his forehead, and looked away. His lack of reaction to the mutilation of the amber-gatherers had surprised me greatly; his passionate disquietude when he spoke of Erika disturbed me even more.

'Her blood is thin, her complexion pale. It is as if a cold wind is blowing through her, day after day. It is drying her out, icing her up, stiffening her joints and cracking her bones. And as you know, Herr Stiffeniis, the aged *die*.'

I thought only of Erika's vitality. The fierce grasp of her hand on my shirt. Her childlike insistence that I take notice of her strength.

'Is there no cure?'

'Of course there isn't!' the doctor snapped.

'And yet,' I flung back at him, 'you promised that you would cure her.'

'Medicine is a cruel art,' the doctor stated flatly 'Paracelsus coined the phrase, I believe. We often say what we hope, rather than what we know, to be true. I encouraged her to come here, so that I might chart the progress of the disease. I even thought I might be able to help her. The science of teratology is slowly making progress . . .'

260

'What is that?' I asked.

'The study of monsters,' Gurten replied. 'Erika Linder is a perfect example, is she not, Herr Doctor?'

'Erika is one in a million,' Heinrich replied, his eyes sparkling with excitement. 'One in *many* millions, I believe. Certainly, she is unique in Prussia. In the whole of Europe, too, perhaps. Could I ignore what Fate had casually thrown in my path? I am a scientist . . .'

'So what are your *scientific* plans for her?' Gurten asked sarcastically.

Heinrich did not flinch.

'I intend to publish a paper describing the rapid degeneration of her bones.'

'The French will welcome your contribution,' Gurten said with a cozening smile. 'No doubt they'll invite you to take her on a tour of French universities. A *stravaganza* lately come out of Germany. That would look good on the posters. What are you waiting for?'

Heinrich stared very hard at my assistant before he chose to answer.

'Is there a doctor who, in his own short lifetime, can measure the ageing process in another human being throughout the course of that person's life? It is a rare opportunity, and I will not let it slip. Physiologically, Erika is in a state of decline. Her strength is failing, her bones are becoming friable, though her mind is as active as that of any girl of the same age. I have made drawings, and taken plaster casts. A number of scientific journals know of the work that I am doing here.'

Gurten took a step forward. Again, I had the impression of two dogs eyeing each other before the tussle.

But Heinrich struck again.

'I intend to dissect her the instant Nature takes its final toll,' he said.

At that point, he turned to me. 'Now, is there anything else, Herr Stiffeniis?'

'I'd like to see those drawings that you mentioned,' I replied.

Edviga had spoken about a mysterious stranger who had made proposals to Ilse, offering to draw her face. Had Ilse been telling the truth on that occasion? Might Heinrich have been the unknown artist?

He opened a drawer, took out a folder, placed it on the desk.

'They are highly technical, as you can see,' he said, pulling out a sheet of paper, laying it out on view, showing none of the reluctance that I expected. 'These are the finger joints,' he commented, while I admired the fine lines and delicate hatching of a life-sized sketch. 'I have made similar studies of her toes, knees, ankles, the wrists and . . . and so on.'

There was even a portrait of Erika's face – lined, wrinkled, baby-like – but not the face of a baby, as I now realised. I put it aside, and asked to see the plaster impressions of her arms and legs.

'Have you made drawings of other people, too?' I asked him. 'The amber-girls, for example?'

Heinrich looked up, surprise clearly written on his face.

'Their injuries will hardly change the path of science,' he said. 'There are very few bodies such as Erika's to study. Plaster casts are not the best way to measure physical change,' the doctor continued, going over to a large wooden trunk in the far corner, throwing open the lid. 'But in a case like this one, alterations over a period of time are all too evident.'

He lifted out two large flat squares of white plaster, and laid them on a side-table beneath the window. 'Erika's left hand,' he explained turning the casts over, reading the dates which were written on the back. 'The first was made when she was ten. This one, instead, was made just a year ago.'

He looked at me for a moment, then he said, 'Well, Herr Stiffeniis, what would your untrained, but undoubtedly *sharp*, eyes lead you to say about these two casts?'

I studied the imprints for a moment.

'The later hand is smaller than the earlier one,' I said.

'Ageing of the ligaments, contraction of the knuckles, clear signs of arthritic complication, and a consequent shortening of the reach,' Dr Heinrich commented. 'This is the hand of an old woman. If you run your fingers over the surface of the plaster cast on the right, you may be able to tell me something else.'

I did as I was told, feeling the lines and the contours beneath my fingertips, unpleasantly reminded of the touch of Erika's skin as she tried to tear the piece of amber from my grip.

'It seems to be scratched, the surface bumpy and uneven.'

'That is wrinkling, calcification, clawing of the finger joints . . .'

'This is all very well, Herr Stiffeniis,' Gurten suddenly burst out. 'But what is the point, except to say that Erika Linder is more and less than she appears?'

Dr Heinrich smiled, but there was no humour in it, as I quickly realised.

'More, and less,' he repeated. 'Now, sir, you have hit on something! The great question in teratology is exactly that. Is Erika more, or less, than one might expect? And how, exactly, does she differ from her contemporaries? Is she a throwback to an earlier, more primitive form of life? Or is she a precursor of an otherwise unknowable future human development?'

Gurten opened his mouth to reply, but Dr Heinrich held up his finger. 'Allow me to finish, if you'll be so kind. No living thing is a fixed, unchangeable entity. Every creature alters in continuity from birth to death. One egg is much like another, but no two chickens are identical. What's so marvellous about Nature is its infinite variability. There seems to be an evolutional process at work . . .'

'According to Lamarck!' Gurten interjected.

'You are well informed, sir,' Heinrich confirmed. 'His Fourth Law states that everything gained or lost by the circumstances to which a race is exposed over a long period of time is passed directly to the new individual by the reproductive process . . .'

'Isn't this French atheism?' Gurten objected.

Dr Heinrich studied his opponent's face.

'How would you account for Erika's aberrations?' he asked. 'Her mother is normal, and the lady reports that her mate, let us call him, was a violent man, but physically average.'

'The heavenly plan . . .'

'Ah, Linnaeus,' Dr Heinrich murmured to himself, as if he had finally managed to plant his feet on firm ground in relation to my assistant. 'Are you a Linnaean, too, Herr Procurator?'

I did not have the time to reply.

'The heavenly plan,' Gurten repeated with insistence, 'is *not* invariably perfect. Indeed, Linné suggests that this is the basic cause of all natural differences. The casual encounter of random destinies, the source of all human imperfections, derives from the consequences of original sin . . .'

'Isn't this theology rather than science?' Heinrich asked him with a scowl.

'Are the two so very different?' Gurten replied. 'New species are always forming. They are an integral part of God's universal plan!'

Heinrich knitted his brow again.

'More perfect in being closer to God's final design for them? Is that what you are saying, sir?'

'Isn't that what you Lamarckians are looking for?' Gurten replied. 'An understanding of the mechanisms of perfection? Isn't that what you are looking for in Erika herself? Just as you are trying to trace it in the pieces of amber that she has added to your collection.'

'Amber?' Heinrich echoed, uncertainly, as if the whirlwind arguments of Gurten had spun off at a tangent.

'Amber containing insect insertions.'

Heinrich seemed not to know how he ought to answer.

'Such precious amber', Gurten raced on, 'is destined for the Royal Academy of Science in Berlin. The French agreed to send it there, on the condition that Prussian scientists reveal whatever they may learn to the equivalent Academy in France. Napoleon's financial needs are more immediate, however. War costs money. Today, Spain is eating up the profits from his amber, but a great deal more will be required tomorrow when he turns on Russia. And yet, there are men in Paris, I have no doubt, who would give their fortunes to establish the primacy of their scientific discoveries. Missing links in the chain of creation preserved in amber may be lost to them because of a treaty hastily signed. That is what they fear.'

'I do not see what that has got to do with me,' Dr Heinrich protested.

'The amber with insertions does not go to Berlin, sir. The local supply has suddenly dried up. No one seems to know where it is going. Except for Erika Linder.' Gurten pointed his finger at the doctor. 'The girl swears that some of the pieces she found are in *your* possession, sir.'

I looked aghast at my assistant.

He had gone too far, too fast.

That is, I had let him go beyond my control. He was like a strong dog, and I had let out his leash. *I* should have been conducting the investigation. *I* should have been asking the questions. If anyone were to threaten and cajole a witness, *I* would do it, but only if I judged his answers to be reticent or insufficient. But Gurten had stolen the initiative away from me. He had helped me greatly in the past two days, but he had overstepped the mark, and I could not let such interference pass unnoticed. It displayed an irascible weakness of character. In my report to the judicial authorities in Potsdam, I would be obliged to note these excesses.

'Dr Heinrich,' I said, stepping between them, determined to continue more calmly, 'let me rephrase the question. Did you purchase amber of a scientific nature from Erika Linder for your private studies? Erika claims that she has given you many pieces,' I countered, before Gurten should presume to do so in my place.

'Erika Linder is a congenital liar,' Dr Heinrich replied smoothly enough, 'along with her more serious congenital problems. It is true that she offered to *sell* me interesting pieces of amber. As a way of repaying me – so she quaintly put it – for my care and my attention. But the girl gives nothing away for free, I promise you, sir. And I cannot afford to pay what she is asking.'

Was Erika the congenital liar? Or was the doctor?

'Have you bought amber from any other patients, Dr Heinrich? When I came here the other day I showed you a piece that I had discovered hidden in the corpse of Kati Rodendahl. I know for certain that many other girls are selling pieces such as that one to dealers and collectors here on the coast.'

'I have bought nothing,' Heinrich said.

'And what about the amber stolen from the local church which once formed part of the collection of Jakob Spener?'

'I've no idea what you are talking of,' he said. 'I did not know that amber *had* been stolen from the church in Nordcopp.'

'Do you know Ilse Bruen, then, or any girl calling herself Megrete, or Annalise?' I insisted, despite his continuing denials, hoping to provoke him by the vehemence of my accusations. 'I suspect them all of having stolen the amber from the church. Such pieces would cut a fine figure in your collection . . .'

'My own is hardly a collection,' Dr Heinrich replied with a flash of irritation. 'I do have four or five pieces, but they came to me with my father's blessing. I did not purchase them from Erika Linder, or from anyone else.'

'May we see this collection, sir?' I asked.

'Most certainly,' he replied. 'I have so few, I keep them here on my desk.'

He turned away and opened up a little oak casket, from which he extracted a large magnifying glass with a horn handle. Then, he handed me a small orange lozenge.

'Look at it against the light,' he counselled.

The amber was less than a quarter of the size of the piece that I had removed from the corpse of Kati Rodendahl, and it was clearly imperfect. One half of it was a mottled, pitted, milky white, like a bad tooth.

I held it up, and studied it for a moment or two.

'It contains a common ant,' I stated.

'Quite the opposite,' the doctor countered briskly. 'It is *un*common, *un*like any ant out there in my garden today. It is undeniable evidence of the progressive improvement which Nature has worked on all the primitive creatures which it first nurtured.'

He produced a second piece. 'Compare this one.'

It was larger, clearer, almost lemon-coloured, and shaped like a tear-drop.

How long had it taken for that lump to form, I asked myself, *as the lymph of the tree imprisoned the minuscule creature that could just be seen as a small, dark blob at the core of the gem?*

'Here we see the remains of another little tragedy,' he commented. 'This ant was drowned, embalmed, preserved for eternity. Just like the other one, of course. But they are *not* the same. Not at all! Concentrate your attention on the antennae. They are longer, finer, more similar to the ants that we see today. We may safely assert that the first creature is older in the Chain of Being. With the slow passage of time, something has altered significantly. But what? That is the mystery which perplexes us.'

If tragedy there had been, as he suggested, the passions and struggles of that event had been transmuted into timeless immobility.

'I think of myself as a scientist,' he said, 'yet there is something truly magical in an amber enclosure. These pieces are tiny windows into the past.'

'They show the incredible variety of creatures that God has created since the Flood,' Johannes Gurten stated more calmly. 'Amber is God's gift to Prussia. It allows us to see the simple perfection of the world as *He* initially conceived it.'

I had heard similar sentiments expressed by Edviga.

'What about the rest of this collection of yours?' I asked sharply.

Never taking his eyes from mine, Dr Heinrich felt around with his fingers in the casket. He pulled out two more humble pieces of amber, and gently set them down on the surface of his desk. He might have been a man who had just been ordered at pistol-point to drop his own weapon.

'This is it,' he said with a wry, challenging smile. 'And you are disappointed, I see. Is this the way you formulate your accusations, Herr Procurator? By taking literally the accusations of a wretch whose second nature is to lie? As if *I* were the criminal? Colonel les Halles is convinced that he has caught the murderer, as I am sure you know.'

'The evidence he has gathered is worth as much', I said dismissively, 'as the accusations Erika has made against you. And yet, I believe that you may have added weight to his flimsy arguments. He sent over something for you to analyse, he told me.'

He looked at me sharply. 'The bones from the Ansbach farm, you mean?'

'Exactly,' I replied.

There we were, three Prussians in the same room, each one vying to provide the French with the guilty party. Gurten would have handed over the doctor to them without a second thought. Heinrich was in a position to pull the noose tight around the neck of Adam Ansbach. I, on the other hand, was undecided. I wanted definite proof. I would have handed over either one of them, if only I could have demonstrated his guilt to my own satisfaction.

'Those bones are human,' he said.

My heart sank.

How many bodies had been buried in that pigsty? How many women had been slaughtered there?

Amber was uppermost in the mind of every person in the area, except for Adam Ansbach.

'Human?' I repeated.

'Without a doubt.'

Was les Halles right? Was Adam guilty? Or was Heinrich heaping coals on the fire, blowing hard on the flames which seemed intent on consuming the Ansbach farm, and the people who lived there, thus ensuring his own safety from the same accusation?

'Do you know what surprised me most of all?' Heinrich demanded energetically, as if he believed that the news should surprise me, too.

'What?'

I fully expected a catalogue of horrors about the way the bones had been smashed, or about the manner in which they had been severed.

'There was not a single female bone among them.'

I could not speak. My tongue seemed moulded to my palate.

'No female bone?' I said at last. 'Can you be sure?'

'Quite certain. Men's bones are quite distinct. And these were the bones of men who had not been walking on the Earth for quite some time,' he added. 'Marrow is the principal, nay, the *only* means of saying anything about the age of bones, whether human or animal. If marrow is still present, the creature died within living memory. By the time they've been in the ground for a century, say, all traces of marrow have disappeared. Consumed by worms and mites, presumably.'

'Are you saying that the bones are a hundred years old?'

'At the very least,' he replied. 'In ancient times, that pigsty may have been the centre of a battlefield. Or the chosen burial ground of our Teutonic forefathers. I am speculating, of course.'

In my mind's eye, I saw Adam Ansbach set free, while the dark shadow of the murderer hovered just beyond the edge of my vision. The presence of Ilse Bruen's body in the pigsty remained to be explained, but of two things I was certain: no other woman had died there, and Colonel les Halles had sent an innocent man to Königsberg. At the same time, another unavoidable question rose up to confront me. If Adam was not the killer, who was? Could he be standing there before me?

'I am pleased to hear you say so, Doctor,' I said.

Despite this compliment, the doctor's face seemed to lour resentfully.

'And I would be most grateful, sir,' he said, carefully weighing his words, 'if you were as scrupulous in your own investi-
gations, as I have been in mine. It is all too easy to sling mud.
We are all vulnerable to casual misinterpretation in this place.
Our position, *vis-à-vis* the French, is a fragile one, to say the
least. And now, sir, if you have finished, I have work to do!'

Outside, the street was crowded with amber-traders.

I turned on Gurten and grabbed hold of his arm.

'Do not dare to interfere like that again,' I warned him.
'Never question a suspect with such an open show of vehemence or hostility. If you are to play the part of the bull mastiff,
you will do so because *I* have instructed you to do so, and for
no other reason. Do you understand me?'

I expected a show of penitence, or fright. After all, his career
as a magistrate would depend on how I chose to assess his
aptitudes, and report them to our masters.

But Gurten did not excuse himself. He strode along at my
side, stepping out of the path of other passers-by at the very
last moment, as if daring them to bump into him.

'Are you listening to me, Gurten? You can't . . .'

Suddenly, he turned and stared at me.

'The doctor is guilty, sir.'

It was not a question. He spat the words out in a fury.

'How can you make such a wild suggestion? We have
nothing against him, except for Erika's testimony. And I know
well enough what that . . .' I swallowed back the word *child*, 'I
know that the girl is able to deceive.'

'That may be true,' he agreed. 'But she was terrified, sir.
Witnesses tell the truth when terror takes possession of their
senses. She was not lying about Dr Heinrich.'

'We have only her accusation,' I hissed at him. 'What sort of
magistrate will you become if you are prepared to trade one
Prussian for another so easily?'

'Prussian?' he said. His eyes were huge with surprise. 'That
man is in league with the French, sir. They need our amber to

sustain their theories, they are carrying it off to France. That's why nothing important is reaching the Royal Academy of Science in Berlin. They're stealing our most precious treasure, taking it to France. Baltic amber contains the history of the world. And Heinrich is giving it to them.'

'Very well,' I said, prepared to hear him out before correcting him again. 'But what proof do you have of his involvement in the trade? On what specific *evidence* do you base your accusations?'

He did not hear me. That is, he did not heed me.

'It is a perfect triangle,' he said. 'The girls smuggle amber out from the camp with the connivance of the French soldiers. Or they steal it from a church. Then, they pass it on to Erika. Those pieces go to men who appreciate them, men like Dr Heinrich, and then they go to the scientists in Paris.'

'It is not a crime to believe in the theories of Lamarck,' I challenged. 'Nor to inherit a few poor bits of amber from one's dying father. Nor is it against the law to study human deformity and attempt to cure it.'

Gurten did not hear a word. 'He is blowing smoke in your eyes, sir. He is lying to save his own skin. Those trifling pieces of amber in his study are irrelevant. They are not enough to sustain his theories. And why would Erika lie in this specific case? She says she has sold him many precious pieces . . .'

'No judge would believe her,' I interrupted him. '*I* do not believe her. No sensible man would take her word as gospel. Now, what other "proof" do we have?'

'The victims were mutilated by an expert hand,' Gurten replied at once. 'He is a surgeon, educated in anatomy, skilled with a knife. Perhaps the girls became too greedy in their demands. They may have threatened to tell the Prussian authorities that he was buying up amber which belongs to our country. Perhaps he decided to cut Erika out of the equation, and deal directly with the amber-gatherers. I believe that he is the killer . . .'

'This is too far-fetched,' I said dismissively.

'As doctor to the French camp,' Gurten went on relentlessly, 'he lacks no opportunity to make the acquaintance of the workers from the coast. The French trust him, and so do the girls. Indeed, for some of them it was a fatal mistake.'

I recalled my first conversation with Dr Heinrich. We had talked about our work, and our shared sense of regretful submission to the French. I would not give him up without convincing evidence of his guilt.

'He has faithfully served the local community for years,' I replied, playing the Devil's advocate. 'He was here before the French arrived. He amputates limbs, it is true, but his real talent is the making of artificial replacements. Against all odds – despite the obstacles posed by the French occupation – he continues with his scientific studies, as any serious doctor should. It makes me proud to think that there are Prussians who still go about their business as if the French had never come to hinder them.'

Though I spoke on behalf of the doctor, I realised that I was defending myself.

'Are we – you and I, that is – are *we* not hampered in our investigative task by the ambiguity of our relations with a foreigner who has possessed himself of us, and all that is ours? Are we guilty of a crime?'

Gurten did not answer immediately. We had pulled up in a doorway as the argument raged. His eyes were on the people passing up and down the street. 'Heinrich may believe that his scientific studies are more important than any other thing on earth, sir. That is what I fear.'

'I do not follow you,' I said.

'He is a Lamarckian,' Gurten said again. 'He believes that the Enlightened culture which the French are trying to impose on us is an upward step – an inevitable gain – for Prussia. An evolution. There, sir! That's what Heinrich would call it. He would explain himself and his actions by saying that he is working for a better future. But he is still a collaborator.'

'He is not alone,' I said abruptly. 'And you should never forget it, Gurten. If we wish to pursue our chosen professions here in Prussia – if we are *allowed* to do so – it can only be within a context in which the interests of the dominant foreign power are always pre-eminent.'

He stiffened, stared at me.

'What if we can find the necessary proof?' he said. 'What, then, sir?'

Was the apprentice throwing out a challenge to his master?

'I would be prepared to bet that he has published something on the subject,' he rushed on. 'Heinrich is a believer in the merits of Lamarck, but even in France there is frantic debate going on about the validity of those theories. Heinrich must have given his drawings and writings to someone. Indeed, he spoke openly of the fact that he is in touch with various scientific journals.'

Was this the stuff of which a magistrate was made? Gurten's initiative was undeniable, his thoughts were bold. He did not hesitate to posit that a man might kill for the sake of his own advancement in the hierarchy of learning. Was this another one of his good intuitions?

'Where would you look for proof?' I asked him.

'In the French scientific press,' he replied at once. 'That man is passing Prussian amber on to them.'

I considered this proposal. 'Isn't it a bit like trawling in the sea for a rare fish? You might spend your whole life at it, and never catch the species you are fishing for.'

'Knowing where the rare fish dwells is half the hunt, sir,' Gurten replied.

He was so determined, I did not know how to deter him. It might be better to let him run. On a loose leash, as my father said when the hounds had caught a scent. Either he would catch the prey, or he would come quietly back to heel. And I knew of a library where French scientific journals could be consulted. Count Dittersdorf in Lotingen was an avid collector of anything scientific. He had provided me with that copy of the *Procès-verbal de la visite faite le long des deux rives de la rivière Seine, le 14 février, 1790* as I struggled to understand the implications and dangers of the animal excrement fouling the streets of my home town.

'There is a place close by,' I said, 'where you might test your theory.'

Even as I made this announcement, I realised the temptation to which I had just exposed myself. Dittersdorf's library was in Lotingen. It would be the perfect excuse for me to return home, and visit my wife. I would be testing a theory, after all, not abandoning my task there on the coast.

'Where, sir?' Gurten was bright-eyed, watching me in a sort of impatient ecstasy. The fact that I had admitted the possibility that his idea was worth the testing seemed to have quelled the fire in him.

'Lotingen,' I announced.

Gurten's mouth fell open with surprise. 'Shall we continue the investigation there, sir?'

I was sorely tempted for a moment.

Then again, Adam Ansbach and his mother were in Königsberg. A French judge might decide their fate before I could do anything to help them.

'No,' I said at last. 'The doctor's declaration regarding the age of the bones that were found in the Ansbach pigsty changes everything. I must speak to les Halles about Adam and his mother, and I need to do it now.'

'Don't you think that we should force the doctor into saying more, sir?'

I had begun to fear the passion with which Gurten threw himself into proving his theories. And I could hardly leave him there in Nordcopp, knowing that he might be tempted to pick up the argument with Dr Heinrich in my absence.

'You go on to Lotingen,' I said. 'And I will come to you there.'

By the time we reached the North Gate, I had told him how to find Dittersdorf, where to contact Knutzen, and what he

274

was to say to Helena on my behalf. At that point, our ways would part. He would take the next coach to Lotingen, I would return to the coast.

'Monsieur Magistrate!'

A French voice called out my name.

'Monsieur Stiffeniis!'

Standing by the office door at the foot of the tower I saw Sergeant Tessier. He was waving his hand in the air. He might have been waving a signal-flag, but he was holding up a letter, instead.

'I've been searching for you for over an hour, monsieur,' he said, coming towards me at a trot, his plump face red, swollen with the effort, holding out the missive in front of him like an overweight Greek athlete carrying the sacred flame the last few strides to the top of the steep summit of Mount Olympus.

I took the note, turned it over, and realised immediately what had made for such a marked, servile change in his attitude towards me. The envelope had been closed with red wax, and over the seal, in a flamboyant hand, was the name *Louis-Georges Malaport.*

I broke the seal.

16th August '08.

FOR THE EYES OF MAGISTRATE STIFFENIIS ONLY.

The coach which brought this note is waiting for you. Colonel les Halles has been informed of your departure by means of the daily despatches. There is something you must see here.

L.-G.M.

'A waiting coach is mentioned here,' I said waving the paper.

'It is just outside the gate,' the sergeant pointed. 'It was sent to the coast, but Colonel les Halles said that you were here in Nordcopp.'

'Thank you for your help, Tessier,' I said.

275

For one moment, he seemed disappointed, as if he were bored and hoped that some excitement might be brewing. He had seen the name and seal of General Malaport on the note, after all. He sighed, saluted, then marched away as if he had just received a worthy commendation after a particularly arduous battle.

'Herr Stiffeniis?' Gurten appeared at my shoulder.

'A sudden change of plan,' I explained. 'I must go to Königsberg. You go on to Lotingen. I will be in touch with you soon.'

He nodded, then bowed.

'Thank you for your faith in me, sir,' he simpered.

For a moment, I thought he wished to take my hand and kiss it. We looked at each other in silence for some moments. I was perplexed, he was radiant.

'You should not be excited at the thought of hunting down a Prussian,' I reproved.

'It isn't that, sir,' he said, a warm smile on his face. 'It's just that . . . well, I did not expect to have the pleasure of making the acquaintance of Frau Helena.'

24

Königsberg Castle is a dark and gloomy place.

As the coach drew up in the shaded courtyard, my spirits drooped.

The Royal Guard had gone. Some to the grave, without a doubt, while others had thrown their death's-head shakos in a heap on the cobbles before they fled to the Tsar in Russia, or to those remote and secret hideouts where our rebels gather in the East.

In their place, a regiment of French *chasseurs* now occupied the castle courtyard. They were wearing faded blue jackets which had certainly been slashed at by Prussian sabres. Their bright red caps by contrast, being evidently new, had felt nothing sharper than the prick of a hatter's needle. These foreigners lounged upon the steps, comfortably straddled the ornamental cannon, or propped up as many door-posts as they had been able to find. Knots of them coalesced around the parade-ground, as if they had just come off duty, or were waiting to go on. Their muskets stood in upright piles like tents, the new-regulation bayonets glinting. They smoked and spat and swore out loud, jostling, pushing and shouting as if each one of them were the King of Prussia. The vast cobbled square, once the hub of ordered Prussian military life, had become a shambles. To add to the disgrace, piles of rubbish rotted and stank beneath the windows from which they had been unceremoniously tipped.

'Monsieur le Général is on the second floor,' the driver called, as I jumped down.

I ran up the broad stone staircase, well aware that the general would be anxious to hear my report. Louis-Georges Malaport had made himself at home in the city governor's apartments. At the far end of the long room, a small fire smouldered inside the baroque depths of an immense marble fireplace, the sputtering flames like a ship's lamp glimpsed in the vastness of a dark ocean. Cold enough in August, I did not like to think of that room in winter. The ceiling was almost invisible, the ogive arches lost in a permanent twilight high above my head. The walls were thick, roughly plastered, the stone floors shiny and slick with damp. Maps and standards hung from the walls, almost as heavy with age-old mould and clogged dust as the faded material from which they had been made. Three pointed windows, very tall and very narrow – the ancient stained-glass panes as cracked and opaque as the lead that fixed them – let in no light at all.

Like a desert island in that calm, cold ocean stood a vast black desk.

A silver candelabrum with a dozen tall candles gusted to no effect in the flurrying currents of chill air.

'Herr Stiffeniis,' a voice groaned from behind the mass of flickering lights.

Louis-Georges Malaport appeared to be even more thoroughly exhausted than when I had seen him last. Was it only five days before? His uniform was so weighed down with medals – I noted that he was prominently wearing that of a Commander of the Legion of Honour – he seemed to sink beneath their weight. His large bald head was more bowed than ever, his rounded shoulders more sloped, more stooping. His tiny hands were joined together, as if in supplication. Those grey eyes fixed me with their glaring intensity.

'I've been expecting you,' he said, inviting me to sit, continuing to stare at me in silence for longer than was polite, as if he expected me to blurt out everything that I had discovered.

What should I tell him? And what I should keep to myself?

Those questions had occupied my mind as I travelled to Königsberg, and tried to make sense of what I had learnt in

Nordcopp: the dead amber-gatherers, Jakob Spener's treasure, the shadowy figures of Annalise and Megrete who had stolen part of it, the rank corruption of the French soldiers, the illicit smuggling of amber of a scientific nature, the role that Erika Linder had played in the trade, my suspicions about Dr Heinrich. I had struggled to shape these elements into a convincing whole, but something always jarred, as if some vital piece of the narrative was missing. My principal aim was to demonstrate the innocence of Adam Ansbach, but the absence of any other person to accuse did not help me.

General Malaport asked me nothing, however.

He looked down, stretched out his fingers, then laid them flat on a scuffed and dirty pile of papers that were spread out before him on the table.

'These come from what remains of the police archives,' he began, pushing the documents across the table towards me. A moment later, he shifted the candelabrum as well, as if I might need it.

Could such miserable scraps have come from a Prussian police office?

'French rule was enforced here with great difficulty,' he announced, as if a general overview of the situation were somehow necessary. 'Indeed, there had been a widespread breakdown of law and order. Most of the town watch abandoned the city when our army approached, along with what remained of the Prussian garrison. In the last ten or eleven months, there have been sporadic outbreaks of looting, vandalism, the wanton destruction of public offices. Many important civic matters, together with some hideous crimes, have been obscured or overlooked in the chaos. Only now are the facts coming slowly to the light. My task, as you know, is to re-establish civil order, and guarantee the safe transport of amber back to France.'

There had been rioting in the city that winter. The grain harvest had failed for the second time since Jena. Trade with England and Russia had been hampered, as Bonaparte insisted on the adoption of his Continental System. There had been unrest in the whole of Prussia, but especially in Königsberg, where a slice of stale black bread was considered a luxury. Most families made much with a quarter-loaf where they had once made light of a whole.

'Surely the situation is now in hand?'

General Malaport pursed his lips, and frowned.

'In hand, you say? Three months ago, a mob set light to the building where the criminal files are kept,' he continued, gently massaging the bridge of his nose. 'A great deal was lost, though fortunately some material was salvaged. Including this file. It was brought to my attention just yesterday. As soon as I saw the contents, I knew that you had better read these papers, too.'

I held up what remained of the fascicle.

Three pages held together with a loop of twine. The first was a handwritten document in square, childlike German italics – full of blots, smears and crossings-out. The second appeared to have been more carefully written out by a professional hand. The last page was nothing more than a torn scrap with a scribbled note in pencil. In addition, the top page had been severely scorched, as had sections of the two underlying pages, particularly at the bottom of the second sheet, where the flames had taken hold. There was a charred diagonal line, and the words below it had all dissolved away to ashes.

'Read them,' he instructed me. The candlelight struck harshly at his harrowed cheeks. His hooded, unblinking eyes fixed on mine with the solemn intensity of a toad stranded on a water-lily.

I obeyed.

. . . on the Pregel bank beneath the . . . .
bridge. Throttled with a length of wire . . . .
. . . . no sign of interference with the skirts (she was
wearing no drawers), though there was not a . . . .
. . . . ual violence . . . .
. . . . . the lower left
forearm, and the hand were missing . . . .

.... *like an empty bag containing bones, and nothing else.*

A doctor was called to certify the dea . . .

The fragment ended there.

'A murder?'

'A murder,' he confirmed.

'This paper is not dated,' I objected.

'Read the other one,' he answered brusquely.

Again, I obeyed.

Lomse District, 26th April 1808.

<small>CRIMINAL INVESTIGATION 3/05/08 B (REF. MURDER FILE)</small>

Reporting officer's statement: The remains of another young woman were found at half past nine this morning. The corpse was blocking a drain outlet beneath the Grünen Brücke bridge, and was removed of necessity by workers from the city Water Board. It should be noted that a similar discovery was made – not fifteen feet away – beneath the very same bridge just four days ago. As in the previous case (ref. CI 3/05/08 A), the victim had been garrotted with a length of thin wire. It is not clear whether both of the murders were committed at the same time – the second corpse being overlooked on the first occasion – or whether the very same place had been chosen to dump the women's bodies on two distinct and separate occasions. Nor is it clear, given the decomposed condition of the two corpses, which of the two was the first to die . . .

'Two corpses in the same spot?' I said, holding up the paper in my trembling hand.

Had it all begun in Königsberg? Before the killing started in Nordcopp?

'Two,' he confirmed.

'Have the bodies been identified, sir?'

281

'No names are mentioned in those fragments,' Malaport admitted quietly.

Suddenly, his temper flared. 'The cleansing power of flame. We know this, and nothing more. Two women murdered a short while ago in Königsberg. There may be other corpses – previous cases, or subsequent ones – about which we still know nothing. The archives and the city records are being thoroughly examined on my specific orders, though nothing has yet emerged. The great problem is that few of our men read German, Stiffeniis. One or two from the Saar and Alsace regions are doing what they can.'

He did not move an inch, but sat as still as a snake ingesting a large prey. His eyes never left mine, nor did they blink. It was as if he were waiting for me to say something that he evidently expected me to say.

'Two dead females,' I said, and my voice sounded hard and callous, even to my own ears. 'This is nothing new in Prussia, sir. Nor, I believe, in the rest of the empire. Both of them were garrotted. And by the same hand, probably. What connection can there be with Nordcopp, if not for the fact that they met a premature death?'

I turned to the second sheet, noting that the Police in Königsberg appeared to have adopted Professor Kant's system of recording witnesses' statements. The policeman's prompts and casual observations were recorded, and every spoken word was scrupulously included in the declaration.

Doctor's interrogation: a naval surgeon living close by was immediately called to examine the body in the culvert.

Q. How did this person die?
The evidence is there for all to see, Officer. This creature died as the result of strangulation by a means of a tight ligature binding around her throat. That rusty wire did for her, I shouldn't wonder. It is still there, and quite impossible to undo. Her eyes and her tongue are popping out.

Q. How long has she been dead?

How long, sir? I can give you no close estimate of how long she may have been left to rot in this here culvert. From two days to a week. Two weeks, perhaps. The outer tissue of the corpse, the skin covering her body – here and here, can you see? – has largely fallen away. Comes off in strips and patches, it does. The whole thing is riddled with maggots, worms, and the like. Decomposition accelerates to a marked degree when quantities of bilge water are present, I've observed at sea. This corpse was found in the main city drain, remember, sir, so there's the contents of that drain to take into account as well. Mainly organic and faecal matter. Can't you smell it?

Observation: a small eel wriggled out of the corpse's nose to everyone's surprise.

Apart from the general decay, there is more evident damage to the upper left arm, which hangs as an open flap around the bones, and an even more profound cavity in the area of the left shoulder. The tensor muscle and the bone of the scapula are nowhere to be found. Which does not amaze me. Such severe, localised damage is caused, as a rule, by animal scavengers. Starving dogs and rats are plentiful here by the docks, and if that shoulder were sticking out from the drain, that is where they would attack it . . .

'Who was this doctor?' I asked.

'I cannot say,' Malaport replied. 'The police in Königsberg never name the doctor, surgeon or dentist who is called to inspect a corpse, unless the case is brought to trial in a law-court . . .'

This was another one of Professor Kant's innovations. It served, he said, to protect the identity of the professional witness from intimidation by anyone else who happened to be involved in the eventual criminal proceedings.

'This case never got to court,' the general concluded.

'Have you any idea who compiled the notes?' I asked him. 'Surely the policeman would know the name of the doctor?'

General Malaport sniffed loudly. 'If there was a signature, Stiffeniis,' he said, 'it went up in smoke. I doubt that any Prussian policeman would own up to having written it, especially now that the French authorities are taking an interest in the case. The same thing goes for the doctor. You might start your enquiries on that count, of course.'

I was already making enquiries in my own head.

Had I found Annalise and Megrete?

Two women murdered in the port area. The amber-trading district was close by, just on the other side of the Grünen Brücke bridge. Was that what the two women were doing there? Selling off the amber they had stolen the month before from the Church of the Saviour in Nordcopp? Was that why they had been murdered in Königsberg? And had the killer then retraced the girls' steps to Nordcopp in the hope of finding more amber of the sort that they had been offering?

Malaport was talking on, regardless of me.

'To my mind, the similarities seemed striking. With what is happening out on the coast, I mean to say. Even to a rough old soldier like myself, who is more at home with maps and provisions and the daily running of the garrison. I could not avoid making a direct deduction. That's why I sent for you.'

'You are convinced that it is the work of the same killer,' I said, having already come to the same conclusion.

'Can it *not* be?' he replied more forcefully. 'You have been investigating those more recent murders on the coast, Stiffeniis. In both those cases, the victim was a young woman. In both cases, the corpse was interfered with after death. That is, the body was purposely mutilated. And certainly not attacked by rats or dogs! Here in Königsberg, too, some part of the body had been removed and carried off for reasons that we can only guess at.'

I was impressed by what he said.

I had never considered the act of mutilation as the prime objective of the crime. General Malaport proposed that the mutilation was an end in itself. He had, so to speak, turned the case on its head.

'Clearly,' he continued, 'the murderer selects his victim on the basis of a particular anatomical detail which he appears to covet. Having quickly despatched the woman, this heartless butcher then possesses himself of the physical item in question. Sex does not come into it.'

He stopped and peered at me for some moments in silence.

'What do you make of it, sir?' I asked.

'What do *you* make of it, Stiffeniis?'

I was thinking of Dr Heinrich in Nordcopp.

I saw the moulds and braces, the artificial limbs that he made, hanging on his surgery wall. The drawings he had made. Heinrich was interested in the mechanics of the human body. I remembered Gurten's ire and the hypothesis that he had advanced: that the doctor's avidity for amber containing animal insertions knew no limits. Was anatomy, then, what truly interested him? And would he go to the trouble of securing examples of the bones and joints that were his livelihood by committing murder?

'This person is interested in human anatomy,' I replied. 'Female anatomy.'

On hearing this, a trace of a smile seemed to settle on his lips.

'Herr Procurator,' he said, his eyes shifting to the paper in my hand. 'Read on to the very end.'

I turned my attention to the third and final sheet of paper.

Scrawled with a blunt stub of graphite pencil on rough brown paper, the handwriting sloped riotously away to the right in a downward slant. I had to turn the note this way and that to catch the light, and I moved it even closer to the candle on more than one occasion to make it out at all.

'It is the list of a watchman,' General Malaport explained.

We had spoken French all the while. Did he know German, too? Had he read the papers for himself, or had some more qualified person told him what the documents contained?

19.00. Started out checking workshops in the Königstrasse district.

20.30 Robbery reported in the butcher's shop in Zeebruggestrasse. Two sides of beef and several strings of sausages removed. Proprietor to make a statement tomorrow.

22.50. Three persons stopped on the Grünen Brücke bridge – two women and a man. Rowdy behaviour. The women were shouting drunk. The man was not. The women's papers were in order, as were his. Sent them on their way, telling them to make less noise. The man sneered something as he turned away. I took his name and gave him a further warning. Flighty fellow. Gave his name as Herr Vulpius . . .

'Vulpius,' I said out loud. 'This is the first name that we have come across.'

As my eyes fell upon the smoke-darkened page once more, a most surprising fact caught and held my attention. When questioned by the officer, Vulpius had described himself in a way that was at once bland, yet terribly disconcerting. Bland in the opinion of a humble policeman who was probably uneducated beyond being able to read and write, and who appeared to make nothing of the declaration uttered for his benefit.

Vulpius's description was most disconcerting to myself, however.

My eyes seemed to burn another hole in the page as I studied the line in question.

Herr Vulpius describes himself as a scholar, a follower of Manual Cant.

Had the name of Herr Professor Immanuel Kant, once so famous throughout the world, dwindled so quickly into the twilight of the past? Evidently, the name meant nothing to the officer who had written it down and made two crass mistakes in just as many words.

Was Vulpius studying at the university in Königsberg? And what exactly did he mean when he spoke so determinedly of himself as a follower of Kant?

'Herr Stiffeniis?'

I heard my name called out again.

Looking up, I saw the puzzled frown on the general's rugged face.

'Is something troubling you?' he asked.

'I was simply wondering whether anyone has managed to speak to this man.'

Malaport shrugged his narrow shoulders. 'I was short of soldiers when I came here. Not a day passes, but I lose some more. The Königsberg garrison is being cut back to a bare skeleton. The war in the Peninsula, as you know, is taking its toll on our resources. You'll have to find him for yourself, I'm afraid.'

General Malaport settled more comfortably into his chair.

Resting his elbow on the desk, he stroked his narrow chin and stared at me.

'So, tell me, Stiffeniis. How do you intend to proceed?'

25

My memories of Königsberg were stark.

The images fixed most clearly in my mind were black and white.

Four years earlier, late one afternoon in February 1804, I had taken the same route in a coach with Sergeant Amadeus Koch. As we were driven along the quay towards the Baltic Whaler inn, snow was falling heavily. Gale-force winds rocked the vehicle on its leather springs like a flurry of hard punches. Solid ice imprisoned every barge and lighter, every fishing-boat and three-master confined within the narrow harbour. No ship entered Königsberg, or left it. Nothing moved on the quay, apart from our coach. No man worked on ship, or on shore. The warehouses were all locked and barred. The city was suffering the worst winter in over a century.

Everything had changed for the better.

I could not deny it: the French had wrought the change. My eyes, ears and nose confirmed the opinion. The quay was as busy as an ant-hill. Dock labourers bounded up and down the wooden gang-planks to the moored ships. They charged in and out of holds and storerooms, heaving boxes, barrels and sacks on their backs – not a man was idle. The sky was a bright cerulean blue; harmless pink clouds sat on the rim of the horizon like billiard-balls against the bottom cushion. The sea was also blue, though of a darker, altogether greener hue, its surface crisped and crinkled by a gentle breeze that promised wind-filled sails and swift navigation.

No contrast with the past could have been sharper.

The French demanded industry and efficiency. The Baltic Sea provided them.

Wherever I looked, I saw what was expected. Ships coming and going, as the companies required, as the merchants requested, as the captains who sailed those vessels with their bulging holds held dear. It was as if every individual action was well thought out, full of purpose and utility, promising a handsome profit to the commonwealth.

A similar sense of purpose possessed me, though I was not so sure that I would reach the destination I had set for myself. I had asked General Malaport about the amber trade before I left him. What interested me more than anything else was the means by which Prussian amber was transported to France.

He regarded me with surprise for a moment, but then he replied, as if such avid curiosity on my part were entirely natural. 'Nothing has changed very much,' he said with an open-armed gesture. 'Prussia used the sea, and so do we. At least, within the Baltic basin. The British are blockading the straits of Denmark, but that is hardly my concern. The amber reaches Königsberg – from Nordcopp, let us say – and having been worked to the required standard, it is loaded onto a schooner which will carry it along the coast to Danzig. From there, land transport to Paris, though slower and more costly, is the safest way.'

Suddenly, his eyes narrowed with suspicion.

'What does the movement of amber have to do with anything?'

I groped for an answer that might make sense to him.

'I was wondering about the commercial ties that exist between Nordcopp and Königsberg, Herr General,' I replied. 'We know for certain that Prussian women have been murdered in both places. Those killed in Königsberg may have been involved in the amber business here. As was the case in Nordcopp. That's what I was thinking. Is it the amber industry which ties the crimes together?'

I chose the word 'industry' with care, then I asked another question, as if it were a logical consequence of the first.

'Does amber of particular interest arrive in Königsberg as well?'

'What d'you mean by that?' he enquired, looking like a hungry infant who had just lost sight of the spoon and his pap.

'Pieces which contain things provoking curiosity,' I said. 'Small creatures, tiny insects, plant fragments, and so forth. They have fallen out of favour with the jewellers, it seems, though scientists throughout Europe show no sign of waning enthusiasm. Where would such unusual pieces go, sir, before being sent to Paris? I mean to say, they must be separated out from the general commerce somewhere.'

I did not mention the convention drawn up between Berlin and Paris.

Nor did he.

Indeed, I wondered whether he knew of its existence.

His large head wobbled on his shrivelled neck. 'Procurator Stiffeniis! Is a general of the high command supposed to know every detail involved in the transportation and the commerce of amber? I see that you are disappointed. I cannot say what happens to it. Frankly, I do not care. I know that amber arrives from the various sorting-stations, and that it is distributed to the local workshops which we rigidly control. We don't receive as much as *we* – by which I mean myself and Colonel les Halles – would like, but measures are being taken on that account, as you know. Amber arrives each day, and a few days later – a week at the most – it is ready to be shipped. Then, like any other commodity, it is taken to the port. We run a regular ferrying service aboard armed gunboats. I can tell you nothing more precise than that.'

He stared at me again in that disconcerting manner that he had. Then, a sudden smile erupted on his toad-like face. 'Come sir, this apparently innocuous question about the transportation of amber – special pieces, and so on, and so forth – that's not what you really wished to ask. There is a different "merchandise" down at the port which needs to be "transported", so to speak. Am I not correct, Herr Procurator Stiffeniis?'

I had no idea what he was talking about.

He shrugged. 'I suppose that you Prussians have your own secret sources of information. You are a magistrate, after all. We watch you, but you watch us, as well.' He breathed out noisily through his nostrils. 'Very well, then. The murder suspects that les Halles sent up from Nordcopp are being held at the port, as you correctly surmised. They will be transported aboard the next available convict ship. They are destined for the labour camps.' He sat back, and waved his hand dismissively in the air. 'I will not condemn them to death without more substantial proof of guilt. The discovery of the file relating to those corpses here in Königsberg counsels prudence. The boy has been spared an imminent meeting with the hangman, but only on that account.'

As he spoke, he slid open a drawer in his desk.

'Adam Ansbach's file is still open,' he said, waving it at me. 'I cannot ignore the fact that a mutilated body was found in his pigsty in Nordcopp. Nor can I forget that other human bones were buried in the same ground. If he should prove to be the guilty party, I will not hesitate to do my duty.'

I sat up straight.

'Colonel les Halles sent those people here to you, sir, without waiting to hear what an expert witness would make of the bones,' I protested. 'Dr Heinrich, the surgeon in Nordcopp, assures me that they are ancient. No living member of the Ansbach family had been born at the time the bones were buried.'

'But they were living on the farm when the corpse was discovered. Is that not correct, Herr Procurator Stiffeniis?'

I mumbled something to the effect that his statement of the facts was accurate, though I had grave doubts about the identity of the murderer.

'Can you offer me a more likely candidate for the noose?'

'I cannot,' I admitted. 'For the moment, anyway.'

'Furthermore,' he said, looking over the papers in the file, 'I am bound to act on the consequence of what has happened since. Magda Ansbach', he specified, reading out the name, 'bit off the ear of one of the guards while under custody. Her son then attacked the guard in defence of his mother.'

He blew out noisily, vibrating his lips at the immensity of the crime.

'What else can I do? Forced labour is letting them off lightly.'

'I suppose you have no choice in the matter,' I conceded.

'None.'

'And if I wished to speak to them?'

'You would not be allowed within a mile of them,' General Malaport continued. 'Still, I did appoint you to conduct this investigation, Stiffeniis, so I must forget that you are a Prussian, and tell you what I would be reluctant to tell my own men. You want to know where they are being held, I suppose?'

'I know where deported convicts are collected,' I replied, unable to suppress a smile. 'It is a secret to no one in Königsberg.' I was thinking of the ruined warehouse in the outlying district of Pillau, which I had visited four years before. I had gone there to speak to a murderer who was about to be deported to the wastes of Siberia. The cold, the squalor and the violence of that night could still provoke an involuntary shiver.

General Malaport returned my smile, but shook his head.

'Do not assume that we are careless, sir,' he warned me. 'Nothing here is as it was. We must be on our guard against those nationalists who continue to plague our efforts. The news from Spain is fanning the Prussian rebels' flame ever higher. Those condemned to labour camps are dry straw added to a fire. It could blow up into a raging inferno, unless we douse it quickly.' He beat his fist three times on the table as if to extinguish a spark. 'I will allow you access to the area where the deportees are kept. I can do no more for you. Whatever else you wish to do, whatever else you hope to learn there,

Herr Procurator, you must do it on your own initiative. Silence and discretion are the key words.'

Half an hour later, I found it easier to enter the military section of the harbour than General Malaport had led me to expect. A soldier standing guard at the gates seemed far more interested in the bread and sardines that a pretty wench was offering him from a covered basket than he was in the *laissez-passer* that I surrendered up for his scrutiny.

'Berodstein's warehouse?' I asked.

'Down by the harbour light,' he mumbled, his eyes half on his lunch, half on the woman.

I folded up the general's note and began to walk along the quay.

According to the information that I had gleaned from Malaport, three ships would be sailing out of Königsberg that day. A sleek black cutter had just cast off from the sea-wall. It was being manoeuvred out into midstream with the assistance of two long-boats, each manned by six men working the oars. It was a warship of some sort, armed with cannon fore and aft, a line of grappling hooks hanging over the rail. A huge *tricolore* waved defiantly from the stern-pole, making it impossible for me to spy out the name of the vessel.

I walked on, making careful observation of what was going on beside the ships which were still being loaded. The larger of the two, *L'Eugénie*, was a square-sailed brigantine, while the smaller vessel – her large triangular sails flapping idly in the breeze – was an armed schooner of the type that General Malaport had mentioned. I was unable to read her name or port of origin. The name-plates on the prow and stern had been tarred over. A sizeable cargo of Prussian amber was destined to be carried off that day by the French, it seemed, and all in the name of war-reparation.

I stopped to let a cart pass, stepping carefully around another wagon which the labourers were unloading. Wooden packing-cases slid down a plank onto the cobbles for the waiting hands which would carry them aboard the ships once the teller had counted off the number against his bill of lading. Glancing at the boxes piled up on the quay, I saw that many bore addresses in Paris, most of them in the area around Place Vendôme. I had been to Paris, I knew that this was where the great majority of the Parisian jewellers had their workshops. I did not see a single crate for the Royal Academy of Science, the Society for the Encouragement of Industry, nor any other scientific institution inside or outside the French capital.

I tried to imagine the fortune that those boxes must contain.

Halting beside a very large man in a leather apron – a Prussian overseer whose loud voice marked him out – I thrust my *laissez-passer* into his hand.

'Which way is Berodstein's warehouse?' I asked him.

'Straight on, sir.'

'Are these ships full of amber?' I murmured.

'All of them,' he replied in an undertone, glancing warily at a French sergeant sitting on an iron mooring-bollard a short distance away. 'All that's left in Prussia now is shit,' he hissed.

Had he been to Lotingen and seen the streets, I wondered.

I saw the sign painted on the side of a large wooden shed at the end of the dock. It was written in English: FABIEN BERODSTEIN – PRECIOUS HARDWOOD EXPORTS.

No English ship was tied up on the wharf, of course. I could only imagine them sitting somewhere out beyond the visible horizon, tracing out with their prows the liquid barrier that the French had hoped to impose on them, and which, instead, now confined the French to a narrow, navigable coastal strip. Of course, Herr Berodstein might sell his precious woods to France, but his trade did not appear to be brisk. Indeed, the sight of a band of armed French infantrymen standing by the doorway suggested that the trade in exportable hardwoods had ground entirely to a halt.

They were a prison detail, and I was obliged to show the paper signed by General Malaport before I was allowed to enter what was, in effect, a prison. To my surprise, however, the warehouse contained no French soldiers.

'Fabien Berodstein. Born in Alsace of a Prussian father. Half French, half German,' Malaport had informed me, reading from a paper. 'Almost bankrupted by the British blockade. Provides space and surveillance for criminal deportees waiting out on the quay. He would have built a hardwood gallows for Prussian rebels, if that was what we had asked him for. Whether he helps you or not will depend on which of his national souls prevails today.'

That day, Berodstein decided to play the Prussian. Especially when I told him that I was a magistrate. He glanced at the note, then glanced at me.

'What can I do for you, Herr Stiffeniis?'

A stained leather notebook lay before him on the table, next to a lighted lantern. Despite the bright sunlight outside on the quay, it was as dark as Hades in there.

'I want to know when the prisoners will be transported.'

His face was waxy yellow in the light of burning whale-oil.

Two younger men emerged from the shadows as I spoke. They took up places like sentries just beyond his shoulders. They did not speak, and looked to me like twins – of equal height, the same narrow build, their faces dark and harrowed like shrivelled apples from the same bitter tree. They stood behind their master like well-trained guard-dogs, watching me sullenly.

'The ships are expected any time,' he said, and looked towards the door, as if he expected the captains of the vessels to appear before him that very instant.

He shrugged, and peered into the dark interior of his warehouse.

Pale faces pressed against the metal bars of a door.

'They've been here since yesterday,' he said without prompting.

As my eyes grew accustomed to the gloom – the blazing sun outside was as far away and forgotten as the celestial planet was from the Earth – I saw the careworn faces, the curious eyes staring out at me. Perhaps it was the echoing sound of Prussian voices that drew their attention. Perhaps they thought that I had come for them.

The prisoners themselves did not make a sound.

The warehouse had been divided in two distinct halves by a high wall of rough-hewn planks with the metal gate in the centre. On this side, there were stacks of hardwood trunks, others of sweeter-smelling Scandinavian pine, waiting, I presumed, for the departure or defeat of the French, and a return to normalcy before Herr Berodstein would order them to be cut. On the other side, through the narrow aperture of the gate, I saw a crowd of men and women sitting in groups upon the wooden floor, or stretching out disconsolately on ancient tree-trunks, waiting for Destiny to take them where it might. The atmosphere was muggy, heavy, odoriferous, a dense concentration of sap and seasoning wood, musty sea and salt, the faecal stench that wretches left in their filth, and without a change of clothes or air, might provoke. Was there a latrine on the other side of the wall? Was there a place to wash? As I looked, a rat came running along the top of the barricade. Piss, shit, poor food, vermin, close confinement, abundant filth. Unless the ships came soon, the number to deport would quickly start to fall.

'How many are you holding?' I asked.

'Two hundred, more or less,' he said. 'From all the gaols in East Prussia.'

'Where are they bound?'

Berodstein closed his leather notebook with a clap.

The heads of his helpers snapped sharply in the direction of the sound.

Neither moved an inch. They stood stiffly at his shoulders, and seemed to quiver with the effort. Their eyes met mine, their nostrils flared. They looked from me to him, then back again, staring with the fixity of terriers, waiting only for a word from their master before they tore me to shreds.

'Where are they going?' I said more sharply, rapping my knuckles on the table.

'Abroad,' he muttered, opening his book, flicking carelessly through the pages.

He was fifty years old, I would have said. His face was the same pale colour as the Scandinavian wood that he sold. His hair was thick and white, delicately streaked with blond swaths, tied up in a bow.

'When are they leaving?'

His gaze was fixed unflinchingly on the barred door, and the silent prisoners.

How did he keep them quiet? I wondered.

'*La Pléiade*,' he read. 'Out of Hamburg. Should be here today. They'll go where she goes. My job's to load them on the ship, and make sure they don't cause any bother. I have no say about the route . . .'

A howl of pain cut through the air.

Berodstein leapt up, his chair scraped loudly on the floor. The notebook fell, as he reached for the lantern. Then, he was gone, racing round his desk, muttering wildly. The twins went trotting at his heels without a sound.

'Easy, my lads,' he snarled over his shoulder, snatching up a stick, striking it against the bars, holding off the mastiffs with his other hand. 'There, there,' he said, looking through the bars, reassured by what he saw. 'Everything's as it should be. Come! Keep an eye on them, while I finish with the gentleman.'

'Are your charges troublesome?' I enquired.

No one had asked for so much as a drop of water. No one had protested about the way that they were kept, nor about the prospect of their imminent deportation to an unspecified destination.

Berodstein sat down. 'Call yourself a magistrate, do you, sir?' he chortled, looking at me with a puzzled frown. 'Königsberg's full of patriotic scum. A hot-bed of rebellion, if you ask me. More troublemakers here than rats. And the port is worse than all the rest together.'

'Are the prisoners the only thing you handle?' I asked obliquely. 'Unsold wood apart, I mean.'

'What else would there be?' he replied, lifting up the lantern, shining it into my face, as if my question had excited his curiosity. 'After something special, are you? You can find a bit of anything here on the docks.'

'Quality amber,' I said, keeping my voice low.

'Got some strange ideas, you have, Magistrate,' Berodstein replied, his stare more hostile than before. He snapped his fingers, and the two boys quietly appeared at his side, their eyes fixed immovably on me. 'That job belongs to the Frenchies,' he added dryly. 'They guard it and load it and ship it themselves. Don't need help from me. Not so far, anyways. You work for them, it seems. You should know what they are like.'

I attempted a bold smile.

'I am engaged in private enquiries of my own,' I admitted conspiratorially. 'There may be Prussian amber that takes a road that does *not* lead directly to the French wharf. Special amber. Amber that the French send somewhere else . . .'

'You're on the wrong road,' Berodstein interrupted rudely. 'If you want to know about amber, ask the French. Or the jewellers out in Kneiphof. I have heard there's plenty knocking about down there. And a lot of it the French don't know about.'

He lowered his lantern, rested it on the table.

'Now, sir, if there's nothing else, me and my lads have got things to do before that ship gets in.'

'Are they your sons?' I asked, hoping to prolong the conversation.

The sound that came from the throats of the twins made my hair stand up on my head. There is a wild dog in Africa, I have read, that makes a sort of bestial howl that has been mistaken for human laughter. Herr Berodstein looked at this brace of young hyenas, then burst out laughing with them.

'Ain't never shagged no she-wolf, me,' he said roughly. 'She was mother to 'em. Who the father was, I cannot say! I found them in Siberia ten years back. I was up there buying prize wood for the Brits. Saw these eyes peering out at me from behind a juniper bush. And nearly lost a thumb just catching them. I brought them home, but God knows where they came from. I don't need no whips to keep the peace, sir, not with them two. Deportees, nationalists, thieves, it's all the same to them.'

He pushed the general's letter across the table, as if to say that the interview was over.

'I want to speak to one of the prisoners,' I objected.

'Request reluctantly refused,' he said, beating his clenched fist on his chest. It was the Frenchman coming out in him, I suppose. His lips pursed tightly, he rolled his 'r's, aspirating his 'e's like an Aeolian harp, though he was speaking German. 'No one talks to no one here. Forbidden! Those are the rules! The French were clear on that account. There are rebels in the midst of this lot. If there's trouble here on the dock, I'll lose my warehouse. I want them quiet, and I want them orderly. They know it to their cost.'

'I have General Malaport's permission,' I insisted, waving the paper at him.

My appeal to French authority failed dismally.

'I do not think you have, Herr Procurator.' The words thundered from his lips. 'That note says you can come in here and ask me about the prisoners. *My* prisoners, I repeat. Now, I've told you what you want to know, and there's an end of it. You'll not speak to any man. Not while I'm in charge of them. They're my responsibility while they stay on Prussian soil. I won't have riots. I won't have Spain breaking out in the port of Königsberg. Not if I can help it.'

His words were wild, but what came next was wilder. He was on his feet in an instant, lantern in hand, rushing to the barred gate in a fury, calling for me to follow, shouting at his lads to bring me if they had to.

I did not linger, feeling their hot breath on my collar.

'Just look at them!' Berodstein exploded, wiggling his finger angrily, inviting me to step up to the gate and see what he was looking at, holding up his light to aid me.

I heard the sharp intake of the twins' breath.

Wounded prisoners were stretched out on the floor. Those crushing close to the door pulled back like a widening ripple where a stone has landed in a still lake. I searched the frightened faces for a glimpse of Adam Ansbach, but I did not see him.

The stench which entered my mouth and nostrils was like a physical blow.

Berodstein dropped his lantern closer to the ground, pointing. 'There, sir,' he said. 'Look at that one! That's a Prussian rebel, that is.'

I squatted down, the better to see the man that he was indicating.

His face was deathly pale above bruised eyes. His cheeks and chin were stained dark red with coagulating gore. Where blood still flowed, it gleamed more brightly. He had been severely beaten. The tip of his nose was hanging on by a strip of skin, nothing more. His lips were black – crushed, torn and mangled. Streams of froth dribbled from the corners of his mouth and flowed down his jaw. Each time he breathed, red bubbles blew out of his mouth. His head lolled, and I glimpsed a hole in his cheek. The edges were serrated, ragged, the teeth showing through.

'Pretty, ain't he?' Berodstein sneered.

Suddenly, the man collapsed. His face fell with a sharp crack into a large metal bowl. His hands were tied to the wall. If he was going to fall, that was where he would land. Over a bowl of dirty water.

'He's in the shit, so to speak,' Berodstein laughed.

The animals behind me began to howl.

As the man gasped for air, I saw the horrid traces of brown slime on his skin.

'That's where they piss and shit,' said Berodstein.

Suddenly, he was shouting at the other prisoners. 'If I catch you doing it anywhere else, you bastards, you'll get the same treatment!'

'What crime has he committed?' I asked.

'He was talking,' Berodstein snarled, as if it were obvious. 'Talking to the other prisoners. I will not have it! I set my boys on him, I did. They've got their mother's teeth. Most terrible weapons, that's what they are.'

As he spoke, he patted one of the twins affectionately on the shoulder. Like a jealous hound, the other one pushed his brother aside, seeking equal favour from their master.

'They smell rebellion, sir. Don't like it any more than I do. I had to drag them off. They'd have killed him otherwise. There's always one or two that won't be told. Born rebellious, they are. I spot them, and I set my boys on them. It keeps the others in their place. By the time the ship comes in, these Prussian scabs will be glad to get away from here, wherever they're sent.'

It came to me in a flash.

I slid my hand inside my bag, grasped the rolled-up bundle of papers lying at the bottom. I pulled them out, and waved them in his face.

'Your secret's out, I'm afraid,' I said.

Berodstein's eyes flashed wide with alarm.

'What are they, sir?'

They were the seditious handbills Gurten had brought from Lotingen, the ones naming me as a collaborator of the French, damning me as a traitor. I did not tell him the contents, obviously.

'General Malaport must be warned of the danger,' I lied. 'He must read for himself what is written here. Your beasts have attracted attention. Our nationalists have got it in for you. You're on their target-list, I'm afraid, Herr Berodstein. I'd look about most carefully when you leave this place tonight.'

'Me, sir?'

'They say they'll do to you what you have done to them!' I said, pointing in the direction of the prisoners with the scroll of papers.

'Where did you find those sheets, sir?'

His face had drained of colour. His boys began to whimper at the sight of him. I could not see their ears beneath their long black hair, but would have sworn that they were flattened against their skulls, the way dogs do when danger threatens.

'Hanging outside your door,' I said. 'The rebels know what goes on here. They have decided where to start their own *guerrilla* war in Königsberg.'

There was no need for me to say more. Berodstein's hand was on his heart. He opened and closed his mouth, but not a word came out. His Siberian 'hounds' stood close together, eyes fixed on the father who had rescued them from the wilds and generously brought them back to civilisation.

'Regarding General Malaport,' I said, 'there's one thing in my power to do.'

'What's that, sir?' Berodstein spluttered.

'I may not tell him,' I said. 'It all depends on you.'

'Me, sir?'

I let him think on it for a moment only. No repressive measures would be taken by the French against him, his boys, or his warehouse. Prussian prisoners would continue to go to the convict ships, and he would still be paid.

'Give me the passenger-list,' I snapped.

Berodstein swiped up his notebook from the table, his expression as black as coal.

'Here, sir. This is it.'

'Show me the page. Hold it up!'

'It's this one, sir.'

I ran my finger down the list.

'*Magda Ansbach*,' I read out loud.

'Canal-digging down in Hook of Holland,' he said. 'As I said, she's going out today on *La Pléiade* . . .'

'Where is the son?' I asked him, speaking between clenched teeth. 'Adam Ansbach. They were supposed to be deported together.'

'Next page. Got another boat due in tomorrow. *Le Petit Caporal* out of . . .'

'Where is she bound?' I asked.

'French Indies, sir.'

I handed back the book.

'Cancel out the name of Adam Ansbach,' I said, watching carefully as he sat himself down at his desk, slid upon a drawer, took out a jar of ink and a mangy quill, and began to do so.

'Write Adam's name on the list of *La Pléiade*.'

Berodstein raised his eyes to mine.

'These are official orders. Changing names on the lists is a punishable crime, sir.'

'Do it.' I waved my papers at him.

He took a deep breath, then he obeyed.

He reached inside the drawer again, took out a pot of sand and sprinkled it over the ink. He wheezed hot breath onto the page, then shook the sand away, and handed me the book.

'They'll go out together, if the wind holds fair,' he said.

I held up the roll of handbills up, grasping them in my fists.

Piece by piece, fragment by fragment, I began to rip them up, cancelling my own name, cancelling out the names of my wife and babies, the threats which had been aimed at us. When not one readable bit remained, I threw the pieces into the air.

They fell to the floor like flakes of dirty snow.

26

'Go to Kneiphof,' Berodstein had said.

How many times in my life had I heard that phrase?

The very first time, I was still a very young child. No more than five or six years old, playing hide-and-seek with my brother, Stefan, I had taken refuge beneath the table in the kitchen when I overheard a conversation.

'You tell him to go to Kneiphof!' the housemaid squealed with laughter.

'That rogue don't know where Kneiphof is!' the chamber-maid grumbled.

I asked my father what they meant.

'Kneiphof, Hanno?' he replied brusquely. 'You'll learn soon enough.'

General Wagramberg's wife explained the riddle some weeks later. While taking tea and biscuits with my mother, she chucked me playfully under the chin. 'God bless me, Hanno,' she said with a smile, 'you *are* growing. It won't be long before you're charging off to Kneiphof.'

I asked her what she meant.

'It's a popular saying in Königsberg,' she laughed. 'A man goes to Kneiphof to purchase a pledge for a person that he holds very dear. From the jewellery shops. Which signifies that he is about to be engaged. It means that he intends to marry, and eventually become a father.'

It is an old Prussian tradition. The matrimonial pledge is a setting of fine Baltic amber. My mother had an elaborate *complet* – necklace, pendant, earrings and bracelets – that my father gave her when he proposed. The amber gems were large, translucent, smooth, round. The gift was from a shop in Kneiphof. The tradesman's name was impressed in the blue silk lining of the jewellery-case. But for the life of me, I could not remember it.

I had bought Helena a diamond ring when I proposed to her, instead. It came from the shop of a noted merchant in the city of Hamburg: three rose-cuts, one quite large, and two flanking smaller brilliants. Helena was overjoyed when I presented her with the box, though surprised when she opened it.

'A clean break with outmoded tradition, Hanno,' she said ironically, smiling as she slipped the ring onto the middle finger of her left hand.

We were married three months later.

I walked across the Kramerbrücke bridge to the leafy isle of Kniephof, which is the oldest part of Königsberg. The buildings there are made of crumbling wattle and timber for the most part. In that location, Leonard Euler posed his famous puzzle relating to the seven bridges which link the island to the city: could one cross them all in turn without crossing the same bridge twice?

I was thinking of a different problem as I stepped off the bridge.

The puzzle which tormented me was always the same: illegal amber, amber containing insects, the women who died transporting it, the person who had murdered them. Nordcopp, Nordbarn, Königsberg. How did all the pieces fit together?

I turned left on the cobbled quay, my mother's amber treasure again in my thoughts.

What was the jeweller's name?

The town across the water was a delightful vision, despite the damage to the castle caused the previous year by the French bombardment. And Kniephof was a tranquil spot – few people about, though it was a warm, balmy evening. The sun was low and slanting, the river-bank was tree-lined, it was cool in the shade. The castle bells struck five, but I was reassured by that. Our shops rarely close before six or seven in the evening. Long shadows stretched out from the shops by the waterside.

They were jewellers' shops. All of them.

I walked along the row, glancing in at the windows, looking up at the signs.

My thoughts returned to Nordcopp. Much of the amber in these shops had come from that shore. It was stained with the blood of Kati Rodendahl and Ilse Bruen. Tainted with the sights and the smells of the coast where they had worked. Behind each polished cabochon, I saw the mangled face of Hilde Bruckner, labouring over her grindstone. Each flash of light from those glistening amber jewels was like forked lightning striking the sea, reflecting the fear in the eyes of Edviga Lornerssen, who risked her life every time she prodded the pebbles with her stick, or reached too far with her heavy net. And deep inside those stones, at the very heart of them, lay the secret of the man who was butchering the women.

Klaus Flugge & Son.

I halted.

That was the name inside my mother's presentation case.

The shop was small, the window bowed, the mullions sagging out like tired knees. Honeycomb panes of glass, as round as wine-bottles, were grey with age. Two flickering candlesticks flanked a blue cloth. On this dark field, amber had been laid out on display. A double row of oval beads with a gold clasp, the centre piece carved as a cameo. Little wooden trees held earrings *en girandole*, dangling amber grapes. Before the war, the style was much in vogue. Helena possessed a beautiful pair made up of clustered amethysts and pearls. We had been obliged to trade them for a sack of flour and some pork chops not long after Jena.

No amethysts or pearls for Flugge & Son.

Every jewel in the window was amber, as if they cared for nothing else. The range of colours was vast: pale yellow, dark red, streaked orange, intense chocolate brown, and every shade in between. I peered more closely at the goods on display, looking for a fern, a leaf, some trace of animal or insect life. There was not one relic of the Garden of Eden in that window.

I pushed the narrow door, and a bell clinked.

Two ruffled heads bobbed behind the counter. One white, the other dark brown. Two men bent over a pewter tray containing beads of amber. They looked up as I closed the door. Left eyes pinched tight closed, their right eyes took stock of me by means of a metal tube like a miniature cannon. A tight metal band held these instruments of torture to their heads.

'Am I disturbing you?' I enquired.

Like a pair of showmen in the theatre, they simultaneously pushed these cannons onto their brows, and smiled in welcome. I might have been viewing two portraits of the same person made at a distance of a generation. Their faces were of a type, but vigour, colour and animation were absent from the face of the younger man. The old man's hair was thick and wiry, dark as teak. Clear grey eyes peered keenly out of deep, dark sockets. Bushy eyebrows, a strong nose and large mouth denoted character, the ability to smile and encourage, or to issue a sharp rebuke. The son's portrait was the pale ghost of his father's, as if the artist had failed to assert what he intended to show.

'Come in, sir. You are most welcome,' the older man said.

They were dressed like matching funeral busts in a country chapel: a black blouse, a white collar that was stiff and high, white gloves on account of the precious material they were handling. And that strange optical headwear.

'Herr Flugge?' I asked. I smiled and added: 'And *son*, of course.'

'How may I help you, sir?' the old man asked.

'Amber, naturally,' I said, pointing at the mound on the tray.

Those stones had been polished until they shone like rubies. I imagined them passing through the hands of Pastoris, being honed to a polish by his crippled girls. Now, they were about to be selected, modelled and set by the gloved hands of Herr

Flugge and his son. Afterwards, they would go into the window, or be displayed on the shelves behind the counter, the value rarefied by the velvet pads and red morocco cases in which they would be sold. Then, a well-heeled man would come along, and the jewel would go to the lady who was waiting for it, the sweetheart to whom it had been promised, according to General Wagramberg's wife.

Flugge Senior picked up the tray and rolled the amber beads around. 'They were brought this morning,' he said. 'We've not seen such a crop in a long while. It has been an excellent season on the coast.'

'Excellent,' the son echoed, his glove moving in a slow sweep over the goods, an unhappy smile traced on his face.

'Unforgettable,' I added, thinking of the mutilated corpses that I had seen in Nordcopp, and the others I had read about in the reports which General Malaport had shown me.

'My father came here many years ago,' I said.

'What is your father's name, sir?' the old man asked.

'Stiffeniis,' I replied. 'Ignatius Stiffeniis . . .'

'Of Ruisling,' he said quickly. 'I remember all my good customers. How is your good father, sir?'

'Well enough,' I lied, not mentioning that my father had died in 1804.

'Father has an excellent memory,' the young man said.

'It must be almost forty years ago. I was working for my own father then,' Herr Klaus continued. 'Now, my son, Paulus, works for me. The wheel comes round for all of us, Herr Stiffeniis. Fathers and sons. Your father came here once. Now, you have come to Kneiphof looking for a pledge,' the old jeweller said with a knowing smile.

'Not exactly, sir,' I said, thrusting my hand into my shoulder-bag.

I found the kerchief that I was looking for. With a flourish, I held up Kati Rodendahl's amber in my thumb and forefinger, then set it down on the tray with the other beads, which seemed insignificant by comparison.

Klaus Flugge stretched out his hand, as if the creature imprisoned within the amber might still be able to sting him.

His son took a step back from the counter.

'Have you seen anything like this before?' I prompted, imitating the son's sweeping gesture with my hand.

The elder Flugge's stupor was evident. He flashed me a furious glance. His hand shot up and snapped his eye-piece into place. His head ducked down over the tray, where he froze for quite some time, peering deep into the heart of the transparent golden coffin in which that massive insect had been entombed for many centuries.

'A splendid example,' he murmured. 'But what is it an example *of*?'

'Who can say?' I made a helpless shrug. 'I know nothing of the genus, or the species. That is not what interests me. I . . .'

'May I look?' asked Paulus Flugge, who was a full-grown man, forty years old at the least. He bent and examined the creature through his eye-lens, shoulder to shoulder with his father, while I watched. I did not say a word. My questions could wait until they had made their examination.

Herr Flugge murmured something to his son, making a noise that might have been the buzzing of that wasp when it flew through the air an eternity ago. Paulus nodded, then whispered something back, something that I did not catch.

'One question, sirs,' I said, 'then I'll leave you to your work.'

Klaus Flugge raised his head, and fixed me with his viewing instrument.

'A moment more, I pray you.'

Might their scrutiny bring forth some intelligence which would be of use to me?

I held my silence.

And yet, I thought, they ought to be bombarding *me* with questions. Had I found the amber on the coast? Purchased it? And if so, how much had it cost me? The law made plain that such a piece should be consigned to the State. That amber was contraband, and they certainly knew it. Unless I had inherited it, they could only assume that I had had it from a Frenchman, or from a Prussian smuggler.

Still, they made no objection.

They continued to exchange opinions in whispers. That is, the father talked, while the son nodded, reaching out for a stick of graphite, with which he began to make some marks on a sheet of paper. It seemed to me that the less the father spoke, the more furiously the son began to draw.

'Gentlemen,' I interrupted, attempting to explain my presence there.

Klaus Flugge held his finger up for silence, never shifting his eye from the paper on which his son was working. Some minutes passed, the graphite stopped moving. The two men looked at one another, then at the sketches, of which there were two. Then, they both stood up to face me.

The artist seemed drained by his efforts. The father's eyes shone brighter than before. He lifted up the paper, and offered it for my inspection.

'Here you are,' he said with evident satisfaction. 'This is the design that we propose, sir. You won't find anyone along the row who'll do it better. Such a startling creature requires a setting which is bold and daring. It has not survived the ravages of Time to be closed up in the dusty cabinet of some French museum. Or worse, to adorn the mantelpiece of some functionary in Paris.' Klaus Flugge bridled, as if such a destiny were unthinkable. 'You'd be shocked to know how many of our national treasures have been carried off.' He let out a sigh, laid his gloved hand flat on his chest, and added: 'Thank the Lord, this one is in good hands. I would not dare to ask you where you got it, sir. We consider it a privilege to behold such a marvellous piece of Baltic amber.'

If I showed surprise at the warmth of this reception, Herr Flugge betrayed no sign that he had noticed it.

'These are traditional designs,' he said, holding up the paper. 'This one is very popular. We've done quite a few along these lines. Your specimen is larger, of course. But the other customers were highly satisfied. Paulus is a master of his trade. We call this model "The Prussian Eagle". Set in gold, of course. Silver will not do. The reddish tint of the amber would overwhelm it. The nugget can be firmly fixed in place by the eagle's breast feathers. And held – here and here – by the talons.'

He looked at me uncertainly.

'You'd like to see the alternative? "The Hohenzollern Crown" is always dear to our hearts.' His smile grew brighter as he described the effect. 'Imagine the cushion – that's the amber. Imagine the royal garland – purest gold – resting here upon the cushion. Oh, it will be stupendous. My son has really done it justice.'

Paulus Flugge glanced up, then modestly lowered his head.

'Then again, sir,' Klaus Flugge continued suavely, 'we are here to serve *you*.' He bowed, then added quickly: 'Many gentlemen come with an idea already fully formed. We are happy to content them. We've seen some fine insertions recently, but this one is the finest of them all.'

Klaus Flugge seemed greatly pleased with himself and his son.

Most of all, he seemed bewitched by that polished carbuncle of amber.

'This jewel will be a tangible symbol of our history,' he went on lyrically. 'Prussia, the Baltic Sea, the treasure which lies beneath it. Amber is the soul of Prussia. Nowadays, *foreign* hands have dared to desecrate this precious rarity.'

His Adam's apple took a sudden dive inside his high, stiff collar.

'If you desire it, sir,' he rushed on, 'a fraternal emblem might be implanted on the underside, two swivels – here and here – transforming it into a secret symbol of nationhood known only to the wearer. And to others of a like mind.'

A secret symbol known to others of the same persuasion . . .

Did rebels wear insertions to identify themselves? And did Herr Flugge serve such men? Had I discovered the secret path that smuggled amber took? Our own Prussian nationalists?

'I am not here to commission a jewel,' I admitted. 'The woman who owned this amber was murdered. I am a magistrate, and I am investigating her death.' I looked from the father to the son. Their eyes widened, their brows creased. Those shocked expressions made them seem more markedly alike than I had previously noticed. 'I came to ask for information. That is all that interests me. I was wondering whether you had ever been employed to set such a jewel as this one. But you have answered me already.'

I picked up the amber nugget, and clasped it in my fist.

'Do not be alarmed,' I said. 'I did not intend to trick you, sirs. Nor would I arrest two Prussian craftsmen for a misunderstanding. Yet, it is evident that you have had vast experience in handling amber containing creatures. This was found in Nordcopp . . .'

'Nordcopp?'

Oddly, it was Paulus who spoke. If fright subdued his father, the same fear seemed to embolden him.

'Two women have been murdered there,' I explained.

'Are you working for the Prussian authorities?' he asked.

The incisiveness of his question surprised me.

'They know that I am investigating the matter,' I replied in the vaguest terms, afraid that greater honesty would inhibit them even more.

'So, you are working for the French,' the son concluded, as if he were a magistrate and had just read out a capital sentence. As he spoke, he gathered up the amber beads by the handful, carelessly dropping them into a glass jar like so many boiled sweets. Did he wish to save his precious stock from contamination with the piece that I had shown them?

'Your father admitted that you have set a number of similar pieces,' I pressed on. 'Who brought them here? And where would someone obtain a piece like this one?'

Paulus Flugge turned aside.

'That French officer, don't you remember, father? That piece containing . . .'

'An ant,' the old man insisted. 'A tiny, tiny ant. There wasn't much to see, but he was delighted. *Excentrique* was the word he used.' He tilted his head, and stared at me, frowning so hard that furrows appeared on his brow.

'We did the work,' said Paulus, picking up the tale. 'We knew that the decree had just been signed, of course. Even such a trifling piece should not have left the country, but what were *we* to do about it? Can a Prussian challenge a French officer's right to do exactly as he pleases?'

'Hardly,' I agreed.

'And now, here you are, Herr Magistrate, with your fine example. We will not be asked to break the law in this case. You want information. Information which we do not possess, unfortunately for you. What more have we to say to each other?'

He considered me to be a traitor, without a doubt. I could not change his opinion, but I would not let the opportunity slip.

'But you said you have created other jewels of this type. Patriotic emblems, let us call them. How many have you made?' I insisted. 'Your father spoke of each piece being different . . .'

'Setting amber is our trade,' Klaus Flugge flared up in support of his son. 'Every piece that we make is distinct and original. We pride ourselves on that fact. That is what I meant. Nothing more.'

'You described amber as the "soul of Prussia", and I quote you.'

'All true Prussians think so,' he replied disdainfully. 'Unhappily, it is ours no more. You know that, sir, coming from Nordcopp. The French have made great changes, we have been told.'

I held up my hand to stop him.

'Herr Flugge, I am interested only in the murdered girls. I don't care what your business is. Amber of exceptional value is involved in the crimes. But look here,' I pulled my album from my bag, and began to flick through the pages, searching for the rough sketch I had attempted to make of Kati Rodendahl without the mutilation. 'Have you ever seen this face before?' I asked, holding up the picture.

Her eyes were closed, her cheeks were hollow. I had not been able to disguise the fact that she was dead. And they knew it. They stared at the portrait, their magnifying lenses growing out of their brows like monstrous warts, but both men shook their heads when I insisted on an answer.

'What about this girl?' I asked, turning to the sketch of Ilse.

They boggled at the triangular cavity in the girl's throat, but neither spoke.

Perhaps they were too shocked to speak. And yet, I thought, it was more than possible that girls like Ilse and Kati had made their way from Nordcopp to the shops in Königsberg, selling what they had managed to steal.

I turned the page.

There was Edviga. Whole, well, bright eyes sparkling. Clearly alive.

'Have you ever seen this woman?' I said, hoping for little, expecting less.

Their heads turned, one to the other. An unspoken message passed between them.

'I remember that scar,' Klaus Flugge admitted. 'It did not mar her face in the least. We have seen her here. Not recently, of course.'

'How long ago?' I asked.

'Shortly after Jena, as I recall,' the old man said, musing as he said it, and I remembered what the son had said about his father's remarkable memory.

'Two years ago?' I quizzed him.

'Not quite so long,' he said. 'She came from the Samland peninsula.'

So, I thought, Edviga Lornerssen had worked elsewhere collecting amber, and for quite a while before she came to Nordcopp.

'Did she bring you amber?' I held the sketching-album

propped against my chest like a reading-stand, hoping that the sight of Edviga's face would spur him on to marvels.

'What else?' Paulus Flugge intervened. 'We deal exclusively in amber.'

I asked myself why the Flugges were now so ready to talk of Edviga. Was it because that portrait was clearly not the picture of a girl who was dead? Or, having imprudently revealed the fact that many of their customers were nationalists, had they decided to give me a titbit to keep me happy? By doing so, they would distance themselves from any suspicion regarding the girls who had died.

'Where does your amber come from, sirs?'

'Now, that's a question that we can answer,' Flugge Senior replied. 'We purchase raw materials from the Königsberg Guild, sir. They pay the French, then they distribute it to us. Not to jewellers alone, please note, but to all the men who use amber in their trades. Makers of soap and furniture polish, for example. Mixers of medicines, paints and balms. They use powder made from broken bits and fragments, most of them. Amber of the best quality must be entered in the register of the local Guild. And in our accounts-book, too. Then again, sir, very occasionally, a young woman . . .'

'Most infrequently,' Paulus stressed.

'. . . walks in through the door, bringing a piece of amber . . .'

'Not quite through the usual channels,' Paulus added.

'And she asks if we would like to buy what she has for sale.'

'But most infrequently . . .'

'I wish to see your registers,' I said, interrupting this duet.

A thick book in a heavy red leather binding was brought out for my inspection. I felt my heart sink. What did I expect to find? There would be lots which was of no use to me at all, and nothing of what truly intrigued me, that is, amber containing insects, amber which the Guilds were no longer allowed to sell.

'This volume covers the last ten years,' Klaus Flugge announced. His confidence seemed to have returned to him. 'Month by month.'

I spent some minutes sifting through the pages. The Flugges bought roughly six pounds of amber every month, slightly more in the months before Christmas. Each time a purchase was recorded, there was an ink stamp and the signature of the emissary who had brought the goods, together with the signature of Klaus or Paulus Flugge. The emissary signatures for the last twelve months, I noted, were French, as were the exorbitant prices paid. The cost of unfinished amber had tripled in a year. Nothing that might be of help to me, however. The only thing of interest was a certain fussiness which the father and the son displayed, meticulously noting what they did with their monthly allowance of amber. Handles for knives and forks made up the bulk of their work, together with frames for miniature pictures and compact mirrors. They made twice as many earrings as bracelets and rings. Those pages reflected the changing tastes of Prussian fashion – brooches were out, lockets were in – though ever more frequently the name of the purchaser was French. In one instance, in March 1808, just five months previously, Messrs Flugge had acquired '*two large lengths of solid amber – dark red in colour, streaked with yellow veins, opaque*', as the description read. These had been transformed by Paulus Flugge into '*two virile members, almost life-size*' on the order of a French *chasseur* whose name was Captain Noel Laganarde. The price agreed upon was fifty-six thalers '*per item*', which more than equalled the average monthly earnings of the shop. Nothing in the register suggested that the Flugges had ever set a piece of amber containing an insect in a patriotic clasp, or bought a piece of amber on the sly.

I closed the ledger.

I could have made a nuisance of myself. That is, I could have come back in the company of French soldiers, and turned their shop upside down. Or I could have reported them to General Malaport, suggesting that they might know the names of seditious elements that might be worth arresting. Then again, I could have had their names struck off the Guild's list of registered amber-jewellers. I could have closed their shop, for ever.

But I did none of these things. Rather, I compressed the threat that I represented into a few words as I prepared to leave the shop. 'If I need any further information,' I warned them, 'I'll be back.'

I expected no reply, but Paulus Flugge had something still to say.

'We'll be here, sir,' he said, his mouth set in a defiant fashion. 'If you ever do decide to set that splendid piece of amber, Herr Stiffeniis, you know where to bring it, and what will be made of it.'

I opened the door, and the bell tinkled.

I stood outside and listened as the sound faded away.

Lamps were being lit along the Kramerbrücke bridge. I saw a lamp-lighter going over with his stick, a large dog meandering at his heels. There were French soldiers guarding the near end of the bridge now. They were chatting quietly, smoking their pipes, spitting occasionally into the water, their duty more of a pleasure than a burden. Down along the bank, a man was fishing with a perch-pole. The town across the water was lost in shadows, except for pinpoints of light which dotted the mass of buildings that lined the waterfront.

I had learnt something, after all. Scientists were keen on amber specimens with insect insertions, but our nationalists were keener. Illegal pieces of amber were smuggled from Nordcopp by the girls who worked there. Edviga Lornerssen was one of them. She had hinted as much: 'we go to Nordcopp, but sometimes further.' When they found something special, they came to Königsberg. Had the girls who called themselves Annalise and Megrete come with stolen relics from the church?

And was it here that they had met their Nemesis?

27

Vulpius.

His name was in the documents that Malaport had shown me. He had been stopped by a night-watchman in the company of two women on the Grünen Brücke bridge. The following week, two bodies had been found beneath that same bridge. For want of soldiers, the General had let him slip away. Vulpius had described himself as a 'follower of Kant'. That was now the only lead I had.

Immanuel Kant had taught at the Albertina University in Königsberg for fifty years. If Vulpius really were a 'follower of Kant', if he had ever registered as a student, or taken an examination at the university, he would have left some trace behind him. But it would not be easy. The Albertina was one of the largest universities in the German-speaking states, second only to Göttingen. Despite its isolation on the Baltic coast, Königsberg had managed to attract as many as five hundred students a year, and every one of them was obliged to study theology and metaphysics. The lists would be enormous.

The afternoon was drawing on as I walked beside the River Pregel. The low sun cast a sheen of sparkling gold across the rippling waters. Public offices generally close at four o'clock, and I was afraid that the Registration Office might have shut up for the night. Still, I pressed onward, hoping to find one clerk who was as serious as Professor Kant had been, a dedicated man who would still be at his desk despite the hour, ready and willing to point me in the direction of Vulpius.

The great door to the Examinations Hall was wide open.

In the quadrangle, a man was going already around with a spill on a long stick, lighting lanterns. Over one of the doors on the far side was a large blue enamel plaque. The word SECRETARIAT was written in gold. A smaller sign had been inserted into a slotted frame on the wall: AUTUMN SEMESTER ENROLMENTS IN PROGRESS.

A group of young men were loitering outside. Three of them appeared to be playing hopscotch on the cracked flagstones. I hurried over, skipped inside the door, and found myself caught up in a mad scrimmage. I might have been standing on the docks of Königsberg harbour as a sailing ship from Tallin disembarked its passengers. At least two hundred persons were milling about inside the large room. Their buzzing voices were a constant droning undertone, broken now and then by a sharp cry, 'Next!' and the setting-to of all these combatants in a cruel, mysterious free-for-all, as they pushed towards desks which had been set at regular intervals around the large room.

The French had brought the orderly queue to Prussia; the students of the Albertina did not seem to like the concept. Men in long black gowns wandered in and out among the crowd, waving canes, trying to keep order of a sort, shouting out as they went: 'A civil engineering ticket! Tickets for mathematics!' or 'Two for physics! Two more for physics!'

I watched transactions going on all around the room.

A heavy hammer-beam roof rose high above the heads. The yellow-painted walls were filled with wooden boards on which a million pieces of paper had been pinned and posted higgledy-piggledy, one on top of the other. Above these written notices, a number of heraldic devices and brightly coloured coats-of-arms and a large fresco of a growling bear filled one wall, while dour, dust-encrusted portraits of long-dead academics loured down from the other walls, sternly disapproving of the lively assembly of modern youths who evidently wished to join their hallowed ranks.

But something else surprised me.

The Albertina had been renowned for theology and metaphysics. The Pietists had ruled the university for centuries; nothing else had ever been taught there. But I had heard the ticket-sellers, and now I saw the signs above the registration-desks. They were all for scientific disciplines. Was I in the wrong university? There seemed to be no exception. ANATOMY. METALLURGY. MEDICINE. CALCULATION. CHEMISTRY. MEASURES. The air was hot and heavy with the smell of young bodies, old clothes, stale tobacco smoke. It was like the cattle-market in Lotingen on the first Friday of the month. In front of each desk, students pushed and tussled, shook their horns and stamped their hooves, edging forward, tickets in one hand, money in the other, eager to be enrolled on the lists before each course was filled.

Only one desk proved an exception to the rule.

In the farthest, darkest corner of the room, a large, fat, red-faced man was seated all alone at a table. He was writing on a sheet of paper by the light of a candle, oblivious to the noise and the rumpus, totally untroubled by the urgency of everything that was going on around him. Above his head a small notice had been pinned to the wall: PHILOSOPHY / THEOLOGY / METAPHYSICS.

Here was the man that I was seeking.

He did not look up as I made my way through the crowd. Nor as I stood before him, waiting to catch his eye. While the secretaries of the other faculties listed students' names and scribbled receipts for the payment of fees to the university treasury, he went on with his private task. His name was written on a folded card: Dr Narcizus Rickert. Sitting behind a wall of books, he was writing furiously on a sheet of paper.

'Doctor Rickert?'

His head jerked up, and he quickly covered what he was writing.

'Do you wish to enrol?' he wheezed incredulously.

'I . . . I am interested in the courses of Professor Kant,' I began.

The black eyes of Narcizus Rickert did not flicker as I spoke. They peered out at me from under a heavy granite cliff of a forehead, like glistening stars in a stormy night sky. A tattered academic wig was perched on the crown of his head like a washed-out handkerchief.

'Kant ceased teaching here in '96,' he said.

'You miss my point, Herr Rickert,' I corrected him. 'I wish to know about the courses in Kantian philosophy at the university today. Indeed, I am looking for a follower of Professor Kant, and I wonder if he may be enrolled here at the moment.'

Doctor Rickert set his chin on his shoulder. Rolls of fat bulged out from his jowls. He stared up at me and said: 'Just look behind you, sir. Can you see anyone else in the queue?' He did not wait for a reply. 'It's been like this all week. And today is the final day for registration. If you feel like signing up, you'll have the whole place to yourself. Philosophy is dead in Königsberg. No one's interested in thinking any more. Just look at them,' he snorted, waving his hands dismissively. 'For them the world is a thing to weigh and measure.'

He glanced at me, as if to gauge my reaction to this diatribe. Any man, it seemed, who was interested in philosophy ought to share his opinion.

'Science,' he sneered again. 'French poison.'

I tried again. 'Regarding the person that I am looking for.'

'Are you certain that he hasn't signed on for something else?' he suggested with an airy gesture. 'Something more modern, I mean to say.'

'His preference is definitely for Kantian philosophy,' I insisted.

'Are you, perhaps, the first butterfly announcing the coming of Spring?' he asked rhetorically, taking up his pen again, pulling out a fresh sheet of paper, covering up what he had been writing before. 'Just tell me your name, sir, together with the name of this other person, and I will joyfully enrol the pair of you.'

I wondered whether the confusion in the room had dulled his hearing.

'You misunderstand me, sir,' I said, leaning over the table, raising my voice. 'I am not here to enrol. I am looking for a person who has probably studied here, who may still be studying philosophy here. Kantian philosophy, that is.'

Doctor Rickert dropped his pen, and picked up a large leather-bound book.

'Kantian philosophy?' he repeated. 'That simplifies everything.'

He flicked through the pages of the volume, then turned it around and held it up to me. The book was long, narrow, thick. The left-hand page was plain, containing the title and description of a course, together with the themes and subjects which the tutor intended to tackle in the first semester. *An Introduction to the Works of Immanuel Kant*, I read. The right-hand page was a narrow grid of ruled lines: a wide space had been left near the margin for the names of the participants, a line of boxes to the right of it, where their absences and presences would eventually be recorded as the course proceeded. The course had been planned for Wednesdays, three hours, starting at 3 p.m.

Where the tutor's name should have been, the space was blank. And so was the page where the students' names ought to have been listed.

'No names,' Doctor Rickert explained. 'No one to look for.'

I was stunned.

Doctor Rickert dropped his ledger heavily on the table. The page on which he had been writing was now exposed beneath the brown leather cover.

'*Draw blood out from the large vein. This will give the sacred Entity more energy on which to feed . . .*' I read.

I looked up uncertainly. What was the nature of the subject in which he had been so deeply involved when I approached his desk just a few moments before? Like every other young man of my generation, I had read Gottfried Bürger's poem

322

'Lenore', Goethe's 'Bride of Corinth', Ossenfelder's most famous work. I knew what vampires were reputed to drink. Did the 'sacred Entity' that Rickert was interested in belong to the same sinister genre?

Rickert looked at me intently. 'You are not from Königsberg, I take it.'

'I come from Lotingen.'

'You are lucky to find yourself at my desk,' he said quickly, leaning forward with a smile. I counted seven brown teeth, three above, and four below, which were incapable of containing the stale smell of onions. 'For a small consideration, I may be able to provide you with the information that you looking for.'

'Consideration?' I repeated.

'A paltry fee,' he said. 'The usual student rate.'

'Which is?'

'Two thalers, as a rule, sir. That is, two thalers *per* operation.'

'What would this involve?' I asked.

Herr Rickert smiled, then rubbed his eyebrow with his fingernail. 'You have studied, sir, I can see that. You know how a secretary earns his keep. For a tiny fee, all will be revealed. Where a lecturer keeps his room. What time his lessons start. All the changes to the timetable. I'll provide your paper, ink, books. Find you a bed, or a lady to wash your collars and socks. The usual services,' he winked.

'I do not need such services,' I replied. 'I am not a student.'

He raised his hand to stop me. 'But you are looking for a student. A man who is interested in Kant. Is that it?' He edged forward, lowering his voice. 'You are searching for somebody who is a little . . . elusive, let's say. Well, that is more unusual, more costly. Five thalers, sir. Just five thalers, and I will tell you where you can find a man who is interested in Kant, but does not choose to register at the Albertina.'

I thought I could guess where he intended sending me.

'You cannot believe', I objected, 'that any Kantian would try to work his way through the chaos of the Kantstudiensaal?'

'You know it already, do you?' he said, and he seemed disappointed.

I had been to visit Kant's archive the previous year. The money that Kant had left in his will for the conservation and arrangement of his papers, books and publications had been woefully misspent. I had never seen such a disorganised tip. Serge Lavedrine and I had spent a night searching through the so-called 'archive' for a paper that Professor Kant had written in his youth. Before we could even start, we had had to drag the archivist in a drunken stupor from a tavern.

'I will not pay money for such useless information,' I said.

In the course of this exchange of opinions, my hand had slid into my pocket in search of coins, then slid out again as I realised the waste that such a donation would constitute. Herr Doctor Rickert had followed my every movement, and he must have understood that his thalers were in the balance.

'It would be money well spent,' he replied sullenly. 'If he is a . . . Kantian, you'll find him there, I'm certain.' He seemed to imply much more than he actually said. His eyes flashed nervously around the room, as if he feared being overheard, though there was no chance of it. I was the only person within a mile of the philosophy desk. 'All the true followers of Kant go there,' he added in a whisper. He bit his lower lip with his brown upper teeth, and made a thoughtful sucking sound. 'I could even look in the university back-lists for you. Could this person have registered at some time in the past? I can check back as far as 1800, though I'll have to go to the general deposit, which is now kept up at the castle.' He grimaced, then lowered his voice again. 'It is as if they wished to carry off the history of this institution. The French, I mean. A new era has begun, and they will not let us forget it!'

I slipped my hand into pocket, pulled out my purse, counted out two thalers, and dropped them into his open, waiting hand.

'The usual fee,' I insisted.

Dr Rickert's fist closed around the coins like a spring-trap.

'Very good, sir. Now, to work, to work! About this person

that you are looking for.' His voice was bubbling with excitement. 'What did you say his name was?'

'Vulpius,' I replied.

'Vulpius?' he repeated thoughtfully, playing his forefinger against his flabby lower lip. 'A most unusual name. Does he have a Christian name?'

'I know him only as Vulpius,' I said.

He nodded energetically, writing it down on a slip of paper. 'And where can I get in touch with you, sir?'

'I . . . I don't know as yet,' I answered hesitantly. General Malaport had mentioned that a bed would be found for me in one of the dormitories in the castle, but the last thing I wished to do was to sleep in the company of French soldiers. 'I arrived in town just this morning. I haven't had the time to make arrangements.'

Dr Rickert looked up quickly. 'No place to rest your head for the night, sir?' A new light flickered in his black eyes. His face was animated by concern. 'As it happens, you are in luck! I rent rooms in my own home. The best one's free at the moment. Just five thalers per week, if you take the last lodger's sheets. Unfortunately – for me, that is – he stayed for two nights only. Came to sit the *viva*, and complete his degree. As a rule, I charge seven. A real discount, sir. Oh, you'll be comfortable. And I should have the information that you want before you go to bed.'

'If the sheets are clean . . .'

'Immaculate!' he exclaimed. 'A boy from an excellent family.'

'Very well,' I agreed. I had placed the coins on the sticky palm of Dr Rickert without knowing what I was buying.

'Very good,' he said, nodding fiercely as he wrote out the address on another slip of paper, and handed it across to me. 'Ritterstrasse is only a five-minute walk from here. I begin preparing dinner as the church clocks strike seven. You can eat whenever you arrive. I will set a place for you, too, sir. My portions are large, I can assure you.'

The services offered by Rickert were inexhaustible, it seemed.

'Perhaps you can assist me further, Dr Rickert,' I said. 'I have a couple of letters to write, and I must despatch them tonight. Might you be able to help me on that score?'

He sat up like a dog presented with a biscuit by his master. 'It would be one thaler per message, including postage. But, well, as you have engaged the room, and as you've also opted for dinner, I think that it could be done for a single thaler. And I'll throw in the paper, pen and ink.'

The paper, pen and ink belonged to the university, but I did not quibble.

'Where are these letters bound for, sir? I only ask because it's getting late, and the diligence will have already left for the more distant provinces . . .'

Was he about to revise his price-list?

'My home town,' I specified. 'Lotingen.'

Dr Rickert let out a sigh of relief. 'No problem. No problem at all. We have a couple of hours in that case, then.'

'May I use your desk?' I asked. 'Or is there an additional charge?'

His expression was composed and serious. 'Oh no, sir. What are you thinking? It comes with the rent of the room. There would have been a small fee, but . . . well, we can skip formalities. You may even use my chair,' he replied, standing up with alacrity, setting out a pen and paper on the table.

I thanked him, and sat down.

I did what I had been meaning to do all day, I wrote a note to Helena.

She was constantly in my thoughts, I said, and the investigation was proceeding speedily. I told her that I was confident of being home before the child was born. Her time would soon be up. If I had not completed my task (that is, if I had still not caught the killer, though I avoided being so unnecessarily explicit), I would request temporary leave from General Malaport, and I had no doubt that he would grant it. I asked her to consign the second note (which would be folded up and sealed inside her letter) to my assistant, Johannes Gurten. I described him as '*manna from heaven*', noting:

> *I know not where he may be lodging, but Knutzen will know. I count on you, my love, having no other means of contacting Herr Gurten.*
>
> *Kiss our little ones for me. I miss them all. I cannot express the pleasure that I feel to think of the addition to our household, who is, at this very moment, growing inside you. Try to keep him/her quiet until I am able to return to you all.*
>
> *Yours, etc. Hanno.*

The note to Gurten was more prosaic.

> *Königsberg – two unidentified female corpses found here. One was mutilated. The other, too, perhaps. Reports unclear about details. Girls from Nordcopp selling amber in Königsberg? Most likely. City alive with rebels/nationalists/dissidents of every sort.*
>
> *I am hunting a ghost named* VULPIUS.
>
> *I hope that your research is more material than mine.*
> *I will keep you posted regarding developments.*

I added Rickert's address, telling Gurten to send his messages there.

All the while, Professor Rickert stood in front of the table, his back towards me, arms folded, feet apart, as if he were on special guard duty. Would he charge me for this service, too, I wondered. If any marauding student from another queue came too close, he stepped forward quickly, waved them off with his fists, ordering them angrily to keep their distance and behave like scholars.

I folded the second letter inside the first, sealed the packet with wax by the candle flame, then I stood up.

'I thank you for your help, Herr Doctor Rickert,' I said.

'It was nothing, sir. Nothing at all,' he replied. 'You have to keep a careful eye on them, you know. Whatever is the university coming to! They're little better than monkeys. Why, they'd be climbing all over the table if you didn't fight them off.'

I knew what was expected of me. I slipped another coin into Rickert's damp palm as I handed him the letter.

'You spoke of two letters, sir.'

'Just one,' I replied. 'Second thoughts, you know.'

Dr Rickert had no such thoughts. He did not offer to refund a farthing of the money that he had already taken from me.

'Your message will be delivered tomorrow morning,' he informed me, glancing at the address that I had written. 'The town is near enough.'

Dr Rickert was correct. Lotingen was close, Nordcopp even closer. They seemed to me like distant planets drawn together by an astral flux that was malign, mysterious. Lotingen with its invasion of flies and foulness, Nordcopp with its mutilated corpses, living cripples and vulnerable women. Königsberg was part of the same impenetrable labyrinth – strange men and stranger trades in the port, the secretive commissions of its jewellers' shops, the cloisters and the halls of its university ringing with a new scientific language, the old ways all but forgotten. And yet, I thought, there was the secret, hidden underbelly of Königsberg, too, where amber was smuggled, bought and sold, and where feverish and rebellious ideas of Prussia's spiritual rebirth were never far away.

'A letter to your wife, I see, sir. She'll be pleased to know that you have found the perfect lodging. Until this evening, then, Herr Stiffeniis. Your humble servant, sir.'

The eyelids of Dr Rickert beat as rapidly as any young lover's might, when the moment of separation arrives. By way of contrast, his joyful expression reminded me of the mysterious sentence about blood and how best to extract it, that he had been writing when I arrived. Then, something that Colonel les Halles had said the other night on the *coq du mer* returned to my thoughts. *Nothing is what it seems in Prussia, monsieur*. What had induced this smiling academic, this thaler-hungry sycophant, to interest himself in blood, and the most efficient ways to extract it from the human body?

The sun was sinking, and it was gloomy out in the quadrangle. I walked through the great entrance-gate, but I did not leave the precincts of the university. I knew where I was going as I turned away from the harbour, and headed into the shambles of the old town.

I knew what I would find there.

28

The library doors were thrown wide open.

A single lantern traced out a cracked mosaic of pummelled, ancient paving stones. A head poked out of a tiny window in the wall, like a guard-dog on a short chain chasing off unwanted callers.

'What can I do for you, sir?'

'I must speak with Herr Ludvigssen,' I answered, recovering from my surprise. Here was a change! The library had been abandoned and forgotten the year before. Now, there was a man to guard the entrance.

'Ludvigssen? D'you know where to find him, sir?'

'If he is still down in the Kantstudiensaal . . .'

'That's right, sir. Been down there before, have you?'

The head ducked out of sight, as if I had just given the correct password.

As I went down the stairs to the basement, as the lanterns grew sparser, and the shadows thickened, I recalled my visit to the university library in the company of Serge Lavedrine the year before. On that occasion, thanks to Lavedrine's perseverance, we had found what we were seeking.

Would I be so lucky on my own, I wondered.

The underground corridor ran the length of the building. It was dark and dank, smelling strongly of mould and mice, dusty paper and rank abandonment. My nerves were tingling and a sort of blind panic seized me by the throat. Was it possible that Kant had failed to record our conversation? It had changed the course of my whole life. It had altered the direction of *his* life, too. I was certain the philosopher had written a note about it, and I did not doubt that his account was hidden somewhere in that archive. All of his extant papers had been deposited there after his death. And Arnold Abel Ludvigssen had been employed as the archivist to catalogue each single manuscript sheet. My nightmare had long been that the man would find my name and learn what I preferred should be forever lost and forgotten.

My steps echoed on the stone flags. Someone might have been following behind me in the gloom, they sounded so loud. My head was a maelstrom of thoughts that made no sense, as I halted before the door of the Kantstudiensaal.

I raised my fist – it felt as heavy as a cannonball – then let it fall upon the door.

'Come in,' a voice called brightly.

It was not the slurred and slovenly voice that I remembered, though the same man was seated behind a large desk. I recognised the long nose of Arnold Abel Ludvigssen, the straight middle parting, the divided waterfalls of greasy black hair which fell on either side of his long, pale, narrow face. He peered short-sightedly over the top of his pince-nez like a frightened hare.

'Can I help you, sir?'

No light of recognition shone in his eyes, and I was glad of that. Twelve months before, he had been the picture of destitution. Drunk then, he was sober now. The state of the room had altered, too. It was as if a Baltic gale had blown through the place, sweeping up the mountain of manuscripts and books, and depositing them magically in perfect order on the shelves which ran around the walls. He had accomplished a task that would have daunted Hercules. A rubbish tip had been transformed into an archive which was manageable, though vast. The same purifying wind had blown over him. He looked fresh, clean, new, as he came running from behind the desk to meet me.

'I am an investigating magistrate,' I began to say.

331

'You've come about the stolen papers?' he asked, and his left eyelid began to flicker nervously.

'I am conducting an enquiry on behalf of General Malaport,' I specified.

I could have sworn I heard his heels click together at the mention of the Frenchman's name. He had been standing in front of me, his body rigid, eyes cast down like a junior officer brought up on a charge. Now, his tense face seemed to visibly relax.

'You are working for the French,' he started to say, and a trill of nervous laughter burst out of him. 'That's a great relief, sir. I knew they'd take the matter seriously in the end.'

'The matter?' I echoed.

Herr Ludvigssen was wearing a new suit of neat brown twill, his shirt was clean, his collar stiff with starch, his tie was a puffy red velvet bow. When drunk, the man had been rude and intractable, but now he was as meek as a puppy, and he was sober.

'The papers, sir. I was very worried. That's why I reported the theft.'

Had he chosen to confide in me *because* I was working for the French? He was the first Prussian to behave in such a manner. All the others had been terrified at the thought of talking to a man in my position.

Before I could ask him what had been taken, he began to speak again.

'I thought that you'd been sent by them . . . My *benefactors*,' he said, a twisted expression of resentment on his face.

'Who are you talking of?' I asked him.

'The people who supervise the archive nowadays.'

'I thought the University ran it?'

'Oh no, sir. Not any more. The Albertina would have closed the place down,' he continued. 'But then . . . *they* stepped in at the eleventh hour. They paid for the furniture, and the shelves, and the desks, but . . .'

'But what?'

332

'They are strict, sir. Mighty strict. Consider this a mausoleum, they said. And dress the part. The archive must be worthy of the man that it enshrines.' An embarrassed smile appeared on his face, and he giggled quietly to himself. 'Sometimes, when I am down here on my own, I have the notion Kant himself has come in through that door, sir. I get the feeling he is watching me. He is a malevolent presence, sir. A threat, I can assure you.'

He spoke as if he lived in a permanent state of terror.

'Professor Kant would be gratified to see the splendid work that you have done,' I said, trying to put him at his ease. 'Who are these benefactors, anyway?'

His mouth opened and closed, like a carp out of water.

'The idolaters of Kant,' he whispered, leaning closer. 'For so I call them.'

Vulpius had used a similar expression about himself when stopped and questioned in the street by the night watchman. 'I am a follower of Kant,' he had said. Had Rickert sent me to the right place, after all?

'Have you ever met these people?' I asked him.

Ludvigssen clasped his hands together. 'Never, sir.'

'Surely, if they pay your salary, someone brings it.'

He shook his head, and breathed in noisily. 'Oh no, sir. I am paid through the Albertina Secretariat,' he replied. 'That's not changed, though everything else has. Including the notes I get when I commit an error, or put a book back in the wrong place. Arrive a minute late, or close too soon, an envelope turns up.'

'Well, somebody must bring those,' I suggested.

Ludvigssen shook his head. 'I find them on my desk. I've no idea who brings them here. I've asked the watchman on the gate, but he's got no idea, either. It's almost as if the fog had delivered them.'

Ludvigssen shivered as if the temperature had suddenly dropped.

'Were these letters signed?' I asked, wondering whether there might be some rational explanation, an academic committee, perhaps, that had been formed to oversee the daily running of the archive.

'Not signed, as such,' he said mysteriously.

'May I see them?' I asked.

Ludvigssen looked once again beyond my shoulder to the door. 'You are a magistrate, aren't you, sir? Working for the French, I mean?' he said. His eyes flashed bright with fright. '*They* haven't sent you here to test me, have they?'

'I am employed by General Malaport, as I told you,' I answered firmly, 'and I have come here on his business. Now, let me see these letters, if you will.'

He blinked nervously, as if uncertain whether the greatest danger lay in me, or in the unseen watchers. Then, with a deep sigh, he crossed the room and sat himself down behind his desk, reaching down to open the bottom drawer.

As he came up again, holding a sheet of paper, there was something odd in his way of managing it. He had laid the folded paper flat in the palm of his left hand, and he held it closed with the thumb and forefinger of his right hand. 'Open it as if you were lifting up a lid,' he said, offering the paper to me. 'That's right, sir. Just hold it in the same way I am holding it.'

I did as I was told, then raised the top half carefully. There was red wax all around the edges, as if the paper had been sealed like a packet, as if it had once contained something more than words alone.

OFFENCE, I read the large letters. In smaller letters:

Archive closed one hour early on 17th inst. You were seen drinking beer in the Mermaid Tavern. Shirt collar dirty. It has been noted that the frontispiece of the Westphalia edition has been consumed by worms.

WARNING: *Let this be the last time!*

There was neither a date, nor a signature.

Where the signature ought to have been, there was a large bluebottle.

The insect had been squashed, then pressed down hard, leaving the imprint of a finger in the mulch. Fluids had stained a dull brown spot. The crushed contents of the thorax had attached themselves like glue to the paper. As the paper trembled in my hand, a fragment of the wing detached itself and caught against my thumb.

'This was no accident, I think.' I folded the paper up, and pinched it closed.

'Indeed,' he said, putting the note away, taking out another one, handing it to me in the same curious manner.

I repeated the operation.

OFFENCE: *Preface to* Critique of Pure Reason *(1787 Riga edition) incorrectly returned to the shelves containing Social Essays.*

Late in opening 22nd inst.

WARNING: *This is the second time that books have been misplaced!*

No fly had been squashed on the paper. It was a spider this time. A large, long-legged spider, which had been crushed with a thumb, and spread across the page like strawberry jam.

I closed it up, and gave it back.

'Are these accusations justified?' I asked, closing the letter, handing it back.

'They were, sir,' Ludvigssen admitted. 'I have altered my ways. Stopped drinking, for a start.'

'Would the idolaters do what those crushed insects seem to suggest?'

It was cold down there, despite the oppressive heat of summer out in the streets, but a drop of sweat rolled down Ludvigssen's nose and splashed on the surface of his desk.

'I don't intend to put them to the test,' he said. 'Kant's important to them. He must be, mustn't he? Why else would they threaten to squash me like a bug? I must beware of showing negligence towards his memory. I hope I never get another one.'

'How many of these warnings have you received?' I asked.

'I have had four altogether.'

'And are they always signed in the same way?'

'Always, sir.'

Had a band of zealots possessed themselves of Immanuel Kant's archive, I asked myself. Fabien Berodstein's face had contorted in a similar manner at the merest mention of our nationalist fanatics. And I recalled the buttoned mouths and frightened looks of the Flugges, father and son, the instant they realised that I could not be tempted with a rebel's amber pin.

Ludvigssen put the letter back in the bottom drawer.

'But now, sir,' he said airily, sitting up straight, as if he wished to change the subject, 'about General Malaport, and those missing documents.'

'I am here on General Malaport's behalf,' I said. 'But missing documents are not what I am here to investigate. To tell you the truth, I am looking for a person.'

The archivist's face blenched with fear once more.

'A person?'

'Do you keep records of all who visit this room?' I asked him. 'Students, teachers, and so on?'

'I keep a register scrupulously,' Ludvigssen replied, a note of desperation in his voice.

'I wish to see it.'

He pointed towards one of the visitors' desks, inviting me to take a seat, as if the reading of the register might take time. He hurried there before me, pulled out the chair, tucked it in behind me like a perfect footman. A few moments later, he laid the visitors' book before me on the table.

'Where do you wish to start, sir?' His tone of voice was stiff and measured, less warm than before.

'At the eleventh hour,' I said. 'When these benefactors appeared on the scene.'

'That was eight months ago,' he said. 'Just after New Year.'

Again, I noted the frills of lace peeping out from the cuff of his sleeve. His shirt cost a great deal more than I could possibly afford to spend. A generous, but menacing, God had smiled on him. He opened the volume, pointed with his finger. 'Here we are, sir, 2 January 1808.'

I began to look through the pages of the register. When names did crop up, there were not so many of them. There had never been two scholars in the room together, so far as I could see, though the entries were scrupulously kept:

12th/13th/14th January: Bertrand Lupertz. Unpublished notes – Critique of Judgement.

2nd/3rd February: Jeremias Kamansky. Dreams of a Visionary Explained by Metaphysics – rough notes, preparatory sketches, and addenda.

7th February: Tobias Munst. Unpublished letter of Moses Mendelssohn, together with the onion-skin copy containing Professor Kant's reply.

The names were all clearly Prussian.

The date was written at the top of each page, and every sheet was signed twice by the archivist himself, noting the time at which he had arrived, and at which he had left for the night. Then, I turned the page, and read the following note.

9th February: Vulpius. Metaphysics of Habit (Königsberg ed.)

With fumbling fingers, I searched through the register. He was there again on 10th February, and every day the following week, from the 13th to the 17th of the same month. My heart beat painfully as I worked my way to the most recent page on which his name appeared. *21st February 1808.* Six months ago. For some reason, Vulpius had stopped coming to the Kantstudiensaal after that date.

No clue was given to his identity. There was no address. He had arrived one day, come again on a number of occasions – I counted thirteen altogether – then he had disappeared from view. But what was Vulpius doing *before* he came to the

Kantstudiensaal? Had he been living in Königsberg then? And where was he *now*? Had he completed his research in Königsberg, then taken himself off to some other university to continue his studies? Or had he left the city for the north coast?

Had he gone to Nordcopp?

'Here's the man that I am looking for,' I said, tapping my fingernail against an entry, purposely avoiding sounding alarums. 'He came here a lot, it seems. Then, all of a sudden, he came no more. Do you remember him?'

Ludvigssen did not reply immediately. He looked at the book, he looked at me. His face became a stiff, impenetrable mask. 'He did come in frequently for a while,' he said without emphasis.

'What was he looking for?'

'He was very catholic in his tastes, sir. Unsorted manuscript material, sir. Autographs. Notes. Letters. Unpublished writings for the most part. On a whole host of subjects.'

'Is that so?'

Had he found what he was looking for, I wondered.

'Searching through an archive is like searching for silver in a river,' Ludvigssen confided. 'It's hit-and-miss. Sometimes you find what you are looking for. Sometimes you don't.'

I flicked back the page to 9th February.

It was true. Vulpius had started out with the MS copy of one of the better-known titles, but after that he had wandered into the dark unpublished forest of jottings, notes and letters. They were all from the latter part of Professor Kant's life, I noticed, long after the publication of the titles which had made his name a household word. It was the period of Kant's long, slow, mental decline, as I knew too well. If he had written anything about me – I felt a raw dryness in my throat – the pages would be hidden somewhere in the writings from that period.

'Did he tell you what he had found before he left?'

I did not raise my head from the register as I asked the question.

'He did not, sir. He simply came no more.'

338

'But you have a precise idea why he stopped coming here,' I said, observing the shifty look of discomfort which had registered on the archivist's pale face. His lips fell open, then closed tight shut. He clenched his hands together and cracked the joints of his bony fingers.

'He's the one who stole the file, sir. I thought that that was why you had come here.' His voice was rent with emotion as he spoke. 'He carried it off with him, sir. I told the local police, as I mentioned before. I do my best to protect the contents of the archive, but there is only so much that a man can do.'

Ludvigssen's odd behaviour began to make sense. If his rigid controllers had threatened him for minor infractions, how would they react to the news that manuscript documents had been stolen from the archive? And how would they have punished him for it?

'You have not received a warning in this instance, have you?'

'I have not, sir,' he replied. 'But that does not mean that it won't arrive soon.'

I spoke gently, the way that one might speak to a child.

'You must help me, then,' I said.

A film of sweat drenched Ludvigssen's face and forehead.

'You must tell me what you know about this Vulpius,' I said.

It was as if a dam had given way. Words poured from his mouth in a torrent. And I did not doubt that he was telling the truth. Indeed, he was garrulous, abundant in details of every description. But he knew nothing. He had no idea where Vulpius lived. He had hoped that the police would be able to locate the thief. He had been, he said, to enquire at the castle on several occasions, but the police had not been able to add a thing to the little that he knew himself.

The description that he gave of Vulpius reminded me of my little son, Manni, when he came home from a walk with Helena and Lotte. The trees stretched all the way to the sky, Papa! The rooks' nests were armoured fortresses in the tree-tops. The birds spoke to one another in a croaking language only they could understand. They dined on gingerbread and vegetable soup.

'Now, you must describe him to me.'

While Ludvigssen talked, I attempted to sketch the face that he had seen on at least a dozen occasions. As I put the final touches to the impression, I realised that I could have walked out into the street and immediately arrested a score of men on the basis of it. The face of Vulpius was longer than it was round. His chin was pointed, but not so very pointed. More square, as a matter of fact, sir. His hair was brown, but neither very dark nor very light. Brown hair, then. Not so long as to reach his shoulders, nor so short as to reveal his ears. His eyes were so very green that they were almost blue. His nose was straight, pointed, aquiline. His mouth was a narrow slit with very thin lips, except when he smiled.

It made for a slender harvest.

When he finished speaking, and I showed him the face that I had drawn, I saw at once that Ludvigssen did not recognise the man that he believed he was describing. Of course, I asked him what I ought to change.

'Nothing, sir. A perfect likeness. Precise in every detail!'

But when I asked him about the missing papers, we made some progress.

He checked his register, consulted his card file, and moved along the shelves tracing his finger over the reference-codes which were written on the spine of each file or box of papers. Silently, I beseeched the idolaters of Kant to send him a squashed beetle, warning him to speed things up, he was so very slow.

At last, he took down a box, and brought it to the desk.

'Here we are, sir. *C.11–03, pp. 29–37*,' he murmured. 'The stolen papers were the last two in this box.'

The list describing the contents of that file was vaguely descriptive: '*Random notes, meditations, and correspondence of a religious nature*,' it said.

There were half a dozen sheets of writing-paper, each one very thin, yellow with age, scribbled on in pencil, top to bottom, and longwise in the margins too, where Kant had added notes and corrections to what he had already written. I recognised the crabbed script of the philosopher. It was the hand of an old man. His calligraphy sloped away badly to the right, his letters were cramped and often indistinct.

I turned to the last sheet of paper in the file, which was almost blank.

'The Probable Nature of Paradise' was written large, as if it were a title.

Three lines in the centre of the page. Like an epitaph on a gravestone. I read them once, then read them through again. They were almost infantile, as if Kant were quoting or remembering some nursery rhyme. As if his mind were fading into darkness.

If thou couldst but speak, little fly,
How much more would we know about the past!

Beneath this legend, there was a note.

Theological considerations regarding a piece of amber shown to me by Wasianski.

This was the subject that Immanuel Kant had written about in the missing pages.

Amber.

29

The air was heavy with the odour.

Cooking fumes filled the night like virulent marsh gas. As I proceeded through the narrow, winding streets of Königsberg, following the directions that Dr Rickert had scribbled out to guide me, that overpowering aroma conquered every other smell. Except for a slice of black bread and some shrimps in vinegar that I had bought from a stall along the wharf outside Berodstein's warehouse, I had eaten nothing all day. Now, the thought of food pushed everything else from my mind. Herr Doctor Rickert had promised to provide my dinner, and the persistent smell on his foul breath left no doubt of what I would be eating.

Onions.

I turned at last into Ritterstrasse, a narrow alley close to the River Pregel. The smells of fried and boiling onions persisted, but there were other less enticing odours, too. Slops and sewage soiled the ground, and I had to watch out for my boots. This was the poorest heart of the student quarter. Rickert's house was at the bottom of the street. There were no lanterns. If not for a tiny pinpoint of light at the very far end, the street was as dark as a cellar.

The district had figured prominently in the newspapers the previous year. Popularly known as 'the Graves', the houses were tiny, squashed together like overcrowded tombs in a forgotten cemetery. No sooner had the French seized Königsberg than they sealed the area off, and took possession of the dwellings. The invading army had swollen enormously as the town held out against the siege, and defeat brought change. All the Prussian students had been flushed out of the Graves, making way for the swarming followers of the French camp: wives and washerwomen, officers' grooms and servants, saddlers, boot-makers, blacksmiths, sword-smiths, and all the rest of the 5th Army's random baggage had rushed in and laid their hands on every available room.

The colonisation had lasted three weeks only.

The French soldiers had threatened to raze the town, obliterate it from the map of the empire, unless some fitter accommodation could be found, asserting in one voice that the university quarter was no place for the likes of them, the backbone and muscle of the Grande Armée. The houses were lice-ridden, cramped and filthy, the by-ways under-lit and over-crowded, they complained. 'The Graves' was a danger to their health, with one communal privy out back for every twenty-four houses in a row. One day, therefore, the French charged out again, invading all the farms and villages around the city. As they ran out, the Prussians rushed back in: students, half-pay scholars, college cooks and servants, an army of private tutors, university teachers with no fixed tenure, and all who had once owned a house, or sub-let a room there.

The ghosts, as the local joke went, rushed back to their Graves.

It was no place to wander alone after dark.

And yet, as Dr Rickert had promised, a lantern glowed outside his door. I had hardly lifted an iron knocker in the shape of a fist and let it drop, when the door was opened, and the man himself stood before me.

'I was looking out for you, Herr Stiffeniis,' Narcizus Rickert chirped, glancing over my shoulder, as if expecting me to come along in company with someone else. 'Do come in, sir. Everything is ready.'

My host had put aside his dark suit, and wore a bright green smoking-jacket of some shimmering material. He led me into a tiny room, the lumpy walls of which had been papered yellow at some time in the last half-century. Garlands of faded flowers were still dimly evident. The windows were shrouded by washed-out grey linen swaths that might have been spiders' webs; rope sashes painted red suggested they might actually be curtains. Despite the warmth of the evening, a fire blazed in a rusting cast-iron hearth. A covered pot was hanging from a chain, giving off little puffs of steam, the lid chattering quietly to itself like an old woman, filling the room with a most particular smell.

'Onions?' I asked.

'Onion *soup*,' he specified, and seemed quite proud of himself.

To one side of the fire was a small armchair. On the other, pressed hard up against the wall, was a two-seat sofa. Rickert described it as his chaise longue while pointing out the other comforts of his home. 'Small, but neat,' he said more than once, while I looked all around me, noting the smoke-blackened ceiling, patches of mould like the maps of so many undiscovered continents on all the walls, and a precarious piling of thing on thing until it seemed that one thing toppling would topple every other thing. A tiny round table filled what remained of the room. This three-legged table was set for one person with a brown clay bowl, a pewter cup and spoon, and a dark green bottle which would serve as a carafe for water.

Unlike the French, I did not complain.

'I hope that you'll excuse me, sir,' he said, 'but I've already eaten. A particularly painful swelling of the stomach, and a ripping gripe in the bowels, sets in if I eat too late. I'll keep you company, of course. Unless you have already partaken?'

'I made a point of waiting,' I said, my stomach churning on the smell in that enclosed space.

'Just heating it up for you. Ready in a few minutes. Would you care to view your bedroom before you dine, sir?' he asked, as if certain preliminaries needed to be got out of the way.

Had other lodgers made themselves at home, eaten his onions, then fled as soon as they saw the bed without bothering to pay him?

He pointed to a shimmering grey curtain, which was heavy with grease and smoke, then pulled it aside like a theatre-manager who intended to impress with the scene he would reveal.

'Did you shift out when the French came through?' I asked, staring into the narrow cubicle beyond the curtain. My 'bedroom' was six feet long and four feet wide, a corridor closed off by a barred door, which led, I guessed, to the rear of the house where rubbish could be tipped and chamber-pots emptied. If there was a bedroom upstairs, it was his. I knew such 'lodgings' from my own days at the university in Halle.

'Not for very long,' he said with a hearty chortle. 'This is the bit of Prussia that they didn't want. I'd like to see the rat-holes *they* are used to in Paris,' he added with a sarcastic French accent on the second syllable.

He stepped into the alcove, and gently ran his hand over the bed. 'These sheets are fresh. Three nights only, as I told you,' he said again, raising the grey pillow-case to his nose, inhaling deeply. 'The lad was most particularly clean. He sat his doctoral tripos the other day. It went off very well.'

He pinged his knuckle against a large ewer which was standing in a matching bowl on top of a hat-box.

'Water for washing and drinking, sir.'

He flicked his nail against a chamber-pot.

'Freshly rinsed,' he said.

I nodded, thinking that I would need to keep my wits about me during the night. I did not wish to drink from the one when I ought to be drinking from the other. There was no lamp or candlestick, which was no bad thing. In such confinement an outbreak of fire and instant immolation was more than probable.

'And now, sir, if you wish to eat, the soup is on the hob.'

We turned around, the curtain fell on the scene of my nocturnal slumbers, and we were in the kitchen again. I sat down at the table where the plate had been set. He pulled up the armchair and sat himself opposite, reaching for the pot and the ladle, carefully filling my bowl to the brim.

'Did the French leave onions behind to pay the rent?' I asked convivially. 'The streets are full of the smell of them.'

'You have a selective nose, Herr Stiffeniis. The French complained of everything else. Our onions are in good supply this year.'

As he spoke, he gestured impatiently to me to eat.

'Delicious!' I lied, spooning up the thin and tasteless gruel. 'And thank you for pointing me towards the Kantstudiensaal today. It has greatly changed, as you remarked. Do you go there often, Herr Doctor Rickert?'

His eyes gleamed fiercely. 'I would if I had the time. Unfortunately . . . Still, I am glad that noble benefactors have taken the place in hand.'

'Noble?' I queried.

'In a figurative sense,' he replied quickly. 'I've no idea, really. But if that archive were to close, why, it would be as if Kant had died a second time. It had fallen into a terrible state before the French came along and laid another heavy block of granite on Kant's grave.'

'Do you know who pays for it all? The Albertina University does not, as Herr Ludvigssen happened to mention.'

Rickert stared at me, then he winked. 'Good Prussians, sir. Who else?'

'Ludvigssen does not seem to think so,' I replied.

His eyebrows met in a stern frown. 'Is he complaining? I'd like to know what for!'

I broke a piece of black bread. 'The new masters watch him like sharp-eyed, sharp-beaked hawks,' I said. 'He feels threatened by them.'

Rickert's eyes widened. His lips pursed. 'Threatened? They are paying him a decent salary!' he snorted. 'While I'm obliged to rent out rooms to survive . . .' A sickly smile lit up his face. His lips parted, exposing his brown teeth again. 'Of course, sir, it is a great, a very great, pleasure for me to have guests. Guests like you, I mean. Unless we get some students for philosophy, the Albertina will decide to get rid of me next. Then, I'll be obliged to find a sponsor, or take in sailors, soldiers, and the refuse of the taverns. It will be the ruin of me, I can tell you!'

He sank into a fit of sighing depression.

'Did Herr Ludvigssen find a sponsor?' I asked. 'Or did the sponsor find him?'

Rickert closed his eyes, shook his head. 'No idea, sir. No idea at all.'

'Did you manage to find any trace of Vulpius in the lists, as you promised to do?'

Rickert's eyelids flickered rapidly. 'Did you discover nothing at the Kantstudiensaal?'

'Vulpius had been there pretty frequently, but Ludvigssen had no idea where he might be living.'

Dr Rickert put his hands to his head and pulled fiercely at his hair. Blond on the crown of his head, it was dyed as black as coal around his ears. Even Pietists fall prey to vanity, it seemed.

'Goodness me! I thought we'd solved that little problem. That's where I send anyone who, you know, expresses an interest in Professor Kant nowadays.' He pushed his lower lip out in a show of uncertainty. 'But, sir, I made it clear, I think. The . . . the money which you gave me was for pointing you towards the archive.'

'The money which I *paid* you', I repeated more severely, 'was to ensure that you searched through the Albertina registers.' If I hoped to get anything out of him, I would need to show the same regard for cash that Dr Narcizus Rickert did.

He poured me a beaker of water like the perfect host.

'I wouldn't like you to feel that money has been squandered, sir,' he murmured. 'I did look, and would have given you my report in time. Vulpius has never been enrolled in the schools of theology or philosophy. Not in the last ten years, at any rate.' He pursed his lips and thought for a moment. 'Still, you really should have found him there at the archive. If he is a true follower of Professor Kant, you'll find him nowhere else. They all go there . . .'

He spread his arms wide, his palms turned up to heaven, like the plaintiffs who sometimes appear before me in the court-house. 'You will remember, sir, the price that we agreed on does not, cannot, guarantee the successful outcome of the research. One can only try. Do one's best, so to speak. What did you particularly want to know about him?'

'His address,' I said.

He rubbed his hands, then asked me: 'Have you ever actually met the man?'

'Never.' I lifted the water to my lips, drained it off, then stared into the thick bottom of the glass, as if the information might be found there. 'Have you ever met him?'

'Me, sir? Vulpius?' His appeal to me was not so much of surprise, more of alarm. 'Can you believe, Herr Stiffeniis, that I would not have told you everything and straight away?'

There, that was the point. Could I believe what he chose to tell me?

He knew about the recent changes at the Kantstudiensaal. He must have realised that the archive had become a potent symbol of nationalist resistance, the hub and focus of a movement which had found its inspiration in Immanuel Kant. I recalled the concern that General Malaport had expressed regarding the presence of Prussian rebels in Königsberg. *They are everywhere,* he had said. To the local French authorities, the archive might seem like little more than a pathetic attachment to a former glory, a long-forgotten library where the books and papers of a deceased Prussian philosopher were kept. It was a small bone that might be thrown to the Prussians without losing any sleep.

But what if the danger was real? What if the Kantstudiensaal was the place where the rebels congregated? And more to the point, what if Vulpius was one of them?

I was shaken from my reverie by the voice of Rickert.

'May I ask, sir, why you are looking for him?'

I hesitated for some moments, then I started to tell him precisely who I was, and exactly why I was looking for Vulpius. That is, I told Dr Rickert what I wanted him to know.

The boot was on the other foot.

Dr Rickert leant back in his seat when I had finished.

'I heard about those bodies that were found beneath the Grünen Brücke bridge,' he murmured thoughtfully. 'It's only a three-minute walk away from here. It was the talk of the town 'til the French hanged a gang of saboteurs who were trying to mine the docks. Five of those men were living right across the street from here. Can you imagine that, sir? By the time the commotion blew over, those poor women had been forgotten. What was it, a couple of months ago? And now you say they think that Vulpius was involved in the murder? A Kantian scholar?'

I did not give him time to collect his thoughts. 'The French suspect him. It is in their interests to blame everything on a Prussian. They've set their sights on Vulpius. But you and I, sir, why, *we* are Prussians. We know where our duty lies. I have always been a fond admirer of Immanuel Kant.'

On that count, at least, I was only telling half a lie.

'Me, too, sir,' Rickert pitched in enthusiastically.

'Just like Vulpius, a Kantian through and through,' I insisted. 'I must find him and warn him of the danger. And I must do so before the French manage to get their hands on him. That's why, Herr Doctor, it is imperative that you help me to locate him.'

I gave him time to think on my proposal by finishing off his soup. But evidently, Rickert needed more time, placing his own survival in the form of cash earned on one side of the balance, and the life of Vulpius, Prussian nationalist, on the other.

'I may be able to help you find him,' he said at last.

Thinking back on that evening in Rickert's house, I often puzzle over what actually happened. Along with the other things that he offered me – bed, soup, water, conversation – had Rickert set out from the start to feed me privileged information that I would never have unearthed without his help? Was his performance chicanery? An attempt to squeeze more money out of me? Or was it, instead, a form of fear, a sublimation, a means of indirectly providing me with information that he would rather not have told me, and which he would never admit to having personally given away?

Then again, was it something of an entirely *different* nature?

'Do you know Salthenius?' he enquired, his voice low, his head bent close to mine. 'Daniel Lorenz Salthenius.'

The name was familiar.

'I studied at the University of Halle,' I replied. 'Salthenius was once the Professor of Philosophy there. It was long before my own time, of course.'

Doctor Rickert clapped his hands like an excited child. 'Correct! But he was more than a philosopher. Born in Sweden, Salthenius was forced to flee for . . . Well, sir, let's just say that serious allegations were made against him. He found refuge in Halle, where he was converted to Pietism by Philipp Jakob Spener himself. Later on, Salthenius moved to Königsberg. He taught for many years here at the Albertina University and his lectures were packed, sir. Just imagine those days. All those students looking for bed and board at any price . . .'

His eyes flickered, lost in a dream of endless beds and cauldrons of onion soup.

'I do not see what this has to do with Vulpius,' I reminded him.

Rickert raised his finger. 'One moment, sir, I'll get to it. In 1740, his world was turned upside down. Malicious voices were raised against Salthenius once again. In Sweden, he had been condemned to death. In Königsberg, they satisfied themselves by removing him from the Albertina. But in the meantime, he had met a young scholar who was just beginning to make his own reputation.' He stopped short, and stared at me. His eyes were two bright, interrogative lamps. 'You know who I'm talking of, do you not? I discovered a note from Immanuel Kant in the university archive, asking whether he might visit Salthenius.'

I did not see where his reminiscences were leading.

'A letter that is not in the Kantstudiensaal,' he clarified, tapping his closed fist against his chest. 'I *alone* know what Kant asked Salthenius . . .'

'A philosophical problem, I imagine.'

He vigorously shook his head. 'Kant asked Salthenius how to contact Satan!'

It had been a long, frustrating day. I did not have the strength to argue with a madman and I had no intention of resurrecting Kant, or the Devil. I would not go down that road. It is always a problem in Prussia: relax your guard and the Devil leaps out at you as if he is something real and tangible. There, I thought, that's one thing the French will *never* rob us of: our fascination with the diabolical.

'Why would Kant ask Salthenius about the Devil?' I forced myself to say.

'He fled from Sweden, bringing that terrible knowledge along with him.'

'But Salthenius became a devout Pietist,' I objected. ' I have never heard of a Pietist who worships the Devil.'

'Salthenius was never his familiar,' he protested. 'He never bowed to Satan. He tried to use the power of the Devil for the good of Prussia. For the good of all of us!'

He shook his finger in my face.

'If only we had found the spiritual strength to learn from his teachings! Kant tried, believe me, sir.' Were those tears of passion glistening in Rickert's eyes? 'When you came by today, asking about Kant,' he said, 'I took it as a sign. A potent sign, though I did not fully understand it.'

'A sign of what?' I felt unable to withdraw from the delirium of his attack.

'You are looking for Vulpius to save him from an unjust French accusation. Vulpius is a follower of Kant. Kant ignored the false accusations against Salthenius. And you have come to *me*.'

'But you have told me nothing about Vulpius,' I replied, attempting to shatter the brittle chain of his strange logic.

'Not yet, Herr Procurator Stiffeniis. Not yet.'

He rose suddenly, and went over to a small wooden chest positioned near the fireplace. Dropping down on one knee with a grunt, he raised the lid. The chest was full of papers.

There were hundreds of sheets crammed in haphazardly. Some were crushed and bent; others were twisted, folded, ripped. When he closed the lid, and returned to his seat, he was holding a small pewter saucer in one hand, and a bundle of papers in the other. The sheets were shaking as if they had a heart that was tremulously beating of its own accord.

'Here we are, sir,' he muttered, beginning to lay the sheets on the surface of the table one at a time, folding out the pages that were bent, smoothing this one, removing creases, aligning them edge to edge, spreading a second layer over that one, until he had covered the entire surface, like Lotte when she made a sandwich-cake.

Then, he set the pewter plate exactly in the centre of the table.

'Just there,' he murmured to himself. 'That's right.'

I tried to see what was written on the sheets, but it was impossible. The contents seemed to be a jumble of words and symbols scrawled and scribbled by a childlike hand in what might have been red ink. It had turned a dull dark brown. Many of the words and letters had run, or smudged, where ink appeared to have bled into the paper.

'What are these messages?' I asked.

'The words of Satan.' He stared at me hard. 'Salthenius transcribed these messages in his own blood. As the Evil One required him to do.'

Was Rickert totally mad?

He was staring at me from deep within himself. He might have been peering out of some dark cavern. I felt a sudden repugnance for Prussia, and all things Prussian. Wasn't it better – simpler – to deal with someone like les Halles? The Frenchman was driven by a blunt materialism that was uncompromising. His hands were dirty. His concerns were finite. His gantries and pulleys were too large, or too small. They worked, or they did not work. His *coq du mer* would penetrate the sea-bed, or the sea-bed would repel it, send it back, obliging him to make more trials, more calculations.

And when his engineering science had found the answer, the solution was there for all to see.

For an instant, I prayed that France would impose its practicality on Prussia. That Bonaparte's men would cancel out the multitude of devils that continue to haunt us.

'It all began with this,' said Rickert, waving a flimsy piece of paper in the air. 'It was folded up inside the syllabus that he wrote in 1737. You know the Pietist principle? *Bußkampf*. A man must win his individual struggle with the Devil if he hopes to enter the Kingdom of Heaven. Salthenius had a greater plan: he challenged the Evil One to tell him everything that he wanted to know.'

'And what did Salthenius ask?' I said at last.

Herr Rickert held a different note out to me. I took the paper from his trembling hand, and read the single sentence.

Anti-Christ will come from Paris . . .

'He told Salthenius that Bonaparte would come before the Corsican was even born!' he murmured darkly. '*He* can tell you what you want to know, sir.'

Was this what it had come to? A devil-worshipper was going to tell me where to find Vulpius, having consulted his friendly household demon? I was prompted to take up my bag again, pay for what I owed, make my excuses, and leave him to it. What was to stop me? In retrospect, I realise that there was only one reason: I am a Prussian. The Devil fascinates us all. Without exception.

'Daniel Salthenius speaks to *me*,' he continued. 'He placed that paper where I would find it. I was chosen . . . Chosen! Look here, sir,' he added sharply, pointing his finger like a magician's wand at the mass of papers on the table-top. 'This is our correspondence. From beyond the grave.'

He planted his elbow on the table, opened wide his left hand. His right hand came up holding a fruit knife. With one swift, deft stroke, he cut a nick in the pad of skin between his thumb and forefinger.

353

Draw blood out from the large vein. This will give the sacred Entity more energy on which to feed . . .

He dropped the knife on the table, and tilted his hand over the pewter saucer.

Blood ran like a gleaming rivulet down the length of his forefinger, and into the receptacle. With a rapid mechanical gesture – as if he had done it many times before – he pulled his finger away, pointed it to the ceiling, and wedged my table napkin over the knife-cut.

'There,' he said, 'that is more than sufficient.'

He closed his eyes, and a beatific smile appeared on his face.

I heard the buzzing of a fly, then realised that he was making the noise with his lips.

Then, he began to write, dipping his fingernail into the blood. *Write?*

Do we form our letters, or do they form themselves? Do our eyes contribute to the act of writing? His eyes played no part in it, and the results were adequate proof of the omission. With hesitation and uncertainty, laying fresh blood over stains that were old, dry, faded, he traced three circles and a triangle. With the same mechanical impetus as before, his finger suddenly pointed upwards. He removed his hand, using the napkin to wipe away the blood again. He had, it seemed, finished.

Dr Rickert glanced down like a man possessed. Two small circles like eyes. A larger circle beneath it, like a gaping mouth. A medium-sized triangle, which might have been a rough approximation of a nose, except for the fact that it was where the right ear would have been. There was not much more to see on that paper.

But Rickert seemed pleased with himself. 'Not far,' he said, tracing out the patterns in the air. 'Not so far away at all.' He made a loud tutting noise. 'I don't suppose you see it, sir. You don't know Königsberg as well as I do.'

'Königsberg?'

He nodded. 'It should not be difficult to find the man. Can you see the pattern, sir?' he asked. He edged forward on his chair, pointing out the salient features of his drawing. 'These circles are the bastions of Königsberg Castle,' he announced. 'The large one is the main tower. So, this direction here is south. This triangle lies east of the castle, then, but it is close to the castle wall. Have you ever been down that way, sir? It is something of a maze. Still, this shape is distinct and I can tell you the names of these three streets. They form the Haymarket triangle. Vulpius is right here, on the corner. All the signs point to it . . .'

I stared at the bloody stains on the paper. Mystic signs. Magical ciphers. Maps written in human blood. 'I hope you will not judge me rude, sir,' I was just able to say, 'but it has been a very long day, and I really *do* need to catch up on some sleep.'

I winced as I said it. Even so, I thought, better to rest my head on a pillow where someone else had laid his head for three nights only than to spend another half-hour in my demented landlord's company.

'Quite right, Herr Magistrate. I'll make your bill up right away,' he said, and beamed a honeyed smile at me.

He did not dip his finger in the blood to make the bill. He did the sum in his head, instead, then explained it to me point by point. Five thalers for my bed, two more for dinner, one for the letter I had asked him to despatch to Lotingen.

I had already done the sum; our tallies did not match.

'Those ten thalers more,' he patiently explained, 'are for services of an *extraordinary* nature.'

I paid without argument.

Later, I lay down on my narrow bed without undressing.

Alone in the dark, the odours of that house were almost tangible. The musky, sweaty smell left behind by the tenant who had filled that space before me. The heavy, ingrained filth of ages in the mats and curtains. The acidic tang of the chamber-pot which I had removed to the farthest corner. The lingering greasy sourness of the yellow sheep-fat candles with which Dr Rickert lit his abode. The persistent sweetness of the boiled and basted onions. Plus, other traces of the sharp and the bitter which I did not care to identify.

Somewhere in the night, a dog howled. Somewhere close at hand, another hound wailed back. In Italy, when dogs cry out at night, the people get up from their beds and sit on the doorstep, waiting for the worst. Howling dogs, they say, are the early heralds of an earthquake.

In Prussia, we think differently.

Our dogs howl when the Devil comes to call.

30

The large one is the main tower.

Rickert's words echoed in my mind as I walked into the shadows of Königsberg Castle. The towering brown-brick edifice loomed high above me, cancelling out the sun, transforming the warm morning into a cold and gloomy twilight. All the administrative offices of the occupying forces had been located inside the fortress, including the office of the French military police.

As I passed beneath the archway, I recalled the February night four years before when I had entered Königsberg Castle for the first time. A necromancer had been waiting for me down in the dungeons, and I had seen him communicating with the soul of a dead man. I shivered at the memory, as I presented my identity papers to the guard.

Two smaller circles . . .

Every time I came to Königsberg in search of a murderer, I was obliged to deal with evidence of a sort that no sane man should act upon.

Did the Haymarket triangle exist, as well?

The police office was on the far side of the square. I entered, identified myself, showed my papers, asked my questions about Vulpius. He had been reported by the Königsberg nightwatch in the company of two women near the Grünen Brücke bridge, more or less in the same spot where two female corpses were later found. They knew that a man named Ludvigssen had accused Vulpius of having stolen two sheets of paper from the university library. They knew nothing more than I knew.

'Was Vulpius ever traced?' I asked the clerk.

The French soldier looked at me, then elbowed the man sitting next to him.'Well, if you'd care to wait, Monsieur Magistrate,' he replied, grinning savagely, 'we'll order the 12th Dragoons straight back from Spain to look for this thief who stole two bits of paper belonging to . . . what was his name? Professor Gant?' I could still hear their laughing when I left the room.

I stood once more in the cobbled square outside the fortress.

The Haymarket triangle lies east of the castle wall . . .

I had no other lead to follow. I went the way that Rickert had indicated. The area was dirty, badly run down, with signs of the heavy French bombardment still in evidence. The houses were ancient – some were made of wood which was rotten, frail and slanting. The streets were narrow, many cobbles were missing, having been used as missiles during the rioting. And yet, for all the dirt and broken panes of glass, there were housewives slopping soap and water on their doorsteps, and sweeping dust into the gutter with their brooms in the interests of cleanliness.

I stopped and surveyed the scene.

The jutting corner-house at the lower point of the Haymarket triangle was the one that Narcizus Rickert had mentioned to me the night before. I felt sure that he must know the place. Even so, I crossed the road and stopped in front of the house. Several rugs were draped over the railings, and a middle-aged woman was rolling up her sleeves. The hairs on her forearms glistened in the early morning sun like fields of corn, and in her right fist she brandished a carpet-beater.

'Does Herr Vulpius live here?' I asked with no preamble.

Bunching up the fat around her eyes, the woman peered at me through two tight slits. 'Are you a friend of his?' she retorted.

I was stunned. Rickert had evidently drawn blood from the correct vein.

'Is he at home?'

'Doubt it,' she said.

I was surprised at the news. It was not yet nine o'clock.

'Has he gone out already?'

'Gone out? Who knows if he'll be back? Comes and goes, he does,' she said dismissively. 'People go missing all over the place in Königsberg.'

'Has something happened to him, d'you think?'

She put her hands on her hips, and stared at me. 'I was talking of fly-by-nights that don't keep up with their rent! Herr Vulpius is usually as regular as clockwork. I will say that for him. But you can never tell.'

'Ah,' I said.

'You might well say *ah*!' she muttered sarcastically. 'Left all of his stuff, he has. Gone off, the Lord knows where. I can't throw his things in the street, can I? Too much of it for a start. Books, clothes, and I know not what else! I can't afford to be prosecuted if he takes it into his head to come back again. Nor can I let his rooms to any other tenant while they are still occupied. Maybe I should get the police to look for him.'

'I *am* the police,' I said. 'And I am looking for him.'

Her sour expression softened in a flash. 'What did you say that your name was? Mine's Poborovsky. What's he done? I won't have criminals in my house.'

Frau Poborovsky laid her hand upon her breast as if to calm herself.

'It's nothing so terrible,' I reassured her.

'You'd better come in, then,' she said.

It was a decent house. A respectable, clean-looking house. There were religious prints and framed psalms on the white-washed walls. The furniture in the raftered living-room was old, but solid: black wood dressers, matching high-backed armchairs with Berlin beadwork seats.

She did not invite me to sit down, however.

'He's been living up on the first floor almost twelve months,' she said, nodding at the ceiling above her head. 'Never once invited me in. Do you want to see the apartment, sir, before you call the bailiffs?'

359

I had no intention of calling anyone, certainly not the bailiffs.

I followed her bulky bottom up the narrow staircase.

'Do you know Narcizus Rickert?' I asked, while she searched through the large assortment of keys that dangled from her *châtelaine*.

She looked at me with a frown. 'Who, sir?'

'Herr Doctor Rickert. He rents rooms to students, too,' I said. 'Is he a friend of yours? Or of Herr Vulpius?'

'Don't know no one of that name,' she said with a shrug. 'We are so many in this trade. And Vulpius don't have visitors, sir.' She turned and stared me. 'Now don't you think that's strange? A young man with no friends?'

How had Rickert found the address, I wondered. Was he personally acquainted with the 'idolaters of Kant' that he had spoken of? Was that why he had sent me to the Kantstudiensaal? I was lost for any other explanation.

'Did Vulpius come to you from the university?'

She squinted. 'How should I know where he come from? Word gets out. I've no idea, and never asked.'

As she turned the key in the lock, I asked: 'How long has he been gone?'

'A week, ten days . . .'

'And he has disappeared before, you say?'

She looked at me for some moments, as if considering what to confide.

'He's like the lark in spring,' she said. 'A few days here, a few days there. A few days missing, then he's back again.'

I would have liked to examine the room alone, but there was no avoiding Frau Poborovsky's company. She seemed to be as curious as I was. There was an observable hesitancy in the way she advanced so timidly into what was, after all, her own property. Clearly I had provided her with an undreamt-of excuse to explore the room of her absent lodger.

'Just look at the dust!' she exclaimed.

I looked, but I was not so shocked.

Vulpius was relatively tidy, so far as I could see. There was a large bed in the corner. The sheets were thrown back, and one of the blankets was trailing on the floor. A small table and three chairs were positioned by the window. The table was piled high with books and papers and an empty plate, as if he ate and studied at the same time. Shirts and stockings were scattered haphazardly over the backs of chairs and on the carpets. I stepped across to the table, and began to handle the books, looking at the titles, while Frau Poborovsky slid open the drawers of the dresser to see what Vulpius kept inside.

Would I find the stolen manuscript pages of Immanuel Kant hidden somewhere in the heap, I wondered. Goethe's *Apprenticeship of Wilhelm Meister*, a recent publication by Schiller, novels and romances by other lesser names. Anthologies of poetry, a number of philosophical tracts. I picked up Göckel's *Lexicon Philosophicum*; evidently Vulpius knew Latin. There were patriotic pamphlets, too. Fichte's *Address to the German Nation*, plus other more incendiary appeals to Prussian national sentiment.

A folded newspaper caught my attention. It was a copy of the *Königsberger Zeitung*. A brief item on the front page had been boxed off with a bit of red wax crayon, as if the contents had meant something to the reader.

FRENCH REQUEST ASSISTANCE

A murder on the north coast. A young woman. No name has been released, but the French authorities in Königsberg are treating the matter seriously. General Malaport, commander of the Königsberg garrison, has requested the help of a Prussian magistrate with local knowledge to investigate. It is thought that a request will be made to the district of <u>Lotingen</u>. An able magistrate is living there, a young man who made his name in Königsberg four years ago, when he was called to assist the aged Professor of Philosophy, Immanuel Kant.

Readers will recall that four people were murdered in our city in the winter of 1804 . . .

The article reported at length on the facts relating to the events four years before, rather than saying anything about the murder on the amber coast. And yet, one thing was inescapable. I felt my heart and pulse begin to race. Vulpius had underlined *Lotingen*. I had been chasing him for one day only, but he had been collecting news regarding me for a longer period.

Another news-sheet had induced Vulpius to use his red wax crayon again. *Le Clairon militaire de la Baltique* was produced on rag paper of the poorest quality. A single large sheet folded in the middle, then folded again. It was cleverly printed in disjointed quarters, so that the reader could read four pages in a row, then turn the entire page, fold the paper the other way, and read the remaining four. I might have missed the inner fold, except for the fact that my eye was caught by the sequence of letters which formed my own name.

'*Hanno Stiffeniis has been ordered to conduct the murder enquiry . . .*'

One thing was clear to me. The French had made a hulla-baloo of my name and my history, perhaps to make my name digestible to French officers who might, otherwise, have made life difficult for me. At the same time, they had exposed me to the criticisms of my fellow-countrymen, who would damn me as a traitor.

Magistrate Stiffeniis – a married man with three young children – is a long-time resident in Lotingen in the canton of Marlbork. His wife, Helena, is expecting a fourth child late in the summer. Just last year, together with the eminent Parisian criminologist, Mon. Serge Lavedrine (who is currently attached to the 7th Chasseurs as a colonel), Magistrate Stiffeniis investigated the massacre of three small children in Lotingen, and was instrumental in cancelling out the vile, false accusations which had been brought against the French garrison there. Local insurgents had spread rumours which enraged the town's inhabitants, suggesting that the massacre was the work of French soldiers. General Louis-Georges Malaport speaks highly of the Prussian magistrate, and says that he is confident that the current scare on the north coast will soon be brought to a successful conclusion. Mon. Stiffeniis is a man of sound judgement and worthy of our trust . . .

Me. My family. The fact that Helena was pregnant.

The same facts had been reported in the nationalist broadsheets that Gurten had brought to Nordcopp. The French article had been printed *before*, however. It had been issued the day after I met General Malaport in Lotingen. It was not a coincidence. The *Clairon militaire* had provoked the Prussian nationalists to respond.

Who should I fear the most, the French, or the Prussians? Or Vulpius, perhaps, who seemed to have taken such an interest in me?

I turned to Frau Poborovsky, who was holding a pair of stockings against the light.

'Can you describe him, ma'am?' I asked.

She turned to look at me. 'Vulpius? Describe him?'

'Physically. His build and general appearance, I mean.'

She paused to think, a finger on her lips. 'Well, he's quite tall. Your height, more or less. Slender figure, a bit thin and wiry for my taste, but he has a good pair of calves, I'll say that for him.'

'The face, Frau Poborovsky. Is there anything that distinguishes him?'

She rubbed her hands together. 'He is quite handsome. Charming manners, too. Thin lips, a shapely nose, a good square chin, good teeth, a broad brow and . . . oh yes.' She pointed her finger toward me. 'His smell, sir. I could smell it on his hair and hands. It lingers in the air when he's at home.'

'What smell?' I asked.

363

She brushed her dress off, as if the smell were clinging there as well. 'Wax, I would say, sir. Once I told him that he smelled like a church at Christmastide.'

I needed something more visible than a smell to go on. I drew out my sketching-pad and turned to the page which held the face of the man that Ludvigssen had described to me.

'Is this him?' I asked her.

The lady's eyebrows rose in perfect arches. 'This, sir? Vulpius?' she said. 'As similar as a cat and a mouse, perhaps.' She clasped her hands and her shoulders drooped. 'This man's eyes are round and small. Herr Vulpius has a pair of eyes . . . well, they are very different. These lips are thick . . . Oh no, sir, this cannot be Vulpius. You are looking for the wrong man.'

I had realised that Ludvigssen had been of no great help. But how inaccurate had he really been? And how precise was Frau Poborovsky being now?

I went across and opened up the tallboy dresser. The smell seemed to unwind and unfold from the cupboard, like a snake uncoiling. It was not the sour smell of camphor which Helena and Lotte used at home to ward off moths. This smell was sweeter, almost medicinal, and there was a mild aromatic edge to it.

I hesitated.

Was it similar to anything I had encountered in the house of Dr Heinrich? I inhaled more deeply, held it in my nose and throat, then let it go. It was not dissimilar, I thought, though I could not be more precise. I looked more attentively at the contents of his wardrobe. Vulpius dressed well, though there was nothing remarkable about the long brown winter cloak, the green velveteen frock-coat, or the blue fustian jacket which were hanging there. Beneath the long tails of the overcoat, I noticed a round box the size of a skillet. I bent down, removed the lid. Empty.

'Do you clean his rooms as part of your fee, Frau Poborovsky?'

'No, sir. He said straight away that he would clean up after himself.'

'Usually a man renting rooms is glad to have that service done,' I insisted.

'He didn't want me moving things, he said.' She did not seem upset at this rebuff. 'Jealous of his things, he is. And secretive, too. But I came in when he was out. One day, I had to . . .'

'Why was that, Frau Poborovsky?'

'The smell again. I didn't know what to make of it. So I used the spare key.' She wrinkled her nose with disgust. 'He keeps them in the bottom drawer of his desk . . . ugh!'

I turned my attention to the drawer and opened it, while she took a step backwards, shaking her shoulders like a professional actress.

The drawer was full of jewellery boxes. Though differing in size and colour, all the containers appeared to have come from such a source. I picked one up, removed the lid, and looked inside. Something was wrapped up carefully in a bit of tissue paper. I opened it up, and stared at the contents.

A strip of paper was fixed inside the lid, on which was written in a neat hand: *Phylum: anthropoda. Class: insecta. Subclass: pterygota. Infraclass: neoptera. Order: coleoptera – (Linnaeus, 1758).*

'A beetle,' I said.

Frau Poborovsky was standing at my elbow.

'Why keep dead insects in a box?' she asked. 'It's not the only one, sir. There's something of the sort in all of them. I looked in three, then I looked no more. As if there were not creeping things enough, even in the most well-kept house.'

'He probably collects them,' I said, though my thoughts had taken a different direction.

Those letters sent to Ludvigssen. The crushed insect with which each warning was signed. Had Vulpius sent those messages? And if he had, why steal a manuscript from the very same archive? What did he hope to learn from Kant? And what did Baltic amber represent for him?

'I almost hope he don't come back,' Frau Poborovsky muttered. 'I could let the attic to two or three young men . . .'

'The attic?' I repeated, turning on her.

'He rents the attic, sir. Uses it as a workshop.' Her lips twisted and crinkled with disgust. 'You don't suppose . . .'

'It will be full of crawling creatures, I'm sure,' I said, intending to visit the attic alone. 'Bugs and slugs and spiders. Revolting things with fifty or a hundred legs. Shall we go up?'

She hugged herself, and let out a little squeal.

'I'll go alone then, ma'am, if you don't mind? If the bailiffs are to be called,' I reminded her smoothly, 'it may be best if we have a clear idea of the task that faces them. Do you have the key?'

Frau Poborovsky unlatched a key from her bunch, and pointed me up the final flight of stairs. There was no other door up there, she said, I could not miss it. I left her on the first-floor landing, and made my way to the top of the house by means of an uncarpeted staircase until a narrow door prevented me from going further. I put the key into the lock, and turned it twice.

It would not open.

Was Vulpius in there?

I listened at the door for some moments. It was so very silent, I thought I could hear the worms inside the wood. Then, I tried the key again. I could feel the lock turning, but the door refused to budge, no matter how I pushed it. I went back down three stairs, and bent to examine the bottom of the door. A thin band of light was shining beneath it. That was when I noticed a bit of string which passed beneath the door, peeping out at me like a rat's tail.

Had Vulpius used some secondary means of barring entrance to his domain?

I took my clasp-knife from my bag, slipped it under the door, and found that there was indeed some hindrance near the string. I jabbed forward with the knife once or twice, and the obstacle gave way a little. Then, I tried the door again. As the door swung back, I saw a wooden wedge with that piece of string attached to it by a knot. Having closed and locked the door, Vulpius employed this simple but ingenious stratagem to safeguard the contents of his *workshop*. That was the word that Frau Poborovsky had used.

'Is everything in order, sir?' Frau Poborovsky called from below.

I reassured her that it was, while I pushed open the door.

Two eyes stared at me.

My heart had leapt into my throat. They were the eyes of a pretty young woman. I let out a deep sigh as I stepped inside the room. I closed the door carefully and blocked it with the wedge, as Vulpius himself might have done.

Then, I turned around and examined those eyes.

It was a painting. An oil, no larger than a linen handkerchief, which made the face exactly life-sized. The surface was oddly rippled in some indefinable way, executed in a style which seemed distinctly old-fashioned. Certainly, it was from another era. A young woman with a powder-white face, high cheekbones, piercing black eyes, and a strange blue-and-white cap on her head. A gold ring dangled from her left ear.

Her eyes seemed to follow me as I began to explore the place.

Ancient rafters rose to a point ten feet above my head. A murky gable window at either end let in light. There was a lantern, but I had no need of it. Even in the gloom, I could see what Vulpius was engaged upon. Along one wall was a shelf lined with glass jars. Some were large, some were small. All of them gleamed in the half-light. Each one contained a quantity of pale yellow liquid, and some dark object. I could not put specific names to the contents, but I could see that they were insects, most of them from foreign climes. From Africa, India, other exotic places. Beetles with horns and others with more legs than I, or Frau Poborovsky, would have had the heart to count. Unlike the bugs in the boxes in the room below, the jars had not been labelled. There were no titles in German or Latin, no dates to indicate where, when or how the samples had been collected. As if the scientific data did not interest him, but rather the exotic shape and the *genus* of the creatures.

I turned away from the exhibits, and began to examine the rest of the attic.

Other glass jars contained live creatures: black slugs, green worms, a long-legged spider with a thick pelt of brown hair that was larger than a plum, a beetle with two large horns on its head. He probably purchased them from the ocean-going ships in the port. Some were in the last, twitching stages of life. Wherever he had gone, Vulpius had left his private menagerie to starve to death. There was nothing sentimental in his hoarding, that was evident. Each jar was empty and bare, except for the life form that it contained. There was no moss, no grass, no stick or stone, which might have made the occupant feel any more at home in its cold glass prison. Vulpius seemed intent only in watching those creatures live, grow and die.

A keen eye, I thought, *but a heart of stone.*

For the rest, the contents of the workshop were – I felt some degree of relief – works of the imagination which he had committed to paper. I am a fair artist, but Vulpius was a gifted illustrator. Large sheets of paper were spread out on an angled desk, where he appeared to be working on some project which I would have been hard put to describe. He favoured the use of a blood-red chalk – the sort they call *sanguigno* in Italy – which he appeared to have moulded and shaped with his finger, having laid it on the surface of the paper.

The top sheet was a large-scale drawing of a frog's leg, the skin stripped away to reveal the muscles and tendons in the act of jumping. Next to it, a drawing of a human leg in matching scale, performing the same action, as if man and frog were of the same size. The frog's upper leg muscle made the man's seem puny in comparison; the man's calf was immense beside that of the frog. And on the very same sheet, he had created a hybrid model, combining the jumping power of the frog with the marching power of the man. It was an impossible dream, yet it seemed to attract and fascinate the man that I was searching for.

The man that I had already met?

The casts and drawings Dr Heinrich had made of Erika's limbs would not have been out of place in that workshop. In my mind's eye, I saw him bending over that work-top with a red chalk-pencil in his hand. I could imagine the interest with which he would observe the creatures in their jars, humming quietly to himself as he went about his task, totally absorbed in it, as he had been when he showed the plaster casts to Gurten and myself. I remembered what Gurten had said. *The doctor is guilty, sir.* Once again, it seemed, my assistant had been pointing in the right direction.

I turned to another drawing, and felt a sense of shock and revulsion. Indeed, I felt my stomach heave. He had moulded the legs and wings of a house-fly onto the body of a man, as if both fly and man would benefit from the adaptation. Sheet after sheet, there were dozens of these bizarre representations. I went through them quickly, looking for some drawing of Erika, convinced that I would find the final connection between Vulpius and Dr Heinrich, whom I had thought to leave behind me in Nordcopp. Would it not be ironic if I found in Königsberg what I had sent Gurten to look for in Lotingen?

But there was nothing so obvious.

I dropped the papers on the table with a sigh. I was surrounded on all sides by a bizarre and cruel vision of grotesque Nature. But as my eye swept over the room and its contents, I let out an involuntary cry as I spotted something familiar on a narrow shelf at the far end of the attic. Treading carefully, as if the sound of my footsteps might make that mirage disappear, I went towards the far wall, and stood there staring for some moments at what was on display.

Amber.

An entire collection. Dozens and dozens of pieces. Some of the lumps were the size of boiled sweets, others were as large as a closed fist. But it was what the amber contained that was so breathtaking. The flies and other nameless insects caged inside were unlike anything that I had ever seen before in my life. Could such creatures once have crawled upon the ground, or taken wing on a sky that was the colour of lead and stank of the sulphurous fumes of volcanoes in endless eruption?

I recalled the horror of Helena the night before I was torn from Lotingen, the description she had given of an enormous insect disappearing into the open mouth of baby Anders. She had described a creature such as these, a creature unlike anything that might be found in the house, or in the garden. I held the very creature she had seen in the palm of my hand. I beheld a host of them. Though dead and trapped inside the golden amber for countless centuries, they seemed no less terrible. If those creatures had ever moved on Prussian soil, I thought, this was no vision of Paradise. It was a nightmare.

Which of those pieces belonged to the Spener collection?

And who had brought the others from the coast?

Kati and Ilse? Megrete and Annalise? Edviga Lornerssen?

And if he had taken those treasures from the girls, why had he slaughtered them?

I had found the killer. Half man, half beast, a hybrid creature of a more primitive age, like the strange things that he pawed over. A doctor, who cured the sufferings of the amber-gatherers; a beast, who mutilated their corpses.

I pulled up with a start.

I was facing the portrait on the wall.

By some devilish artistry, the pretty young girl had disappeared, her angelic face transformed into a bone-white skull. Only the gold ring dangling from her ear remained unchanged. I eased closer to the portrait, realised that there were, in fact, two portraits overlaid, the lower one visible through narrow slats in the surface of the upper canvas. As I went beyond a certain point, the picture began to dissolve, then it suddenly snapped clear, and I was staring at the face of the beautiful young woman once again.

As I left the attic, I did as Vulpius would have done. I positioned the wedge close beside the door, and placed the string at the side of the door-jamb before closing the door. When the key was turned and the lock snapped shut, I pulled hard on the string and tugged the wedge back into place.

Frau Poborovsky was waiting at the foot of the stairs, her eyes wide with alarm.

'Nothing . . . strange up there?' she asked uncertainly.

'Books for the most part,' I reassured her. 'But I wonder where I might find him. You say he had no friends. What about acquaintances at work, perhaps?'

She curled up her bottom lip, and shook her head.

'I can't think of anyone. Apart from that letter of reference . . .'

'Letter?'

'When he signed the lease for the room, I insisted on a character note from a person of respectable standing in Königsberg.'

I felt a flush of excitement. 'Do you have this letter?' I asked her.

She shook her head again. 'I clean out regular.'

'Do you remember the name of the person who signed for him?'

She crossed her arms, and thought for a moment. 'I can't recall it now. Still, I do remember thinking he was Dutch, though.'

'Dutch? What makes you say that?'

'It was the name. De-something-or-other. You know the way they have them funny shoes, and funny names? The gentleman had a shop down in Schwartzstrasse.'

31

Turning into Schwartzstrasse, I pulled up sharply.

It was as if Frau Poborovsky had opened Vulpius's wardrobe again.

That smell.

The same pungent aroma that clung to Vulpius's working clothes. Cloying and sweet, it invaded my throat, and sat heavily upon my stomach. Frau Poborovsky had said that it was constantly on his hands and hair. A most peculiar perfume that he favoured, she believed. It was certainly distinctive, but she was wrong in thinking that he wore it as a pomade.

Tall, dark warehouses lined the far side of the street. They had been abandoned for some time by the look of them. The doors were barred, the hatches closed, the joists and pulleys used for heaving sacks to the upper floors were orange with rust. Even so, the street was busy. On the near side there were mechanics' dens, a blacksmith's yard, workshops of endless variety. Saws rasped and buzzed from one door, beating hammers exploded from the next. I paused outside a barrel-maker's, and heard the creak and shriek of staves being bent, the rattle of iron hoops, the thumping of wooden mallets. Up above my head, seagulls screeched forlornly. Perched on roof-gables, they stared fixedly north in the direction of the Baltic Sea.

I worked my way along the street, following that smell.

There had been more fragrant scents there in the past, it seemed. Hand-painted signs offered spices from the Indies, tropical fruits from South America. But then the French had arrived and the British naval blockade had put an end to foreign trade. Where pepper, nutmeg and other rare vegetable extracts had once been ground and packaged in paper sachets, mackerel were now being smoked on strings hung over a charcoal-pit. The view through the open doors of the smoking-yard was like a still-life painting from the Low Countries: bright glowing embers in strips on the ground; hazy blue smoke on a dark ground; silver-glistening, dead-eyed fish.

But that other smell kept coming back to me.

I lost it for an instant as I passed beside a carpenter and his lad who were making coffins beneath an ancient sign. PRECIOUS WOODS – INTAGLIO WORK, it read. They were rooting through a mound of cast-off lumber which had just been tipped out onto the cobbles. A lanky man in rags with a skinny horse and makeshift cart was dumping broken doors and scorched planks onto the pile, whistling through his gap-teeth while he worked. Wood-shavings, glue and varnish filled the air.

But not for long.

I caught the scent again, then lost it immediately.

The doors of the next shop were thrown wide open. Three men were hard at work. Their faces seemed to be melting in a lather of sweat. Old sacks covered their bodies and heads. They were filling large glass jars with vinegar and baby eels, which twisted and jerked away as each man grabbed a writhing handful from a tub, and tried to press the reluctant creatures into their little glass coffins.

I lingered for a moment, remembering.

One of our serfs had been sent to Königsberg to collect the leather harnesses for a new coach. When he returned to Ruisling, he brought back a jar of pickled eels for my father, saying that they were considered to be a great delicacy. Father, Mother, Stefan and I had sampled the eels that evening, and been sick for three days afterwards. Helena had expressed a craving desire for pickled eels one morning recently, as pregnant women sometimes will.

Very soon, her time would be up . . .

373

I had never felt so helpless. I thought of her swollen belly. The child would be gathering his strength now. He, or *she*, would be preparing to fight his, or *her*, way into the world. I ought to have been there. And maybe I would be there soon.

That distinctive smell grew stronger.

Smoked fish, scorched wood, pickling eels could not hold me back. Like a prized red setter, I caught at the richer, more celestial, aroma floating on the warm air, and I rushed on down Schwartzstrasse. It pushed all other smells aside, persisting long after they had faded. Had I walked that street at night – had my eyes been blind – I would still have been able to follow it to its source.

Bright red letters on a white background, the hanging sign looked relatively new. I stopped and read again what was written on the trade-sign. DeWitz WaxWorks – Death Masks On Request.

I breathed in deeply.

It did not smell like the beeswax that Frau Poborovsky probably used to polish the dining-table in her parlour. Nor did it have the clinging greasy odour of the tallow rushes that she certainly used to light her rooms. This stuff had a sharp, almost bitter, scent that anyone might have remarked upon if Vulpius carried it into his lodgings.

A handcart was parked in front of the door. Ready to depart at a moment's notice, I surmised. They must carry wax to a customer's home. It seemed unlikely that grieving relatives would bring a body all the way here to make an impression of the face alone. I decided immediately how I would present myself. I would invent an uncle, then sacrifice him. He had died that very morning; I wished to have a death mask made.

I pushed on the door. A dangling bell clanged and jangled as I entered.

I might have been stepping into a church. The warm wax worked its spell on me. Can any Christian soul resist it? It seemed to promise warmth and light and eternal life – despite the suggestion of death, and the hint of funerals that inevitably accompanies it. The low, barrel-vaulted ceiling of the work-shop was made of ancient smoke-stained bricks, and it was as long as a country chapel. There even appeared to be side-altars sprouting off on either side. Light shone out of these openings, tracing elongated human shapes in stark silhouette upon the opposite walls.

'Is anyone there?' I called.

Large cubes of grey wax were stacked like blocks of ice against the walls on both sides of the entrance. Clouds of wood-smoke filled the air. As I called again more loudly, the figure of a man emerged from the swirling smoke, as from a fog, coming to meet me in an unhurried manner.

'May I help you?' he enquired.

He was tall, slender, rakish. Not yet fifty, I would have said. Wisps of long blond hair dangled in a goatee beard from his pointed chin. He had carelessly thrown a brown cloak over his shoulder like a French *chasseur*, and wore a red wool cap pulled down tightly over his forehead. His bright blue eyes gazed into mine.

'I am looking for Herr DeWitz,' I announced.

'You have found him,' the man replied with a pleasant, welcoming smile. There was a croaking catch in his animated voice. He spoke German well, but clearly it was not his native tongue.

'You . . . you are not Prussian, sir,' I said, dithering about the best way to begin.

Having got so very close, I did not intend to startle Vulpius into flight.

'You have a good ear, sir. I am Dutch. From Delft. But no,' he apologised quickly, his face taking on a more lugubrious aspect. 'You have more urgent business certainly. A death in the family, I suppose?'

I toyed with my mythical uncle, then decided to be blunt.

'No, thank the Lord,' I replied. Then, lowering my voice, I took a step closer. 'I am a Prussian magistrate, sir. I am conduct-ing an investigation. Is there somewhere we may talk in private?'

He did not seem surprised or alarmed at this request.

'Come with me,' he replied, turning away, walking into the smoky interior.

I followed him in silence, taking careful note of my surroundings. In the first vaulted room through which we passed, two very young girls were sitting beside an open fire on a which a large pot of wax was bubbling. These children were making domestic spills, dipping long reeds one by one into the pot, then placing them in an upright rack to harden and dry.

'We're getting ready for the winter,' DeWitz informed me, turning to the right, leading me into another brick-vaulted tunnel, where an old man with a badly bent back and large, skeletal hands was feeding brushwood kindling into a fire beneath a large brass boiler. A set of long, slender candle-moulds were laid out on a work-bench beside him, the wicks pulled tight by dangling weights at either end of the mould.

I fought off the suggestion which rose immediately to my mind. Plaster casts of candles of differing dimensions hung from the walls. It was all too easy to make comparisons with the surgery of Dr Heinrich and the plaster casts of Erika Linder's arms, hands and legs. All too easy to reach a wrong conclusion, and see what I wanted to see.

I chased after DeWitz.

At the far end of this long low hall was a table and four stools. The proprietor of the waxworks sat down, made himself comfortable, and invited me to do the same with a sweeping gesture of his pale right hand. He poured himself a glass of water from a carafe, sipped from it, then he looked at me. 'Will this do you for privacy? You are very mysterious, sir.'

'I . . . I saw your sign,' I said, hesitating again. My greatest fear was that Vulpius was somewhere in the vicinity. 'Death masks . . .'

'A minor branch of the trade,' he replied. 'We don't do more than four or five a week. It is going out of fashion. Candle-making takes up the greatest part of the general business. All shapes and sizes. All qualities, of course. The denser the wax, the longer they burn, the more they cost.' He sipped again, apparently waiting for me. 'It is thirsty work.'

It was extremely warm in the manufactory. It would be a decent place to work in winter, I thought, but the numerous fires, the smoke, and the heavy scent of perfumed wax clogged the stifling air.

I leant over the table.

'I am looking for a man named Vulpius,' I said very quietly. 'I have been informed that he works for you.'

DeWitz stared hard at me. 'Vulpius *sometimes* works for me,' he replied.

'Is he here just now?' I asked.

'He is not,' he said.

'Do you know where he is?'

'Again, Herr Magistrate, I must say no.'

The tension drained out of me. Frustration took its place.

'But you know where I can find him, surely?'

DeWitz did not move, his glass poised close to his lips.

'I have no idea,' he said at last. 'To tell you the truth, I am beginning to lose my patience with him. He should be here, he should be working, but I haven't seen him for . . . what, a week? More, perhaps. What day is it today?'

'Thursday,' I replied.

'It is at least ten days since he was here,' he decided at last.

The deaths of Kati and Ilse fell within that time span. And Dr Heinrich had been in Nordcopp – not Königsberg – as I could personally testify, in the same period.

'What does he do when he does come to work?' I asked.

'He is a modeller,' DeWitz replied.

'Of candles?'

The answer came after a while. 'He is employed in the laboratory.'

'The laboratory?' I repeated. 'And what is that?'

DeWitz looked at me, and he smiled more pensively. 'Have you a good, strong stomach, sir?' he asked.

I nodded mechanically, thinking that he was talking of mortuary masks. I had seen the operation done on two occasions in my youth: my father's mother first, then, a decade later when my brother, Stefan, died.

'I know that wax is applied to the cadaver's face . . .'

DeWitz shook his head. 'Not that,' he said dismissively. 'It might be better if I show you what we do here, rather than explain it. You are a magistrate, after all. You'll have seen sights that other men find shocking. Is that not so, sir?'

There was an air of presumption in his manner, almost a challenge.

I rose to my feet at once. 'Where is this place?'

We went back down the hall, turned left, then right, and left again. At the end of the tunnel there was a broad double door. And a warning sign: KEEP OUT – ON PAIN OF DEATH. Someone had sketched a skull, and a pair of crossed bones in the form of a knobbly letter X. The symbol reminded me of the *memento mori* carved on ancient tombs in country churchyards.

DeWitz pounded three times on the door.

Each knock was separated by a second of silence.

He waited for a few moments before pushing the door and going in.

The room was larger than any of the others. Six or seven people were working there. Two of them were women. One of them was stirring a large bowl of what looked like plaster, but that activity seemed tame in comparison with what the other workers were doing.

'I have a licence,' DeWitz said quickly. 'From the police, and the Albertina, too.'

'I certainly hope so,' I muttered.

In the centre of the room, a man in a leather apron was standing by a table. He was working with a short knife, removing the heart from a dead body which was naked. The butcher was so thoroughly caked in blood that his apron was black. Spots of blood were spattered on his arms and his face.

'A male,' I murmured, noting the grey, lifeless sex of the corpse.

'Fresh from Lobenicht poorhouse this morning,' DeWitz informed me. 'We make the most of what we can get.'

'What are they doing?' I asked him.

'They're making models for the university,' DeWitz replied with a short, ironic laugh, as if he had sensed my doubts. 'What else would they be doing?'

Someone began to sing in a high-pitched female soprano.

'Tu 'nce si nnata co' le rose 'mmano . . .'

A second voice picked up the melody of a song that I had heard before.

'Are they Italian?' I asked, nodding from the blood-soaked man with a human heart in his hands to the singers and the other persons employed in that charnel-house. To make it worse, two small boys were tending a fire and the cauldron for melting wax that was suspended over it.

'Indeed they are,' DeWitz explained with a raising of his eyebrows. 'From Florence, most of them. Though the carver over there,' he indicated the man with the human heart, 'his wife and his daughter, who both have lovely voices, are all from Naples.'

'What are they doing in Königsberg?'

'They are artists,' he replied. 'Florence and Naples are cities with a refined and ancient tradition in modelling wax. They can fashion a crib that will have everyone who sees it weeping on Christmas Eve. *Voi siete artisti, non è vero*, Pasquale?' he called over to the man, who was scraping and levering with his knife, extracting some other organ from the cavity of the corpse that lay wide open before him on the table.

'*Verissimo, capo!*' the Neapolitan replied without looking up.

DeWitz turned to me and shook his head. 'I went to Italy many years ago,' he said, 'intending to learn the waxy art myself, but it is not learnable. Either you have the talent, or you don't. I did not . . .'

'Does Vulpius have it?' I asked.

'Oh yes, he does,' DeWitz replied enthusiastically. 'He's one of the best, though relatively new to the trade. I had him making plaster casts for me at first, but when the Italian workers arrived, we needed extra help to meet the terms of the contract.'

'And Vulpius volunteered?'

'He did, sir. Displayed a rare skill, too. He is a student of medicine, and is working here to pay his way. His knowledge has been useful. His anatomical drawings are precise. That is, they are precious to me, as you can imagine.'

I had seen the drawings in Frau Poborovsky's. Bizarre, they might be. Monstrous, too. But they were incredibly lifelike and marvellously detailed.

'You mentioned a contract,' I said.

'Science is all the rage at the university now,' he replied. 'It all began with the arrival of the French . . .' He turned and stared aggressively at me. 'I know what Prussians think of them, sir. But not everything they bring is bad.'

I was inclined to agree, though I did not like to hear such talk from a foreigner.

'What is this contract for?' I insisted.

'A medical museum, Herr Procurator,' DeWitz replied with a broad smile. 'The Albertina is enlarging its faculty. I was working on a similar job in Paris before coming here. I spent two years at the Observatoire National. These men and women came here with me. They have been imported, so to speak. It is easier to import people into Prussia nowadays than it is to bring in tea or coffee. No Prussian artist is their equal. Except for Vulpius. They are incredibly skilled in modelling the human anatomy. You'd be amazed at the sort of detail they are able to reproduce in wax. Just look here, sir.' He led me over to a table where a middle-aged woman was working on a model of a hand. '*Con il tuo permesso*, Maria. Will you look at that? Have you ever seen anything like it?'

In my head a warning voice sounded.

Dr Heinrich had been there . . .

Dressed in a brown overall and bonnet, the lady was working by the light of a lantern with a magnifying mirror. Even in this fierce blaze, I was able to distinguish the real from the false by one token only: one hand was finished; the other was not. The hand from the corpse was laid out on a square of pale satin cloth. The loose skin had been peeled away from a central incision, and rested in two triangular red flaps, exposing the veins, the nerves and the bones. The artist had already formed the general shape of the muscles; she was laying thin strips of purple wax over the fleshy pink mound between the thumb and forefinger.

'She'll form the veins one by one, then ripple them to suggest the contours and pulsing shape of blood-laden vessels. When all is perfect, she'll weld the additions to her model by means of heat,' DeWitz explained.

'But the cloth is real,' I challenged.

Like the real hand, the model was laid out on a piece of satin.

'Wax!' DeWitz proclaimed, as if the thought bewitched him. 'The magic of wax and gum arabic. They build the model up, layer upon layer. And when it is quite finished, it goes into the storage room to set hard.'

He pointed to the furthest, deepest part of the vault.

In the gloom I could just make out long shelves piled high with covered objects. In the centre of the space were a number of long tables covered with white drapes. It looked to me like a ward in an epidemic hospital where all the patients had died.

'As the gum sets, the wax takes on a permanent glaze,' he explained. 'Once that is done, the exhibits are ready to go on public display. Within a year, Königsberg will be in a position to open the doors of its very own wax museum.'

I remembered seeing something of the sort in Paris in 1793, though those exhibits were real: the decapitated heads of common criminals and nobles ranged side by side in gore-splashed baskets beneath the guillotine.

'A lurid spectacle for the curious,' I muttered.

'Not at all!' he protested vehemently. 'Have you been to Florence, sir? Have you never seen La Specola, the museum of the Duke of Tuscany? It is a waxen mirror of life and death, the finest scientific collection in the world. Duke Peter-Leopold of Hapsburg-Lotharingen was an enlightened scholar of the first order. Public dissection of the human body was odious, he declared, and he decided to prohibit it. But doctors and surgeons still needed to be trained. They had to know in detail the mechanics of life and death. So how were they to learn? There was only one way, sir. By cutting up human bodies. There is no lack of common criminals in Florence, you might think. But how many bodies does a medical school require in the course of a year, Herr Procurator? The number disgusted Duke Peter-Leopold, and it continues to horrify the religious authorities in Königsberg. The Pietists object to capital punishment for fear of condemning an immortal soul to Hell. They prefer long prison sentences, hard labour, much prayer, and the possibility of eventual penitence. I am their salvation,' he added archly. He seemed to pulse with pride at the thought of such admirable human and scientific progress.

I trembled also, aghast with a sense of horror.

Had the jaw of Kati Rodendahl and the larynx of Ilse Bruen passed through their hands? Had the Italian woman working patiently on that lifeless hand worked on the amber-gatherers, as well? Or had Vulpius attended to them? Had he made models of the pieces that he had heartlessly ripped from the living?

My doubts melted like hot wax. Heinrich was leading a double life. And the name of his double was Vulpius! He was not concerned with amber alone. Nor with the ancient creatures that it contained. Malaport had guessed. 'He is interested in anatomy,' the general had said. 'Female anatomy.' That would explain why Dr Heinrich was so enamoured of the amber-gatherers.

Had Erika's deformity saved her from a similar fate, I wondered. Was he more concerned to study her than to cut her up into little pieces?

'How many bodies do you need to make a single model?' I managed to ask.

DeWitz looked at me with a complacent smile. 'Just to make that hand,' he said, glancing at the modeller as if he were talking about the manufacture of a bit of furniture, 'Maria will have used at least a dozen. A fair-sized medical school will work its way through a hundred bodies every year.'

I asked him where he found them all.

'In times of war, supply is plentiful,' he said with a shrug. 'In times of peace, any person, male or female, who dies in the poorhouse ends up here. Any corpse that is found within the city limits. All executed criminals are brought to me. That body over there belonged to a nameless vagrant.'

'So, the authorities approve . . .'

'They know that time will end our work,' he insisted. 'When the museum is complete, public dissection will still be necessary, but the need will be greatly reduced. Young doctors will learn about the human body from wax models, then they'll attend a dissection or two to learn in detail what they are about. If cutting up meat were the only criterion, they could work for a week in a butcher's shop!'

'Isn't that what your workers are doing? Chopping up . . .'

'That is not exact!' DeWitz objected, staunchly defending Enlightened science. 'Dissection is an extremely wasteful business. The body is hacked to pieces, decaying in a very short time to a state where it is fit for burial, and nothing else. As you see, I have seven artists – eight, when Vulpius is here – working from a single body. That corpse will keep them busy for days.'

'Supplying bodies would be a profitable trade,' I began to say.

'Oh no. There's no shortage of supply,' he interrupted quickly again. 'While poverty is rife, Nature's toll is a heavy one. Disease, illness, accidents . . .'

'Are female cadavers easy to come by?'

'Two a penny,' he replied bluntly. 'A peasant will sell the body of his mother, wife, or daughter for a pittance. We rarely bother to buy them, though. The port is a hive of prostitutes. We get one or two a week from that source.'

So why did Heinrich–Vulpius kill and mutilate the amber-gatherers?

I could not shake off the image of Kati Rodendahl's face, the cavity hacked in Ilse Bruen's throat. What I had discovered in DeWitz's workshop should have given me a sense of triumph. But I felt nothing of the sort. Another question rumbled in my mind, instead, and not even DeWitz could answer it. *Was there some connection between amber and the mutilations?*

And if so, what might it be?

'You have been most helpful, sir,' I admitted. 'I have just one final question, then I will leave you to your work.'

'Questions seem to be your business,' DeWitz smiled broadly. 'You did not come to order a death mask, or purchase candles. And my anatomical models would not hang well on your parlour wall. What can I do for you?'

I took my sketching-album from my bag.

'Does this remind you of Herr Vulpius?' I asked, showing him the picture that I had drawn with Ludvigssen's help.

'Not a lot,' he replied quickly. 'Indeed, not at all.'

I flicked to the next page, and the portrait that Frau Poborovsky had helped me to make. The two faces had little in common, but I hoped that he might be able to resolve the enigma for me. If DeWitz recognised either face, I would report the fact at once to General Malaport and the French.

But the Dutchman showed no enthusiasm for the second portrait, either.

He turned back to the first, and his uncertainty seemed to mount even more.

'I cannot say that either picture resembles him much,' he said, as he handed the album back. 'The second sketch . . . well, there is a tenuous likeness, but it's very slight.'

I took the album from his hand, turned to a blank page, then handed it back to him.

'With your experience in handling human flesh, you must be an expert physiognomist,' I said in a categorical way. 'You can accurately describe a face, and draw it, too.'

DeWitz frowned, as if he were considering the proposal.

Then, his hand dived into his pocket, and came up holding a piece of charcoal.

'You exaggerate my skills,' he replied. Nonetheless, he began to trace the contours of a face with rapid, dashing strokes on the paper. 'I am not the artist in this workshop. We do not use drawings as a rule, though Vulpius sometimes makes a sketch for his own use.'

The portrait that DeWitz produced was smaller than the others. But as the features began to materialise in a flurry of lines and hatchings, I almost led myself to believe that I saw the eyes, nose and lips of Dr Heinrich taking shape upon the page. There was an ironic, slanting set to the mouth which recalled the proud, bluff confidence of the surgeon of Nordcopp to my mind.

The work was quickly finished.

His sketch showed no resemblance to the other portraits, however. This Vulpius was thin, gaunt. His cheekbones were high, his gaze challenging. His chin was speckled with a dark stubble.

Dr Heinrich?

'I hope you find him,' DeWitz remarked. 'He's in no trouble, I hope?'

I should have expected the question. 'No trouble,' I replied neutrally.

The Dutchman took stock of me. 'Vulpius knows the secrets of the human body, Herr Procurator. He is a first-class artist in the modelling of wax. A stickler after perfection. Why are you looking for him?'

'Why?' I snapped my album shut and remained in silence for some moments. 'For the very reasons you just mentioned. He is an anatomist and an expert modeller.'

32

I laid General Malaport's *laissez-passer* flat on the counter.

'I must send an urgent message,' I announced.

The French corporal sitting behind the despatch counter looked up. His uniform appeared to have been used for the purpose of greasing axles. His *képi* tilted down over his right ear as if he had just been walloped by his superior officer. There was nothing military about his appearance. Nor did his counter inspire confidence. A mound of letters lay scattered in a haphazard heap, a dagger planted upright in the wood like the sword in the oak of German legend.

'Are you a Prussian?' he said, propping his elbows on the counter, looking me up and down, as if to assess the value of my clothes and boots.

'A Prussian magistrate,' I specified.

'That doesn't change the rules,' he warned me in laboured German. 'If you want to send a despatch by way of this office, I'll have to read it first. Censorship.'

I tapped my forefinger on General Malaport's letter. 'I would advise you to read this authorisation with care,' I said in my very best French.

He glanced at the contents, then let out a sigh.

'General Malaport, right. Save us a bit of time, that will. Got a date with a Prussian sausage,' he added, as if it were a task of unimaginable importance.

As he reached for a pen and a despatch paper, I saw what he was talking about. On the table behind him lay a piece of black bread, and a garlic-seasoned sausage which he had probably sliced with that same dagger. The slender blade was greasy with pork fat.

'What's your name, then?' he asked carelessly.

'I can write my own messages,' I replied.

'Name,' he insisted, dipping his pen into the inkwell.

'Hanno Stiffeniis of Lotingen.'

'Stiffeniis?' he asked aggressively, dropping his pen, and clasping the handle of the dagger as if he meant to attack me with it. 'Lotingen?'

I pointed my finger at Malaport's note.

'My name is written here,' I insisted.

'If that's the case,' he replied, flicking at the letters in the pile, using the filthy blade of his knife to turn them over one by one, 'a message came for you this afternoon.'

Suddenly, he jabbed hard, and held a letter dangling on the point of his blade.

'Here we are,' he said, jerking it away as I reached out to take it. 'We don't get much mail with Prussian names on. Fear of the censor, I suppose. All too busy plotting, aren't you?'

I could have seized the knife, and rammed it down his throat.

I struggled to control my temper. Every contact with the French was a trial. Daily humiliation of this sort rankled most of all. The more lowly the soldiers were, the greater their pride, the worse their disdain for us. That a clerk could be so arrogant to a Prussian magistrate acting on behalf of a French general was beyond belief.

He let the letter drop on the counter.

'Thank you,' I said, snatching it up, turning away.

I expected a note from Helena, but I recognised the plain upright hand of Johannes Gurten instead. Could this be his reply? Already? I had consigned the letters to Rickert just the evening before. I felt a rush of anxiety. Had something happened in Lotingen?

I broke the seal.

Herr Stiffeniis,

I arrived safely, and can report that your wife and children are in good health, according to your clerk, Herr Knutzen. He found me decent lodgings at an inn close by your office, and directed me to the estate of Count Dittersdorf. That gentleman placed his library at my disposal, as you requested, and I began to examine the collected editions of the various French journals which are in his possession.

So far as I can tell, there is nothing published which relates to Erika Linder, nor any description of a medical condition similar to hers, but there is a great deal written on the subject of Baltic amber!

Until three years ago, there was little mention of it in the French papers. Almost none, indeed. But since the invasion, articles have been appearing regularly in the most important Parisian scientific publications, i.e. Le Moniteur des sciences, and Le Journal pour l'encouragement des industries. This seems to support my conjecture that there is serious scientific interest in amber in French universities, and suggests that restrictions on the exportation of Prussian amber containing insects are being widely flouted.

French scientists are particularly interested in the creatures contained in amber because they play an important role in two conflicting theories, as regards the laws of the Natural World and its Ancient History. As everyone knows, the debate centres on the contrasting opinions of the Swedish naturalist, Linnaeus, and the Frenchman, Lamarck, concerning the classification of animal species.

Amber has assumed a central role in the proofs and counter-proofs since Baltic amber first came flooding into France in 1806. Clearly, large amounts are now being smuggled into France. This we knew. What we did not know is: a) the extent of the trade; b) the precise nature of the amber being actively sought; c) the vast amount of money which is available for the purchase of any amber specimen which seems to provide another link in what they call 'the Chain of Creation'.

And now we come to Dr Heinrich.

I turned the page.

Johannes Gurten had made himself master of the complex world of French science, as he had promised, while never losing sight of his objective, which was to find the proof that Dr Heinrich had killed the women on the coast. I had been reluctant to follow his reasoning. We had both been right and wrong, I thought. Gurten had been right to point an accusing finger at Heinrich, wrong in suggesting why he might have killed. In Königsberg I had found the true motive. What would Gurten say when I told him that Heinrich was not in league with the French, but with our own Prussian nationalists?

I read on:

A fair number of the best-illustrated articles about amber in Le Moniteur *appear to have been submitted by an unidentified expert. The editor employs the term 'our correspondent in Prussia' to identify the mystery writer. In one instance, referring specifically to amber as a fertility symbol, the writer mentions the town of Nordcopp as a place where the ceremonial blessing of the swollen womb of a pregnant woman with an amber insert has been carried on for centuries. If this fact is commonly known, I have never heard it. And who was more likely than a doctor in Nordcopp to have discovered this pagan practice? And in the next issue, the same writer mentions the use of amber containing animal insertions by 'wise women' to induce the spontaneous abortion of an unwanted foetus. In the very same geographical location! I would swear that one of the illustrations in* Le Moniteur *(19.01.1807) is <u>the very same piece of amber</u> that we observed together in the surgery of Herr Doctor Heinrich.*

I have finished my work here, sir, and will immediately return to Nordcopp – I believe that I may safely anticipate your instructions – where I will keep the doctor under surveillance.

I will be staying in my old room at the Pietist convent.
In faith, Johannes Gurten.

My heart was in my throat. Gurten had returned to Nordcopp. He might be in danger. I was well aware of his impetuous nature. At the same time, I was glad that somebody in Nordcopp knew about Heinrich, and what he was up to. When the case was concluded, my official report would reflect the facts. I would not decry Gurten's merits in order to exalt my own more feeble achievements. He would be given all due credit for his labour.

'I need that despatch form,' I snapped.

The clerk frowned resentfully, and put down his bread and sausage. His fingers were slick with grease as he pushed a paper, pen and a cob of red wax across the counter. That note for Gurten would be tainted with the stink of pork and garlic.

'*Vulpius is the name that Dr Heinrich uses here in Königsberg,*' I wrote quickly. '*Do not alert him to our suspicions. I will come to you on the coast at the very earliest opportunity.*'

I read again what I had written.

For a moment a wave of doubts washed over me again. I was doing exactly what the French expected me to do: I was handing them a guilty Prussian. I had searched the room of Vulpius. I had seen his drawings, the obscene transformations that his graphite had worked on animals and men alike. I saw again the contents of the storage jars, the organs and other appendages floating in a sea of yellow spirit. He was fascinated by all monstrous forms, and had studied Nature for no other purpose. I shuddered to think of the laboratory of DeWitz, and the gruesome work that Vulpius had been doing there. Had I seen anything in Königsberg that I had not already seen in Dr Heinrich's house in Nordcopp?

Before I closed the despatch, I added three words to Gurten.

'*Prudence – prudence – prudence!*'

Had there been more space, I would have written more along the same lines. But I was afraid of communicating the fact to Gurten that I was not in complete control of the situation.

I melted wax in the flame of the candle next to the inkwell, and sealed the note.

'This must be delivered by the first transport going west,' I ordered sternly. 'If it arrives quickly,' I added, 'General Malaport will not be told of the reek of your breath, or the deplorable state of your jacket. You are a disgrace to the colours that you wear.'

The man threw me a startled look.

'It will leave in twenty minutes, sir,' he said in a subdued whisper.

As he began to brush the crumbs from his chest, and wipe his greasy hands on his trousers, I turned away. At last, there was a man who appreciated the power of General Malaport. But it was a hollow victory. I regretted the erosion of my own authority as a Prussian magistrate, and resented the need to rely on the fear which only a French name could inspire.

The bells of the city churches were ringing the hour of seven. The light was fading. The days were darkening rapidly as August drew towards its close. And yet, my heart felt lighter. With so few days remaining before the delivery of the baby, I could hope to be there at Helena's side, as I had promised her.

Within hours, I intended to consign my findings and the name of the murderer to General Malaport. But there was still one thing that I had to do in Königsberg first.

Dr Rickert.

He appeared to be a sort of recruiter of nationalistic lost souls. He picked them out at the Albertina University, then redirected them to the sanctuary of the Kantstudiensaal, where they would meet other like-minded individuals.

I turned towards 'the Graves', and began to walk quickly along the quay.

Early that morning, I had heard Rickert moving about in his sitting-room. Before leaving the house, he had called through the greasy curtain: 'Until this evening, then, Herr Procurator. Bread and broth will be served at seven-thirty prompt.'

His honeyed voice was servile, ingratiating.

I replied with nothing more than a grunt.

I had had no intention of ever returning to that mean little house in the dark environs of the Albertina again. I had played my part in a farce the night before. The charade with the ghost of Salthenius had embarrassed me at the time. Now, instead, I realised what that performance had meant.

Rickert knew Vulpius.

There was nothing supernatural about it, no need for dripping blood, contact with the dead, or the drawing-up of pacts with Satan. He would tell me where the killer was. Königsberg? Nordcopp? Hell?

The sky had been very grey that morning. The sun had barely shown itself all day. There had been an occasional rumbling of thunder, an odd flash of lightning. As I hurried forward, a mountain range of black clouds was massing on the far horizon out at sea.

Edviga had been in the water all day long. Her arms and legs would be stiff and tired with the endless labour. Her stomach cramps would be more frequent.

I don't know where the notion came from. No sooner there, it was gone, like a mouse scuttling behind a cupboard. The thought of Edviga hid itself away behind the more reasonable concern which took its place: *Helena.* The baby would be fully formed by now, kicking out impatiently whenever the fancy took him or her, waiting for the cramps and the labour to start, waiting for the waters to break.

Waiting for me to come home . . .

As I was walking along the quay towards the Albertina, and Dr Rickert's house, my eye was attracted by an unexpected flash of light on the far bank of the river. The bow-window of Herr Flugge & Son was gleaming like a faceted gem in a single, piercing ray of sunlight. On impulse, I turned sharp left, strode across the bridge, and stepped off it in Kniephof.

There was something that I had to do.

I had to rid myself of the guilt and shame that only a wayward husband can feel. I had thought of Edviga Lornerssen and the dangers she was facing on the Baltic coast. Then, and only then, had I remembered my wife, and the baby who would soon be born.

I walked across to the row of jewellers' shops.

The previous evening, my eye had been bewitched by two objects standing next to each other in the window of the shop of Andreas Borkmann. The first was a silver rattle for a baby; the second, a tobacco-box for a man. They were so very different, and yet, I thought, there was a temporal connection between them. Many birthdays would have to pass before I could think of buying my son a tobacco-box.

This was the moment for a silver rattle.

It was almost a tradition in the Stiffeniis family.

Almost . . .

I had been given one that was made in the shape of a whistle, the rattle comprising little balls of Italian coral. My brother Stefan's was made of mother-of-pearl, and it contained balls of agate. When I left my father's house for the last time, those rattles were resting on the mantelpiece in the drawing-room, as if they might be called into use at any moment.

My first child, Manni, had never had a rattle. Nor had my daughter, Süzi. And baby Anders had been lulled to sleep by the firing of French cannonades. It was time to revive the family tradition. The new baby would have a silver rattle with beads of amber.

I emerged from the shop five minutes later. In my hand, a pretty box tied up with a bright green ribbon. As Herr Borkmann placed it in my care, he had assured me that the toy would ward off any fear the child might have of the dark. As I walked across the bridge towards the Albertina University, I heard the rattle tinkle with every step that I took. In the network of streets and alleys leading down to Rickert's house, I was tempted to shake the rattle as I went. Black thunderclouds had settled on the town, cancelling out the day. Nothing had changed since the night before, except, perhaps, that the smell of onions was less strong.

It was very dark as I approached the house. Rickert's window was one of the few in the street not lit by a candle or a fire. If he had not returned, I would have to wait for him out in the street. As the first drops of rain began to splatter on my forehead, I hurried forward, intending to shelter in the doorway. But as I ran, I realised that there was a feeble light in the window. With a surge of hope, I thought that Rickert, after all, might be at home. So eager to escape from him that morning, I pounded with my knuckles on the door, more eager still to be admitted from the rain.

Dr Rickert did not answer.

I knocked again, thunder clapped, rain pelted down.

He did not come.

I stepped to the window, pressed my nose against the grimy glass.

The half-moon of a palm and three fingertips had touched the glass and left a streaking mark. I looked at it more carefully, and saw that the striations were red. My heart sank.

I peered inside again, so far as the dirt and dust on the window would allow.

The fire was a dull glow, a cooking-pot suspended over it. So, Rickert had returned, and had been cooking soup for dinner. Indeed, the untidy breakfast table I had left behind had been cleared, and freshly set with bowls and spoons. I stood on tiptoe, cleaning the condensation of my warm breath from the glass with the sleeve of my jacket.

Then, I spotted him.

First I saw the soles of his feet. His naked calves protruded from behind the sofa, where the rest was hidden. I crushed my face against the window-frame, trying to see around, or beyond, the obstacle. His upper body was twisted, as if in trying to escape he had slipped, then been struck as he attempted to rise again. The cut extended from his left ear, beneath and beyond his larynx. His white face was floating on a dark red lake. So much blood had discharged on the tiles, it was hard to believe that a single drop remained inside his body.

Frantically, I pushed against the door.

As I did so, I realised that it had been left open.

I cannot say which came first.

The sensation of swimming in a dark green sea, or the thought which flashed through my mind.

He is in Königsberg.

33

'Stiffeniis.'

The voice was soft, almost beyond hearing.

A cloth of some sort clung like skin to my nostrils, mouth and ears. It was damp, and I choked on the mouldy stink of it. I tried to shift my hands, but I could not do so. They had been tightly tied across my chest, and bound at the wrists.

I was caught up like a fly in a spider's web.

'Stiffeniis,' that voice called out again.

I opened my eyes with difficulty. The cloth binding was tight, but I could just make out something through the weave of it. I might have been peering through a thick fog. A vague dark form towered over me, dimly lit on one side only by a flickering candle.

Vulpius.

'You thought that you were hunting me,' he said. 'But I was hunting *you.*'

The last thing I remembered was seeing Rickert on the tiled floor. The front door was ajar. I had ventured in. Then, I had been struck down. Afterwards, I suppose I had been bound and gagged. Unlike my erstwhile host, I had not been murdered.

Not yet.

'I know that you can hear me,' he went on. 'You are here to listen to me, Herr Magistrate.'

The accusation rose unbidden to my lips.

'You killed Rickert.'

'*You* killed Rickert, Procurator Stiffeniis.' His voice was a rasping growl. 'You listened to him. He would have told you anything for a handful of coins.'

'He thought that he was helping you,' I replied. 'He hoped to save you.'

Silence greeted this remark. When he spoke again, his voice was an angry cascade.

'Helping me? By telling you where I was living? Tracing a map of the street in his own blood? What a remarkable talent I have wasted!'

I ought to have recognised that voice, but I did not. The cloth had been so closely wrapped about my ears, I had to strain to hear him.

'You knew him,' I insisted.

He hovered over me like Death.

'Rickert and I had never met before tonight, Herr Magistrate. Satan told him where to look for me. At least, that's what he told me. And d'you know what? It may even be true. I have no idea how he found me. What strange times we live in!'

A violent spasm of shivering shook me.

At any moment, a knife might slice through my throat. His knowledge of the human body was unequalled. As was his eagerness to kill, dissect, anatomise, mutilate. I gasped for air, but that wet rag clung to my mouth. I was afraid, but it was not fear of pain alone that tortured me. *He* would decide when to kill me. *He* would choose the method of my despatch. *He* would dispose of my corpse as he wished.

'What do you want from me?' I challenged him.

My inquisitor did not hurry to reply. Indeed, he seemed to consider carefully before he chose to speak. 'What do you want from me, Herr Stiffeniis?'

'You have been murdering women on the coast,' I accused.

'Is that what I've been doing?' he spat back sharply.

Was he toying with me?

He repeated every word that I said. Like an echo running round the dome of an empty church. My voice returned to me, a pale, thin shadow of its former self. I spoke, and he repeated what I said. He did not answer my questions. Instead, he asked a question of his own.

'You killed them, Vulpius.' I stepped out onto thin ice. I was determined to use his real name, no matter how he might try to disguise his identity from me. 'Or should I call you Dr Heinrich of Nordcopp?'

'Heinrich, Vulpius,' he murmured, conceding nothing.

'You killed Rickert,' I pressed on, 'and you'll soon kill me.'

'Kill . . . *you?*' His voice faltered, as if the idea had come to him that instant.

I retched, but nothing issued from my mouth. I swallowed acid, sank back in a faint.

Had the bindings loosened as my body shook?

I tried to move my hands.

Pain exploded, as his boot cracked down on my shin.

'Bones are made of calcium,' he growled. 'They are brittle. Do not provoke me, foolishly trying to free yourself before my eyes. I need no encouragement to cruelty. You should know that by now.'

I gritted my teeth. He was a doctor, a surgeon. He had vast experience of pain. He knew the fragility of human limbs. I had seen the callous professional indifference with which he lopped them off.

'My bones are not so weak as Erika's,' I said, despite the throbbing ache. 'Is that why you let her live? Is that why Erika's body interests you so much? Because she is so different from the others, the ones that you have murdered?'

Again, he said nothing.

Was he gratified to hear that his crimes were known to me, at least?

'I know you,' I said more boldly. 'I know what you can do.'

'Do you really?' he replied sarcastically.

'I know your house. I visited your surgery,' I pressed on. 'I know about the amber that you covet. The worthless bits you showed to me in Nordcopp; the treasures that are hidden here in Königsberg. Amber stolen from women that you murdered and butchered ruthlessly. Using Erika Linder as your go-between. Promising to cure her in exchange. She told you what the women had found in the sea.'

I paused for an instant, but he said nothing.

'She has been arrested,' I went on quickly. 'She is in the hands of the French. She will tell them everything. Just as she told Gurten and myself. You approached the women. You took what you wanted. It was so easy for a doctor. You stole their amber, then you robbed them of their lives without a second thought!'

The bonds cut sharply into my wrists and throat. That foul rag was choking me. I shifted my head, trying to ease the pressure on my lips, struggling to breathe. If I could have freed myself, I would have murdered him.

'You have been slaughtering women here in Königsberg, too. Two girls from Nordcopp stole amber relics from the local church. Megrete and Annalise. They did not dare to try and sell those pieces there, of course. But here in Königsberg they thought that they were safe.'

He seemed to be listening, waiting for me to go on.

'Was that what you were celebrating when you were stopped by the town watch last April?' I probed more gently. 'That night you intended to lay your hands on amber of incredible value for the price of their two miserable lives. Amber from the collection of the venerable Jakob Spener.'

Silence.

Would my throat be slit without an answer? Without knowing why he had hacked those women to pieces?

'Johannes Gurten knows,' I blurted out.

Doubt seized me by the throat. I had sent my young assistant to Lotingen. His work done there, he had taken it on himself to return to Nordcopp.

'Have you murdered him as well?' I asked.

Silence hung as heavy as an axe above my head.

Suddenly, he spoke up: 'You are well informed, it would appear.'

His voice was calm, his tone distant. Dr Heinrich's reserved detachment had surprised me the very first time that I spoke with him. We were fellow Prussians, and we were obliged to serve the French in a professional role, yet he avoided any reference to the unsavoury fact which united us, as if it did not interest him at all. Now, I thought, I understood his motive. He was working for himself alone. By seeming to help the French, he had acquired the freedom that he sought.

'I still don't know why you mutilate women,' I said.

'Is that all you want to know?'

'That is all there *is* to know!'

I could barely see his outline through the gauze which masked my eyes.

'Don't you want to know what I discovered about you, Herr Magistrate Hanno Stiffeniis of Lotingen?'

There it was again. He answered me with a question, throwing my arguments arrogantly in my face as if they were his own. What more did he have to hide? Why torment me before he murdered me? Was this another aspect of his malevolence? First, he would amuse himself. Then, he would kill with whatever came to hand, wherever he happened to be. A windswept beach, a stinking pigsty, on the muddy banks of the River Pregel, in the tiny house of Narcizus Rickert.

I felt a tremor shake my limbs. Having killed me, he would take what he desired. Cutting, hacking, carrying off the bits that fired his madness. I had to humour him. And yet, exasperation got the better of me.

'What can you know of me?' I protested. 'I told you very little when we met in Nordcopp. You know only what les Halles and the French have decided to let you hear. A Prussian magistrate sent from Lotingen to investigate the crimes of which you are guilty.'

I heard the squeak of tensing leather.

He seemed to be crouching close beside me.

His breath was warm. It penetrated the cloth that clung to my face.

'I saw the newspapers in your room, but they could tell you nothing . . .'

'I knew of you *before* they sent you to the coast,' he stressed. 'I learnt of you from a different source. A most reliable one . . .'

The odour of his body was stale, musky. There was not the slightest hint of wax. Frau Poborovsky had said that she could smell it always on his hands, hair, and clothes. He had not been to work in the last ten days. Had the smell faded away? Had he sloughed it off, as snakes are said to change their skins?

'You went to the Kantstudiensaal yesterday,' he said. 'I followed you there. You did not find what you were looking for. That particular manuscript had been removed for safe-keeping, let us say.'

'You stole it. Then, you sent Ludvigssen those crushed insects . . .'

'Could Kant's legacy be trusted to a drunkard?' he snarled suddenly. 'The French would have closed the place. The Albertina is in their hands already. They have laid their greedy paws on everything else. Now, instead, the Kantstudiensaal is open. Kant's books and his manuscripts are cared for in the manner that they merit. The true spirit of Prussia will be preserved. For ever . . .'

'Like flies in amber?' I hissed.

The dark shape of his head loomed close to my face.

He let out a heavy sigh.

'Now you are beginning to make some sense, Herr Stiffeniis.'

'That document you took from the archive,' I said. 'It was something Immanuel Kant had written about amber. Why did you remove it? Why remove *that* document, and no other?'

The sound of our breathing was audible.

I sucked air in gasps through the stifling gauze; he breathed slowly, regularly. There was no doubt in my mind. My life could be snuffed out at any instant, and at the slightest provocation.

'I thought you might have understood by now. Professor Kant was the first to comprehend the significance of amber,' he said at last. 'He saw the way ahead. Late in life, but he saw it.

He understood what others have always failed to see. What *you* have failed to see . . .'

His voice faded away.

'I read the note in Ludvigssen's catalogue,' I said. 'There was nothing of a scientific nature in what Kant had to say.'

'*Regarding a piece of amber shown to me by Wasianski,*' Vulpius recited precisely. 'Kant had never taken much of an interest in the natural sciences. But when Wasianski showed him that unusual piece, it was as if the golden light of the amber had illuminated him. The note is very short – two pages – you are right about that. But what intuition! No one has ever explained *who* and *what* we Prussians are. Nor what Prussia is. But then, Professor Kant turned his mind upon those questions.'

I heard the scrape of a boot, the swish of clothes as Vulpius moved away. Some moments later, the sharp crackle of a piece of folded paper being opened.

'And you hold the key to his meaning, Stiffeniis.'

He began to read, and I was obliged to listen.

Was it the confusion in my head? The pain in my skull? The muffling curtain about my face? His voice worked its way inside my brain. Professor Kant might have been reading to me from beyond the grave.

'*Wasianski showed me something memorable today,*' he read.

I thought at first that he had caught a butterfly, the way he held it tightly trapped inside his closed fist. And yet, it is winter. Some worm, or creeping thing, I thought, as we sat together before the parlour fire. As a special favour, Wasianski reported, a friend had left an object in his keeping for the day. Wasianski wanted me to see it. The next morning, the owner intended to sell the treasure in the Kneiphof district.

'Dear Kant,' Wasianski began, 'have you ever seen the like of this?'

His voice was trembling with excitement as he showed me what was hidden in his palm: a piece of amber, the size of a large plum. It glowed like a small transparent sun, the glistening, yellow colour of honey fresh from the hive.

And there was something darker at the core . . .

It took my breath away.

'It is from the Baltic,' Wasianski said. 'Just look what it contains!'

I had never seen anything so luminous. A living flame enclosed within, it seemed to spark and flare as it refracted light. I had seen slight fragments of vegetation and minute flies contained in shards of amber, but never anything to equal it.

The insect swept every other thought aside. Not for an hour. Nor a day. But for many weeks altogether.

Had such a brute once taken wing on Prussian winds? It was horrid, fascinating. Longer than my thumb, it might have been made of the hardest steel – a suit of armour with six legs, a single horn, two sets of wings.

Where had it come from? When had it lived? What dangers had it outfaced before it drowned in liquid amber? Invincible, aggressive, cruel, there was no hint of conscience in that design. It was fashioned for survival. Nothing more.

Could God invent such a thing?

'It is our history,' I said.

But even as I spoke, another thought was taking shape in my mind. An idea which induced a sense of stupor and fright. Planted there by a young man who came to see me recently, having just returned from France. His words echoed in my head; that monster of Nature glistened in my hand. I saw what Wasianski could not see. I saw what no man had ever seen before, I think. I alone had spoken to the youth. I alone had listened, as he walked with me around the Castle Walk that foggy afternoon. He had opened up his heart to me. I had looked into his thoughts, and what I saw there was dark, cruel, primitive. I had the same impression as I gazed upon that insect trapped in amber.

The fixation will not let me be.

Is it possible, I ask myself? His dark soul; that extinct creature frozen in time? Not a vision of the past, but of a possible future?

I must speak to him again. I must know what has become of him.

I stare at the creature trapped inside this stone, and I see a visible darkness. What would happen if this monster were to free itself and fly away? What if it is nesting now in his mind and in his soul? What would the consequences be for all of us?

'This document is dated November 1803,' Vulpius added. 'That is, a short time before the killings began in Königsberg, and Professor Kant sent for you. You will see the connection, I think. When the French ordered you to go to Nordcopp, it seemed as if the ghost of Kant had issued you a further challenge. But you did not see it that way. Betraying yourself and the "darkness" that Kant had seen inside you, you set yourself to help the French, enabling them to possess our amber and crush our primitive hearts.'

And for that sin I must pay with my life.

And yet, his reasoning was false. I had not betrayed Kant. Nor helped the French to take possession of my country.

The words tripped lightly from my lips.

'I am not helping the French . . .'

'Just listen to yourself, Herr Magistrate!' he snarled.

I had set my foot on a slippery rock.

'Prussian women were being murdered on the coast,' I said, changing direction quickly. 'That was all that I knew when I was ordered up to Nordcopp.'

'You did not know that the French were building machines? That they were planning to strip the coast of amber?' he stormed, his anger mounting. 'You have seen them at work, Herr Magistrate. Their theft grows day by day. Yet you ignored what they were doing.'

'I saw how Prussian women were being butchered . . .'

'They had to die,' he snapped impatiently.

'Why?' I shouted. 'Why?'

He did not react. Or would not. As the silence stretched out, hope began to flutter in my breast, and a sort of desperate madness took hold of me. Why had he taken me prisoner? Why did he let me live? I had something that he wanted. Whatever it was, it might just save my life.

'We can help each other,' I suggested. 'Don't you want to know what Kant left out?'

Time stood still.

'Continue,' he snapped.

'What do you think Kant saw in me?' I asked, carefully weighing my words. 'What connection did he make between myself and the piece of amber that Wasianski showed him? *That* was the reason he sent for me, and no one else, four years ago, to investigate the murders in Königsberg.'

I said no more, but waited for his answer.

'I want to know,' he said at last.

I took a deep breath.

I could smell my own sweat. It was sharper than the stink of the binding cloth and the cloying odour of putrefaction in that place.

'I witnessed an . . . an execution,' I said.

I had to force myself to speak. When it came at last, my voice seemed to come from the centre of the Earth. 'I saw a man beheaded by the guillotine. Blood spurted out of his neck like vapour from the blow-hole of a whale,' I said. And then, in a whisper, 'I hoped that the flow would never end.'

I fell headlong into the nightmare from which I had tried in vain to escape. I told him what I had confessed that day so long ago to Professor Kant. I had been in the Place de la Révolution in January 1793, when the Parisian mob put their king to death. That day my life had changed for ever. I described what I had seen, and what I had felt. It was not an ordered narrative. I re-evoked the violent rush of emotions which possessed me as I stood at the foot of the guillotine. The buzz of vulgar tongues. The dizzy ecstasy of expectation. The execution order

405

finally given, the explosion of a drum-roll. The thunderous beating of my heart. The sudden shriek, the metallic scrape as the blade fell free.

The fountain of blood upon my face. The coppery taste of it upon my tongue. The immense power of Death. My unquenchable desire to see life taken.

Again, and again, and again . . .

I felt anew the passion of that day. I relived it all in perfect detail, wondering where the tale had been hiding. In which dark antechamber of my fetid soul had it lain fallow? I pulled it out like a horrid trophy, and threw it at the feet of the man who meant to murder me. I did not intend to let him think of me as his victim. I wanted him to think of me as his brother in blood.

'Kant saw the same implacable cruelty, the same heartless ferocity, imprisoned in that piece of amber. The hideous insect trapped inside the stone. Wasianski saw a marvel. Kant saw a monster,' I concluded. 'He thought at once of me.'

The light seemed to ebb before my eyes.

The death-blow must come now.

I did not strain against my bonds.

An image filled my thoughts, instead.

A memory, rather . . .

I was in the garden. It was early morning still, the light was brilliant. I was on my way to work. I stopped by Helena's roses, and saw a fly caught tight in a spider's web. Later that day, I had been summoned by General Malaport and sent to Nordcopp. But it was the fly that gripped my thoughts. I felt as that creature must have felt. I was helpless, mortally trapped in a suffocating web of Heinrich–Vulpius's making. Like the spider, he would wait until the fight had drained out of me. That is when they kill.

But no blow came. That voice came, instead.

'Professor Kant saw the future in you,' he said.

I was stunned. Had he accepted the deal? Had he taken what I had to offer?

'Prussia will not be born again on the field of battle,' he murmured. 'Generals, armies, cannon, frail flesh. These things are gone for ever. Jena proved it. Our revolution will . . . Listen to me,' he hissed sharply. 'Could any man, except Professor Kant, have divined it? Our ideals will stem from amber. Our weapons will be wax and flesh. Can you imagine that? You have been to the workshop of DeWitz.'

What was he saying?

DeWitz, the workshop, Prussia's spiritual rebirth?

'I have been there,' I said uncertainly. 'I have seen the models for the university.'

'There is much else, besides.'

What did he mean?

'DeWitz showed me examples of . . .'

His voice cut brusquely over mine. 'That place is dark and damp. It is a womb, Herr Stiffeniis. DeWitz knows nothing. He would not recognise the creature taking shape before his eyes.'

I was lost. He was talking in metaphors.

The dark, the damp, creatures forming in the womb . . .

A hand settled heavily on my arm.

I froze. My scalp tingled madly with fright. My clenched teeth ached as I prepared to die. A knee crushed down upon my chest, holding me firm. Did he intend to cut my throat, as he had done to Ilse? As he had slaughtered Rickert? Would he drive a wooden stake through my heart?

A thousand terrors flashed through my mind.

An instant passed, then he removed his knee.

Was he hovering above me? Was that his game? Would he slaughter me the instant that I attempted to rise and escape from that place?

'Vulpius?' I hissed again.

My voice rebounded off the walls. Somewhere a rat skittered across the floor. Or had Vulpius made that sound? Was it part of his strategy – like the spider lurking in my garden – before he struck the final blow?

'Vulpius?'

Had the offering of the secret, dark side of my heart failed to placate him?

My breath burst out in a painful rush.

'Vulpius?' I called again, my voice no longer human to my own ears.

And Vulpius replied, as he had done before.

With silence.

34

Was I alone?

I strained to hear him.

I opened my mouth to cry for help. A last appeal for mercy. I gagged against the sodden binding, tried to think, but despair had laid its heavy hand upon my heart.

Was this how I would die?

Like a fly in amber?

Was Heinrich–Vulpius watching me? Was he sitting somewhere in that room, savouring the agony, enjoying the spectacle of my prolonged dying? My breath came in painful spasms, my chest heaved violently beneath my crossed hands. My face was wet. With blood, I thought. My own, or Rickert's? The foul sweet odour of his gutted corpse seemed to meld with my own sour sweat. I retched again, then swallowed hard. If I were sick lying flat on my back, I would choke to death.

I called out frantically. 'Heinrich, are you there?'

No sound, no movement signalled his presence.

I had seen the drawings in his room, the specimens imprisoned in their jars. Insects were his model of perfection. He would act like them. Immobile, half-hidden in the dark, assessing every tiny sign of life remaining in the victim he had managed to entrap. When he was certain of his dominance, he would strike. The spider used its claws, its venomous sting. What means would Heinrich choose to finish me off?

I listened harder, tensing for the blow that must inevitably come.

I could hear the sound of something dripping.

Plop – plop – plop . . .

Then, I heard the smothered, rasping bubbling of air or gas.

The corpse was shifting, stiffening, releasing odours and fluids as it settled into final immobility. Rickert's throat had been slit. His stomach had been gutted. His blood was weeping onto the ground.

Had he left me alone? Had Heinrich-Vulpius let me live?

I clutched at straws to avoid sinking into the abyss. Was he satisfied with our exchange? Had I told him what he wanted to know? The secrets of my soul were mine no more. The murderer knew what Professor Kant alone had known before. He had made the connection with amber that he was looking for.

I started, suddenly.

I would find what I was looking for in the workshop of DeWitz.

Prussia will be born again from wax and amber . . .

What was hidden there? What had I not seen? What had DeWitz not shown me?

My left hand slid free, pulled tight across my chest a moment before. I suddenly found that I could move it. I wriggled like a clutch of maggots freshly spawned. My fingers pushed at the bindings, then tore a hole in the mesh. I felt cold air against my skin. Frantic energy possessed me as I struggled to escape. The ripping sounded like a cascading waterfall.

I froze, listening. If he were there, he must strike now.

No voice shouted out. No footsteps clattered on the tiles. No boot pressed down on my frail bones.

I was alone . . .

I pushed out with both my hands, using all my strength, stretching the restraining material away from my body. More cold air entered. I gulped at it, sucking it greedily into my starved lungs. The smell of Rickert filled my nostrils, making me retch and baulk. If Heinrich had not killed me, that rapidly decomposing corpse would soon have done the job. I tore the bindings from my body, shouting with the effort as the material began to yield. Hands free, I sat up and stripped the wrappings from my face.

A candle burned above the fireplace. The flame was weak, the light a sickly yellow. And yet, it might have been the sun at midday. I was obliged to turn my eyes away. That side of the room was empty. I quickly looked the other way, still fearful of my captor.

Two eyes stared into mine.

They were open wide. His face was a foot away from my own. Yet, he was not looking at me. His eyes were fixed on dark infinity. Had he seen the blow striking down on him? Had he felt his throat being slashed open? Blood had gorged out onto his neck and his chest. It had spouted upwards, then cascaded back, like frothy beer from a freshly broached barrel. His chin was black where the gore had clotted and dried. Another slash had ripped his stomach open. I was lying in his mortal fluids. The net curtain which held me tight was sodden with the blood and the effluents of Narcizus Rickert.

Heinrich–Vulpius had laid me next to the corpse. He had intended to kill me in the same manner. We would have rotted there together until the stench brought neighbours and the police to investigate the cause of it.

Nausea gripped me. I emptied my stomach on the floor.

Heinrich–Vulpius had gone. Wherever his folly had taken him, I could only be grateful that he had chosen to spare me. I had given him what he sought; he had left me with my life. And something more. His words rang insistently in my head.

The workshop of DeWitz . . .

I darted to the door, listened for an instant, then threw it open.

A draught of cold air doused the candle. I was tempted to cry out, but did not. He might be in the passage. I could not see ahead of me. I hesitated to escape. He might be waiting there in the dark. That cold breeze might have been his icy, deathly breath. And yet, I had to go forward. Whatever the risk, I had to do it. Like Lazarus when he rose up from the tomb, I was seized by doubts and misgivings. Not happiness, certainly. I had to hurry.

I leapt out into the passage-way. No one tried to stop me. No shout went up as I darted for the door. No dagger lunged as I pulled it open and ran out into the deserted street. Somewhere in the distance I could hear the sound of a horn-pipe played by a hollow, rasping fiddle and a sibilant, whistling flute.

The river shone like a rippled sheet of glass at the far end of the sloping prospect, and I began to run towards the water. I knew where I was going. Certain of the direction, I ran out onto the wharf. A group of sailors were drinking on the quay beside their barge. One man was dancing with a woman, the others egging them on to worse.

I began to run along the wharf towards the Kniephof bridge. *There is much else besides . . .*

What had Vulpius meant? What was he thinking of?

Vulpius?

My side was aching. I slowed to a trot, but still I pressed on.

Gurten had interpreted the words of Heinrich. He had made sense of the collection of objects in Heinrich's house. He had seen an aspect of the plaster casts of Erika's limbs that I had failed to see. He was convinced that Heinrich was the killer. Heinrich killed to gain possession of the rare and precious amber which would support his scientific theory. Gurten had been right concerning who the killer was, though he had never understood the murderer's motive. He had failed to explain why Heinrich mutilated his victims. I must find the missing piece in the puzzle. And I must find it fast.

I turned the corner into Schwartzstrasse.

Advancing more warily, I hugged the walls, darting from one deep shadow to the next, careful to avoid being seen by anyone who might be guarding the waxworks. The street was deserted, the workshops closed for the night, and yet, the scents of wood and sawdust, paint and pitch, and all the other materials from which our industry is forged hung heavily on the night air. Among those cold and stagnant smells, a fresher perfume picked its way with care.

The warm smell of melting wax.

I stopped before the door of the waxworks.

How should I enter?

It had been hot inside the vault. DeWitz had ordered the air vents to be opened to relieve the discomfort of his employees. A man had opened them, using a long hooked stick. I worked my way along the brick wall of the workshop, searching for one of these wooden hatches. I came to the corner without finding one, then turned down the narrow alley which ran along the side of the building. It was darker there, more putrid than the filthy street. I trod upon a rat, and heard it yelp.

Might there be a night-watchman?

A simple knock on the door, and he would have opened up. Would DeWitz employ a man to guard that place at night? Was there any sane man who wished to steal what the Dutchman manufactured? But then, I saw what I was seeking: a half-moon wooden shutter close to the ground. I tried to kick it in with my foot, but it would not give. A pale halo of light shimmered around the edges.

Somebody was in there . . .

The impulse to run was strong. I could go to General Malaport, and tell him what I knew. He would call out the French soldiers. They would storm the workshop in force. But would they come in time?

Heinrich–Vulpius would flee . . .

Whoever was inside the workshop was making no attempt to hide.

I retraced my steps to the front, raised my fist, and hammered on the door.

Nothing happened for a minute or more. No one came. I knocked again.

Then, I heard the murmur of voices. Not one person. More than one. They were talking – whispering – on the other side of the door.

I rapped harder.

'Signor DeWitz?' a female voice cried out. '*È lei là fuori?*'

'*Sono il magistrato Stiffeniis,*' I answered.

I had learnt some simple phrases when I visited Italy fifteen years before.

The double door creaked, and half of it swung open slowly. Two women stood before me, their eyes were wide with fright. One of them held up an oil-lantern, and I recognised her.

'Maria.'

The woman smiled uncertainly. 'You came yesterday,' she said in stilted German. 'Signor DeWitz is not here tonight, sir.'

'It doesn't matter,' I replied, stepping inside.

'Was that you in the alley, sir? You frightened us. We are working. We thought it was the rats. They love the wax, and lay siege to this place at night.'

DeWitz had said that they worked at all hours when a suitable corpse required it.

'I will not take up your time, I promise you,' I replied, stepping inside. 'Just show me one thing, and I'll leave you in peace.'

Maria had been modelling a human hand in wax the day before. She turned to the other woman, who was older, plumper, her long black hair rolled up in a net which hung heavily on her shoulder. They spoke together in Italian for a moment, Maria explaining who I was, reassuring her friend.

'Is anyone here, except yourselves?' I asked.

They knew Vulpius, and would have let him in without any question.

'There's no one else tonight, sir,' Maria assured me. 'I'm helping Anna. She has a lung to finish.'

'Lung nearly done,' the other woman said in broken German. 'Nothing left for the rats. *È quasi putrefatto.* Urgh!' The look that appeared on her face was one of plain disgust.

'No one wants to work at night,' Maria said with a twitch of her nose. 'But if there's work to finish, well, we have no choice.'

'What about Herr Vulpius?' I asked her.

'Oh, he is different,' she said. 'He'll work any time.'

'Have you seen him recently?'

'Not for weeks, sir.'

I paused for a moment. 'There is a place, I think, where freshly made models are left to set.'

'The cold room.'

'That's it,' I said, explaining nothing. 'Can you lead me there?'

As we passed through the vaults, I noticed the tiny oil-lamps burning in every room beneath a brass cauldron so that the wax would not set hard during the night. And in the main work-room the other woman returned to her table, where a lamp and a mirror illuminated the puffed-up lungs on which she was working.

We stopped before a small wooden door.

'Here you are,' Maria said, and handed me her lamp.

As the door swung gently open on its hinges, I stepped inside, and looked around. There were four full-length figures in the centre of the room. They were laid out beneath white sheets which served as dust-covers. There was no other door, no room leading on from this one. This was the innermost sanctuary of DeWitz's workshop.

The cold room.

No cauldrons bubbled there. It was cooler than the other rooms, but not cold. Neither was the chamber large, though it was cramped, and full of things. In the weak light of the lamp I could see that there were shelves on three of the walls. They were loaded down with objects, each of which was covered with a cloth. They might have been packages waiting to be collected from a post office. Signs hung at intervals on the walls: BONES/SKELETAL COMPONENTS. MUSCLES, TENDONS, CARTILAGES, EXTENSORS. LUNGS/FINE TISSUE. ORGANS. MEMBRANES. BRAINS.

I peeled back the sheet which shrouded the object on the nearest table.

A naked man, life-sized, was reclining on his back. He might have been peacefully sleeping, except for the fact that his snaking innards were exposed to view. No man could survive for long in such a state. Intestines had uncoiled onto his chest, arms and lower trunk to form a sort of vast amphitheatre. Deep down in the centre of the arena itself, the complex mechanisms by which the stomach functions were on display.

I raised my hand, covered my mouth, swallowed hard.

No blood, fluid, bile or mucus obscured the horrid spectacle. As a teaching instrument, the inanimate wax model would undoubtedly be useful. The statue was a monument to the combined miracles of Art and Nature. I recognised the hand that had fashioned the plaster casts of Erika Linder's limbs. There was the same precision in the detail, the same impeccable realism. But surely this was not the piece that he had been talking of.

I threw back the second dust-sheet, and held up the lantern.

An aged woman.

A head of braided hair – was it real? – a wrinkled face. From the point of her chin to the soles of her feet, the skin had been stripped away from the body, revealing the bare bones of the skeleton beneath. Large red-and-blue knots bulged along her arms and legs, together with the major blood vessels which connected them to her heart and lungs.

Where were the muscles?

It was a sort of abstract of a human corpse, and I recalled the French word that DeWitz had used to describe the models for the Albertina. *Écorché*. The French verb means 'to flay; to lay bare'. The effect was more pronounced in this particular instance. The wax model illustrated in infinite detail the cyclic flow of blood around and through the avenues of the body. Anything which was irrelevant had been eliminated for didactic purposes.

I pulled away the third sheet.

Relief. Disappointment. Nausea. I felt all three together. DeWitz had spoken of the governing principle in the making of such models. Here was vivid evidence of how they were constructed. A wire frame had been shaped in the figure of a

416

child – the unfinished piece appeared to be a boy aged eleven or twelve. Lying comfortably on his left flank, the skin and fat had been removed from his arms, legs and stomach, exposing his maturing muscles, and the conformation of his developing sexuality. Finer details in the form of the internal organs and the bodily mass were being added as each item became available, though the calves and the feet were still no more than bare metal wire.

Was this what Heinrich–Vulpius wanted me to see?

He had been so intensely mystical when he spoke of it, yet I saw nothing which could represent in any way the rebirth of a fallen nation.

I replaced the dust-sheet over the boy, and turned to the last table. I hesitated for an instant, then threw the sheet back.

A naked woman.

She was large-boned, muscular, strikingly beautiful.

I had seen such women on the coast. Their robust yet graceful physical structure, the harmony of the hips, their well-shaped legs and the long muscle-honed thighs. Indeed, I corrected myself, I had seen many of them.

Before, and after, death.

The face was only partially finished. It was a miracle of gory detail. The skin had been stripped away – perhaps, it had yet to be put on – revealing the underlying features, the muscles, fat and tissue, which would give it form. The upper teeth and the lower jaw were missing.

Kati Rodendahl . . .

A large triangular section was lacking from the throat and the larynx.

Ilse Bruen in the pigsty . . .

The women in Nordcopp had told the truth about the artist who was obsessed by the anatomical perfection of their bodies. Heinrich had picked them out, noted the pieces that he was searching for, murdered them at his own convenience, then brought the specimens to Königsberg. He had still not found the time or the opportunity to model them in wax. I felt a tremor of revulsion course through my body. Were the missing parts kept in jars of distilled wine, together with the other creatures, in the attic of Frau Poborovsky?

Was it all so simple?

A maniac obsessed by a particular type of woman, possessed of the necessary artistic skill to reproduce her model, desperate only for examples on which to base his work? What was the finality of it all? What could he hope to achieve? I could see nothing that was revolutionary in the scheme. Could he hope to defeat the French army and send them packing with a wax model of a woman, no matter how perfect he might make her?

I pulled the sheet away entirely, exposing the figure.

The wax woman was naked below the waist. Her legs were long, graceful, strong, but the figure was incomplete. In the triangle where her legs joined her trunk, there was a large gaping cavity. I felt a painful jolt.

The womb.

I remembered something that DeWitz had told me about his modeller.

'He is a perfectionist. He'll not invent a thing when Nature can be called upon to provide a perfect specimen. He recently mentioned the case of a woman who will certainly die before her time is up. He called her the new Eve . . .'

A pregnant woman, her belly swollen with the child that she was carrying. The one thing missing: an unborn foetus.

Edviga Lornerssen.

I recalled the way she asked about my wife. I saw again the gentle and protective way in which she laid her hands in her lap as she listened to my replies. She had even mentioned the fact that she feared for the effect that cold sea-water might have upon a child. I had had the right intuition: Edviga was asking about Helena, but she was thinking of her own baby.

Edviga Lornerssen was pregnant. She had gone to speak to Dr Heinrich. He knew about the baby growing inside her. The perfect foetus for the perfect Eve.

He would strike again in Nordcopp.

35

'What did you see there?'

The voice of les Halles was brusque.

I stood at his side, looking down on Nordcopp beach. Everything had changed during my short absence. A dozen braziers had been set up near the waterline. These fiery beacons cast a pink glaze on the rippling black waves that broke upon the shingle. Thirty paces out, the steam-pumps of the *coq du mer* were chattering furiously. Piston-driven rods flew up and down, sucking up the sea-bed, sending the sludge hissing through a series of filters, spewing the water back to where it had come from. A rotating canvas belt fed stones and shale into a long, narrow flume which carried it onto the beach, where the detritus cascaded noisily into a metal tray. The amber-girls were working there, throwing unwanted pebbles higher up the beach, dropping fragments of amber into sacks which dangled around their necks. Their nets and spears were gone. They were obliged to work bare-armed, bare-foot. French soldiers pressed close around them, making sure that nothing was stolen.

Once, they had seemed to me like goddesses.

Now, they looked like humbled slaves.

Colonel les Halles surveyed the field of battle. Sweat rolled off his brow and trickled down his chin, running under his collar like dark rivulets of blood. His cheeks were gaunt, his cheekbones scuffed with oil where he had tried to brush away the sweat with the back of his filthy hands. His face was the painted mask of a warrior. He was fighting the final skirmish in his war against the Baltic Sea. He had violated the sea-bed, illuminated the shore, triumphed over gravity with his ingenious pipes and pumps. His machines would work all day, and through the night, digging endlessly for the precious amber that was buried beneath the shallow waters.

'Well, Stiffeniis?'

His patience was short. His mind was on his own task, not on mine.

I began to tell him what I had done the minute I arrived in Nordcopp.

'Why didn't you report your discoveries to me?' he snapped. 'He could have murdered you, as well.'

His questions were intelligent, rational. My behaviour had been neither. I had ridden hard from Königsberg. Three hours in the saddle, the horse almost lame by the time that I reached the town. I had gone immediately to Heinrich's house. Afterwards, I reported what I had found to Sergeant Tessier in the North Tower. Five minutes later, aboard an open carriage with an armed escort, I was racing through the dunes towards the sea and Colonel les Halles.

'You cannot go alone,' Tessier grumbled.

But I saw the truth in his eyes. He did not trust me. I was a Prussian. Prussians were devious, dangerous. I must be carried directly to his superior, while he went off to verify what I had told him. For all he knew, I might be mad.

'Why did you enter that house alone?' les Halles demanded.

His eyes were red, he had not slept all night. The blazing orbs of a man possessed. They peered out from his smoke-blackened face with demonic energy. Success was the only reward that he craved. Amber was there to be taken; he would take it.

I envied him.

Had I conducted my investigation into the murders half so well? Had I saved a single Prussian life that might have been saved? Or was I, on the other hand, assisting the French to strip my native country of its wealth?

The killer had beaten me at every stage, but now I knew for certain who he was.

'I wonder why you took such risks,' he said with a loud sigh. 'This was not a contest between the two of you alone. A duel, let us say. The aim of your enquiries was to put an end to these disturbances, restore the peace, and let me to get on with my job.'

I could not tell les Halles why I had been so foolhardy. I had feared to lose far more than just my life. My soul was in the balance. My integrity. I had to outface Heinrich, and get back what was mine. By confessing what I had revealed to Kant, I had persuaded him to spare my life in Königsberg. But now, I wanted that secret back.

No ghost must haunt me.

'And why would he leave the front door open?' les Halles frowned. 'It is almost as if he wished you to find what he had left behind.'

His eyes flashed up into mine.

'Is that his game, do you think? Is he playing with you?'

My first impulse had been to call Gurten from the Church of the Saviour. But in the pale glimmer of the moonlight, I had seen the dark gap between the frame and the door. It was a clear sign of the killer's presence. He had used the same trick on me in Königsberg, luring me into Rickert's house.

Like a fool, I rushed into the trap, slamming the door back on its hinges, crashing it against the wall, announcing my arrival.

'You expected to meet the doctor,' les Halles summarised.

'I saw two hands,' I said. 'Gripping the bottom of the door like talons. The body was in the kitchen, I could not see it from the hall. But those eight fingers caught the ray of a moonbeam. Blood had run beneath the door and formed a pool of glistening darkness on the tiles. I stepped into the room.'

A loud, dismissive grunt confirmed what he considered to be my foolishness in entering the house alone. 'What had he done to the corpse?' he asked with barely controlled impatience.

'The right side of the skull had caved in. Blood and brains spilled out . . .'

I could not finish. I saw once more the blue, metallic sheen that the moonlight cast on her skin. The blood seemed as heavy as molasses. It had congealed in the folds of her face and neck. The skull had been crushed by a massive blow. White fragments glinted like pinpoints in her tangled brown hair. She had been bludgeoned to death with one of Heinrich's plaster casts. It lay in smashed and bloody pieces beside her body. The ample breasts which had barred my way to the doctor's surgery but a week before had settled heavily to the side, pulling her body aslant. Her white linen blouse was piebald black with blood.

Can one feel relief at the sight of a corpse so brutally slaughtered?

I breathed more easily as I stared into those lifeless eyes. They were not Edviga's, as I had feared. I recognised Frau Hummel. Dr Heinrich had murdered his housekeeper.

'Had he mutilated her?' les Halles insisted.

'She was not what he was looking for,' I said. 'He is only interested in the girls who gather amber.'

'You said that there was more than one,' les Halles prodded, impatiently.

'Indeed,' I said. 'There is another room where Heinrich performs his surgery. The same room where he makes casts of human limbs from gypsum and wax . . .'

I paused.

There was a smell of wax in the surgery, but it was nothing like as strong as the smell of wax in the house of Frau Poborovsky, nor could it ever hope to compare with the overwhelming atmosphere of DeWitz's workshop.

I took a deep breath, preparing myself to tell the worst.

'He was tied to a chair,' I said. 'He was sitting at the desk . . .'

'But how did he die?' the colonel snapped, as if the deed did not interest him. He wanted facts, and nothing more.

'Face down in a bowl of plaster,' I replied, equally brutal in my description, recalling the large blue bowl in which Heinrich had been mixing plaster when I called on him in the company of Gurten. 'Heinrich held him down until he drowned, then left him where he sat. The plaster had set hard and fast. It was a horrid way to die,' I said. 'The agony was long. His wrists were deeply cut as he tore against the rope. This killer likes to torture his prey . . .'

Whenever I thought of Heinrich, that word rose spontaneously to my lips.

'He used the plaster of Paris like the resin which forms amber,' I continued. 'It smothers, chokes and kills the victim as it hardens. Just like the insects trapped inside it.'

Colonel les Halles let out a groan of dubious perplexity.

'Never let it be said that Prussians lack imagination!' he exclaimed. 'And what do you think he had in mind when he mutilated those women? Is it not the inspiration of the moment which guides his cruelty?'

I admired the practical nature of his thinking.

'If the victim's face had set fast inside a bowl of plaster,' les Halles ploughed on, 'how did you recognise him?'

The only source of light in Heinrich's surgery was a candle on the mantelpiece. The tallow was almost out, burnt down to a stub, but there was flame enough to see what had happened.

'I recognised his jacket,' I said. 'The same dark brown riding-jacket that he always wore. And the ring on his finger. A cornelian with a swan and the initials J.G.'

Heinrich had murdered my assistant.

Johannes Gurten had returned to Nordcopp, as I instructed him, but he had ignored the warning that fright had inspired me to add: 'Prudence – prudence – prudence!'

He had paid for his rashness with his life. Heinrich had pushed his face into a bowl of plaster, and held him there until he was dead.

'You know his name, then?'

'Johannes Gurten was a trainee magistrate,' I told him. 'He had been sent to Lotingen to serve his apprenticeship with me, but when he learnt that I was engaged on a case in Nordcopp,

he took it on himself to follow me to the coast. He had been
. . . helping me, let's say.'

'Did he not go with you to Königsberg?' he enquired sharply.

'I assigned a different task to him. Concerning Heinrich. He
was to search for information . . .'

'I knew nothing of this person,' les Halles interrupted me.

'I knew you would not let him into the camp. I did not ask.
I, too, have had my share of obstacles,' I reminded him, without
insisting that those obstacles were of his making.

'I suppose you have,' he agreed, looking out over the shore.

Down below, the machines continued to thump and pound
like a dismal orchestra playing some strange, heathen symphony.
Pride gleamed in his eyes, however. Nordcopp shore was where
he wished to be.

'Very good, Stiffeniis,' he said. 'Now, let's conclude. What
about the other one?'

I thought I had misheard him. There was a great deal of
noise. The sea, of course. The thundering engines of the *coq
du mer*. The rushing water in the flume, the crashing of the
pebbles as they clattered into the metal tray, the shouts of the
French soldiers as they urged the women to work without
respite. The sounds of labour on the Baltic coast had been for
ever amplified.

'I did not catch what you said,' I apologised.

He turned on me, his face a mask of angry impatience. 'You
have said nothing of the third corpse in the house. Surely there
were mutilations in that case?'

'Third corpse?' I repeated in surprise.

My legs turned to the consistency of the fine sand beneath
my feet. Cold sweat erupted on my body, as if I had that very
moment emerged from a nocturnal bathe in the Baltic Sea.
This was the news that he had been expecting to hear. This was
the part that interested him. Not the corpse of Frau Hummel.
Nor the body of Johannes Gurten. There was another corpse,
about which I knew nothing. A mutilated corpse.

One of the amber-girls . . .

'You reported to Malaport's office, did you not?'

'The minute I arrived in Königsberg . . .'

'You did not go back to him, I take it?' He wiped the sweat from his upper lip with his thumb and forefinger. 'Before you left to come here, I mean.'

'I did not think . . .'

'If you had gone to Malaport, he would have informed you that another worker has gone missing. Shortly after you departed,' he hissed. 'Edviga Lornerssen. The girls who shared the hut with her reported her missing. They came to me like a bunch of frightened rabbits. They did not want to be killed as well, they said. They were preparing to leave.' He opened his arms in a gesture of helplessness. 'I let them go, but no dead body has been found so far . . .'

He did not finish, leaving me to draw my own conclusions.

I did so, but I could not find the strength to put them into words.

'I searched the house from top to bottom,' I said. 'I found two bodies only. Then, I went at once to seek out Tessier and tell him what I had discovered.'

Les Halles turned to me.

'Why kill *those* two people, Stiffeniis? Why would he murder your assistant, and his own housekeeper?'

My ideas were clear regarding Johannes Gurten.

'If he had tried to confront the doctor, or arrest him, Heinrich would have had no alternative but to kill him. Frau Hummel may have accidentally witnessed the slaying of my assistant,' I said. 'If that was the case, then she, too, had to be silenced.'

Les Halles shook his head.

'There must be another corpse hidden in the house or the garden,' he repeated stubbornly, a note of acidity in his voice, as if he did not trust me to search the house properly. I had thrown the name of the murderer at his feet, but that was not enough for Richard les Halles. There was a hitch, and it threatened to distract him from the work that was going on along the shoreline.

425

'That house must be turned inside out,' he growled impatiently.

There was no corpse hidden in Heinrich's house. He had never bothered to hide the evidence of his crimes. He could have thrown Kati Rodendahl into the sea, but he had left her corpse on the shore where she was bound to be seen. He might easily have buried Ilse Bruen beneath the loose sand of the dunes. Instead, he had abandoned her body carelessly in the pigsty of the only farm in the district. He had left the corpses of Rickert, Gurten and Frau Hummel where he had slaughtered them. If he had ripped the child from Edviga's womb, he would have left the body for the world to see.

'You won't need me in Nordcopp,' I said. 'I want to look in Edviga's hut. She may have left some clue behind to tell us what has become of her.'

I wanted to be alone when I discovered what he had done with Edviga.

I wanted to be alone when I met Dr Heinrich again.

36

Except for a single light, it was dark out on the water.

Moonlight cut black chasms between the wooden slats as I crossed the pontoon bridge and clattered up the ladder onto the platform. The huts were shrouded in darkness, and they appeared to be deserted.

An untrimmed lantern guttered in the centre of the space, as if the women had been whisked away by some spirit even more malign than Colonel les Halles. I could make them out, labouring on the shore beneath the flaming braziers to turn the Frenchman's dream into reality.

The forgotten lantern gave off a slanting plume of trailing black smoke.

I raised the glass, adjusted the wick, then went forward, my footsteps beating on the wooden boards like a muffled funeral drum, towards Edviga's hut. It was on the far side of the compound, looking over the sea; she had pointed it out to me the day les Halles had let me speak to her. The smell of the sea was strong, stagnant, almost rank. I might have been on a seaweed-covered rock at low tide. The wooden cabins reminded me of the lean-to huts where fishermen hang their fish to dry along the northern shore. They were very old – the ancient wood dark, cracked, warped – very different from the new huts where the French had installed themselves, where I myself had slept. Being so close to the sea and the spray, those huts had soaked up more water than the timbers of a sailing-ship.

I stopped outside her lodging, listening for any sound.

Waves were breaking gently in a shimmering silver line along the shingle *haf* a quarter-mile out from the shore. Farther down the beach came the rude suckling of the *coq du mer*, the sharp exchange of orders being shouted, the muted murmuring of the women's voices as they worked together, learning the new task which would render them unemployed the instant they had mastered it.

The air was fresher than it had been for many a night. The first hint of summer's imminent end, I thought. The Arctic ice would soon invigorate the wind as autumn came. That gentle breeze would turn into a howling gale, racing down from the north, sweeping away the stale odours of the stagnant sea. It would soon disperse the fetid air of that long summer.

I pushed the door open, and entered the cabin.

The air was heavy with the odour of damp clothes, and with the acidic smell of the bodies that had worn them. The lantern lit up four trestle beds, the general clutter of the women who had been living there together. Clothes and clogs lay in great disorder on the floor, as if they had been hastily thrown aside. Earthenware cups, metal spoons and a covered pot set down in a circle in the centre of the room. The other women had run off, leaving everything as it was. Their cots were stripped bare to the bones of their latticed wooden frames. Only the cot in the farthest corner remained untouched, the covers thrown back, exposing crumpled bedding, as Edviga Lorncrssen had left it.

I began to search the room more thoroughly, concentrating my attention on the area around that bed. Apart from the bedclothes, some traces of the girl's presence remained. A flimsy printed woodcut was fixed to the wall above the spot where her head must have lain. A female saint, I thought at first, wondering whether Edviga might have been a Catholic. I had never asked about her beliefs. And yet, religion of any sort seemed at odds with her desire to bury a piece of amber with Ilse Bruen, and with the superstitious ritual she had performed over the corpse of Kati, covering her nudity with a blanket of fur, surrounding it with a scattering of amber fragments.

I held the lantern up, and looked more closely at the picture.

A pretty young woman dressed in a long dark cape with a hood. She might have been another one of the amber-gatherers. The image did not seem to have any religious significance. Nor did the nail on which it had been crudely impaled suggest any sign of reverence.

Not a saint, then. It was simply a decoration, like the strings of sea-shells which dangled from the ceiling, and the misshapen tangles of driftwood which hung from the walls like stags' heads in a hunting-lodge.

Edviga's amber-gathering gear was draped over another rusty nail. Her stout jerkin and stiff leather trousers dangled in a careless twist, as if the uniform had been peeled off in one piece from her body. Like the shell stripped from a shrimp.

Beneath, neatly aligned, stood her heavy thigh-length boots.

As I lifted the lantern, I caught a glimpse of something peeping out from beneath the bed. It was dark and triangular. Bending down, I saw a medium-sized wooden box that was partially hidden in the shadows. I pushed the bed aside, and pulled it out. It was the sort of box that they use for packing roundels of cheese. Two large initial letters had been unevenly burnt with a red-hot iron on the lid.

E.L.

It was not locked, and I carefully opened the lid. My fingers hovered in the air for a moment, hardly daring to touch the contents. What did this mean? Were these the clothes that she had arrived in? Were they the clothes that she would have worn if she had left of her own free will? I lifted up a crushed green bonnet, which I set down on the floor. A dress had been carefully folded beneath it. Printed with a pattern of pink flowers, that poor faded frock had seen a good few summers. It was, indeed, little more than a rag. Had Edviga nothing better to show for her labour on the seashore? I saw her in my mind's eye. Any other woman would have been demeaned by those poor garments.

Not Edviga.

I laid my fingers on the dress, shifted it aside, and examined the contents of the box. I was surprised by how little it contained. No bag, no shawl, no vest or stockings, no keepsake from home, no letters. There was nothing except for a pair of cracked leather pumps, one of which had lost a buckle. Having removed the contents, I turned the box over, wondering if something might be hidden under it. A tiny fragment of stone clattered onto the floor. I picked it up between my thumb and finger and held it to the light.

It was a dense, dark red. Very dark, indeed, but it was amber. A piece of no great value. Of all the valuable amber that had passed through her hands, was this the only fragment she had kept for herself? Had she left it in the box, asking her friends to bury her and it together in the sea if anything should ever happen to her? I replaced the clothes, and the chip of amber, closed the lid, and made to slide the box back into its place beneath the bed.

Something scraped on the wooden boards.

I pushed the box aside, fell to my knees, and peered into the darkness. Almost hidden in the corner, an object glinted. I stretched forward, felt cold metal, then pulled it out. I turned it over in my hands, examining it more carefully in the lamplight. It was an implement of some sort. A tool connected with her work, perhaps? Fashioned neatly from an amber-worker's rake, it had been transformed by a blacksmith. All the teeth had been removed from the rake – with one exception – leaving a flat grip which fitted snugly into the palm of my hand. That one remaining tooth protruded as a sharp prong about five inches long. When I closed my fingers around it, that prong jutted out from between the closed fingers of my bunched fist. It was an ingenious tool. Or was it a weapon? Did she take it with her when she left the camp at night? Did she carry it to protect herself when she went to Nordcopp?

She had left it behind when she met Dr Heinrich . . .

That thought was like a hammer-blow.

It tolled the death-knell of my hopes of finding the girl alive. In a panic, I dropped to my knees again, thumping the lantern down on the wooden floor. I brought my right eye close to the floorboards, and sighted along the plank. Splinters stood out like the spines on a hedgehog's back. The crazed grain of warped wood was a maze of rival lanes running away in the same direction. I was looking for blood. For the stains of Edviga's blood on the soft wood. For darker traces which might have found their way into the grain, distinguishing one anonymous, narrow track from the guilty one next to it.

But there was nothing. No blood. No sign of violence.

No clue which might tell me whether the girl was alive, or dead, or where she might have gone.

I stood up, dropped the metal implement on the bed, then bent again with a sigh, intending to retrieve the lantern from the floor. The flickering light glared brightly in my eyes. Then, a dark shadow moved over me.

I glanced up.

There was a silhouette against the canvas of the doorway.

'Edviga?'

My lips closed in silence as the shadow stepped into the room.

Wet clothes clung to that body like a second skin. Water formed a shallow pool around the naked white feet. That figure had come upon me silently. Every fibre in my body tensed as I struggled to make sense of it. The night before, he had let me live in Königsberg. Now, it seemed, he had dogged my heels, and followed me to Nordcopp. Had he decided that I must die, as well?

Dogged my heels?

Surely not. He must have reached the town before me. The instant I slid down from the saddle, I had gone to Heinrich's house and discovered the bodies. I had touched the lady's cold cheek, and clasped the stiff hand of the other corpse, concluding that they had both been dead at least an hour.

'You got here quickly,' I managed to say.

'Quicker than you think, Herr Magistrate,' he answered with an enigmatic smile. 'I am here, there. I am everywhere.'

It was a strange thing to say, and it jarred with what I knew. He had been in Königsberg the night before. He must have

431

returned to Nordcopp in the early hours of the morning. He had killed Edviga, and now he had come to kill me, too.

He took three steps into the light, and shook the water from his hair. Some drops touched the hot glass of the lantern, sizzling loudly as they instantly turned to steam. He seemed to shimmer. The effect was unexpected. His face was bright where I expected dark, distorting shadows. The lantern projected a honeyed gold glow on his pale skin. His brow was smooth, as gently curved as a dune of wind-planed sand. His cheeks stood out like perfect halves of the same round apple. The contour of his lips was soft and delicate. His short hair sat stiffly on his head, which glistened with tiny liquid sea-pearls. I recalled the first time I had met him, meditating in the Pietist convent in Nordcopp. Then, too, he had seemed to emanate light.

'You came from the sea.'

'You came by land,' he answered swiftly

It hardly mattered where he had sprung from. He had evaded the guards on the landward side of the camp, that was all I needed to know. Edviga had told me how the girls came and went at night, walking along the ancient harbour wall submerged a few feet below the shallow waters of the bay. They went that way to Nordcopp, carrying amber, meaning to avoid the rude attention of the French soldiers on the gate. It came as no surprise that he knew the route. He knew the amber-girls, he knew their secrets.

He had murdered them.

He seemed imperturbably calm. Relaxed, but concentrated. Was this the effect of transcendental meditation? Or was the act of murder his Nirvana, joy in the destruction he had wrought in the doctor's house three miles away?

It was time to pick up the conversation we had broken off in Königsberg. Now, the questions would be different. Even so, I could not predict whether his replies would clarify the situation, or confound me all the more.

'Why kill Dr Heinrich and his housekeeper?' I asked.

My voice was firm. The shock had quite drained out of me. He was the very last person that I had expected to encounter. And yet, I wondered, had some seed of doubt been planted in my heart from our first meeting? Instinctively, I had tried to keep him at a distance. Even so, I should have known. I should have realised who he really was.

He smiled, his teeth tinged yellow by the flame which flared up from the lantern.

'You disappoint me, Stiffeniis! Is this the dull procedure that they teach in Prussian law schools?' He made a grimace of disgust, which distorted his handsome mouth. 'I expected you to start with the other deaths. The ones that you were ordered to investigate by the French. Don't you want to know what you were really up against?'

His words flew rattling through my head like a flight of cawing crows. What did he mean? What more remained to be said about the murders that he had not already told me in Königsberg?

My mind was in a whirl.

He knew me intimately. What I had told him freely, and what he had extracted from me by force and guile. He probably knew a great deal more, and weighed it more objectively than I could ever do. He knew the darkest secret of my soul. I would have killed him to retrieve it. Surely, he knew that, too.

I called myself to order. I must concentrate on the one undeniable fact in my possession: Dr Heinrich was not the killer that I had been seeking.

'Let us begin, then, with my error,' I said. My voice sounded calm enough, but my heart was pumping furiously. 'I thought that I was on the trail of Dr Heinrich. I believed that he had taken me prisoner in Rickert's house last night. But then again, I thought I saw your corpse an hour ago in Nordcopp.'

He threw back his head and laughed.

The lantern played new shadows over the surface of his face. Dark pits with gleaming needle-points replaced his eyes. His mouth became a black and toothless trough. This ugliness was a revelation. I saw him suddenly for what he was: a sinister creature who had crawled out from the sulphurous pit.

'Do not blame yourself, Herr Stiffeniis. You saw what you were inclined to see. You can blame my ability to produce convincing illusions, if you're feeling generous.' Clearly, he was pleased with his own ingenuity. 'While dressing up the corpse in my jacket, I was moved, believe me. With his face set fast in plaster, and my seal-ring on his finger, Heinrich looked as *I* would have looked if he had murdered me!' A gasp of emotion issued from his lips. 'You know, I actually said a prayer for my soul, while standing over what appeared to be my own body.'

He shrugged his shoulders.

'I used every trick the theatre can inspire. The dark setting, pale moonlight shining in through half-closed shutters. A single, flickering candle. Like a symbolic, flailing soul. I knew you'd be enticed by the open door. Who can resist it? Did you enjoy that moment? You thought that *I* was there, and that you might be able to prevent whatever was about to happen. It's fair to say that I outwitted you at every turn, Herr Stiffeniis. Noble thoughts buoyed you up, I know. Your young assistant had been taken prisoner, probably murdered. You couldn't save him, but you would take revenge for his life. You hoped to wash your own hands clean in the murderer's blood.'

Suddenly, as if the slide had changed in a magic lantern, his face was a mask of rage. 'You sacrificed Gurten, your newly acquired assistant. You offered him up to the killer as final proof of your theory. You knew that he would go to Nordcopp the instant you told him that you, too, suspected Heinrich of the murders. Could he stay in Lotingen, safe inside a library? Of course he couldn't! A young man with great ambitions. You *knew* what he would do. Isn't that what went through your mind, Herr Magistrate? Is that not what you felt when you saw his – *my* – corpse?'

Could I offer a word in my own defence?

'Gurten does not exist,' I said. 'He never has.'

He took no notice.

'Heinrich appeared in Königsberg.' His voice was raw with excitement. 'Or so you thought. Exactly as I *wanted* you to think . . .'

'Why?' I asked, hardly daring to hope that he would clarify his motives. 'Why lead me to believe that Heinrich was the murderer?'

His eyes lit up with surprise, and a smile flashed across his lips. 'He was perfectly placed to kill the women. How warmly you embraced the notion when you spoke to Erika in the cells! She was terrified. She knew the victims, and she thought that she'd be the next. And she suspected *him*. Don't you think a creature such as her might feel and see things that you aren't able to?' He fixed me sternly with his gaze. 'Who knows, Heinrich may well have been a murderer. Why not? I mean to say, the truth could well be this. If that's the case, then *I* have done what you lacked courage to do. I stopped him in his tracks.'

He continued to make light of me for his own perverse amusement.

'You killed the women,' I stated plainly. 'You murdered Heinrich, and you slaughtered his housekeeper. Your actions are crystal clear. It is the motive which escapes me.'

'Everything must be plain and simple. Explanation. Justification. Motivation. No ambiguity must remain. Reason is everything. Am I right, Herr Procurator? People are dead; there must be a killer. And if so, what can he say to explain his crimes?' He laughed again, nodding as he did so. 'I agree with you. After all, I *am* your assistant. I'll give you a valid reason, then. Heinrich wanted amber. At any cost. Like everyone else on the coast, French or Prussian. He'd have committed any outrage to lay his hands on the pieces that he wanted.' He twisted his lips derisively. 'Indeed, he has done so heartlessly. In the interests of science, so to speak. He tricked a helpless cripple, promising to cure her in exchange for amber. Can you believe that he possessed those paltry bits he showed to us, and no others?'

My thoughts flashed back to Frau Poborovsky's attic.

The amber collection on the shelves. Some pieces large, others small, containing an incredible menagerie of unknown flies and insects. I had been in no doubt that Heinrich had collected them. That he was Vulpius. Yet Heinrich had never been there. The amber did not belong to him. Nor did the drawings, or the collection of creatures floating in the jars of preserving wine.

Johannes Gurten had assembled that collection.

The realisation froze the blood in my veins.

Who was this man? What did he want from me?

He slowly shook his head from side to side. 'Impossible to found a theory on so little, Herr Stiffeniis! Heinrich believed that the origins of life could be found in amber. His interest was scientific, his ambition limited. I ask you, can a man have a heart so *impure* that he will see no more in godly nectar than the confirmation or denial of the theories which inspire him?'

'You accused him of collaborating with the French,' I replied. 'You went to Lotingen to look for those articles. You sent me details of the essays you had found there, concerning amber.'

He shrugged dismissively. 'I might have found such evidence if I had bothered to read the rubbish he had written. Or *not* written. Who knows? I will not deceive you, sir, on that point. I did not look for proof. Nor did I disturb your friend, Count Dittersdorf. Dr Heinrich probably told the truth when he said that he was waiting for Erika to die. He would have written a pamphlet describing that ambiguous creature to the world, half child, half crone. He would have printed out the lurid diagrams of her twisted bones, cracking and crumbling into dust. That's what *real* scientists do. But you are right, Herr Stiffeniis, we have no evidence that Heinrich ever passed his studies on to the French. Neither in Erika's case, nor concerning Baltic amber.'

He stretched his shoulders, twisted his head on his neck. His wet clothes hardly seemed to trouble him, though he was surely frozen to the bone. The water was cold enough, and now the night chill came creeping damply off the sea.

'I am not like you, Herr Magistrate,' he said. 'I have no need of proof. I watch, and I judge. I know what's what. Heinrich would have killed to gain a piece of amber that he wanted. Indeed, he may have done so. Other girls have been murdered on this coast. He would have killed, I think, for an example containing a previously unknown insect.'

Gurten raised his forefinger questioningly.

'I see the flicker of doubt in your eyes, sir. Has he done so? Is *this* the truth? We cannot exclude the possibility. In Nordcopp, as you know, the world revolves around the hub of amber. If you want a reason for what you saw this night in his house, I'll give you it. Amber, amber, amber.'

He shook his head, and laughed again.

'Heinrich saw what wasn't there. In amber and the creatures it contains, he found truths of no importance whatsoever. Like you, Herr Magistrate, he was looking for facts and certainties. He needed vast resources of amber for his studies. He thought of them as fragments of a complex puzzle. This made him dangerous.'

'Dangerous?' I echoed. 'Whom did he endanger?'

Gurten turned his head towards the open door.

The glassy darkness of the sea rippled in the light of the moon.

'The ignorant are always a danger,' he snapped, glaring back at me. 'And those who doubt are still more dangerous. In the pursuit of certainty, they say and do the most misleading things. They forget what amber really is. They fail to recognise what amber represents for Prussia.' He turned aside again. 'I have *no* doubts, *no* illusions. I know what I must do. Heinrich had to be eliminated. And when his housekeeper tried to save him, I killed her, too. It was a truly touching scene!'

He frowned, and pinched the bridge of his nose.

'Those plaster casts make wonderful weapons,' he remarked. 'I grabbed the first one from the wall, strode into the kitchen, and hit her with it. Dr Heinrich had done an excellent, solid job.'

He stared defiantly at me, as if to study my reactions.

I stared back, searching for clarity, finding none.

'Do you not agree, Herr Stiffeniis, that punishment should suit the crime? I pressed the doctor's face down into the plaster until the fight went out of him. And while his nose and throat were filling up, while the cast was setting hard, I whispered in his ear and told him what the point was. Herr Doctor, I said, this is how your precious insects felt when they sank and drowned in amber resin. He had studied the creatures fixed inside their transparent coffins. In that instant, he realised what it meant. I only hope that he was grateful. He learnt a great deal more in a handful of seconds than he had garnered from a lifetime of futile observation.' He smiled, and added: 'Now *that* – I am sure you will agree – was a most appropriate way for him to die.'

Revulsion surged in my throat. I baulked, swallowing the acid stuff that spurted up towards my mouth. I must not give way. I must humour him, encourage him to talk. He had to tell me what I wanted to know. What had he done with Edviga Lornerssen and the child that she was carrying in her womb?

'You did not kill me last night', I said, 'because you wanted me to see what you had made in DeWitz's workshop.' I paused for an instant. 'I have seen it. But what was I supposed to make of it? Why kill the girls who work on Nordcopp shore to make that model? You spoke last night of the destiny of Prussia. I saw nothing of the sort in that strange waxwork.'

He clapped his hands like a delighted child. 'Now the real investigation begins, Herr Magistrate! So, you found the place. I would have expected you to lose yourself in the maze of Königsberg – all those alleys, lanes and bridges.'

He knew that I had been there. He knew that I had found it. Did he not recall what we had said the night before?

'Ask on,' he encouraged, his tone sarcastic. 'I will hide nothing from you.'

'The pact we made,' I said. 'Last night I helped you understand what Kant intended when he wrote those pages about the creatures trapped in amber. Now, you must help me. That creature you are creating in DeWitz's workshop. What has it to do with the future of Prussia?'

37

'I call her Eve,' he said.

'Who is she? *What* is she?'

He raised his chin, eyes half-closed. Sweat or water ran trickling down his forehead. It split into two separate streams that ran down either side of his nose. His tongue shot out and caught the flow.

Suddenly, his eyes blazed into mine. 'You have seen the women,' he said passionately. 'The women of the Baltic coast. As they enter the sea in those strange outfits. Like pagan goddesses. Working with their prongs and nets. Surely, Stiffeniis, even you can understand the attraction that they wield?'

On the far horizon, a pink haze began to tinge the purple sky.

'Contact with amber, and with the primitive organisms preserved within it, has transformed them,' he said slowly, carefully, as if he were outlining a thesis. 'They are superior beings, Stiffeniis. They are strong, resilient, an ancient memory of what Prussians used to be. They stand firm against the wind and the waves. The sun cannot harm them, nor can the freezing winter cold. They breathe the densest fog, ignore the driving rain. They are immune to storms. All they know is amber and the dour struggle for survival. The strong live, the weak die. They are creatures of another time. Other German women are as larvae in comparison with them.'

I remembered gazing on the statue made of wax, and thinking of Helena.

My wife and those working women were creatures from two different worlds. No similarity existed between them. My wife's slender limbs and narrow hips denied the motherhood within her. How could she carry a child? When I saw the *écorché* that he had made, I had thought instinctively of Edviga Lornerssen: strong arms, powerful legs, the physical presence, the jolt that I had felt as she stepped into my cabin.

'The French are changing everything,' he said. 'Machines, engines, pumps. Useful, efficient, but nothing more.' He passed his hand across his face, as if to cancel out that vision. 'Our women are no use to them. But *we* know what they are. We must become like them. We must generate children in their likeness. Children who are immune to pain and suffering. Children who will not bend with fear, or shrink with remorse. Children who will fight to the death. You have seen the creatures enclosed in amber, Stiffeniis. Professor Kant was galvanised at the sight of them. He understood what had happened. He grasped the true implications of the Flood. The loss . . . They are the original forms, closest to Almighty God, and His Creation. He made them so. In His own image. Pure aggression. Sanctified cruelty. God is not so mild as we have come to think. We celebrate His meekness, we adore Him as a sacrificial lamb. But the creatures that He made were powerful. He shaped them to survive, and dominate.'

He clenched his fist and held it up, as if to explain the inexplicable.

'Prussia is finished. Our army has been dismantled, our arms confiscated. But all is not yet lost. The Prussian soul must break out from its amber tomb and live again. We must create a new species of man. That's what we must do. Men born from the loins of women such as those who work here on the coast. Men born of amber. Men whose instincts are savage and primitive, like those fearsome insects nestling deep inside the soft, transparent resin. We must cancel out all mystification. There will be no room for sentiment, no space for conscience, or for pity. We must cultivate the bestial core. The raw barbarity of our ancient souls. Until that spirit lives again, we will be slaves. Of the French. Of others.'

This was true madness. No grotesque scowl, no lolling mouth howling senseless obscenities, no inexplicable undirected rage. Instead, a careful, reasoned belief in the impossible. Madness was stamped on the face of Johannes Gurten. He was handsome, glowing, transported, youthful, serene in the spiritual intensity which animated him. The strength of unalloyed conviction.

'How?' I asked in a whisper. 'How can this come about?'

'Let it happen,' he replied slowly. 'Let the French do as they please, while our scientists find the means to defeat them. Nature can be moulded. As Monsieur Lamarck has discovered, Stiffeniis, Nature moulds itself according to its circumstances. This is the challenge that we face. Implant a soul of iron in a human form that is invincible. *This* is the path that we must follow. We must implant a buzzing insect where the frail human heart once held sway. Our scientists are the finest in the world, but they must be shown the way. A working model. That *écorché* in DeWitz's workshop will be transformed by Prussian science into flesh and blood. When it is finished – and it will be finished very shortly – we'll waste no time on hare-brained plots and futile opposition. We'll leave all that to the Spanish. We will spread the news to all those Prussians who love their country, those who are ready to create a new Garden of Eden in this land on the Baltic shore. We must look to our glorious past if we intend to form the future. Amber holds the key, and Kant knew it.'

He smiled in my direction, an expression of evident triumph lighting up his face, as if he had revealed a palatable truth to a friend who would surely understand his feelings.

'What have I to do with this scheme of yours?' I asked him. 'What exactly do you want from me?'

Gurten made a loud clicking sound with his tongue.

'Poor Magistrate Stiffeniis,' he said with an affected air of concern. 'You thought that I had come to learn from you. The opposite was true. I came to teach you how to face a truth that you are trying constantly to deny. Embrace your destiny, sir.

Family, work, a peaceful life in a country town . . . You are not these things. Sooner or later, the black insect nestling in your soul will free itself. I hoped that you would find the truth that Kant discovered in you. He saw the human form enclosing a ravening beast. You are as transparent as amber, sir, there is a black spot at the core. You hide the abyss in your soul. That's why you became a magistrate. You think that you are safe in there, appearing to be on the side of what is Just and what is Right. But you deceive yourself. The sight of blood, the smell of it, attracts you terribly. Irresistibly. You cannot stay away from it. Murder stalks you.'

I felt the impulse welling up inside me.

'When I read that the French had handed the investigation to you, I was already here, and I was very busy.' He laughed to himself. 'You can imagine what I was up to, can you not? A great many corpses are needed to make a detailed anatomical model. The French had no idea, of course. They realised that women were disappearing without a trace, but . . .' He shrugged. 'Well, what did it matter? They thought that the girls had run away, carrying the amber that they had stolen. But then les Halles arrived on the scene. Women disappearing? A Prussian killer on the loose? He wanted the killer to be stopped. His motive was obvious, of course. He was afraid the French would be blamed, that it would go ill with him when he tried to rid himself for ever of the women, and replace them with his machines. But what was to be done? Les Halles spoke to his general, and Malaport had a bright idea. What about that Prussian magistrate, the one who was called to Königsberg by Kant? That clever fellow had already worked with the French, and he had proved his usefulness. A French criminologist had written excellent reports about him. If he can find a suitable Prussian suspect, Malaport declared, and if he hands the killer over to us, all our troubles will vanish into thin air.'

He stopped.

'Could I refuse them?' I protested.

'Who *can* refuse them?' Gurten continued. 'That was why I wanted to be at your side. I hoped to temper your enthusiasm, Herr Magistrate, and call forth from your soul the beast that had taken refuge there.'

He roared down from his pulpit. I sat meekly in the pews. I wished to ask about Edviga, but I hesitated to do so. If I asked him outright to tell me what he had done to her, he would only plunge me deeper into confusion and mystification. But there was one road left. He offered me no alternative. I had to try and play him at his own game.

'You must take me for a fool,' I said. 'Did you believe that you had got the better of me last night? I would have told you any lie to save my life. And so I did. I led you to believe that we are two of a kind. You fell for it. You let me go, did you not? So, tell me, which of us is the greater fool, Johannes Gurten?'

For an instant, I saw a shadow of doubt flash upon his face. 'I care not what was said last night. You have seen my work in Königsberg. I know that you will wish to see my *écorché* completed. If you are true to your own heart, you will rejoice in what I do. Otherwise, you'll have what every homunculus deserves: endless pain and suffering.'

He flexed his knees and bent to pick up something from the floor. It was dark and sopping wet, like his clothes. He had brought it with him, whatever it was. He snatched this packet up, then rocked it gently in his arms.

As if it were a newborn baby . . .

In that instant, I ceased to breathe.

His eyes held mine.

I looked back with horrified intensity.

The fingers of his right hand pushed inside the sack. The canvas moved, as if the contents had suddenly come to life. He partially withdrew his hand, holding something small, tightly wrapped up in a dark-stained cloth. It had once been white. Now, it was grey, where water had soaked through it. But there were darker stains as well. Dark brown. Reddish brown. The colour of blood . . .

And I could smell it. It was mineral sharp, saltier than the sea. The package was no more than ten or twelve inches in length. If it was what I thought . . .

When had he killed Edviga?

Where had he left the body?

I heard her voice inside my head. Begging me to hide a piece of amber on the corpse of Ilse Bruen before the French threw her body into the sea. Asking me to do the same for her.

Gurten threw aside one fold of the swaddling cloth. It was seen and gone in a flash. A tiny face. A lump of blood and gore. The head of a child barely formed.

Inside my breast, a tempest roared.

I had failed in everything.

'What have you done with Edviga Lornerssen?'

His eyebrows formed a double arch. His eyes and mouth gaped open.

'Edviga?' he asked, his voice a hollow whisper.

Suddenly, he laughed out loud. 'Herr Stiffeniis,' he admonished, 'have you forgotten the name of your own wife? Do you fail to recognise the face of your very own son? Who is this Edviga that governs your heart?'

I heard a Frenchman speaking once of an event on the battlefield. A friend had been decapitated by a cannonball, he said, yet they spoke for half a minute before the poor man died. What cry of protest could I raise? My head had just been blown away, and I was helpless. I could see, but I was in another world already. What sense remained in words?

And yet, I heard him speak.

'I went to Lotingen,' he said. 'But not to visit your Count Dittersdorf. Nor to read his dusty French journals. Surely, sir, you remember the message for your wife? Which I delivered, as you instructed me to do.'

He paused, laughed, found something funny in what he had said.

'It was Helena that I was interested in. She was carrying something that was valuable to me. Where would I have found

444

the crowning jewel of my new Eve, if not where *you* had put it, Hanno Stiffeniis?'

He held the package up and stared at me.

I heard the sharp intake of air through his nostrils.

I did not breathe. I felt no movement in my chest. No beating heart, no lungs expanding and retracting. I had no need of air. My blood was boiling.

'Do you share my joy?' he asked. 'Or do you suffer like a poor homunculus?'

I could not shift my eyes from his ironic smile.

My hand stretched out and found what it was looking for. An object that I had discarded on Edviga's bed. It slipped comfortably into my outstretched palm. It might have been formed for my hand, and no other. It was my hand, not my brain, that drew back suddenly, then struck forward.

The pointed blade arched through the air like Death's scythe.

I pushed past his heart and into Infinity.

The sound was liquid, solid, a bucket overturned, a pile of clattering wood. My hand was deep inside his breast, blood spurted out and bathed my face. I pulled away, then thrust again to finish him off.

That smile never left his face.

As I pushed forward, he staggered back.

He opened his mouth to speak, and blood poured out like a crimson cataract, cascading onto his shirt and his vest. Then spluttered words.

'It will not end with me,' he gagged. 'We are . . . the Devil's brood.'

Even in death, there was something twisted, false, and devilish about him.

I knew that I had killed him. I rejoiced in the deed, and Gurten knew it. His eyes peered into mine. He saw into my soul, I think, and knew what I was feeling. And in that instant, the creature dwelling in the black depths of my heart looked at him without a grain of pity.

The handle of the weapon seemed to sear my skin.

I let it go, watching as his hands came up to clutch and hold it. He staggered backwards.

I matched him pace for pace, my face two feet away from his.

His shoulder smashed against the door-post, he spun away from me, falling heavily against the door. The handle of the weapon scraped a terrible dirge as he slid along the door, and staggered out into the air.

I followed quickly, but it happened in an instant. He seemed to buckle, then run forward. In an instant, he was gone, falling headlong off the platform into the sea. I saw him sink, then bob and float, then sink again. Then, he disappeared for ever beneath the waves.

I darted back inside the hut.

The package was gone. He had carried it with him into the bay.

I ran out again, scanned the oily waters, looking everywhere. I saw nothing. The Baltic Sea had opened its mouth and swallowed him whole.

And my dead son along with him.

38

Dawn came on by slow degrees.

Pitch black in Nordcopp, the heavens were indigo as I raced through Frombork. An hour later, a streak of speckled salmon-pink lit the far horizon, glinting off the tiled roofs and the distant spires of Lotingen. The clouds had formed themselves into puffy purple balls, like a hundred plums laid out on a large tray. Beyond the town, a lone star glistened over the sea, like a beacon.

Hunched in the saddle, sighting between the mare's sharp ears, cutting every bend as closely as I could, saving every inch, I galloped forward. But why was I hurrying at all? I could have stopped to count the blades of grass along the roadside. Nothing would alter.

I was hurtling towards a massacre.

That I knew.

Gurten had mentioned Helena and my son. But he had said not a word of Manni, Süzi, or Anders. Nor had the name of Lotte cropped up. Only one question remained to be answered. How deep would the chasm be?

That I did not know.

I approached town by the East Gate, cursing as the bay mare lost her footing for an instant on the ancient, rounded cobbles of the hump-backed bridge. Then, I reined in hard at the guard-post. The animal wheezed, I panted, we gave off one united cloud of steam and sweat. Without a word, I thrust my papers at the soldiers. A corporal, two privates, all bleary-eyed with sleep. They must have been on guard all night.

Suddenly, their eyes were wide awake.

I cannot say what they beheld. Dust and filth, without a doubt. Tiredness to outmatch their own, perhaps. But what did they make of my expression? What terror did they see upon my face?

'*Allez, monsieur,*' the corporal murmured, ignoring the rumpled papers in my outstretched hand.

I followed his gaze, saw a black slash across my right thigh. Blood had oozed from what appeared to be a deep cut, and it had stained my linen ducks. I had no remembrance of this accident. Had I jabbed myself with the riding-crop? Had a thorn-branch ripped at my leg as I flew by in the darkness? Might I have fallen from the saddle at some point along the road?

'*Faites donc! Monsieur, allez, allez!*' the Frenchman cried angrily.

He jerked his head away, and whacked his hand on the horse's rump.

I almost fell as the animal spurted forward.

I reached the market-place two minutes later. My office stands on the far side of the square. The briefest glimpse: windows gleaming like brass plaques in the frail first light of the rising sun. I dug my heels with force into the mare's wet flank. The staccato clash of hooves rang off the walls, echoing beneath the covered arches. The offices and shops were all locked up, the street deserted. A sentry raised his hand in warning as I galloped past the General Quarters, but he did not shoot, or cry out, as I veered around the corner into Frederickstrasse and charged for home.

Five minutes more, skittering gravel behind, hooves thumping on the sun-hard surface of the lane, I caught a first glimpse of my destination. The sight was lost to me at once as the lane ran downhill into the Dittersdorf estate. A light mist streamed through the lowland woods, rolling like billowing steam across the dew-damp lawns and the open meadows.

Death was too light a sentence, Gurten had decided.

I had left the coast without going in search of les Halles. There had been no time. As I wrested a horse from the enclosure

448

at the camp, I told the flat-nosed ostler to send word to his superior officer that I was on my way to Lotingen.

'Tell him I have killed the murderer,' I said. 'And that my family is in danger.'

I knew les Halles would follow me to Lotingen. I knew that he would bring armed soldiers with him when he came. For all the good that it would do. I had to be the first to enter the house. I had to go alone.

The mare was almost spent. She galloped mechanically onward, loping stiffly, shifting heavily, this way and that. When the gravel path veered left towards the house, she slid away again, and almost threw me off. I did the first sane thing that I had done all night: I slackened the reins and let the animal canter. Long before I reached the garden gate, I had slowed her down to a walk, approaching the house more warily, taking stock of what I could see. It was not that I was afraid. Rather, I realised the futility of haste.

I slid down from the saddle, and my legs buckled beneath me. My right thigh quivered and quaked with fierce pain. After galloping relentlessly for over three hours, I was as exhausted as the mare. The reins slipped from my hands. The mare loped off to the far side of the lane and the long grass growing there.

I steadied myself against the garden gate. My head weighed down as heavy as a millstone. I had to force myself to raise my eyes and look towards the little house that I had once called home. The mist was thicker in the dell. Helena often remarked that they had not picked the healthiest spot to situate that house. 'It will be the death of all of us,' she joked, because she loved it so. The roses beneath the kitchen window had shrivelled up and died in the summer heat-wave. The hazelnuts and the apple trees seemed alien, hostile.

All was motionless, suspended, silent.

The windows were six dull blanks, the curtains tightly drawn, the shutters closed. The blinds excluded everything, enclosing everything within. Visitors not welcome, those windows proclaimed. The general impression reminded me uncomfortably of the family mausoleum in Ruisling, though no wrought-iron gate had yet been placed before the door to keep the living out.

Another world began beyond my own front door.

The gate fell open. The old familiar creak. The rusty hinge. I suppose I must have shaken it loose with the violence of the emotion which threatened to overwhelm me. I had been entrusted with the investigation. I had been commanded to put a stop to the killings, to halt the travesty of mutilation. But Gurten had followed me to my own door. He had desecrated my house. He had carried Death along with him from the coast. There was little I could do. Bear witness. Assess the horror. Take leave of my wife and children. Do my best to compose and dress the fragile corpses. Before any other person entered the house.

I stood before the door, hesitating.

In some deep recess of my mind, I heard it.

My brain did not react. My animal spirit may have done. Suddenly, everything juddered to a halt. My blood lay stagnating. No room for thought. Energy drained out of me, like water from a lock. My lungs were empty. I was as immaterial as the morning mist. Had I heard the ghost of something brushing over the stone tiles in the hall?

The sound repeated. Slightly louder. On the other side of the door.

The bolt slid back. The inner bar was removed.

I crouched and bunched my fists as the door swung open.

A frightened whisper sounded to my ears like thunder.

The dawn light painted her cheeks, nose, lips in delicate pastel shades of blue. She seemed less tall, less strong in such domestic garb.

That frock was Helena's . . .

I recognised the lustrous pale-blue taffeta, the sprigs of pink blossom, the simple lace collar of the gown that Helena sometimes wore when she went out walking. I had brought it back from Hamburg several years before. I had never seen it worn before with one of Lotte's grey sack-aprons.

'What . . . are you . . . doing *here*?'

I had to swallow, could not speak. It went beyond the powers of my imagining. Edviga and Gurten were in league together. She barred the entrance to my own home. And Helena's gown was not the only element in the transformation. I had never seen her hair let down before. It hung in lustrous golden curls which graced her brow, her neck, and shoulders like ripe wheat, or amber of the purest hue. Only the livid scar on her left cheek proclaimed who she truly was.

What right had I to call myself a magistrate? This case had swallowed my family whole. And still I had failed to see the truth. Johannes Gurten could not have done it all alone. Edviga Lornerssen was the creature who would be his prototype. By means of her, a Garden of Eden would be created anew on Prussia's shores. Amber had united them. She had led her naive companions into his wily net. She had seduced me to confide in her the delicacy of Helena's state. She had lulled me into confidentiality. And all the while, I had convinced myself that *she* was expecting a child, that *that* was the child which Vulpius had set his sights on to complete his horrid work in wax.

Together they had schemed and planned. Together they had done it. Helena had been the target. Helena, and the child that she was carrying in her womb.

Blood roaring through my temples, my hands came up, hovering at her throat.

'You knew what he was after, didn't you?'

She stepped back, eyes wide with fright. She could not escape me in the confines of the hall. The only way was out, and I was blocking the door.

'Of course, I did, sir,' she cried, protesting. 'Why else would I have come here?'

As I advanced on her, she cowered in the corner.

I blocked her in, felt the pull of my jaws, my teeth exposed, the desire to rip her body to shreds as a wolf might have done.

'Why, Edviga?'

She stared at me in puzzlement.

'I was afraid. That's why! The French were working on the beach. Colonel les Halles wanted to get rid of us all. You know what he was planning, sir. That's why I ran away.'

We were so close, I felt her warm breath on my face. Once, I had desired such intimacy. That thought now turned my stomach. I pressed my hands against the wall for fear of tangling them around her slender throat.

'I fled to Pastoris,' she went on quickly. 'His girls had been dismissed. Those Frenchmen had taken over the polishing of the amber. The women had been told to leave that night. I decided that I'd go with them. I've got this mark on my face, I can limp like the best of them. Hans Pastoris would never give me away. He took me in. That's what I did, sir. I left my things in the hut. I walked out on the water.'

'So, Pastoris was lining up his lambs to march them out.'

A look of anguish flashed upon her face. It made her seem almost human once again. This was the Edviga that I had spoken with on two occasions. I did not shift my hands, or ease my stance. I would crush her like a viper the instant she spoke of Gurten. I had to know how deeply she was in league with him.

'Hilde Bruckner had them,' she burst out suddenly. 'Ilse had given them to her to keep the night before they found her dead in Ansbach's pigsty. With Ilse dead, she was at her wits' end, sir. Crossed herself again and again, and swore she wouldn't touch a thing that Ilse had handled. Would I take them? That's what she said.'

My head was spinning.

'Take *what*?' I said.

'Ilse's things, sir. She'd dug up her treasures. Ilse was planning to leave as well. She'd left her things with Hilde. Ilse had a man, I told you that. Remember, sir, the one that drew her? We've always hidden our stuff in Nordbarn. We trust the girls. Anything we're bringing out, or taking in. Spener's stolen amber passed that way, I'd wager.' She hurried on, as if to cancel out what she had just said. 'Poor Hilde'd no idea what was in that sack. Ilse had stashed a load of amber, I expected that. But what surprised me more was the . . . the . . . what do you call them, sketches? Two of them, there were. One was a picture of a neck and chin. I realised that was Ilse. He cut her throat out, didn't he, sir?' She sobbed and looked away, but only for a second. 'The other picture . . . Oh sir, it was a . . . a picture of a woman's . . . of a woman's belly, a woman that was carrying a babe. But Ilse Bruen wasn't pregnant!'

Slowly, I let my hands slide down and away from the wall.

Edviga's eyes flashed nervously from side to side, following them down.

A deep sigh escaped from between her lips.

Was that what she had hoped to achieve by telling me her tale? Did she dare to think that I could be placated?

'It was you,' I said.

She shook her head, eyes down. 'I can *never* have a child,' she murmured. 'Still, I thought, it must be one of us. But who, sir? Only the doctor would know for certain. All the girls go to him . . .'

'Go on,' I urged her.

She refused to meet my gaze, as if to spare my embarrassment.

'I knocked on Dr Heinrich's door,' she said more calmly. 'He'd gone away, his housekeeper told me. Gone to buy medicines and stuff for his trade. Back tomorrow, the lady said. Of course, I didn't believe her. He doesn't want to speak with us no more, that's what I thought. Got no time for amber-girls now. He knows we're being sent away. But as I was turning away from his door, another possibility flashed through my mind. It frightened the life out of me, sir. There *was* a woman who was pregnant. But she was not in Nordcopp. Not there on the coast . . .'

Her eyes were wide as she relived the terror of that moment.

'A woman that the killer would be interested in. Frau Helena, sir, your wife. He'd want *their* child, I thought. You believed that you were chasing him, but was he chasing you? He'd set his eyes on everything that you held dearest.'

'And so you came to Lotingen . . .'

The air wheezed out of me as I tried to speak. My chest ached with the tension. Would she finally reveal the horror?

'Frau Helena was in a proper state,' she said. 'Her labour had started, though the babe was not expected for a week or two. The waters broke while I was standing at your door. Lotte was in a panic, the little ones were terrified. They'd seen their mother lying on the floor. I told a lie, sir . . .'

'What lie was that?'

'Lotte thought that you had sent me, and so I said that you had.' As she pronounced this sentence, her eyes lit up with simple pleasure, and a giggle issued from her lips. 'Oh sir, they were so afraid and lost, they'd have welcomed in Napoleon himself!'

'Who was in the house?' I asked, still wary.

Edviga shrugged her shoulders as if it were a silly question. 'The mistress on the floor. The babes around her crying. Lotte doing her best to calm their tears and see to Helena. I dropped my bag, took off my cape, and set to work. Your wife was in a fright, sir. I tried to calm her, saying that you would soon be home. But there was no time to be lost. A decision had to be made.'

I braced myself to hear how my son had been torn from Helena's body. The blood-soaked object Gurten had let me glimpse. The tiny face a dark, twisted pulp of flesh and blood . . .

I saw darkness, felt that I might faint away.

'Are you feeling ill, sir?'

Edviga's voice revived me like smelling-salts. I had to hear her out.

'What did you decide?'

'To send Lotte off with the children. Her brother lives in . . .'

'I know where Lotte's brother lives!' I snapped.

It was the worst scenario I could imagine. Helena helpless. Lotte gone. My wife left all alone in the hands of Edviga.

Gurten waiting somewhere close by. He'd have come to her the instant that the coast was clear.

And then . . .

'Lotte did not want to go, but I persuaded her,' Edviga continued. 'I made Frau Helena comfortable where she lay, while Lotte took the children off to safety. They're still there, sir.'

I saw a single ray of light. The children were safe. And Lotte, too.

'But you stayed here with Helena,' I murmured. 'Alone . . .'

Edviga did not speak, she merely nodded her head.

'Then Gurten arrived,' I cut in quickly.

Edviga stared at me. Surprise traced furrows in her brow and seemed to etch the livid scar more deeply in her cheek. 'It was a good while later, sir. Frau Helena's labour was long and very hard,' she replied obliquely, as if she would not be deflected from her tale. 'The child would not come out . . .'

'But out it came at last,' I countered brusquely. 'Who delivered it?'

Edviga stared at me, her eyebrows arching.

'What a question, Herr Magistrate!' she said, caressing the scar on her cheek. 'I delivered the child, and cut the cord.'

'It was a boy.'

Again, she stared at me transfixed.

'A girl, sir.'

I opened my mouth to speak, but no words came.

I lurched forward, crushing her forehead with my own.

'But Gurten knew. He knew, did he not?'

Her brow was moist, her skin was cool. I felt the corrugation of her forehead.

'Herr Gurten, sir? Why should *he* know? What difference would it make?'

My hands closed round her throat.

'He told me that the baby was a boy,' I managed to say.

'Herr Gurten?' she echoed hoarsely, her voice rising, fingers scrabbling desperately to prise my straining hands away from her gullet.

In that instant, a sharp cry sounded in the house.

I looked towards the stairs.

'Please, sir. Let go of me,' she shouted, pushing hard against my chest.

Her strength, as I have remarked more than once, was equal to a man's. She threw me effortlessly off, and was gone in an instant, darting across the hall, dancing up the stairs. Her feet made the slithering sound that Lotte's generally made. It was as if she had stepped quite literally into Lotte's slippers.

Then, I heard that cry again.

I darted after her, my nostrils filling with the odours of my home: the lingering sweetness of honey, the sharper smell of burning camphor to ward off flies and insects. My eye fell on a basket on the landing. It was billowing with sheets. They were spotted with blood. I stopped abruptly, closing my eyes for fear of what I would find, bracing my hands against the bedroom doorway.

'You did not keep your promise, Hanno.'

The voice that spoke to me was calm, amused. I had heard that mocking note whenever the children did not do as they had been told. Apparently severe, there was a lingering, ironic undertone to it.

'Husband, you have come too late!'

Helena was pale, thin. Like a swimmer struggling against high seas, it seemed that she might disappear beneath the rolling ocean of pillows, sheets and bolsters that covered the bed. Close beside her, Edviga was bending over an empty cot, straightening pillows, the parody of a fairy godmother in some cautionary children's tale.

Helena had loosened one of her breasts from her smock.

I could not see the infant, but I could hear the sound of feeding. Regular, insistent, soothing. Like tiny waves rippling gently on a sandy shore.

'She is so impatient,' Helena chided with a broad smile. 'Don't you want to see her?'

I seemed to float towards the bed in a dream. My hand reached out like a disembodied thing, and shifted back the coverlet. A tiny face, shiny and red. Eyes tight closed, dark curling lashes. A close pelt of dark hair covering her scalp. Two plump cheeks that seemed to have a life of their own. Two bunched fists that moved in tandem as she sucked contentedly. I placed my hand on Helena's brow, which was hot, slightly damp. Her hair was wild, uncombed, a rambling thorn-bush. Her eyes were two bright pinpoints of feverish light. Her cheeks, slightly sunken, made her face seem gaunt and angular. Yet still she smiled. Clearly exhausted, she was recovering with Edviga's help.

'Your daughter could not wait to see the world, sir,' she whispered, casting down her eyes upon the infant at her breast. 'She almost wore me out, I think it's fair to say. I prayed that you would come in time. Of course, you did not. But you did the very next best thing. Edviga.'

She held out her hand, which Edviga took at once and fondled warmly.

'You gave to her the same task I had given to you. Don't you remember? Save the lives of the women on the coast, I said. You have done just that, she swears. And she has saved my life in return, together with the life of our new daughter. Why, she would not even let that young assistant magistrate of yours . . .'

She looked at me enquiringly.

'What was his name again?'

Edviga and I replied in chorus: 'Gurten.'

'Goodness knows what use he would have been to *me*!' my wife exclaimed. 'And yet, he was most insistent, Hanno. I think he was afraid of your reaction. He'd come too late to help. Edviga would not let him in to see the child, though she did consent to take your letter from him. Oh, it all went off so perfectly. She whispered words of comfort in my ear as the little one came into the world.'

Helena caught the girl's eye.

'She was born before her time, Hanno, yet she is beautifully, perfectly healthy.'

She patted the coverlet, indicating that I should sit beside her.

'Don't you want to tell me what you've been up to on the coast?'

39

I told Helena very little of what had truly happened on the coast. But later that morning, I was obliged to admit a great deal more to Colonel les Halles. He arrived outside the house at about half past ten in an open-topped barouche with four armed troopers. Sergeant Tessier jumped out first, kicking down the folding step, eyeing me suspiciously, as if he believed that they had come to arrest me.

Les Halles's lined face bore smudged traces of oil and dirt. He still wore the filthy overalls he had been wearing while conducting the operations down on Nordcopp shore the night before. With his bib and braces, trousers stuffed into his boots, he might have been a fisherman. Certainly, he gave no impression of being a high-ranking French officer. He looked to be what he was: a worker, who had gone without food or rest, and had not seen soap and water in a long while.

'What's all this about, Stiffeniis?' he said, marching to the gate, his manner stern, reproving. 'Given the circumstances, I made all the haste that I could.'

I apologised quickly, and told him that the fears I had expressed on Nordcopp shore had proved unfounded.

'Do I take it that your family is safe?'

His eyes were veined and red with lack of sleep. They might have been cartographer's maps.

'Safe, well, and greater in number than the last time that I was home,' I replied.

A expression of joy lit up his rugged face, and his hand reached naturally for mine. He shook it for longer than I might have expected. His skin was rough, dry, calloused, his grip firm and strong.

'That's the best news I've heard in a long time,' he said. To my surprise, he winked. 'Almost as good as the fact that the *coq du mer* has tripled production in a single night.' But then his gaze took on a more stern and guarded look. 'Now, tell me, what exactly happened on the coast last night. The message you sent to Nordcopp was garbled by the man who brought it. I came here expecting to find . . . well, I know not what!'

I invited him to enter the house, asking the soldiers to wait beyond the gate. I did not wish that Helena should see or hear them.

Tessier bridled, but les Halles quickly put him in his place.

'There's not the slightest risk, Sergeant,' he said. 'In any case, I wish to speak with Magistrate Stiffeniis alone.'

I led him through to the kitchen, sat him down at the table, then heated a jug of Lotte's cider-and-apples with the poker from the cooking-fire. In summer, we put out the fire after breakfast, but that morning was the first real day of autumn. Edviga had left the fire burning, and she had closed the doors at the front and back of the house. A cold wind was blowing in from the coast, sweeping away the warm, humid air of summer.

'Your good health!' he said, emptying half the beverage at a single draught, as if he had eaten nothing for a week and drunk less for a month, fishing with his fingers in the cup for the bits of apple that were resting on the bottom.

'We found no third corpse at the house of Dr Heinrich,' he announced with a sigh. 'Nor anywhere else in Nordcopp. Did you squeeze that out of him? Whether he had killed that girl, and where he might have hidden the body, I mean to say, before you . . .'

An hour earlier, I had watched Edviga close the garden gate.

She had been wearing that gown of Helena's, though it was a trifle short and unseemly, showing off her shapely ankles to all the world. Over her shoulder she carried a bag, which was filled with food for the journey and clothes that Helena insisted she should carry away with her.

'Can't she stay with us a little while longer, Hanno?'

Helena had asked this question in front of Edviga, as if I alone had the power to decide the question.

Edviga and I exchanged looks.

She knew the French would come to Lotingen. She realised that she would have to explain why she had left the camp without saying anything to anyone. She knew what les Halles would ask. Had she carried any amber off with her? If he suspected that there was amber in her bag – Ilse Bruen's treasure was hidden there, I knew, together with my own gift, the piece of amber that I had removed from the corpse of Kati Rodendahl – she would be subjected to a search with inevitable results: seizure of the goods, and a spell in prison. If she were arrested in my house, it would be a source of embarrassment not only to myself, but to Helena as well.

'I think Edviga would prefer to leave,' I murmured.

Edviga did not speak, though she seemed to acquiesce.

'Our little girl will bear her name. Do you agree to that, Hanno?'

I turned to Helena. She held my gaze. She would accept no less.

'It sounds very fine,' I said. 'Edviga Stiffeniis.'

Edviga glowed with transparent joy, like the most luminous piece of amber ever found on the Baltic shore . . .

Les Halles was staring hard at me.

I looked fixedly into the depths of my cup. I could only pray that he would not guess what was passing through my mind, hoping that he would interpret my silence as a natural timidity to admit what I had done the night before.

'Gurten and I had little time for talking, Colonel,' I said at last. 'He did admit that he had murdered Heinrich and the doctor's housekeeper, but he would not say why. He also said that he had

followed me. His intention, as you know, was to show me that
. . .' I could not find a suitable word. 'He told me that it was the
unborn corpse of my son that he had torn from Helena's womb.'
I swallowed hard, remembering the pit of despair into which I
had been pitched when I saw that gory bundle in his hands. 'I
struck him then. It was instinctive. I was certainly not thinking of
Edviga Lornerssen's fate in that moment.'

The Frenchman placed his elbows on the table, and settled
his face in his hands.

'Why do you think he set his sights on you?' he asked.

I shrugged.

'I was hunting him on your account,' I said. 'By order of the
French.'

He plunged his fingers into the cup, chasing the last bit of
apple. 'I am not convinced,' he said slowly, raising the sodden
triangle of fruit to his lips. 'I mean to say, even if he thought of
you as a traitor, I have never seen such ferocity directed against
another man.' He chewed, staring at me as he did so. He shook
his head. 'To rip an unborn child from a mother's womb! As if
he thought that death itself were hardly a sufficient punishment
for you.'

There, he had said it.

He sighed again. 'We did not find his body. My men searched
the water. Some swimming, some throwing grappling-irons
from boats. They covered pretty much the whole of the bay, but
they did not find a trace of him.'

'I saw his body in the water,' I insisted, remembering that
wicked tool of Edviga's firmly planted in his chest. 'Then, I lost
sight of him, and saw him no more. It was dark, the water was
deep, the current strong.'

Les Halles raised his hand to stop me. 'I was puzzled when
the soldier brought me news last night that you had galloped
off to Lotingen, Stiffeniis. He told me that you had killed the
assassin. Then, he said that you feared for your family. It all
seemed a sight too convenient. The murders solved, the killer
killed, though not the mystery of why he chose to mutilate

them. The bodies of Dr Heinrich and his housekeeper, but *not* the corpse of the murderer himself.'

I sat up stiffly in my seat.

'You think that I let him get away. Is that it? And that I told you a neat tale to put an end to the affair! Why would I do such a thing, les Halles?'

'Because you are afraid to hand a guilty Prussian over to the French authorities. Has that not been your greatest fear from the very start, monsieur?'

'Last night on the beach,' I said, 'I failed to tell you something. Not from any reticence, but to avoid wasting precious time. Regarding something that I saw in Königsberg, something which explains the motive behind the murders, as well as the mutilations to which the victims were subjected.'

I told him of my investigation in the city. I described the statue that Gurten–Vulpius had been working on. I also told him how I had led myself to believe that the true identity of the man that I was seeking was that of Dr Heinrich of Nordcopp.

'Everything seemed to fit,' I said. 'Vulpius's medical and scientific interests matched everything that I had seen in Heinrich's house in Nordcopp. His landlady in Königsberg described a man who might have been Dr Heinrich's brother. Even the smell of wax and plaster of Paris was the same.'

'Tell me more about this strange wax figure,' les Halles interjected.

I recounted what I had seen: the *écorché* modelled on the body parts that Gurten had stolen from the corpses; the fact that features still to be added corresponded exactly with the anatomical pieces which had been removed from the bodies of Kati Rodendahl and Ilse Bruen.

'There was a gaping hole in the centre of the statue.' I swallowed hard. '*That* was what he was after. I thought I knew where he might try to procure a pregnant womb. In Nordcopp, from Edviga. But I was wrong. Helena was his real object.'

'Amber did not come into the equation, then?' les Halles enquired, rubbing his knuckles hard against his brow.

'Not directly,' I replied. 'Gurten believed that he was creating a prototype of a Prussian woman that our scientists and doctors would one day manage to produce. He thought that the human species could be improved – like cows, or horses – by selective breeding. His female ideal was based on the women of the coast. Physically strong, and fiercely independent. "As beautiful as any goddess," he said. Now, this is where amber comes into it. He saw a potent symbol: the repulsive insect at the heart of the beautiful amber nugget. If an implacable, primitive heart could be implanted in a well-developed Prussian body, who could hope to oppose or stop them? Gurten's nationalism outstrips any other brand of fanaticism.' I thought for a moment, then I added: 'It was the most dangerous brand of all. According to him, amber offers us a vision of a long-lost Paradise on Earth. The Garden of Eden, it is widely believed by amber collectors, once existed on these shores. The creatures living in that Paradise were fierce, aggressive. They were not influenced by vague ideas of Good and Evil. The only thing that interested them was life, survival. That was the lesson that Gurten drew from amber.'

Les Halles sat in silence.

Then he began to rub his nose, as if some doubt had struck him.

'That's all well and good,' he said at last, 'but why did he focus on you? Why try to steal your unborn child, Herr Stiffeniis, rather than anyone else's? I do not think I am far from the truth if I assert that you must have represented something very particular to him. Now, what do you think *that* could have been?'

I had told the Frenchman more than he needed to know. I had served Johannes Gurten up on a plate. I did not mention the Kantstudiensaal. Nor did I hint what Kant might represent for our Prussian nationalists. Of pages stolen from the university library, speaking of the monstrosity of those primitive creatures trapped in amber, I said not a word. Nor did I tell him of the parallels that the philosopher had made with the black heart pulsing beneath my outward show of moral principles. I told him that I had been taken prisoner in Rickert's house, but not what Gurten–Vulpius and I had said to one another.

'I have no idea,' I lied.

He narrowed his eyes and peered at me.

'You know me well enough by now, Herr Magistrate. You know that I am a practical man, a mechanical engineer. I do not easily follow certain ways of reasoning. A mind like Gurten's, well, I . . . I hardly know what to make of it.' He waved his hands at a swarm of midges that might have been a manifestation of the strangeness he was talking of. 'If I thought I might be able to persuade the emperor to wash his hands of Prussian amber, I wouldn't hesitate one moment. Good God!' he exclaimed. 'You'd think we had violated sacred ground, and that the local gods and devils had risen up as one to protect it. The Spanish have got their claws into us, but they might prove nothing in comparison to these fiends of yours.' He shook his head again. 'I'd have had a hard job believing you, sir, if not for what one of my men dragged out of the sea.'

It was my turn to frown. Had he been hiding something from me?

'You said that you did not find a corpse . . .'

'Not Gurten's, no. But we found what Gurten showed to you, claiming that it was your son.' He turned away and cursed beneath his breath. 'What sort of a devil would think to play such a vicious trick on his neighbour? It would have been kinder if he had tried to murder you.'

'What was it?' I asked, hardly expecting an explanation which would diminish the horror of what I believed I had seen.

Les Halles leant forward over the table. 'A badger, Stiffeniis. A badger cub that he had skinned. It made a fair pass for an unborn child.' He sat back more easily. 'The man was an illusionist, a mighty cruel one. He had set his heart on one thing: he wanted to break yours.'

He stared at me in silence. He expected me to make some comment.

465

I stared back, said nothing.

'He almost managed. Isn't that true?' He breathed out with such force and for so long that he must have risked a collapse of his lungs. 'When I saw that gruesome thing, I realised something terrible was happening. Having seen it, I can comprehend the folly that you have just described, including this mad desire to make a statue based on the anatomy of his victims. How long has it been going on? How many women had to die?'

I shook my head. 'The deaths of Kati and Ilse only came to light because their mutilated corpses were found. Two more were found in Königsberg. God knows how many other victims there have been.'

I spread my hands wide in a gesture of helplessness.

'Or where the body of Edviga lies,' he added. 'If he killed her, too.'

'Impossible to say.'

He pushed his empty cup towards me. 'I don't suppose you've anything stronger to offer me?'

I went across to the pantry. Lotte kept a bottle of sloe gin there for emergencies. I remembered her opening it the day the news arrived that the battle of Jena had been lost. I placed the flagon on the table, pulled out the stopper, half-filled his cup, and pushed it over to him.

His large square hand closed around it like a vice.

'Let me ask you something,' he said, and drank it off in a single draught.

I raised my palms, as if to say that I was at his service, ready to try and cope with him and his doubts.

'When you told the soldier that your family was in danger,' he began, his eyes sparkling bright, 'you thought that he'd been here already. That he had killed your wife, your child, and whoever else was in the house. Very good,' he said, running his finger first around the inside of the cup, then licking it. 'So, why do you think he *didn't* do so? What was there to stop him?'

For an instant I was tempted to tell him that Edviga had saved my wife. But I did not do so. I would have set him on her trail. Then again, if he discovered that I had lied to him once, he would believe that I had hidden other facts from him.

'Gurten–Vulpius was human,' I replied. 'He was not the demon that you seem to think. Obviously, he could not be in every place at once. He left Königsberg long before I did. I had to free myself, walk all the way to DeWitz's workshop, see the statue, then find myself a horse. A common hack from the coaching-inn, as it happens. He had a couple of hours' lead on me, I'd guess. When he arrived in Nordcopp, he killed those people at the doctor's house. Perhaps . . .' The idea took shape as I said it. 'Perhaps he had not even been to Lotingen at that point. He may have wished to kill me first. To clear me out of his path, so to speak. That trick with the dead badger was meant to stun me, and render me defenceless. It almost worked. Having killed me, he would then have made his way to Lotingen and obtained with great tranquillity what he was really after. My wife would have been entirely at his mercy.'

As I spun this fantasy to hide Edviga's role, I wondered whether it was a true reflection of what Gurten had actually done. In reverse, of course. He had come too late to Lotingen. The child had been delivered prematurely. Had he returned to Königsberg to show me what he had actually achieved, then followed me to Nordcopp to punish me for what he considered to be my treachery?

'Let me say one thing, Herr Magistrate Stiffeniis.' The forefinger of les Halles came up and pointed at my heart. 'We'll give ourselves a week. You write your summary of the investigation for General Malaport, and see if you can make some sense of what has happened. In the meantime, I'll keep looking for the corpse of Gurten.' He shook his finger sternly at me. 'That man did not think like any other human being, nor did he behave like one. I'll keep looking 'til I find him. The baby is a girl, you said?'

I nodded.

'I want that child and her mother to sleep in peace in the nights to come!'

40

Light shone forth in fragmented sunbeams which caught the clouds, highlighting the edges, darkening the shadows. The mist began to lift. I could see the fields, the trees, the house. All was calm. All seemed right. The night had passed. Another day had begun. As it must.

I closed the gate and made my way along the lane to town, as I had done almost every day of the nine years that I had been living in Lotingen. I had called the assizes for that morning, intending to conclude the case of Keillerhaus *v.* Gaffenburger, the very same litigation that I had been obliged to postpone the day that General Malaport had sent me post-haste to the coast.

The 'Silly Cow-Pat' case, as I had privately christened it.

My boots crunched loudly on a black carpet of flies and insects. The noise raised my spirits. *That* enemy had been defeated. The night before, a cold wind had begun to blow. It whistled in from the coast like a witch's breath, and instantly all the flies and insects fell dead. That wind had sucked the life out of them. They dropped to the ground like bits of lead, their wings and shells hard, dry, dull in colour.

In no time, the earth was coated with them.

I thought of the creatures imprisoned in the frozen world of amber. They were larger and more monstrous than the ones that I was stepping on.

Could anyone hope to bring that world to life again?

Could any man believe that such bestiality was buried in our minds and souls?

In *my* mind and soul?